THE CRACKED AMULET

Conflicting and competing religions wage holy war, some to get more power and some to persuade people to embrace a gentler vision of an integrated existence. Families are torn apart as violence engulfs the region with its wanton killings and enforced exiles. This is a story of a girl trying to survive and a young man on a quest and their entanglement with an old lady's plan to shepherd slave orphans to freedom.

BOOKS IN THE WEFAN WEAVES SERIES

The Fractured Monolith: Book 2 of the Wefan Weaves Trilogy

The Ruptured Weave: Book 3 of the Wefan Weaves Trilogy

THE
CRACKED
Amulet

By

R B Watkinson

Claret
pr@ss

ISBN ebook: 978-1-910461-06-8
ISBN paperback: 978-1-910461-07-5

www.claretpress.com

I want to say a very big thank you for all the help given to me by my Oxford writers group: Mary Lucille Hindmarch, Brian Nisbet (our dear departed friend), Mick Smith, Sylvia Vetta, Maggie Hartford and Mukta Vasudeva, for they helped to get me where I am today with my writing. Thanks also to my editor Katie Isbester of Claret Press for whipping this book into the polished tome it is now.

To my husband, Paul and my three children Nick, Greg and Suzy for not only putting up with my writerly ways for so very, very long, but for encouraging me every step of the way.

Map of Dumnon

Chapter 1

Spring came early to Kalebrod that year. The leaves spread out in a sudden rush, fuzzing the woods with soft greens that glowed against the gloomy pines. The air smelt of growing things and the rivers ran deep, fast and frothed white with snowmelt.

Coryn tried ignoring the tree-spirit but when it started to waggle its twig-like member at him and pull faces it wasn't easy. Looked as if it had chosen to torment only him today. To Da and Bryn it stayed invisible.

Concentrating on the job in hand, Coryn breathed deep, his eye on the target, feathers brushing his ear. Letting his breath out, slow and controlled, he eased the gut-string free. The arrow rose, soft and silent on the air, then dropped, brushed past soft brown fur and disappeared into the burrow. The rabbit startled and shot off into the undergrowth, flashing a white tail in warning.

'It was closer than the last one, son.' Da wet a finger and raised it to the air. 'You've got to allow more for the breeze. Get a feel for its strength and direction. Practice will do it.'

'A lot of practice.' Bryn grinned. 'But it'd be better if you didn't lose all your arrows down those burrows.'

Coryn had gone to bed excited about his eleventh name-day last night, hoping he'd get a man-sized bow and could finally get trained up properly like Bryn, his big brother. Perhaps he'd even kill his first writhen this spring. They'd soon be coming down out of the mountains. The pale greenish-gray creatures were hard to spot in the forests, but he was sure he had the eyes for it.

He'd got his bow all right, Bryn's hand-me-down, and had practised all morning, but all he'd got was frustrated. If he couldn't even hit a fat rabbit sitting right in the middle of the glade, how was he ever going to help Da protect the farm? Coryn sensed the spirit and looked up.

The tree-spirit grinned at him then disappeared, only to reappear hanging upside down from a twig above Bryn's head. It riffled at his hair. Bryn brushed his hand over his head, flapping away the insect he likely thought was there. The spirit dodged Bryn's hand then riffled his hair again. Despite his frustration a laugh bubbled up that Coryn had a hard time smothering.

There'd been more writhen coming down out of the mountains than ever before over the last year. That's what the rangers said, those who'd come by on their way to or from the border lands. Last autumn, some of the farms higher in the foothills had been attacked and burned to the ground, the people killed or captured. Uncle Haarl had already taken Coryn's cousins off to Kale. He said he might even take ship there for the west, Faran maybe or even Losan. But that'd be a long journey.

Da said he'd never leave the farm. It'd been Granda's and his Da's before him, and the spirits be damned if he'd ever leave the place. Even though they didn't think Ma was quite so sure about staying, Coryn and Bryn had agreed that it wouldn't be right to leave the farm. It'd mean the blood-priests had won, wouldn't it? And that couldn't be good. Anyway, they had their amulets, spirit-blessed and hung all over the fences and buildings to keep the Murecken from finding them.

Coryn pressed his hand against his own amulet, hidden inside a pouch hung round his neck, then he nocked another arrow, this time aiming for the target Da pinned to the tree. He felt for the breeze, how it licked against the left side of his face, then sighted along the arrow. A shade higher than the target, a shade left, he breathed out and released.

'Yes!' Coryn whooped. He'd hit it dead centre.

'Well done, son.' Da patted Coryn on the shoulder. 'Now collect up all your arrows and practise some more. Bryn, you and I have to see to the roof of the small barn.'

'Da! I wanted to take Coryn down to the pool.' His hand shot out. Snatching hold of the tiny tree-spirit, Brynn grinned at Coryn then threw the creature up hard. It spun and clung upside down to a higher branch, chittering in annoyance. 'We might catch some fish for supper.'

'Very well, but don't take off your amulets if you go for a swim.' Da glanced up at the spirit and back at Bryn. 'There's talk of bloodhunter-priests coming up through the mountains into Kalebrod and lacerts along with them. I'd rather not have them sniffing either of you out.'

'But I've no Wealdan, Da.' Coryn tugged the arrow free from the bark. 'Those sniffers won't be interested in me.'

'You might yet manifest it, son. There are no hard and fast rules as to when it appears in a youngster. And we both know you saw the

12

spirit. It's a beginning.' Da pressed his hand against his own chest where his own amulet lay. 'Best be safe, son.'

Coryn touched a hand to his own small leather pouch again. The spirit-blessed stone Ma had found for him a year and a day after he was born felt hard and sure. Some said they didn't work, but Ma and Da held to the old ways.

'I'll take care of him, Da.' Bryn put his arm round Coryn's shoulders.

'You do that, son.' With a wave, Da disappeared into the woods towards the farm.

'Won't the water be freezing still?' Coryn looked up at his brother.

'Don't you know? That's when it's best!' Bryn grinned. 'C'mon.'

Coryn woke in the darkness of the farmhouse with a yell, frightened, but not knowing why.

'Coryn, child.' Ma was there in a moment. She held him tight, rocking him. 'Did you have a nightmare?'

'I don't know.' He felt confused, the scare fading fast.

'Just a dream, a bad dream, but it can't harm you.' Her soft words calmed him down. She kissed him. 'Now, go back to sleep and know I love you.'

She gave him an extra squeeze and tucked him back in bed next to Bryn his fifteen-year-old brother, who thankfully stayed fast asleep. It was embarrassing, Ma treating him like his little sister, Lera, but it was good to feel warm and safe. He soon dropped off to sleep again.

Dawn was a faint hint around the shutters when Coryn woke again in a panic. He sat bolt upright in bed and peered round his room wide-eyed. In the grey light he saw Bryn pulling on his trousers.

'Writhen,' Bryn whispered in his ear. 'The bastards sneaked down out of the western forests. They've already killed the dogs and fired the barn.'

Shaking, Coryn pulled on his own clothes and followed Bryn into the main room. He remembered his night scare and wondered if he'd sensed them coming.

Their father stood at the heavy door squinting out through a long slot made for arrows, his bow drawn, feathers touching his cheek. A thrum and the arrow disappeared through the slot. A screeching howl answered and arrows smacked into the door and shutters. Coryn smelled smoke and heard the animals screaming. Bryn grabbed his new bow and ran over to one of the windows. Easing apart two slats of the heavy shutter, he drew and released. Another howl.

'Well done, son.' Da didn't turn, but aimed and loosed another arrow.

Coryn ran forward, grabbing his new bow and quiver from its peg by the door.

'No, not you too.' Ma grabbed him. She held little Lera tight to her chest with her other arm. Ma's voice sounded strange, all wrong and scary, and Coryn let her drag him into her bedroom. 'You're going in here.'

An axe head crashed through the shutters as Ma pulled him into the bedroom. Coryn heard Bryn scream as Ma pushed him into the hidey-hole under the floor behind the bed and shoved Lera into his arms, making him drop his bow.

'Be very, very quiet.' She put her hand under Coryn's chin, raising it so she could look into his eyes. 'No matter what you hear.'

Lera nodded and stuck her thumb in her mouth. Coryn felt her tremble and he held her tight. He had to be brave for her.

'You look after your little sister, Coryn.' Ma kissed him on the forehead.

Coryn nodded, unable to speak.

A broadhead spear crashed through the shutters and arrows spat into the room with the light of the rising sun. Ma slammed the trapdoor shut and shoved the bed back against the wall. Then Coryn heard her fall against the floorboards with an awful sound. Her cry cut off short.

Lera stayed silent. She clung to him in the dark with one little fist bunched around some of his shirt, her head turned into his chest and her mouth full of thumb. He tried not to shake like she did as he waited in the hidey-hole, squashed against the precious things his parents hid here, pushing his fist into his mouth to keep from crying. Worst of all, he realised he'd taken off his amulet for the night and forgotten to put it on again. Would a bloodhunter-priest find him? He comforted himself with the thought that he'd no Wealdan for a blood-priest to sniff out. Not yet anyway. And Lera was far too young.

Things seemed to fall silent after a while, and he was just thinking to leave the hole when he heard scratchings and snuffles from above. He pressed his back to the wall, feeling a strange spiking sensation against his skin. He pushed the feeling away, trying to concentrate on the sounds. Was it a wild animal? Or, he shuddered, a lacert? If one of those Murecken blood-sniffing dog-like reptiles was about, it'd mean a bloodhunter-priest was close by for sure. That'd be the worst thing ever. Before he could make it out, it had gone.

Coryn and Lera stayed hidden for good while longer. He'd no idea how long. He kept falling asleep and waking up panicked. When he crawled out, the acrid stink of smoke made him cough. He pulled Lera out and held her in his arms. Heavy rain fell from dark clouds, smothering the fires and leaving the house and barns smouldering ruins. They were both soon soaked through and shivering as he searched what remained of the farm.

By the time he had found what was left of Da and Ma the rain had stopped. He couldn't find anything of Bryn. Maybe a lacert and a bloodhunter-priest had come to the farm and had taken him. He couldn't think of anything more awful and sent a wish to the spirits to make it not so, hoping instead that Bryn had made an escape and was trying to get help, or warn the next farm, or something. Coryn held tight to that thought as he did what he had to do.

Building the pyre didn't take half long enough, nor did finding the three-forked willow sticks that would help the Cuinannufen find his parents' spirits and bring them safe to the spiritworld of Annufen. Maybe one day they'd be reborn to another life. A better one. He wrapped their bodies in what cloth he could find and, with little Lera's help, dragged them one by one to the pyre and laid them on the oil-soaked wood. Ma and Da lay close together. They'd have wanted that. He covered them over and hung their stone amulets on the sticks – not that they'd done much to protect them in life. But the Cuinannufen, the spirit-guides of the dead, were real. They'd come for his parents soon enough.

It was only then he realised he'd not seen a single spirit since he'd climbed out of the hidey-hole. And that was strange.

The pyre burned to the ground long before Coryn was ready to go, but he had to go. After all, the writhen might come back. There wasn't anything left here for either him or Lera anyway. Not even their amulets. No matter how hard he looked, he just couldn't find them.

From the hidey-hole, he took the coin pouch and the flask of firewater. From what was left of the cold store he took a bag of oats, another of salt and the last jar of honey. He searched around in the ashes of the farm for anything still more or less whole. There wasn't much. Just some wrinkled winter vegetables from the root-cellar, a hunting knife and a sack. He found a blanket on the line. Ma must have left it there overnight. He didn't know why. It was a bit damp, but he figured they'd be glad of it soon enough. Once he'd filled the sack, it felt comfortingly heavy.

With Lera holding his hand and the sack over one shoulder, Coryn left everything he'd ever known.

Chapter 2

They'd travelled for days. It felt like he'd gone further than ever before in all his eleven years, but Coryn had no idea how far downriver he'd come. Nor did he have any idea how much further it'd take before he got to the sea port of Kale, the capital of Kalebrod. All he knew was that he had to stick to the River Brod the whole way. He hoped Uncle Haarl was still there, then they could all get on a ship and sail west together. That'd be good.

He stopped at a good place for fishing, by a pile of rocks overhanging a pool of still water. A pair of water spirits floated by, both as big as Lera, their hair flowing down their bodies like pond weed, so he knew the place was safe. For now.

Hunger made his stomach hurt. Lera hungered too. He heard her whimper from behind the rock where he'd hidden her. She was a good girl though, and kept it quiet. Coryn had boiled up the last of the oats and given them to Lera that morning.

Evening coloured the big-bellied rain clouds red and purple, just like the bruises all over his body. Coryn tried to ignore all his aches and pains as he lay on the rock with his arm sticking into the river. His hand began to go numb but he kept it there, hoping. He felt a prickle of excitement as the slick skin of a fish slid against his fingers.

'Steady now,' he whispered.

'Steadda now,' Lera echoed.

Taking his time, just as Da had taught him, he cupped his hand under the fish's belly and tickled it for a slow count of fifty. Coryn made a sudden grab for the fish and flicked it up onto the bank. It flopped about in sparkles of water and silvery scales.

Coryn whooped. 'Yes!'

'Yes, yes,' Lera crowed, popping up from behind the rock. 'Fishy!'

He whacked the fat trout on its head with a heavy stone, gutted and cleaned it, then stuffed it into his bag. Now it was time to find a place to stop for the night, a place where he could make a small fire. They'd both eat well today. He rubbed his arm, trying to warm it up again. With Lera clinging onto his back, he hopped from rock to rock along the riverbank.

As Coryn looked around for a good spot to camp, he saw a small fire through the trees. He reached round to put a finger against Lera's lips. She nodded, silent. Cautious, he slipped between the trunks, closing the distance as silent as Da had taught him.

'I've been waiting for you.' A woman much older than Ma sat by the fire. She turned her pale face and stared straight at him through the dusk with bright blue eyes. She held a baby in her arms. 'It's safe, you've no need to hide, boy.'

Wondering how she could've seen him, Coryn stepped out from behind the trunk and into the firelight. He smelled food, something good and hot. His stomach rumbled.

'Food,' Lera whispered in his ear.

'How'd you know I was coming?'

'Sit down, boy.' She laid the baby on a fur cloak and wrapped it up snug. Her trousers and jacket were thick, tight-woven wool. Over the jacket, she wore a long, fleece jerkin, tied in with a wide, leather belt. Her dark hair was braided and looped over one shoulder down to her waist. 'Closer to the fire, you look cold, as does your sister.'

Coryn swung Lera round to his chest and sat as close to the fire as he could, almost close enough to singe his boots. Lera curled into his lap. He could feel her tremble.

'Have some food.' She held out a bowl, but Coryn hesitated. 'There's plenty, I made extra and have already eaten. We'll cook your fish in the morning for breakfast.'

How did she know he had a fish? Coryn sniffed. He sighed, the smell of the fish was strong. His stomach rumbled again so he shrugged and took the bowl. It steamed and smelled of vegetables and herbs making his mouth water. He blew on a spoonful for Lera, then on one for himself.

'You've a name, boy?'

He looked up. Her eyes seemed to stare right into his head, making him feel prickly. He scowled, shoving the feeling away. She jumped and sat back as if she was startled. 'Er, my name's Coryn, Coryn aef Arlean, and this is my sister Lera,' he said round a mouthful of stew.

'Lera.' Lera nodded but kept her eyes on the bowl, her mouth wide, waiting for the next spoonful.

'We're going to Kale,' Coryn blurted out. 'We've an uncle there. Our farm's been attacked and our parents are dead.'

The ache speared into him, fresh as if it had all just happened. He'd not said it out loud like that before. Somehow it made it more real and horrible. Lera closed her mouth and looked at him, patting his cheek, then opened her mouth wide again.

'But you have your sister.' The woman nodded and smiled. 'You have looked after her well for one who is only eleven years old.'

Stunned, Coryn stared at her. How could she know that? She smiled again, but looked sad at the same time.

'My name is Birog Llawgoch. I'll escort you to Black Rock. It is both a great sea port and the royal city of Rophet. You cannot go any further toward Kale, there are blood-priests, writhen and a Murecken army between here and there. It will soon be surrounded. You'll find no help there even if you were able to reach it.'

'The royal city of Rophet? But that's leagues and leagues away up north.'

'Yes, we are in for a very long walk indeed, Coryn aef Arlean.' She smiled again. 'But both our journeys will be much, much longer than that, I am sorry to say.'

Coryn wasn't sure what to think about that. He filled Lera's mouth and then his own again.

For two months they travelled hard heading northeast. Over rocky ridges and forested valleys, through rivers and around lakes. They hid in caves and thickets from writhen and Murecken scouting parties. And roaming packs of bandits, that Birog said were inevitable during wars. Then, after breaking camp before night ended, they reached the hills above Black Rock. Just as Birog had promised.

Half way up one long, low hill, they stopped next to a lightning-struck tree standing on its southern slope. In the pearling grey of dawn the air filled with the green-bursting scents of late spring. Right on the top of the bare hill stood a single standing stone. Coryn remembered the one just like it that stood near the barn. It was hard not to cry when the memories rammed into his head.

Birog took the strip of fine calfskin from her belt-pouch and showed it to him. Rolled tight and tied with string, it wasn't much thicker or longer than his thumb. He had seen her write on it most times they'd stopped for the night, when it was safe enough to light a fire.

'You are young, you have seen much and had to mature fast and well beyond your years. Now you have to become a man full grown. See the city below? Go to the sea docks at the northern end of the harbour and get a berth on a ship to Storr. Once there seek out one of the Lehotan Adherents in Storr Haven, a scholar in historical studies. He goes by the name of Daven. Daven aef Kaerin.' She waited for him to repeat the name. 'Give him this vellum. Do not worry how long it takes you to reach him, even if it is years. But show it to no one else Coryn aef Arlean, and tell no one else about it. No one.' Birog kept her voice low but it was fierce and she stared deep into his eyes.

It felt like she could see right into his mind and knew all his thoughts. She'd looked at him like that a lot while they'd travelled. Sometimes she would turn away quick, looking sad. That'd been the scariest for Coryn.

'I don't know if I can leave Lera.' Coryn blurted out the worry he'd been carrying for the last whole month. 'She's all I've got, I'm all she's got.'

'You must be strong, Coryn.' Birog put Lera down on the ground and knelt, giving him a hug. The baby, swaddled tight to her chest, squished between them but, as usual, she made no sound. 'I can get her to a safe place, one where she will be well cared for.'

'But you really can't tell me where?' Coryn looked down into her grey eyes, biting his cheek to stop the tears. He had to be a grown-up, like Bryn. At fifteen, Bryn never cried. If only he'd been able to find his brother, they could have all stayed together for sure. He looked down at the baby's face. Deep green eyes looked back at him. He knelt down and took Lera into a big hug.

'No, I am sorry. I have two or three possibilities in mind. I shall tell the person I place her with to inform Daven aef Kaerin. One day you will be reunited with your sister, please believe me.'

'I don't know how to say goodbye.' His words were muffled in Lera's fluffy blonde hair. A small hand patted his cheek.

'I understand, and so will Lera. I only wish I could bring you with me too. But it is impossible, I have not the strength to carry us all through safely, and for that, I cannot be more sorry.'

'Me too.'

Birog stood and looked down to peer into the misty forest below. She frowned but said nothing. Taking him by the hand, she led him to the fat old lightening tree and helped him up to a narrow crack, twice as high up as he was tall. Coryn looked down into a hollow large enough for him to hide in.

'They are not far behind us now. We must be quick. Hide here and do not move till you are sure they have gone. It is important that you are certain they are well away before you climb out.' Birog waited for Coryn to nod again before going on. 'I have made a new amulet for you. I know you lost the one your mother made you, but this one will be just as good if not better. It will cloak you from blood-priests and block their blood-magik so it is important that you never lose it. You will feel prickles or spikes if anyone uses magik of any sort near you, the same as you felt when we first met. Do you remember?'

'Any magik?' Coryn remembered the funny feeling he'd had when he'd first seen Birog.

'Yes, even the Wealdan. It is up to you to block it, you just have to use your mind to push it away from you. Do you think you can do that?'

Coryn nodded, though he wasn't quite sure what she meant. Before he got a good look at the amulet stone, Birog put it and the roll of velum into a leather pouch, much like the one Ma had made him. All burned and gone now with the rest of the farm.

'Don't worry. The Murecken will not know you are here, you will be safe for long enough to evade them. That at least I can promise you. Trust me.'

Coryn heard the writhen then. Their strange hollow croaks and screeches. Then he heard the howl of something worse cut through the rising mist. A thrill of fear arrowed through him. Lacert. One of the enormous lizard-hounds of the Murecken priesthood. It'd found their scent. He'd known it would.

'But I still don't understand why I can't go with you.' Coryn shivered with more than cold, scanning the trees below the hill, trying to see where the blood-priests were. 'I can walk, you don't need to carry me.'

'I must go through a place where you cannot walk. I can carry these two little ones through the Portal and into the Wefan-flux, no more.' Birog pointed up at the stone, but again Coryn didn't know what she meant. 'I am sorry Coryn but it is very important that this one is not taken by the Murecken.'

Coryn looked down again at the tiny face peeking out from the swaddling that held the baby tight to Birog's chest. The startling eyes gazed at him, like deep jade-green pools, a curl of golden hair made a question mark on her forehead. In all the time he'd known her, the baby hadn't ever cried, hadn't made much sound at all. She was nothing like Lera had been when she was a baby that small. Lera was quiet now though. Too quiet. He wasn't sure he liked it. 'She's special, isn't she?'

'Yes, she is and the blood-priests want very much, but they will not have her, not if I can help it in any way. Nor will they have Lera. Remember, you must not tell anyone about this babe but Daven. Do not tell anyone but him about the Portal either, this is important too. Promise?'

'Yes, I already swore I wouldn't,' Coryn insisted, and he wouldn't. Anything to cross the stinking damned blood-priests. 'And I won't!' He didn't even know what a *portal* was so how could he tell anyone anything? 'Anyhow, you've got Lera too, and she's special to me.'

'Yes, I know how special she is to you. Thank you. From the bottom of my heart, I thank you. Your journey will be longer and harder than I would wish on anyone, Coryn. Please believe me when I say I am sorry for what you will face. If there were any other way...' She sighed and closed her eyes for a moment. Then she reached up and squeezed his hand. 'But there is no other way and you must be strong. Come, it is time to hide.'

Coryn nodded. Trying to be brave like Bryn would be, he waved at Lera.

'Bye, bye, Cowyn.' Lera patted his ankle. 'Lub you.'

Coryn nodded. He couldn't say anything past the lump in his throat. He thought he might cry but, making his shaky body work more or less like it should, he scrambled down into the hollow till the sky was a small patch of blue high above his head. He remembered then how Ma had hid him and Lera under the floor. That made him worry even more. What would happen to Birog, Lera and the baby? Would they be safer than him? Level with his chest, there was a crack as wide as his little finger where the light squeezed in, so he crouched down a bit and found he could see right up to top of the hill. His heart hammered as he squinted out.

Birog had already climbed the hill and now stood close to the tall stone. Twice her height, the stone leaned toward her, looking like it could fall right over and squash her flat. Coryn wanted to cry out, to warn her. As if he'd shouted for real, Birog looked down to the tree. She gave Coryn one last smile and raised a hand in farewell. He raised his own, then dropped it, feeling stupid. She couldn't see him wave.

She'd strapped Lera to her back with another length of swaddling, and his little sister had wrapped her skinny arms round Birog's neck, just like she'd always done to him. Another lump rose in his throat and he had to swallow hard.

Facing the stone with her back to the east and the rising sun, Birog pulled a crystal out from her dress. The light made it spark and flash greeny-blue. Birog was a Lehotan Adherent? Why had she never told him? No wonder the blood-priests were after her. Wouldn't Lera be safer with him after all? Worrying even more, he rubbed some grit from his eyes that was making them leak, then squinted back through the crack with his other eye. Should he do something?

Birog's lips were moving now, but he couldn't hear what she said, then she pressed her crystal against the stone. The howling got louder but she didn't move. A moment later, the sun rose above the mist, high enough to hit the face of the stone, splashing the grey rock with pinkish-gold light.

Then Birog lifted the baby's hand up to touch the standing stone and stepped forward disappearing into the rock.

Coryn stifled the yell that almost spurted out of his mouth by shoving in his fist. How did she do that? Where'd they gone? Right through the rock? Was there a tunnel, a door or something? But they hadn't come out the other side! They'd just vanished!

A moment later, a lacert sprinted up the hill, passing far too close to the tree for Coryn's liking, and crashed into the standing stone. It bounced right off it again.

It couldn't get through. Birog had closed the door somehow and had got away. Coryn almost cheered, but the lacert was too close and he bit down on his tongue. He'd never been so near a live lacert before and it scared him.

Uncle Anky had joined the border guard some years back, and he and his patrol had brought one they'd killed to show all the farmers and loggers up in the hill country what to look out for. It'd been smothered in pine pitch to hide its stink from the sturdy mountain pony but, after they'd scraped some of it off, Coryn had seen the rough scales of its skin, the lizard-talons at the end of its legs, the long snout with its dagger-teeth sticking both up and down outside its mouth, and the slit-like holes it had instead of ears.

It looked worse alive, with its great goggle eyes glowing red in the sunrise and long strings of saliva hanging from its gaping snout. Its talons scraped at the stone as it dug into the soil around it, throwing up great clods of earth and grass.

Then five writhen scrambled up the hill holding short spears and long daggers. Fascinated, Coryn studied them as they crawled, ran and hopped over the rough ground. Their round bodies were covered in various animal skins and their skinny arms and legs were covered in tribal scarring. Some of them had covered their outward pointing tusks with spiked metal caps. A Murecken blood-priest followed them.

Coryn realised it was a bloodhunter-priest, not an ordinary blood-priest, when he saw that the poor horse wore a hood over its muzzle. The special leather hoods were soaked in a pungent oil to stop their horses going mad from the disgusting stink of bloodhunter-priests. Uncle Anky had told his Da about bloodhunter-priests too, about how they'd gone through terrible blood-rites involving lacerts to become what they were. Now here he was seeing one for real.

The bloodhunter-priest got off his horse and pressed his hands against the stone then sniffed at it like the lacert had – sniff, snuffle, snort. Coryn imagined he could hear him, smell him even, the same stink as the lacert. He felt sick.

A horn blew, then a second and a third. The bloodhunter-priest shouted out a command, mounted and galloped back down the hill right past the tree, followed by the writhen and the lacert. None of them sensed he was hidden there. Not long after, a bunch of riders with a pack of dogs sped up and over the hill, spearing one straggling writhen not far from the lightning tree.

Rophetan soldiers. Coryn wanted to cheer again, but stopped himself. It might not be safe yet. Other writhen could be sneaking around, hidden in the bushes and trees.

When the sun had melted all the mists and risen high in the sky, Coryn felt safe enough to leave the tree. He stood by the stone for a long while before he reached out to touch it. The blue-grey rock was hard, rough and very, very solid all the way round, right to the bottom and as far up as he could reach. He couldn't imagine how Birog had got through. He could smell the bloodhunter-priest's stink on the stone. Or was it the lacert's? He didn't know which but likely it was both. It was worse up close.

He tugged open the pouch and rolled the vellum and the amulet into his hand. Something looked odd about the stone: it had a hole through it, like it should, but he could just see a tiny crack spreading up from the hole. Wasn't that wrong? He held it up to the light. Something twinkled inside the crack, a small speck of greeny-blue that flashed in the sun, the same colour as Birog's focus-crystal. That'd be the special Wealdan-magik she'd used on it, he supposed, keeping him hidden from the bloodhunter-priest and his lacert. He'd keep his cracked amulet safe for sure, now he knew it worked.

He put everything back in the pouch and climbed to the other end of the long, sloping hill where the wind hit him, fresh, cold and smelling of salt. Astonished, he stopped and gaped. Down and down, past more long, bare hills, stretched leagues and leagues of water.

'The sea.'

It was enormous, bigger than any lake he'd ever seen, and grey as a stormy sky.

Chapter 3

The biggest, noisiest place he'd ever been to before was the spring market at Halebridge, six miles from the farm. Black Rock was much bigger, busier, noisier and so crowded, Coryn could hardly squeeze through all the people and animals, carts and carriages, so it took forever to get hardly anywhere. Even the tall and narrow buildings were all squished up to use every inch of space along the streets. It seemed unlikely there was enough air to breathe in the city.

Everyone looked in a terrible hurry too, with no time for smiles, let alone hellos. They mostly wore dark colours, though he did spot a few in the greens of Kalebrod woodsmen. He didn't see anyone he knew though, and he looked hard enough. Still, he supposed, he didn't know many people.

The city stank, worse than the barn had ever stunk, even when the old cow had died of the flux. Every street had narrow gullys running down either side of them, full of smelly water. At odd stretches along the road the water disappeared down holes with metal grates over them, no doubt it ran straight into the river. He even saw someone throw a pot full of lumpy liquid right out of a window above an alley. If he'd not had his wits about him, he'd have been soaked in someone's water and night-soil for sure. It was horrible. The river that split to run on either side of the island on which Black Rock stood must be filthy. Nothing like the sparkling clean rivers back in Kalebrod.

Somehow he managed to forget it all though as strange sights and sounds pulled at his eyes and ears, all the way up a steep, wide, road looping up the biggest hill on the island. Lots of people, all wearing bits of red, yellow or orange to brighten up their dark clothes, headed up the hill and Coryn fell in step with them. Birog had said that he'd need to get to the docks on the other side of Black Rock, and it seemed the easiest way to do that was to go right over the middle hill along this wide, looping road. He didn't like the idea of getting lost in some side street or alley. He supposed she hadn't realised some sort of festival was going on and that the streets would be this busy.

A man wearing a long brown robe, covered in ribbons in all the colours of a fire, tied a strip of yellow cloth round Coryn's neck like a scarf. Before he could think of what to say, the man had disappeared into the crowds. Another man, again in brown robes covered in ribbons, shoved a small roll of bread into his hand.

'Come to the Temple of Atash, and you'll have more.' He patted Coryn on the shoulder. 'Atash is a generous God.'

'What?' Coryn looked up from the roll, amazed, but the man had disappeared.

'Eat it before it gets cold. The priests only give out one each.' A boy, not much older than Coryn, gave him a friendly shove. 'Spirits know how they work out who's had one an' who hasn't though. Come on, I'll show you the best place for a good view of the ceremony.'

'Ceremony?'

'Thought you were new by the way you goggled your way up the Royal Avenue. My name's Flick.' The boy grinned, grabbed Coryn's arm and pulled him along up the hill, weaving through the crowds like a fish through weeds. 'The Fire Ceremony, in honour of the God Atash, begins at high-noon.'

Coryn managed to eat the sweet and still warm roll as he was half dragged along, wondering who this god Atash was, sure he'd never heard of him before. But the roll was good and if the priests had more like it, he'd be happy enough to go to this temple of theirs.

They arrived at an enormous square thick with crowds of people, all wearing fire-coloured bits of cloth. On one side was a huge white building, Atash's temple Coryn guessed. Opposite the temple stood the biggest building he had ever seen. The black walls and towers scowled down over the square like stacked thunderclouds. He'd seen it as he came down over the hills, but up close, it seemed even more enormous. He guessed it must be the royal castle. He imagined the king and queen and their court in beautiful clothes eating fancy food off gold plates.

Flick guided Coryn round the edge of the square towards a water-trough standing in one corner. They climbed onto its wide stone edge. Over the heads of the jostling crowds, they had a good view of the temple's front.

'Them there are the everlastin' flames.' Flick pointed up at the taller tower. 'The Fire of Atash. We're to witness the ritual rebirth of the flames.'

'If they're everlasting,' Coryn asked, looking up at the squat building with its two stubby towers at each front corner, 'why do they need to be reborn?'

'Eh?' Flick screwed up his face. 'I dunno. Hadn't really thought about it before. See it's a new religion round here. We only started hearin' bout them no more than a year or so ago, an' they only finished the temple a tenday ago. Knocked the old Lehotan Haven down to build it. The priests tell us plenty but I ain't ever really listenin'. Thing is, most of us only listen 'cause they feed us.'

'I've never heard of a god called Atash.' Coryn licked the last delicious crumbs from his fingers and wondered what good a god was when there were spirits and each other to rely on.

'Seems he's a generous god, always givin' us poor folk food, specially street children like me.'

'Street children?'

'Ones as haven't got no parents or home,' Flick said. 'You got parents? A home?'

'No, I – I don't.' Coryn's gut twisted, and he scowled at the temple, trying to get angry. Being angry helped make the pain go away. Sometimes. 'They died...back in Kalebrod.'

Flick nodded. 'You've not told me your name.'

'Oh, Coryn – Coryn aef...'

'Just the one name'll do.' Flick waved his hand toward the temple. 'See on the platform in front of the temple, that 'normous bronze bowl?'

Coryn nodded. The bowl, polished to a golden sheen, stood in the middle of a wooden platform built against the front of the temple half way up the broad steps.

'It's a firebowl.' Flick grinned. 'You wait till they light it! They did all this last spring too, right the same time as Belttainne. The one they did in autumn, same time as Mabon, is different. There're more people here this time too. Don't suppose there'll be so many out on the hill for the Belttainne festival any more. Look! The temple fire-priests have started!'

At the front of the platform two men, wearing narrow yellow robes reaching their knees with baggy trousers underneath, began spinning long ropes. Fat knots at the end of the ropes burned with smoky flames. The ropes whirled round in hissing circles of flame, up, down, round and round, in more and more complicated patterns. It looked amazing, and Coryn clapped and cheered along with the rest of the crowd. Some yelled when the fires got too close though.

Then men on stilts, wearing outfits covered in long fluttering strips of fire colours, came through the tall temple doors, crossed the platform and walked down the steps into the crowds. They carried pairs of small torches and kept swallowing the flames of one only to set it alight again with the other. Coryn wondered how they could keep doing it. Surely the flames must burn their mouths?

A group of players, sitting just below the stage, made music on horns and drums. It got louder and louder, so loud Coryn could hardly think. Then it suddenly stopped. And everyone stopped moving and speaking.

'That one there's the High-priest,' Flick whispered, pointing.

Out of the tall double doors of the temple strode a thin, pale man followed by two other men, all wearing narrow, long black robes lined with shiny red cloth. Each of the priests carried a bushel of kindling. They surrounded the chest-high firebowl and bowed in unison as a drumbeat began again, slowly at first, then faster and faster till it sounded like thunder rolling through the square. The priests began chanting.

Coryn felt a build-up of pressure just behind his eyes, but it wasn't really hurting so he ignored it, not wanting to miss a thing.

The drum roll continued on alone and a priestess rose like a queen from the firebowl wearing a long dress made of the same shiny red cloth that lined the priests' robes. She wore lots of jewels round her neck and bare arms that flashed like fire. The priests put their bushels of kindling into the firebowl, right around the priestess so she was covered almost to her waist. The priestess then lifted her hands to the sky.

'Atash!' She screamed and a flame burst from the big red jewel hanging round her neck. The flame ran up her arms and filled her hands with fire. Some people gasped, some even screamed. Flick laughed and cheered along with most of the rest.

The pain in Coryn's head got worse, feeling like spikes poking through his skull. They pricked at him all over his body too, pushing him against the wall. He gritted his teeth and grabbed hold of the pouch feeling the shape of the amulet Birog had given him and trying to push the pain away. It surprised him how quick it eased off.

He opened his eyes to see the priestess bring her hands down and bend to push them into the bushels of kindling inside the bowl. She stood again and the fire on her hands had gone. Two of the priests came forward and lifted her out of the firebowl just as white hot flames roared up into the sky. The crowds all cheered and the spikes and prickles disappeared.

'Better than last year I'd say,' Flick said loudly in Coryn's ear. 'Come on, there's a fair north of the sea docks, on the sandflats, with proper Belltainne celebrations, horse racin' an' everythin'. Coming?'

The musicians had started playing something people could dance to, and the fire-dancers spun their ropes again. Coryn shook his head. 'I'll come with you to the docks, but I've got to get the first ship I can that's heading to Storr.'

'Storr? But that's leagues away. Don't know how many tendays of sailin', an' a bad journey this time of year with winter storms and the like. What you want to go there for?'

'So's I can see my sister again. And I've a message to deliver.' Coryn pressed his hand against the pouch again. 'It's important. Very important.'

'Must be to go all the way to Storr for.' Flick squinted down at him. 'Still, family is important. If you've a sister there, you gotta join her. You got coin for a berth?'

'A what?'

'A berth. Passage.' When Coryn still looked blank, Flick went on. 'It's payment for travel on a ship. Somewhere to sleep onboard.'

'Oh, yes. I've got a bit of coin.' Coryn pulled at the second pouch he'd pushed inside his trousers.

'No, don't take it out. There's pickpockets, thieves an' toppers all over. I should know.' Flick grinned, then grabbed hold of Coryn's hand and pulled him down from the trough.

'But...'

'If I wasn't around to help you get that berth,' said Flick, dragging Coryn across the square, 'you'd be skinned and left in an alley by midnight. You're nothin' but a sucklin', with no more sense than a babe.'

'But why are you helping me at all?' Coryn asked as they wove through the crowds, through a huge arch and down another looping road. 'I mean, I'm real grateful and all, but you don't know me. And what's a topper?'

'A topper? A topper's someone who uses the rooftops like roads an' burgles houses through the attics, an' I'm one of the best.' He grinned.

'As to helping you, I suppose it's 'cause I've only a sister left to me too. An' you're from Kalebrod, like me.' Flick smacked his chest with his palm. 'We homeless Kalebrodians got to stick together.'

'You don't sound like anyone from Kalebrod.'

'Been here long enough to sound Rophetan.'

'How'd that priestess make the fire, and how come she didn't get burned? Was it magik?'

'What? Nah, they don't use magik! Atash is against magik. His priests say it's evil an' only the evil use it. On account of the blood-priests bein' magikers everybody's believin' them. All magikers should be rounded up and taken to the temple for cleansin', the priests say. Sometimes, a few get brought out of the temple, an' they get burned to death.' Flick stopped and stared down at Coryn. He leaned down and whispered in his ear. 'Didn't used to be that way though, even got to hide believin' in the spirits an' that nowadays. An' how'd you know if'n the priestess used magik anyhow? You a magiker?'

'No, I've no magik. Anyway, magik isn't evil, it depends how it's used. That's what Da and Ma always said. Anyhow, though I've no magik, I know what it feels like.' Flick looked at Coryn funny, so he explained. 'It feels like spikes pricking into me when magik's used. I felt it just then, when the priestess made the flames. So the priests are lying.'

Flick looked at him a long while. 'Best you did leave this place then. I'm thinkin' me an' my sister should be doin' the same. Only Laru won't hear of it. She keeps findin' youngsters and bringin' them in to look after. Like we can barely look after ourselves as it is. Come on.'

It didn't take long for Flick to find a ship taking passengers. Coryn was to board with a whole crowd of other Kalebrodians at dawn to catch the morning tide. He'd paid half the berth, or rather he'd given Flick the money and he'd paid the First Mate. The second half was to be paid on safe arrival.

'Thanks, Flick.' Coryn smiled up at his new friend as they walked back into the city from the docks. There was plenty of coin left in his pouch and he gave it to Flick. He had another pouch hidden in his boot, proud of the fact he'd not mentioned it. Turns out he wasn't quite the *suckling* Flick thought him to be.

Flick didn't question it. He pushed the pouch under his shirt and brought Coryn home to meet his sister, Laru, by way of a market to buy bags of food. There, curled up in the attic of a tall, narrow building that smelled funny but was warm and dry, Coryn slept well. With a full belly and a roof over his head, he was happier than he'd been in a long time, and adventures on the sea filled his dreams.

Chapter 4

Katleya and her uncle hunted. It was the tail-end of winter, and the snows had begun melting on the lower mountain slopes. They were high up in the foothills of the Ruel Mountains and had stopped at the edge of the leafless woods half filling a valley. Below, the River Stam tumbled in a rush over rocks between narrow, reed heavy banks. Due west, a few leagues downstream, lay their home, the village of Laeft ofer Stam in the far western reaches of Rophet.

'So, tell me what you see.' Uncle Yadoc looked at her then back down the slope.

Katleya pushed out the tip of her tongue and moistened her lips, tasting the frigid breeze sliding down off the mountains. The earth smelled of ice, browned fern, moss, nibbled grass and wild animals. She spotted the tracks of rabbit and fox, even a spirit, a little shy, brown earth-spirit peeping out from a burrow, but that wouldn't be enough for her uncle.

She moved her head a little from side to side and leaned into the wind. It wasn't necessary but it helped her concentrate. Then Katleya opened her Wealdan.

Too much.

Searing light flooded in, swamped her brain, and threatened to drown every sense. She gasped, struggling against it. Forcing her focus to narrow, she felt the light fade to something more bearable. Then she could see, or rather, sense the individual gossamer threads of Wefan. The strands of energy trellised through the trees, laced the grass and leaves, and latticed the rock and earth. Each pattern stretched a little way out into the air creating a nimbus of light, an aura she'd been learning to read. If she concentrated very hard, Katleya could almost hear the soft hum the Wefan made as it coursed through everything. She crouched, laying one hand on the grass. The thrum and tingle of Wefan felt strange and wonderful at the same time.

'You should know how to stop letting it overwhelm you by now, child. People will notice you gasping and flapping about like a landed fish. Trackers and hunters should be silent, unknown at all times, no matter what skills they use,' Uncle Yadoc repeated. Yet again. 'Now, tell me what you see.'

Stung by his rebuke, Katleya turned away, pulled the wide brim of her hat down low to hide her flush, and searched. Where animals had passed she saw the slight damage done to the patterns of the energies in stems, blades and leaves, even on mud, stone and sand. She recognised what had passed by and how long ago by how they'd affected the Wefan. They led her to the actual spoor, which she could see using ordinary sight. The cloven hooves of a herd of deer. The clawed paw of a mountain cat standing well over three feet by the size of its pads. The prints of a wolf pack.

The breeze stilled as she looked over the river. Here, the fast flowing water distorted the strands of Wefan, sending them, and any that floated loose in the air above, into a constant state of flux. It made them almost unreadable and what lay on the opposite bank hard to see. She turned to her uncle.

'Nothing this side of the river.'

He nodded and led them on. They forded the river, stepping from one slippery rock to the next, where the water ran shallow but swift with icy snowmelt. Then the contamination of Wefan by writhen alerted all her senses.

They had left an obvious trail. Staining the strands of Wefan with a disturbing murk. As if their *wrongness* infected the patterns of everything they touched. Katleya paralleled their route noting when the spoor of clawed yet human-shaped feet were joined by the prints of a pair of unmistakeable wide, square-toed boots.

'Writhen passed through here.' Katleya flared her nostrils. She could almost smell the acrid stink of the twisted creatures. She hesitated, reading the trail with care. 'Three. They came past here a day ago. A Murecken blood-priest is with them.'

A shiver ran down her neck. Writhen coming down from the mountains so early was bad enough, but a blood-priest too and so close to the village? And so far from the Kalebrodian border? Katleya gripped her short-bow a little tighter. 'They worked their way along the river here. Then turned back up the ridge over there.'

'Yes. I see the tracks now.' Uncle Yadoc followed close behind. 'Where do they turn, child?'

Katleya walked on then pointed northwards to a slope of rocks and furze. 'Right here. Then on through that birch copse.'

Uncle Yadoc looked at the tracks. He nodded, almost smiled as he turned toward her. His steel-blue eyes gleamed against his bronzed skin, leathered by the wind and rain of over sixty years. 'You've done well. Three writhen and a Murecken blood-priest as you say.' He crouched low and traced one of the scuffed prints left in the soft soil. He stood. 'But you still need more practice. Not now, however. It's time to return home. The light will soon fail and I've no wish to meet a blood-priest face to face. We must also warn the village. Come, child.'

A short while later they came out of the trees and drank from the brook where a stand of ice-tarnished goldenrod feathered the breeze. Uncle Yadoc led the way again. He stepped through clumps of frosted bull rushes, his boots crunching into frail ice where it silvered the tracks of deer.

Katleya, glowing from Uncle Yadoc's praise, placed her feet in his tracks, watching out for snares hidden along the rabbit runs by Luffe and his sons, Aeffe and Coulfe, earlier that evening. She didn't want to annoy them, though it'd be funny to hear them swear. She wondered what elaborate new oaths they could possibly come up with, ones that she could learn. She flicked her plait back over her shoulder and stretched her legs to mimic Uncle Yadoc's long stride.

A while later, Katleya saw columns of chimney smoke rise into the evening sky, then the scattering of thatched rooftops that made up Laeft Village, peeking above the new walls of river stone and tree trunks. It looked snug and safe in its little valley.

'It's time to leave Laeft.' Uncle Yadoc flicked her a look over his shoulder. 'We'll warn everyone but I'll not wait for them to decide what they'll do. A blood-priest means only one thing. They're after people with the Wealdan. People like you. And not long behind them will be the Murecken army.'

Katleya knew all about the likelihood of being hunted by Murecken bloodhunter-priests. She'd been trained well by Uncle Yadoc since she came into her Wealdan. Trained to hide it from everyone and everything. But to leave Laeft? She couldn't imagine living anywhere else. And how could Uncle Yadoc ever leave his beloved smithy, his metalworking? It'd be like the great oak of the village green tearing up its roots and trundling off to settle itself up a mountain – just plain wrong. She walked a little faster so she could see his face, trying to read what hid in his eyes. His thoughts stayed hidden, as usual.

Studying him made her realise again how different she was from him. His hair spiked from his head, straight and coarse, black as the peaty soil of the foothills mixed with the iron of horseshoes. His beard, more iron than black, spiked thickly from his chin. He was a large, stocky man well built for his work, with huge hands covered in the scars of his trade. Nothing like her. She stood tall for a girl and some called her skinny. Her skin refused to tan, even through the glory days of summer. Her curly hair was a very pale blonde under its dye. Another secret Uncle Yadoc made her keep, only saying that her mother had had the same hair and it'd got her killed, then refusing to say why. She wondered what Aeffe would think if he ever saw her real hair colour. No one round here had such blonde hair. He'd probably just try to get his hands under her clothes all the more if he knew.

Not for the first time she wondered about her parents. One day, Uncle Yadoc had said long ago, he would tell her everything. Katleya still waited. She looked up at him again.

'We're leaving? For certain?' She pulled her hat off to scratch an itch. The icy air tickled at her scalp.

'We'll take the cart to Black Rock. Sell off the last of the young stock.'

'But I've not got the colts to saddle yet, only the filly's ready.'

'From there we'll take a ship to Storr.' Uncle Yadoc ignored what she'd said. His voice was so low she had to strain to hear it.

'Storr. But that's in the Elyat Sea. That'll take months by sea sailing all the way south and round Deorc's Cape then all the way north again. Isn't there any way over the mountains?'

'The Ruel Mountains are impassable, you know that, Katleya. What with winter lying thick on them still. Besides, they're full of cave dwelling creatures that'd eat you soon as look at you, and do I have to remind you they're also full of writhen and blood-priests? Maybe even blod-gemen too. I've told you what the Murecken do to men they capture haven't I? Twist them with blood-magik till they know nothing but madness and hunger only for death.' She nodded, her face twisting at the horrible idea of it. Uncle Yadoc bent his head down, laying a hand on her shoulder. 'Now, tell me in detail how we'd travel to Storr. Have you the map in your head?'

'As I said, ship would have to sail leagues south past the coast of Kalebrod, past the southern reaches of the Ruel Mountains, past the empty lands east of the Diaphos Mountains, round Deorc's Cape then north past Selassi.' Katleya had her uncle's various maps clear as day to her mind's eye. She liked the feel of his big warm hand on her shoulder, strong and safe, it soothed the turmoil of her thoughts. 'After that we'd pass a lot of other port cities going north along the Sutherne Sea coastline till we got to Torralt's Neck. We'd pass through that narrow bit of sea and so reach the Elyat Sea. Storr Island is in its western reaches just off the coast between Losan and Albane.'

'Well done, child.' Uncle Yadoc gave her a fleeting hug.

'I've never seen the sea or the royal city.' Katleya imagined Black Rock to be magnificent. She had heard all about its tall black castle, the new-built Fire Temple of Atash and the great seaport full of ships from distant and exotic lands, from peddlers and from the Rophetan border guards. The soldiers had come up from their forts to sweep the hill country after the fall of Kalebrod to the Murecken. Looked like they needed to make another sweep.

'You'll have to be even more careful when using your *talent* till we're on Storr, especially in Black Rock. The Atash priesthood is against any magik use and things are getting bad there for anyone who's a bit different. I've heard there's been a lot of burnings. It's long past time you went to the Ostorr Haven anyway.' Uncle Yadoc began walking on again. 'They'll do a better job of teaching you than I, and you're of an age to begin your studies at the Haven, child. In truth, you were the first day you discovered your Wealdan last year. Some come into their Wealdan by twelve and are packed off to one Haven or another for training.'

'My studies?' Bewildered, Katleya skipped ahead to look her uncle in the eye. 'You've never said anything about this before and what's a *haven?*'

Uncle Yadoc stopped, raised a hand for silence and glared round Hag's Wood as though he'd never seen the tract of coppiced hazel before. 'I made a vow sixteen winters ago, child, when you were first given to me as a tiny babe. One I mean to keep to my dying breath. I'll not let you fall into the hands of the Murecken priesthood. And I can't protect you against their bloodhunter-priests and lacerts alone. I'll wait no longer for her to come for...it could be I've left it too long as it is. I thought I could keep you safe here and I don't like Storr. It's a den of politics and intrigue. Apart from a few, I never knew whom I could trust from one day to the next. I hoped never to return.'

'Come for...? Someone was going to come for me? Who? And you used to live in Storr? How come you never...'

'We will leave tomorrow.' He kept his voice low and gripped Katleya's shoulder with a heavy hand. 'We'll speak no more of this. The Moder will keep you safe in Ostorr Haven.' His eyes, usually so clear and focused, became troubled. Almost sad. He hugged her again, harder and longer this time. 'I've done as much as I can for you.'

'Uncle Yadoc, what are you...'

'Hush, girl.' Uncle Yadoc turned Katleya about and urged her on toward the village. 'You need to dye your hair again, it's grown and I see roots of gold.'

'And that's another thing, when are you going to tell me why I have to dye my hair? Why did it kill my Ma?'

'Soon, I will tell you soon. For now, we must ready to leave.'

And with that she had to be satisfied, though inside she was screaming with frustration.

Chapter 5

Hearing the clatter of a chain on Cutter's Road, Katleya slid into the shadows of the nearest alley between two of the meat shops and waited. They were all youngsters this time, none of them over fifteen, she'd guess. The twenty-four children stumbled through the slush, each shackled by one wrist to a long chain held at the front by a Thief-taker Guildsman, unmistakeable in his black uniform with the orange flame of their fire god, Atash, on one sleeve. Two other Thief-takers strode up and down the chain, cracking their short whips to keep the poor wretches moving. The people on the street gave them plenty of room. A few melted away like summer snow.

Like me.

A voice bellowed through her private shame.

'Hoy, Thief-taker, here's one for your chain.' A butcher shoved a ragged boy of about seven or eight into the road.

The boy tripped and fell, dropping a pig's foot into the filth. With hunger overruling any sense he might have had, he didn't run, but scrabbled after the stolen trotter. A blow to his head opened up the flesh behind one ear and he had joined the chain before the blood reached his shoulder.

'He'll be cleansed by the Fires of Atash, His Flames burn eternal.' The Thief-taker almost sounded like he believed in what he said. 'More every day find that serving the Great God Atash is a better way of life.'

'Hear you've enough boys for your priesthood now. You'll be sending these ones to the border, fresh fodder for the guard to keep them blood-priests from our doors, eh?' The butcher's eyes glinted in the cold light. 'Is it a silver per child and two for an adult you're getting from the army now?'

I hope rats chew on his bollocks!

The urge to throw something at the butcher was strong. Somehow, Katleya kept herself from lifting the hard lump of grimy snow she now gripped.

The Thief-taker grunted and copper flashed. The butcher snatched the coin from the air and slid it into the pocket of his bloodied leather apron.

Muttering rumbled through the crowd, but it faded when a red-robed priest stalked out of the chandler's opposite Katleya's alley. He stopped on the wooden walkway above the mud of the road. She ducked lower and peered at him through the slats of a broken crate. The priest's robes swelled over his stomach, his fire-stone rings glittered as he stroked his oiled beard. He studied the prisoners, stone-faced, as the chain shuffled down the road past him.

During their *cleansing* by Atash, the priests had their pick of the prisoners for the temple. The ones they kept were rarely ever seen or heard of again. Folk had learned not to show any interest in their disappearance. Katleya couldn't tell if this one saw any youngsters worth choosing along the chain. He raised one black-sleeved arm, its orange embroidered Flame of Atash shining bright in the morning sun, to acknowledge the Thief-takers' salutes.

Katleya wondered what they saw in those they chose to keep. Dull brained obedience? Cloak swirling, the priest turned and strode up the hill. A well-fed acolyte, wearing brown and orange striped robes, scurried along behind carrying the priest's goods. The city folk gave them both as much room as they had given the Thief-takers, if not more.

Half way down the alley, Katleya began scaling the crumbling wall of a house, the clanking of the thief-chain still loud in her ears. She had learned how to survive in Black Rock over the year or so of being trapped in the city, learned how to avoid or deal with the street gangs, the Thief-takers and the city guard. But she had lost count of the friends taken or killed by one or the other. She knew only the blind luck of the spirits kept her safe. Not that she'd seen any spirits since reaching the filthy city. She tried to convince herself her hands weren't shaking and forced her fingers into the cracks of the uneven wall, hurrying to climb to the top and reach the precarious safety of the roofs.

Half way up Black Rock's largest hill, Castle Mount, the middle one of the three that made up the island on which the city was built, Katleya rested in a gap between two chimneys. She was glad of the warmth coming through the bricks and thinking that maybe it hadn't been such a good idea to sell her coat along with all Uncle Yadoc's tools. It was too good and too red, it made her a target so she hadn't worn it for an age anyway. Keeping it hadn't been an option. She pulled a rather solid little pie from her shirt pocket, one she had bought from a tray-vendor down in the smith's district, and took a small bite. Her mouth filled with the flavours of pork meat, sage and onion.

The woman hadn't lied. Real pork!

Katleya wrapped it back up and tucked it away. It'd be something special to share with Uncle Yadoc when she got back. The smell alone should tempt him into eating. Over the roofs and walled gardens of the richer districts of the Mount, she could see the castle. It dominated the city, its tall walls splashed with torchlight, built from the black rock for which the city was named. Opposite, on the edge of Royal Square, stood Victory Arch and next to it squatted the Temple of Atash. The flames of its beacon on the taller tower glowered against the dusky sky. To the northeast, she could just see where the northern arm of the River Stam tumbled into the sea. She turned to look south. The sluggish and much wider southern arm of the Stam couldn't be seen from where she sat, neither could the hovel where she and her uncle lived.

Spirits, please tell me why we're still in this dump?

They should have left Black Rock long ago. The moment they arrived would have been best, but they could only leave by sea and even a year ago a berth cost a great deal of coin, so much more than they had left after being robbed on the road less than a league from the city. The cost rose with every passing day and every new influx of refugees. It hadn't helped that no one had wanted to hire an old man for metal-working. Then, only a few months after they'd arrived, Uncle Yadoc had got sick. To be old was bad enough, to be sick was unforgivable.

Katleya felt sure her coin pouch finally weighed enough to pay for another healer's visit. It couldn't be soon enough. She got up and moved on up Castle Mount. Worse than surviving in this slag-pit of a city would be surviving in it alone.

Her soft, deerskin boots whispered over slate, wood shingles and clay tiles as she moved through the smoke of countless chimneys. The less time Katleya spent on the streets the better. Normally, she'd circle Castle Mount and stay on the roof-tops of Smith's Hill's western edge, then on to Low Hill the rest of the way home. But she'd wanted to check out the shipping on the sea docks, and then she'd given her word to deliver a message and she couldn't pass up the certainty of more coin so easily earned.

Slithering down a mossy wall into an alley, Katleya peered out over the great, paved space of Royal Square. The last few revellers, wearing evergreen-leaf and red-ribbon garlands, milled round its edges, determined to see the Midwinter celebrations through to the bitter end. Some crowded the pools of warmth around charcoal braziers, others spilled out of the three raucous inns. A few feet to her left, a pair of guardsmen strolled under Victory Arch and down Royal Avenue. The broad street looped down the hill towards the sprawling sea docks. Even from here, the uproar of wilder entertainments from the taverns and doxy houses of the harbour district sounded loud.

On the other side of Victory Arch from Atash's Temple, huddled the smallest of the three inns, its sign showing a man's face in profile wearing an ornate crown. Katleya hurried out of the alley and, with a nod to Sarl, the doorman, went through the heavy door and into the vast tap-room of the Royal Head.

'Is Garve about?' Katleya asked Laru, one of the flustered barmaids and a good friend. She showed her a roll of parchment. 'I've a message.'

'Yup, he's somewhere. Busy as Atash's hells tonight.'

Katleya coughed. After the biting air outside, the fumes from burning tobacco, wood and tallow thickened the air so much she struggled to breathe. She pushed her hat back from her forehead as the heat got to her and looked around. People lounged on long benches listening to music, eating, drinking, arguing. Some even slept. A couple of dogs lurked under the trestle tables, alert for food dropped onto the rushes.

Laru dumped three tankards on a nearby table and scooped up a coin. They'd become good friends after Katleya had saved her from drowning a month after arriving in Black Rock. Shorter than her, but a fair few years older at twenty-four, Laru had taken Katleya under her wing and, along with her brother, Flick, taught her how to survive in the city.

'Garve!' Laru shrilled. Her voice knifed through the noise. 'Katleya with a message for you.'

'Sparks, Laru, where'd you learn to yell like that?'

'Soon learn what you've got to if'n you want to survive, Katleya.' Laru shrugged and rolled her eyes. 'Sold your Uncle's stuff then?'

'How'd you guess?' Katleya shifted and ran her eyes over the room again, hating to think her face that easy to read.

'Got the forge stink on you and a look in your eye. Besides, I hear he's close to gone with the lung-rot.'

'Yeah, well,' Katleya blinked, the smoke making her eyes smart. 'Good quality tools. Every hammer and tong, but I still couldn't get much for them.'

'Everyone's sellin', no one's buyin'.' Laru shrugged. 'The war.'

'That's the truth. Still, I've enough to finally get that healer in.'

'He still don't take to the herbcraft then?'

'It's just not enough, no.'

'Hmm. Could still get you a place here, if'n you're willin' to wear a dress.'

'More likely to knife them than serve them if they put their paws on me.' Katleya scowled round at the sweaty crowd. 'Don't think Garve would like that much. And there's no way I'd ever wear a dress.'

'I'd believe that.' Laru laughed. 'You've a way with knives that I've seen in few others. I only wish I'd had an uncle who could've taught me such skills.'

'Quit your natterin' and get to servin', girl.' A squat bald-headed man bulled his way through the crowd.

'I'll come by tomorrow.' Laru turned and hurried off.

'Message from Master Lugg the Metalsmith, Master Garve.' Katleya showed the landlord the rolled parchment with its black ribbon. 'He said you'd give me twelve docks.'

'Half a sickle for a message? Are you mad, girl?' He glared at her then flipped open a heavy leather coin pouch. 'I'll give you two docks.'

'It's Midwinter. Special rates on a holiday,' Katleya insisted, refusing to back down. 'I'll take ten and not a dock less.'

'You'll take eight and be happy with it, Katleya.' Garve counted out the coins.

'Done.' Katleya gave him the parchment and slipped the coins into the pouch under her armpit, the safest place from cutpurses. She grinned.

She had got twice as much as she'd hoped for and before Garve could change his mind she shot out of the inn. Straight into the belly of a fat man who reeled into her path. He reeked of ale and food stained his green merchant's sash. In full view, a heavy coin-pouch swung below his blubbery paunch. Tempted, her fingers twitched.

Without warning, his fist closed on her shirt and he yanked her close.

'Murak's stinking hells!' Katleya hissed as the linen ripped from neck to navel. 'Let go, blast it!'

'By the Fire-God, it's a female!' the merchant shouted and he roared with laugher.

'Get off me, lump-arse!' Livid, Katleya clawed at the fist and tried to cover her breasts at the same time.

'Blessed be Great Atash, look what I've caught. A new-ripened girl who would pluck me but has been plucked herself!' Lump-arse roared and he tugged at his purse so the thong broke and held it up as evidence.

'That's blasted bollocks!' Katleya landed a sharp kick to his shin, but he wore a pair of thick leather boots and she'd only her soft roof-topper shoes on.

'O hoy, a fresh and lively one too!' Lump-arse grinned through his thick, black beard and gave Katleya a shake that ripped her shirt even more. The cold air bit into her skin. 'My mouth is watering in anticipation of her fair flesh!'

Katleya readied a fist for that but looking up into his face she caught a tell-tale flicker in his eyes and realised Lump-arse had company. Ducking down, she head-butted him in the paunch. Air whooshed from his lungs and he let go of her shirt as he folded to the ground with a pig-like grunt.

A blow skimmed her ribs. It burned forge-fierce but at least Lump-arse's partner hadn't managed to crack her skull. Furious, Katleya whipped round and danced sideways. She slipped her knives into her palms and let the bastard come to her. He had a red-corded hat and a flame on his sleeve. A Thief-taker! So, this was a sweet little set up to catch themselves another innocent for their chains. They would soon see just how sweet she wasn't.

The lean man surged forward and Katleya ducked down and twisted left. She thrust low, well below his belt. A fingers length of fine steel slid straight in, just shy of his bollocks. He doubled over in agony and she slashed into the shadows under his hat. Crying out, the Thief-taker crumpled to the ground and she vaulted over him. Dodging Lump-arse, still winded and yet to get back on his feet, she crossed the square at full pelt.

Her eyes everywhere at once, Katleya pressed the heel of one hand against her ribs and tried to ignore the pain, but it reduced her to quick shallow breaths. As she swung into the alley she felt agony burn across her thigh. She slowed and looked down. Slicked with blood, her trousers gaped open from a ragged cut just above the knee.

How did I miss the blasted Thief-taker's knife?

Then the wound began to hurt like a burn from new forged metal making her stagger and she had to bite down on a whimper. There would be no climbing walls and leaping along rooftops now. She wiped the blood from her blades, sheathed them and limped on.

Close. Too blasted close!

Chapter 6

It is time for me to leave.' Leveen cut off the High-priest's grating drone and rose from the plush, velvet-covered chair by the marble fireplace with its intricate carvings replicating the sigils of Ascian rituals. Arrogant of the High-priest of Rophet to have Murak's art carved where any could see it, even if they did not understand its significance. It would not bode well for the Atash priesthood in Rophet to be revealed as no more than Murecken lackeys. She wondered how such a fool could have risen so high. 'I will pass on your messages to the Atash High-priests of Sellasi and Rialt.'

'You must go so soon? It is a great pity you never have time to stay these days, Leveen el Meera al-Shafi.' The High-priest leered at her. Perhaps he thought saying her whole name would give him some sort of power over her. He was mistaken in his thinking. He stood, waving ring-heavy fingers about vaguely and licking his fat lips. 'I thought, perhaps, you would enjoy looking over our latest culls again. We have found twenty-one with various measures of potency this last month alone and all under fifteen years of age. We have also gathered in a few younger siblings who may have potential given time. So thirty-three in all reside in the cells at this very moment.'

'As I said last time, I am no longer interested in seeing the culls, though I am not surprised by the count. It is no great problem for your Thief-takers and priests to pluck them from the crowds of refugees flooding the city.' Leveen shrugged, knowing what the man truly wanted. 'Just send them on as usual.'

She had gone down to see the child culls the first time she came to Black Rock. In the cells the stink of fear almost drowned the faint scent of the potency in their blood. Leveen grimaced, even that weak trace of the Wealdan had made the blood-madness rise inside her. It had excited the High-priest too, she had seen it in his eyes and her own lust had flared all the higher.

Leveen had thrown him to the ground and mounted him, using him there and then. They had rutted in the dark just feet from the bars behind which the children huddled, any noise they made drowned by the crying and whimpering. At the time, it had sated her need and settled the blood-madness, as it always did. But it had not lasted long enough, as it never did. Not like consuming the blood and flesh of a Wealdan-bearer would. But the culls were denied to her as they were destined for the Murecken priesthood in Elucame.

Making her way to the door, Leveen raised a hand as the scowling High-priest reached for the bell standing on his side table. 'No need to ring for one of your acolytes, I will see myself out. Farewell and may Atash's Flame burn eternal.' She made a shallow bow and opened the door.

'I shall pass on your messages also.' The High-priest rose and bowed, a fraction less than she had, she noted. 'Atash's Flames will burn eternal.'

Leveen smiled, thin-lipped, and fixed her veil in place as she left. Ignoring the skinny boys in orange robes standing to either side of the door, she walked down the torch-lit corridor, imagining the blade of her janbiya patterning the pale skin of his over-fed body, his blood welling up and flowing in red waves down and across the floor. Swallowing the saliva filling her mouth, she had to pause and lean her forehead against the cold stone wall of the dark passage until the blood-madness eased. She almost thought to turn and slake her momentary need on the High-priest or perhaps one of his boys. Gripping the hilt of her knife till her knuckles ached, she made her way down the narrow stairs to a small side entrance of the temple.

As Leveen exited the alley running down the left side of the Temple of Atash and stepped out into the Royal Square she saw a girl dodge with finesse through the last few revellers of the Midwinter feasting. The girl, her clothes ripped and her breasts out on show, staggered at the entrance of an alley and clutched at her leg before disappearing into the darkness. Too much feasting perhaps?

Looking round, she saw a Thief-taker sprawled on the ground not more than three yards from the temple's steps. A fat merchant struggled to his feet nearby. She thought nothing of it till she smelled the blood.

The scent of it punched her in the guts and Leveen needed all her control to stop from leaping towards the two men. She stalked to the Thief-taker's side and saw a knife sheathed in blood half-fallen from his fingers. It spoke to her. Leaning down, she plucked the knife from his limp hand and brought it to her mouth. A touch of the tongue and all was confirmed.

Potency. Such potency it almost overwhelmed her. Though she

knew it was dangerous, Leveen needed to lick more blood from the blade. She shivered at the ecstasy of its taste, felt her eyes burn with an awakening of hunger. At last, she closed her eyes at the moment of realisation, at last she had the means by which to free herself.

'What d'you mean, stealing from a Thief-taker?'

Her leg exploded with pain as the Thief-taker's lead-weighted cosh smashed against her kneecap. Staggering, Leveen whipped out her tulwar and sliced off his head.

Gritting her teeth against the agony in her knee, Leveen tugged the hood of her cloak further forward and struggled back into the shadows. It would not do to be seen clearly in these parts for she was far too recognisable. The merchant had disappeared and all the people still in the square made themselves busy looking elsewhere, hurrying elsewhere. It was good they did as, with her blood up, there was a great likelihood she would take the lives of more should they block her path.

The dodging girl was long gone and Leveen was not in any fit state to go after her. But was that girl the one that was cut by this knife? Leveen could not be sure. She spat onto the Thief-taker's body, cursing the man for her lost opportunity, then she cursed herself for having lost all awareness in that moment of blood-madness.

She would be free of it soon. This Leveen swore to all the gods both old and new.

Thrusting the Thief-taker's knife behind her cummerbund and using her tulwar for support, an almost unforgiveable sin for any pure-blood Shafian, Leveen limped through the arch and down the avenue to the port. It would not do to let the Rophetan soldiers catch her here for the Thief-taker Guild was powerful in Black Rock and the priests might not be able to protect her.

Chapter 7

Katleya hobbled on, grim and determined to keep going till she reached her home.

Ha! Home? No home to me.

She thought on the Thief-taker guild and their thugs. They passed on all the likeliest ones they caught to the border guard, after the Atash priesthood got their pick, of course. They got well paid for it too. The guard needed all the bodies it could get, what with the war dragging on and the border forts hard pressed. Katleya thought she could cope with a bit of soldiering. Maybe. But everyone knew that some of the guild's prisoners got sold elsewhere for much more coin.

A few weeks ago, a Thief-taker captured a girl from Katleya's neighbourhood. Just fourteen and prettier than most, they sold her on to a dock brothel instead instead of the guard. She hadn't lasted long. Katleya heard a knife-fight ended her life before her parents could buy her out. Maybe the quick death was best, like some said, but the haunted look still had to leave her mother's eyes. Katleya hawked and spat to clear the foul taste filling her mouth.

At a scrape from the alley to her left, Katleya palmed her knives. She flattened against a dank stone wall as a pair of glowing amber eyes gazed at her from the darkness. They blinked then disappeared as the feral dog they belonged to slunk away.

Relieved the dog foraged alone – she couldn't see herself fighting off a whole pack, or anything much else – she moved on. Trying to save her soft roof-topper shoes from a soaking, she picked her way over refuse and around stinking puddles. She listened hard but couldn't hear any sound of pursuit.

Not yet.

By the time she reached the river warehouse district the two moons rode high in the black-veneered heavens. Light silvered the narrow spaces between the shacks and glittered on icy puddles and old snow as Katleya limped across the tanner's yard. She looked toward the river.

Has that blasted shack sunk even more?

Another few feet and the upper storey would be in the muddy water too.

The district of tanners and dyers yards, abandoned when the river trade dried up after the Murecken attacks on the hill country, had become a dumping ground for the poorest refugees, like her and Uncle Yadoc. Firelight, seeping between the warped planks of the shack next door, proved more folk had moved into the yard overnight. The gang who controlled this area would be by soon enough to claim coin for their *protection*.

Katleya felt eyes on her as she climbed the ladder to the upper floor. She looked up, giving the boy on the warehouse roof across the yard a wave and the flash of a grin. Half the district would know within an hour what time she'd arrived back and in what condition.

Inside what she'd called home for almost a year, Katleya listened out for her uncle. It seemed the old man slept as no sound came from behind the screen of old stiff hides, none that she could hear over the sounds of the river anyway. Keeping her moves quiet, for he needed all the sleep he could get, she stirred up the banked coals in the large stone firebowl and piled on some sticks. Flames licked the wood as she blew on them and her thoughts flew back to the times she had fired up the forge and worked the bellows for Uncle Yadoc. 'Get that blasted fire going! It's still not hot enough to melt cheese, girl!' He would yell and she would pump all the harder.

Biting her lip, she scrubbed her eyes then hung a small pot of harvested icicles over the firebowl and pushed some larger sticks into the flames. Warmth kissed her skin as she collapsed onto her straw-filled mattress. Katleya flicked a look across the room and saw a rat. A knife flashed and hammered into the floor, pinning the rat through its brain.

Uncle Yadoc stayed blissfully quiet. Katleya bolted upright.

Too quiet!

She hopped across the room. 'Uncle Yadoc!'

His mouth moved, like he tried to say something. Katleya kneeled beside him and leaned over so she hovered above his face.

'A Portal is broken between this world and the Wefan-flux,' he whispered. His eyelids fluttered but didn't open fully.

'Uncle Yadoc, what is it? What do you mean?'

'The Wefan bleeds from Dumnon.'

'I don't understand.'

'Listen, child.' Uncle Yadoc rasped, coughed, caught his breath again. His eyes, fully open, glared at her. 'The time for telling has come. My time will soon be upon me, sooner than I thought possible. You are not yet ready.'

'What? No wait...' Katleya felt reality slipping away as the old man took hold of her hand.

Uncle Yadoc struggled to lift his head up and Katleya saw the grief clogging his eyes. 'Spirits, not like this. I'm sorry, Moder Birog, I have failed you. And Ethlinn too...I can protect this one no more.'

'Who are you talking about?' Katleya's mouth went dry. She put her arms around the old man, trying to help him sit up. Uncle Yadoc spasmed. 'Please, tell me what to do.' Panic clawed its way into her mind.

'Go, you must go...there is...no pain now...I am beyond...' Uncle Yadoc coughed and blood leaked from his mouth. 'Get to Storr...get to Ostorr as fast as you can. Whatever happens do not let the Murecken take you. They must never have you. Never! Forgive me...for failing.'

The whispered words hung on the still air as the old man's hand fell limp to the blanket. His eyes faded and looked somewhere far away. Struggling not to shake, she pressed her fingers to his throat.

Dead. Spirits! He's dead.

Katleya pressed Uncle Yadoc's callused palm against her cheek. She tried to find comfort in knowing his pain had ended, but anger warred with her grief. He should have let her sell his tools before, when the coin would have done some good. She tugged the coin pouch from her under her shirt and threw it against the wall. The useless coins pattered down onto her blankets.

'Stinking blasted city! Why did we ever come here? And you never even told me everything you said you would, blast it! The time for telling has come, you say, and then you blasted well die?'

She heard the faint sound of a bell from the Atash temple toll the midnight hour.

A long while later, emptied of tears and feeling guilt for her rage, Katleya closed his eyes. Uncle Yadoc looked peaceful now. She could almost imagine he slept. Perhaps he dreamed of better times.

She covered him with a blanket. 'Spirits, please take Uncle Yadoc to the deeps of Annufen. Keep him in peace till he's reborn to a new life.'

Katleya fed more wood into the fire-bowl, drew a blanket over her shoulders and stared at the warped wooden walls of the room they had called home since the first thaws of spring over a year ago. When the water began bubbling she rose, pulled a few cocklebur leaves from a bunch of dried herbs hanging from a rafter, threw them into the pot and moved it to the floor to steep. It was good to just do things without having to think. She unstrapped all her knives, stripped off her bloody trousers and examined the wound in her thigh. Much deeper and she could've been crippled.

'Blasted louse-infested rat-gets.' Katleya hissed at the pain. She thought up a few more unflattering descriptions for both the Thief-taker and Lump-arse as she dipped a cloth into the pot. After she had washed it out with the stinging liquid the wound didn't look much better, but at least it looked clean. She wrapped her thigh in strips of clean linen and shifted back to lean against the wall.

Katleya decided she had to see. With Uncle Yadoc's warnings ringing in her head but certain the river running under the shack would hide what she did, as he had always insisted flowing water would, she opened her Wealdan. Easy as an intake of breath, her mind opened to the shimmering gossamer threads of Wefan.

Lost in the patterns of pure energy in everything about her, Katleya let the moment stretch. The Wefan matrices within wood, metal and stone, the tiny half-formed lattices floating through the air like lengths of spider filaments caught in sun beams, all mesmerized her. Shaking out of it, she narrowed her focus and saw the patterns running through her own skin, then deeper, where they wove through muscles and bones. The wound was a jagged slice of dirty grey cutting through the Wefan.

It would be something if she could do more than just *see* the Wefan, she thought. What if she could mend those fragile strands of energy, would that heal the wound? Could it be possible? She thought she could see how it might be done. After a moment, she reached out with her Wealdan and touched the broken strands, tried to join one to the other.

There.

Then pain knifed through her leg and shattered her link into a thousand pieces that jabbed through her skull. Her eyelids slammed shut.

Chapter 8

The crash of metal on metal reverberated through his brain so hard Coryn thought his skull might explode. He tried to smother the rising fear inside. With the promise of freedom so close, it would be a terrible thing for the smith's hand to slip. His life smashed by a hammer just as it looked to begin.

Coryn's mind flashed back to the events leading to his first becoming a slave. Barely a tenday out of Black Rock the pirates had struck. He'd been squeezed into a corner of the hold in their ship for a month or more before reaching the slave blocks of Dal Abar. Wretched and skinny as he was, they'd sold him for a pitiful few coins. The branding and iron collar had likely cost more. His owner, a merchant, had earned his coin back and then some. Whipped into submission and trained up as cook's boy, then guard and scout, somehow he'd survived the harshest desert conditions on the merchant's caravans. So much of his life taken from him, but now he had it back.

'It's done.' The smith levered the collar open and threw it on the growing pile beyond the anvil. The heap of slave collars and chains rattled and shifted, then settled.

Coryn straightened and stroked his neck. Ridged and raw from rubs old and new, it felt strange. Strange how to be free of the weight and constriction of the collar felt almost wrong.

'How do you feel?' Hort asked, stretching out a hand to Coryn.

'Lighter, light-headed, if I'm honest.' Coryn took his hand and let his friend pull him up.

'Is that humour?' Hort grinned. The massive man's eyes gleamed with excitement for his new future.

Coryn shrugged, wondering why he didn't feel that same excitement. He moved away to make room for the next freedman to have his collar removed. Yes, a weight had lifted from his shoulders in every sense, but there was no euphoria. Shouldn't he feel more?

'I heard they're hiring up at City Guard.' Hort turned and made to leave Slave Square, the centre of the ancient slave market area of Selassi. Now put to far better use.

'I heard that too.' Coryn nodded to a Lehotan Adherent who'd looked up from the ledger book he was filling with the names of freed slaves. He looked tired, all the Lehotans did.

'I'm damned sure many others have too.' Hort shrugged and tilted his head. 'And there'll be a limit to how many men they can take.'

Coryn's feet seemed welded to the ground. Eight years a slave, since a boy of eleven summers old, a boy whose life had ended half a world away. He barely knew anything about being free. He couldn't even see his Ma's face any more, or his Da's. Bryn, his older brother, faded in his memories with every passing day as did little Lera, but then she was so young when he'd last seen her how could he be expected to remember her face? It hurt like a knife in the guts though, losing their faces. Somehow it made him feel more rootless, more lost.

Lera. He hoped she was still alive. Somewhere safe. Now free, he could finally look for her, and that made his heart beat a morsel faster. She'd be thirteen, almost a woman grown by now.

His hand travelled to the old sweat-stained pouch hanging around his neck carrying his special amulet and a small roll of vellum. A message both important and secret. It had waited a good eight years more than it ought to have, but it might still have meaning to the man it was meant for. More important, if Birog had managed to keep her promise, that man would know the whereabouts of Lera.

Spirits! I hope so.

'Aren't you coming? You've been given your freedom, man.' Hort paused, looked back over his shoulder, his eyebrow lifted. 'And freedmen can't wait on masters to feed them, we've got to earn coin to buy food now.'

'I know, I do know. But all of a sudden having choices, it gives a man pause.' He should get to Storr, deliver the message and find Lera. He'd need means to travel all that distance northwards. Perhaps as a caravan guard. His laugh was quiet for he knew the work well enough. All the same, he'd need equipment. A sword, knives, a horse, better boots. And a bow. A bow, just like his Da's and his Grandda's before him. Coryn remembered Da's recurve bow being an efficient weapon for hunting on horseback or on foot, in open spaces and in woods. It was powerful, fast and the arrows silent as soft wind passing through spring leaves.

His homeland, Kalebrod, just a narrow strip of land, curling round the southern edge of Rophet, lying hundreds of leagues to the northeast, on the other side of the Ruel Mountains, was inconspicuous on every map he'd ever seen. But he remembered it. Filled with the sound of water from falls, rapids and cataracts. Steep mountains, deep forests, flower-filled meadows, rolling moors, and blue lakes. So different from this damned desert. So very different. He didn't know if he'd ever see it again. It was unlikely.

If he closed his eyes, Coryn could still see Grandda telling stories at the hearthside, teaching Bryn and him how to oil wood, wax bow-strings and fletch arrows. The old man had used his bow in skirmishes against writhen and bandits coming down from the mountains. But then the blood-priests began their raids in earnest. Rumour was they'd got themselves some new Priest-king, one as powerful as some ruler way back in history. He'd set his mind to conquering lands the Mu-recken had once owned, converting everyone to worshipping their blood-hungry god, Murak. No one had noticed just how many had joined his banner, not just bandits, but hill tribes and mercenaries willing to fight for Murecken gold. Using their magik, the blood-priests had tied more writhen to them, and even, so the word went, tadiges, toad-like creatures from the bowels of the Ruel Mountains.

The sparse population of Kalebrod hadn't stood a chance. He'd heard the whole country had fallen to the Murecken a while back. They'd turned on Rophet a year or so ago. Folk here were thankful they wouldn't cross the seas, but it wouldn't contain them, some day they'd work out how to get over the Ruel Mountains and invade the western lands.

For some reason, he had a hunch that Birog's message held informa-tion that'd help the Storrations' up-coming fight against the Murecken.

Hort was right, they should move fast and get those jobs as guards before other freedmen did. 'Time I made my own decisions, I agree. But, if I'm honest, that's what scares all kinds of hells out of me.'

Hort turned back to Coryn and clapped a hand on his shoulder. 'Me too. But I'm hungry and my belly overrides my fear.'

They both broke into laughter. Together they weaved through patient queues of freed men and women still waiting to have their collars removed. So many, Coryn thought, it would take days, tendays, even though almost every smith was hard at the work of it all over the city. He and Hort had already waited days themselves while all the children were seen to first. As he left Slave Square, he wondered if they would keep the name. He thought not.

It felt good to climb the hill of Selassi to the City Guard barracks of his own free will, no owners, no whips. The noon sun heated his shoulders and bare neck. He felt the brush of rough fur against his leg and looked down. Unusual for the dog to be walking so close, to have come into the city at all. It looked up and stared up at him. There was no mistaking it for a desert-bred dog, though it was larger than most at around three feet tall. A deep-chested beast, well muscled, narrow at the hips, with a long tail for balance and large, pointed ears. The battle-scarred damned ugliness of it was enough to give anyone pause. Not a bad thing. It could take down a full-grown man and was capable of killing a mountain lion.

One day he would figure out why it'd begun to follow him all those years ago. Why it still did. He remembered the day well. They'd been heading towards Selassi hundreds of leagues to the south. Coryn eating dust guarding the rear of his master's caravan as usual. He'd been taking a piss in the dunes one sunset, somewhere along the coast between Tashk and Ras Sul, a long way from anywhere, when it had appeared. It had sat there and, just like it did now, stared at him. Uncanny, like it was thinking things no dog should think. It had turned out to be a good hunter though, shadow silent and damned useful to have around for protection.

Some had objected to him, a common slave, having a dog. Yet every time they drove it off, it returned. The ugly, hostile beast refused to follow anyone else. It'd bitten one of the regular guards once, when he'd tried to whip the dog. Coryn had managed to save it from a feathering with ten lashes to his own back. He'd wondered why with every lash. It looked like it would bite him good as look at him a time or two, so he'd not tried to make a friend of it. But he knew he owed the beast. If not for this dog, he'd have been dead many times over. No doubt the dog would leave him when it was good and ready. It just hadn't been ready up to now. Meanwhile, they remained travelling companions neither owned by nor owning the other.

And that felt right.

What felt wrong were these damned gods and their damned priests. What right did they have to go around telling people how to live their lives like that Atash? How come this Murak had to make his followers invade other countries just to get more people to worship him? And

Lehot, what was he about? Promising a better life after you'd died. How about a better life right here on Dumnon? Still, it was Lehot's priesthood getting power here in Selassi that meant he was now free, Coryn had to give them that. Then there was the Mother, a dying goddess, one hardly worshipped any more. Didn't stop her priestesses, or seers, trying to tell folk what was best for them though.

And another thing, who'd ever *seen* any of these gods anyway? Did they exist? Probably just a bunch of priests and priestesses setting up their own little religions and getting folk to follow them just to make themselves feel more powerful. You could see it for sure with that Atash lot. Yes, that'd be about it.

Spirits! Why do people have to make life so damned complicated?

The spirits. Now they you could rely on to be just what they were – undependable, annoying, even dangerous. Coryn had seen them all right, not in the cities, but out where less folk lived. Sometimes they even helped a man, though you had to be careful, never knew what they might want in return. Best part was though, if you left them alone, they'd leave you alone. And they'd no damned priesthood either.

'You brooding again, Coryn?' Hort slapped him on the back. 'Best day of your life and you brood. Wake up, man. Enjoy life now it's yours to enjoy.'

Coryn shook his head, unable to stop the grin plastering his face at Hort's thunderous laughter. They hurried their pace up through the streets of Selassi to a new future.

Chapter 9

The cry of gulls jolted Katleya awake. Beyond the window, the eastern skies pearled, but Black Rock remained quiet while the population slept off the excesses of Midwinter.

'Blast it!' The memories of the night crashed into her mind along with the ache from her ribs and pain of her leg.

Spirits! I knifed a Thief-taker?

The stupid bastard shouldn't have tried to take her. But there would be questions and, with the right encouragement, someone would speak soon enough.

Some weak-willed idiot with rat-piss for brains.

There were plenty about. Katleya sighed, but then hunger weakened everyone. Only real question was, how long did she have?

Katleya climbed down the rickety ladder and out into the thin sunlight of early morning. Heavy snowfall loaded roofs, blurred fences and walls, and somehow managed to hide the ugliness. She shivered and looked back at the tilting shack. Like all the abandoned buildings hereabouts it stood on wooden piles, but when the waters rose high enough, as they did during autumn rains and spring melts, the lower floor flooded. No doubt about it, the place had caused Uncle Yadoc's lung-rot. Already miserable, having abandoned his beloved smithy in Laeft, the despair of being trapped and useless in Black Rock broke him.

A baby began to cry nearby. Katleya knew the mother well enough, a girl barely a year older, with the requisite shadowed eyes and bony body. Everyone got hollowed out here, one way or the other, some fast, some slow.

Katleya kicked at a stone. It spun in an arc, cracked through the ice of a puddle and disappeared with a weak gurgle.

'It's ended then?'

Katleya whipped round. 'Murak's blasted hells, Laru, you shouldn't sneak up on me like that!' She slipped her knives back into their wrist sheaths.

'Sorry, Katleya. You know, one day, you'll be killin' someone before you've realised your knives are in your hands.' Laru shrugged her thin shoulders under her short cloak. 'Anyway's, I promised I'd come by.

The children have missed you these last few nights, thought I might persuade you to visit them, sing a song or two. Maybe teach them a new one. But I see your mind's on other worries. You'll be havin' things to do now.'

'Things to do?' Katleya winced at a man's shout. The baby started to scream.

'Takin' your uncle up to the temple for burnin'.' The older girl tipped her head to one side and she tucked a loose lock of brown hair back under her hood with one bony finger. 'Want any help?'

Katleya closed her eyes for a moment, wondering how Laru always managed to read her so well. 'No, he'd not have wanted the temple. It's the river for him. He'll want the spirits to take him to Annufen. But thanks.'

'Annufen? Ah, yes – the Spiritworld, where spirits wait to be reborn. We left all that behind years ago, when we first got here an' our parents died.' Laru sighed, crossing her arms over her chest. 'Thing is, it's not what we believe in that matters, not here. It's what safest for us to do. You know how powerful the Atash priesthood are now, an' they're gettin' stronger by the day. No one much remembers Lehot, folk just think the old God of Light's changed into Atash or somethin'. Dunno why, they're so different. An' the spirits, they're long forgotten it seems.'

'Yes. You're right, about fitting in I mean, but even so.' Katleya looked up at the shack, then down at her feet. 'Gods seem to come and go, but the spirits will always be there, forgotten or not. Anyway, I've got to do what he'd have wanted, you know, after everything. I owe him that.'

'You'll want help either way.' Laru hitched her skirts up higher and made her way up the ladder.

He had been a big man, but the long illness had wasted away his bulk and they had little trouble lowering his wrapped body down to the ground using ropes. They made a litter out of planks and poles ripped loose from what remained of the yard's fencing and laid him on it.

'No reason to be stayin' here any more, Katleya. Me, I'd want to cut the nose from my face if I were made to live in this dump.' Laru muttered under her breath. She wrinkled her freckled nose as she looked around. 'These old yards stink worse than the North Bridge tenements, and that's sayin' somethin'. Come and stay with us. It's not good bein' alone, not in this city. Not in these times.'

'I'll think about it.'

Now the young mother started to cry along with her baby. The father shouted some more then stomped his way out of their shack. He saw Katleya and Laru watching, scowled then slouched off into the city. Looking for work and food, like everyone else. He'd need the luck of the spirits to find either.

Katleya turned and sighed as she saw the look Laru gave her. 'I will think about it, honest.' But she knew it wouldn't happen, she hadn't any options left to her now.

'You know your problem?'

Katleya waited. 'Go on then, what's my problem?'

'You're too much of a loner for your own good. An' I reckon that's your uncle's fault, keepin' you apart all your life.' Laru tucked the hem of her skirts more firmly into her belt, brushing specks of dirt off the faded blue wool that only she could see. 'To survive, people got to work together.'

Katleya smiled despite the ache in her heart. 'Show me how.'

They heaved up on the poles of the litter and made their way to the nearest jetty. They slid and stumbled through the snow-coated mud. Hidden rubbish snagged at their feet, slowing them more, but still they arrived before Katleya felt ready. They put the litter down at the end of the jetty and she scattered rosemary leaves and oil over Uncle Yadoc's body, then stuck a forked willow stick into one end of the litter and hung his amulet on it so the Cuinannufen, the spirit-gatherers, would find his spirit and take it to Annufen.

Using his battered old tinderbox, she ignited a bundle of twigs and touched them to his wrappings. They pushed the burning bier into the water and watched as the current took him eastwards out to sea. Veils of smoke drifted south.

Opening her Wealdan, Katleya concentrated on finding the strands of Wefan weaving through the currents of the water. Normally, it'd be hard to make them out but here, in the lowlands, the River Stam's sluggish water sent them into less of a flux than the fast flowing streams back in Laeft. Something caught her eye, an unusual eddy in the Wefan near the bier and, as she studied it, it coalesced into a form. An arm, then a head, a torso and a second arm, rose up, as though formed from water and Wefan alone. Not a water-spirit, something else. The figure reached for the bier.

Shocked, Katleya closed off her Wealdan and turned to Laru. But her friend still watched the bier like she'd seen nothing strange or amazing.

Katleya turned back to the river. Had she just seen one of the Cuinannufen? Here? Where so many people lived so close together? She'd not seen any spirits since Laeft, and never one of the Cuinannufen. It made her wonder just how much more Uncle Yadoc hadn't got round to telling her that for him they'd appear in the middle of the day.

Other folk had come out to watch, all silent. A few nodded to Katleya and touched her shoulder or arm in comfort. It wasn't much, but what compassion they had left inside they gave. It made Katleya feel even sadder. The snow began to fall again, small drifting flakes. It didn't take long for the body to disappear toward the river mouth and the sea. The two girls turned and walked back to the shack.

'Join us, Katleya.' Laru tucked her hand into the crook of Katleya's arm. 'You're one of the best roof-toppers we've got an' burglary's one of the few ways left to us to get enough coin for food these days, an' that's a valuable skill. Flick'd agree, you know that. I could teach you more herbcraft too, an' you've still got to finish teachin' me my letters and numberin'. I've got to keep climbin' out of the gutter and I don't mean to do it on my back. I'm already more of a help to Garve so...'

'I'm sorry, Laru.' Katleya couldn't stay silent any more. She shoved her hands into the deep pockets of her coat as flakes of snow began to drift down from the heavy clouds. Her limp had become more pronounced and her wound burned like a forge. 'You're right, you are, but things have got a little complicated since yesterday. I had a run in with a Thief-taker outside the Head. I've got to leave. Since Uncle Yadoc has gone, well...'

'That was you?' Laru didn't sound too surprised. She lifted her face to the flakes and stuck out her tongue. She grinned at Katleya. 'The youngsters love the snow. Me too, I'll admit. Everythin' looks better cloaked under a thick layer of white, don't you think?'

'You knew?'

'I wasn't sure, but I guessed. What'd you expect? It happened practically outside the Head's door right after you left.' Laru's smile vanished and she looked grim. 'I hoped you might want to live with us now your Uncle's gone. But, now...now I'm expectin' you'll be needin' to leave the city.'

'It's probably for the best.'

Laru nodded. 'Suppose they'll be keeping an eye out for you in particular bein' as how you nearly cut the Thief-taker's jewels. Did you know someone sliced his head clean off?'

'What? That wasn't me!'

'No, some tall desert-warrior type took his knife, Sarl said. Then the Thief-taker coshed him in the knee so the desert-warrior shortened him with his sword, or rather his tulwar, I think that's what Sarl called it.'

'Someone stole something from a Thief-taker? Spirits!' Katleya shook her head. 'There was a fat man dressed as a merchant working with the Thief-taker. What happened to him?'

'Ran like Murak's stinkin' hells were openin' up to swallow him, Sarl said.' Laru smirked then indicated Katleya's leg. 'Want me to have a look at that?'

Back in the shack, Laru inspected Katleya's wound, holding the thigh between her hands and squeezing it a little. It felt better than it had last night though it still hurt like a forge burn. She hoped no infection had got into the wound. She breathed in one deep breath and opened her Wealdan to see if the Wefan lines had worsened.

Her jaw dropped at what she saw. The lattice-work of Wefan running through the wound began to knit together, to straighten and mend.

It was like magik.

It is *magik, lard-head.*

'Blasted hells!' Sweet spirits, it blazed! Katleya's hold on her Wealdan broke, sweat prickled across her body and tremors surged making her muscle twitch and spasm. Laru gasped and dropped the leg. She held her head in her hands for a moment, looking like she'd sick up any moment.

'What have you done?' Katleya groaned and fell back on her pallet. 'How have...'

'I've only hurried the healin' up a bit, it's all I can do. But you've never to tell anyone about it, Katleya aef Laeft. I don't fancy bein' taken by the priests and burned to death.' Laru straightened up but still looked green. Her eyes drilled into Katleya with a mix of fierce and serious that she'd never seen in her friend before. 'Yes, I knew you'd know about the Wealdan, you've got a feel about you, an' then when you saw that water-spirit, I knew for sure. It's why I didn't bother to hide it under the herbcraft this time, like I usually do. But I still wouldn't have done it if this shack weren't over the river.'

'I never knew you could do that with the Wealdan.' The pain faded fast, but the tremors took their time to leave Katleya's muscles. 'I didn't know anyone could. By the way, that wasn't a water-spirit. It was one of the Cuinannufen.'

'Durin' the day? Don't be daft. Anyhow, there's a whole lot can be done with the Wealdan an' my skill's only small. I've heard of some things that are truly,' she rolled the word over her tongue, drawing out the sound of it, 'marvellous.'

'There are? Something else Uncle Yadoc didn't bother to tell me. He did tell me touching it, drawing on it, is dangerous though, if you got discovered using it. You shouldn't have done it at all.'

'Drawin' on it can be dangerous, an' that's the truth. Makes me feel sick as a dog for a good while. But for you, I wanted to do it.' Laru collapsed next to Katleya. 'Payment for when you saved me from drownin'.'

'That wasn't something that needed paying for, Laru.'

'Even so. Anyhow, you'll be needin' all your health, strength and wits to get free from this pit an' herbcraft alone wouldn't have done the job half so fast.' Laru smoothed down her dress. 'My gramma told me long ago that there's colleges far to the west an' north, where they teach you to use the Wealdan. Lehotans run them, but they don't only teach about how to worship an' what to believe. Anyhow, we was goin' there when, like you an' your uncle, we were robbed on the road to Black Rock an' our parents were killed.'

Katleya nodded. Laru had told her how their parents had died, but not that they'd been heading for the west. 'My uncle told me about a place.'

'Did he now? Hmm, what was it called?' Laru tapped a finger against her teeth. 'Somethin' Haven, its on the Isle of Storr, or near it. You know, where the High-king lives.'

'Ostorr Haven. And it's on the other side of the blasted world.'

'Not so far as that, but it's a long sea trip all right. It's that or getting' up an' over them practically unclimbable Ruel Mountains. An' no one's goin' that way these days, not when they're full of them blood-priests an' worse. I've heard bigger Murecken armies are musterin' in the foothills and along the border with Kalebrod. Won't be just little bands attacking the Rophetan border any more. No, I reckon your best way out of here now would be workin' for a berth. There'll be ships in dock needin' some poor sod or other to climb the riggin' or scrub the decks.'

'Sounds wonderful.' Katleya grimaced. 'But you've my oath, Laru. I'll never tell a soul.'

'We'll all miss you.'

'I'll miss you all too. If there's any way that you could all leave too...'

Laru shook her head and sat up to look out the window. 'The twins just turned eight, Marky and Lucran are five and Lille is only three. They're too small to work the passage an' we'd never get the coin for that many berths. But you'll remember us. Flick'll miss you too. Startin' to get sweet on you, he was. Specially now you're getting' them buds.'

'Hey.' Katleya poked Laru in the ribs, cursing the blush that warmed her face. 'But I will remember you.' She suddenly felt an overwhelming tiredness and yawned wide enough to crack her jaw. 'You know, since I've got a bit of spare coin, I'll stand you and the little ones some real meat pies if you like, for all your help.'

'I like.' Laru gave Katleya's arm a squeeze. 'Pies with real meat in 'em, hmm? We'd have the luck of the spirits an' all the gods together if we found even one in this dump.'

'There's a woman selling them down in the Smithing District. Real pork, no lie.' Katleya pulled a few coins from her pouch and handed them to Laru. 'She'll be wearing my red coat.'

'Real pork, from actual pigs? I think I'll be takin' a walk down Forge Road then, such a thing needs to be seen to be believed. Or maybe I mean *tasted* to be believed.' Laru paused, heaved out a sigh then got all business-like. 'You'll be needin' to sleep now. A Wealdan healin' always takes the energy out of a body. Sleep and food is the best way to get it back.'

'There's more food over there. I put together the last of it with some other bits the youngsters might like. Nothing I'll need where I'm going.' Katleya pointed to a bag lying against the wall.

'I'm right thankful for it, that's a kindness.' Laru hefted the bag, gave Katleya an awkward hug then left, muttering about extra shifts at the Royal Head over Midwinter meaning she'd lose out on being with the little ones, but with rent and food and all... 'Spirits be with you.'

'Spirits be with you too.' Katleya hoped Laru wouldn't find the extra coin she'd put in the bag till well after she'd got on a ship. She knew

Laru wouldn't accept it if she'd just given it to her, but she and Flick needed it and she didn't, not half as much. On her trip to the docks yesterday she'd discovered a fair few ships in need of crew, not that she'd realised at the time how soon she'd need to leave. As Laru had said, she could work for her berth.

She mixed up some dye and plastered it on her hair, working it well into the roots. Why she still bothered to dye it, she didn't know. Another thing Uncle Yadoc hadn't got round to explaining. She mulled over what he had said though. Birog and Ethlinn. Who were they? He'd insisted she get to Storr fast, and she agreed with that, but why did he think she was wanted so much by the Murecken? Her Wealdan wasn't anything to shout about. Laru's was better, to be able to heal was something special. She was the one who ought to be going to Ostorr. If only the old man had just told her everything straight away. Well, now it was too late.

Spirits! So many blasted mysteries.

The pie she'd bought, what seemed like forever ago, still tasted wonderful. Katleya wolfed it down, her head whirling at all the possibilities of the Wealdan and Wefan. To learn to heal with it like Laru did would be incredible. If she'd known sooner she'd have got Laru to teach her it as well as herbcraft. But here, everyone had to hide anything unusual in case a finger got pointed.

She shook her head. The fact that people could be found who actually taught folk how to use the Wealdan, whole colleges of them, just like Uncle Yadoc had said, amazed her. She felt guilty for not having really believed him at the time, but how could she have known it was true when here you got burned for just being accused of having any magik? Her head buzzed with excitement at a future she never thought to have and Katleya wondered how she could ever sleep with so much to think about.

She dropped off to sleep with pastry crumbs still stuck to her fingers.

Chapter 10

The next morning, before dawn had greyed the sky, Katleya washed her hair free of the sticky dye mess, then checked her reflection in the blade of a knife. A good solid brown, she nodded, satisfied. She dragged on her clothes then strapped her knives to her forearms and shins. Each of the four blades was weighted and sized for her. They were the last things her uncle had crafted in his smithy back in Laeft before they'd left. She slipped her sheepskin jerkin on and stamped her feet into her heavy boots. Even belted in tight, Uncle Yadoc's brown coat drowned her, but it would keep her warm and dry. And it smelled of him. Closing her eyes a moment she breathed deep.

No time for that.

He'd gone with the spirits and she still lived. She had to deal with how things were, not how she wished them to be. Katleya jammed her old hat down to cover her short curls, her long hair cropped for practical reasons soon after they arrived in Black Rock. She checked her small pack had everything she needed: whetstone, flint-box, more of the hazel dye, packets of dried herbs, spare shirts, bloody trousers waiting for a wash and a mend, sewing kit, underclothes and, no, that was it, the rest had gone on food, remedies and gang protection tax. She swung the pack onto her shoulders and climbed down the rope ladder at the back of the shack. Below, a tiny skiff bobbed against a piling.

Almost soundless, she poled east toward the mouth of Stam River. To her left stacks of narrow houses hugged the steep hills of the city and smoke belched into the chill air. It looked dreary in the pre-dawn light. To her right, the distant south bank slipped in and out of view, a blur of fields and farmsteads. Katleya kept to the shallows and shadows of the north bank, threading round pilings and jetties, and hoped no one noticed her passing. She eyed the thickening strand of light between sea and sky and realised she'd have to hurry to catch the ships before they set sail on the dawn tide.

Katleya abandoned the skiff on a muddy bank on the southern edge of the harbour and ran along Broad Street to the docks. The sea-port heaved with squat coastal traders, converted riverboats, big-bellied cargo vessels and tall, narrow ships all jostling for mooring space along the wharves. More lay anchored in the harbour beyond, while fishing trawlers, rowboats and tugs negotiated the spaces between.

'Oi, 'ow 'bout a spin 'tween the blankets, darlin'?' A short woman wiggled her ample bosom at Katleya and grinned showing a mouth dark with missing teeth. 'Do you a special seein' as you're so young, boy.'

Blushing hard Katleya pulled her hat down more and bolted past the tavern ignoring the raucous laughter that followed. She weaved through noisy crowds of doxies, merchants, lumpers, guards, hawkers, sailors and beggars. She hurried past the crumbling Blood Wall, where criminals dangled by their necks from the gallows, their crimes too great for the army. One of the three metal t-shaped posts further on held the smouldering remains of some poor fool accused of using magik, the pyre below it all crumbled to ash and drifting in the sea breeze. Not a week went by but another poor body burned. These days, people had only to point a finger at someone they didn't like and the priests of Atash would come to take and test the accused. Some disappeared, some ended up here.

At the port authority office a line of dejected refugees loaded down with belongings waited. Katleya scanned a long list of shipping and the charges for berths posted beside the heavy doors. The prices had gone up again and she didn't have anywhere near enough coin for even one berth, wouldn't have had even if she'd not given Laru any. But, if her luck held – and she was certainly due some – she'd not need to pay to sail.

A while later, Katleya slogged down to the northern-most dock. Moored to the very end, a lean, fast looking ship rocked on the swell. A tall crewman stood on the gangplank over-seeing a team of lumpers staggering under the weight of oak barrels. A curved sword was strapped across his back and a long knife hung at each hip.

'Hoy there, mister. I heard you're setting sail for Dal Abar this morning and are still short of crew,' Katleya called out.

He turned.

Katleya, surprised, saw *he* turned out to be a *she*. A warrior woman from the deserts far to the southwest with skin the colour of peat soil. A flat turban, worn low over her forehead and over her ears, hid her hair and a sort of short, stiff veil, attached to the turban, masked her eyes but left most of her nose and her mouth uncovered. Though she'd seen a few desert warriors before, none had worn a veil like that.

Nostrils flaring like a dog catching a scent, the woman closed on her. She raked Katleya up and down with her hidden eyes, nodded, then motioned for her to follow and strode up the gangplank. On the main deck she stopped to speak to a hook-nosed man, then strode back toward the gangplank with a half glance at Katleya as she passed.

'I'm the Captain of the Assacar. Pike's the name but the crew call me *Captain Pike* or *Captain*, got it?' The stringy, hook-nosed man drilled Katleya with hard grey eyes till she nodded. 'What can you do?'

'Whatever needs doing.' Katleya had watched and learned on past visits to the docks, she knew what skills would interest the Captain. 'I'm nothing if not adaptable and I've a good head for heights. I heard you needed a rigging monkey.'

'Aye, that's true. But a simple merchantman like this needs versatile sailors. I'm in need of someone who can tally and write too,' Captain Pike stated, his gaze unwavering.

'I can write and number well enough.' Katleya shrugged trying for nonchalance, not sure if she'd succeeded.

'Can you hold your temper even when provoked?' Captain Pike narrowed his eyes. 'There's no fighting aboard this ship. I come down brutal on any brawls. You understand?'

'Yes, Captain,' Katleya agreed. As long as everyone left her alone, that would work just fine.

'You needn't take such care to hide the fact you're a lass either. Take your hat off. Let me get a proper look at your face,' he ordered. Katleya slid the hat off and he razed her body with his eyes till even with her uncle's bulky coat on, she felt naked. 'I take females on as crew if they can do the job as well as man or boy. You've met Leveen. One of the finest helmsmen I've ever had and damned good in a fight too. What's your age and name, lass?'

'Katleya aef Laeft. I've just passed my seventeenth nameday.' Katleya met him stare for stare but she itched to be off the ship. She had no choice but to stay put though, it was the only ship left in need of crew.

'Good, I can see you've potential so I'll take you on, lass. The last rigging monkey we had fell overboard. The sharks ate him. It happens to those taking less care then they should.' Captain Pike leaned closer and breathed fish aromas into Katleya's face. She held her breath and didn't move. With a curt nod he turned and sauntered off, directing his next words over his shoulder. 'Obey orders, learn fast, do the jobs you're given well and you'll fit in. Stay out of the way of the crew while we put out to sea. We'll sort the rest when we've set sail.'

Katleya nodded. After the refusals from the other ships, she'd thought it would be harder to get on board, yet here she stood. Her mood ought to have lifted, but she had a strange feeling she'd made a blasted awful choice. She chewed at her lip as she thought on the reasons why that might be. She didn't trust Captain Pike, no more than she'd trust a spark in shavings, something about him unsettled her, but as she couldn't think of any obvious reason why, she shrugged it off.

The crew scurried around preparing the ship and Katleya moved to the railings to get out of the way. She stared up at the city and along the wharfs.

Blast!

Sudden shock had her ducking below the railings quick as thought while her heart tried to hammer its way out of her ribcage. A Thief-taker strode toward the Assacar, a dockside lumper hurried next to him gesticulating toward the ship. Katleya kept the whore-monger in sight and hoped he hadn't seen her.

They stopped to speak to someone on the gangplank. Katleya couldn't hear what they said but the whore-monger soon stomped off back up the dock. Relieved, she slumped against the rails and waited for her heart to slow. The lumpers pushed the ship away from the docks with their long heavy poles while the rowers, ten to a launch, heaved on their oars to pull the ship out of port.

When they passed the harbour walls, the sails billowed and the ship leaned, cutting through the waves and away from Rophet. Katleya, standing at the rail again, swallowed as tears rolled down her cheeks. She had lost a lot in far too short a time. Her home, her uncle, her friends. Nearly her life.

Too damned much.

Sighing, she turned from the rail.

'What're you snivelling about, lass!' Captain Pike loomed into Katleya's view. His blow staggered her. 'I don't allow any such weakness aboard this ship. If you want to take a man's job you'll have to act like a man. So stop that piss-poor bawling!'

'Yes, Captain.' Katleya felt her cheek burn with his hand print but she managed to hold on to the surge of anger. The spirits only knew how.

'I thought you were made of better stuff,' Captain Pike snarled. He glowered down at her, hands on his hips, feet wide in the typical seaman stance. 'I'd rather have a wild mountain lioness aboard then some weepy-eyed kitten. But I'll cure you or introduce you to the sharks before long, lass. Now go below and stow your belongings. Tacker'll show you where.'

As she turned away Katleya spotted a filthy rat. With reactions honed from keeping the huge city rats away from Uncle Yadoc, her knife whipped through the air and thunked into the deck before she'd taken another breath. The spiky, black furred rodent twitched once, impaled by three inches of quivering blade.

'Doxy spawn! Filthy slum brat! What d'you mean by throwing knives about on this ship?' Pike strode forward, hand raised, ready to strike.

'Lower your hand or you'll skewer it on this knife, Captain Pike.' Katleya stood with her legs apart and tensed but knees soft, a second dagger readied. The blood rushed through her veins, her eyes sharpened, sounds faded and her mind raced. She could swim back to shore. They hadn't gone that far yet. But what then? The blasted Thief-taker Guild would still want her and she'd have a price on her head that'd be hard for the desperate to ignore. 'I've shown you just how good my eye is, that I'm no meek kitten, and that there's no way in all of Murak's stinking hells you'll be able to tame me!'

Captain Pike grinned showing every one of his yellowed teeth and thrust his hands into the wide red-silk sash wrapped round his middle. He turned on his heel and walked off. 'I'll enjoy having you on board, that I will, lass.' Laughter rolled round the deck in his wake.

Katleya blinked with astonishment.

'There, lass.' A broad-shouldered man not much older than her gave her a teeth-rattling slap on the back. 'My name's Tacker. Come below and I'll show you where to stow your gear. Looks like we'll be watch-mates and I think good friends too. I like the look and the sound of you!'

Not trusting herself to talk, Katleya nodded. She yanked her dagger from the deck, cleaned it and slipped it back in its sheath. Then she picked the filthy rat up by its tail and flicked it over the side. Back straight against the stares of the other crew members, she stalked down steep and narrow stairs after Tacker.

In a low-ceilinged area full of barrels, crates and the stink of the long unwashed, a shout of laughter from the crew surprised her on the tail of Tacker's elaborate account of what had just happened on deck.

'Well done, lass! You're a good 'un and I 'ave no doubt you'll turn out a rare seaman.' A squat, muscled man grinned at her. A ragged scar ran down the left side of his face and puckered up his sunken eye-socket. Like the others, he sat on a crate and leaned against one of the roped barrels that lined the walls. 'Leveen was just such a girl as you. Now she's the biggest cut-throat of us all.'

'Never a truer word said, First Mate. Here's a mug of beer for you, lass.' Tacker grinned down at Katleya. 'You wet your tongue now. You'll need it after that run-in with Captain Pike. If any one of us said what you said to the old bugger, why he'd have no tongue to wet!'

The beer smelled as if a horse had pissed in it and tasted no better, but thirst made Katleya take a quick gulp.

'Stop the flapping of your lips, Tacker,' a voice ordered. Katleya looked up. The desert woman prowled down from the gangway and settled onto one of the crates. 'Give the girl a bowl of stew. Do you not see she will soon fall where she stands?'

'Right you are, Leveen.' Tacker smiled and swaggered off into the smoky gloom.

Katleya did feel faint. She'd nothing to eat since the pie the day before and it'd been a long morning and what with the healing Laru had done... only then did she realise how her leg had been completely pain free. She had forgotten about her wound. Dropping her pack to the floor she sat on it and pressed her hand against her thigh. Nothing. Again she was amazed at what Laru had done and even more determined to get to Ostorr Haven and learn how to do it herself. She took more gulps of the weak beer. It improved near the bottom of the tankard, or perhaps it was just her tongue going numb.

'There you go, lass.' Katleya accepted a hunk of flat brown bread and a bowl of broth swimming with onions and barley. Tacker grinned down at her. 'You're a right feisty one and I like that in a lass. It'll be all the more interesting that way.'

Katleya gave him a withering look. She'd met his type before on the streets of Black Rock. She'd practised a lot of her knife work on them. Shaking her head, she began eating.

Chapter 11

The sun lurked behind hazed clouds when Katleya slithered down the ratlines from the crow's nest. Noon meant the end of her watch so she made her way below decks. A tenday had passed since Black Rock disappeared from the horizon and she clambered about as nimble as any of the others. She stepped off the companionway near the galley, exhausted and looking forward to some decent food and her bunk.

Someone grabbed her arm and yanked her into the shadows under the steep stairs.

'There you are, lass. I'm thinking it's about time we got to know each other better and I'm betting you think the same, eh?' It wasn't a question. Hands pulled her close and she gagged on rum fumes as a mouth tried to close on hers. 'Ah, you know you want to be more than just watch-mates as much as I do, lass.'

Spirits! Not again!

'I want nothing of the sort. Get off me, Tacker, you drunken, slag-brained idiot!' Katleya shoved Tacker away. Why were idiots like this always trying to grope their way into her clothes?

'Oh, lass. You've got a need for me and I, sure as all Atash's fires, have it for you. You're a fine looking lass and no mistake.' His voice dropped to a harsh whisper. 'It's better for you to be no virgin in the eyes of the captain. Just run with it, it needn't be for real. You'll thank me for this soon enough, lass, just see if you don't.' Tacker's lips came down hard on hers and he crushed her to him.

Even with her arms clamped to her sides, Katleya managed to slip a dagger down into her hand. She pressed the point against Tacker's groin. He lurched back fearing for his most treasured possessions.

She stepped forward to keep the knife in place.

'Atash's fires, lass. What d'you think you're doing?' Tacker asked with such genuine astonishment Katleya found it hard to keep from laughing. He backed against a stack of barrels till he couldn't go any further. She felt him shift.

'Don't. You'll lose your sacks if you move another inch. Now I've your attention I'll make quite clear a few facts for you. I don't think it's a good idea to become more then just watch-mates. My virginity is no business of yours or anyone else's. And I've not got any blasted *need* for you. Even the thought of being touched by a ratty, pock-faced, arse-wipe like you disgusts me!' Katleya growled out the words low and harsh, driving the message home with little digs of her knife. She hoped he couldn't hear the way her heart pounded. 'I'm sure you'd agree it'd be a terrible shame to complicate our *beautiful friendship* in any way. And I'm sure you'd prefer to keep your sad, shrivelled, little bollocks intact.'

'My, lass, you've a wonderful way with words.' Tacker coughed. 'Ah, I agree with you in every way and that's the honest truth. Apart from the *pock-face* jibe. I take exception to that, lass. So, ah, you'll remove that sharp little blade of yours now, yes?'

'Remember I always keep my knives close.' Katleya slipped the dagger back into its sheath. 'And I sleep light as a cat.'

'I think we'd all do well to remember that, men.' A lantern sluiced the corner with light as Captain Pike's metallic voice broke over the rolling rounds of laughter. 'And that means you more than anyone else, Tacker.'

Annoyed, Katleya turned. A fair number of the crew had closed in without her realising, but then, she'd yet to sort out the many sounds a ship made at sea. They applauded and whooped, evil grins plastering their faces. Had they heard everything?

Spirits, what a nightmare!

'You all mark me now. No one's to touch the lass. By my order.' Captain Pike snarled. 'Tacker, with me.'

Scowling, Katleya shoved through the snickering crew to the galley. Grabbing some bread and cheese from the bowl the cook indicated she turned and found Leveen blocking the way.

'Katleya, get yourself up on deck, girl.' The woman turned and marched off, obviously expecting her to follow.

'I've just finished my watch, Leveen, what's up?' Katleya yawned, but followed her back to the companionway.

'Captain wants all hands on deck.' Leveen was already half way up the steps.

A crowd had gathered on the main deck, Leveen powered through it and Katleya, slipping along in her wake, wondered what the woman's problem was. The crew muttered but she couldn't quite make out what they said. As she passed the mainmast, Katleya saw Captain Pike up on the quarterdeck his arms folded across his chest, his face thunderous. There was a sudden crack followed by a grunt of pain, and she hurried to climb a ratline.

Tacker, tied to the mast and stripped to the waist, had a red welt across his back. Bleak-faced, First Mate Eyeless raised his arm to lay into Tacker again with a length of split rope. Blood dripped from the criss-crossing cuts and with each successive lash his cries of pain got louder. Katleya hissed in sympathy.

'He brought it on himself, girl.' Leveen turned back to the whipping. Katleya was almost certain the woman smiled at the sight. If so, it was the first time she'd ever seen the woman smile. 'He should not have tried to touch you.'

'I'd sorted it already, blast it, this isn't necessary,' Katleya hissed back. She squinted up at Captain Pike, half silhouetted against the bright sky, wondering at his over-reaction. Had Tacker broken some necessary but unwritten rule of sea life she'd not heard of? Maybe fraternizing between men and women wasn't allowed to avoid arguments or fights. The thought of being fought over almost made her laugh, then Tacker screamed again. The captain turned, spotted her on the ratline and scowled even harder.

'It is the Captain's wish, girl. None were to touch you,' Leveen looked up at Katleya. 'His word is law on board this ship. As all the crew know, and as you must learn.'

Katleya said nothing. Angry, she slithered back down the ratline. She'd seen enough, she'd no wish to see any more. It looked like it was over anyway. Someone was untying Tacker and steadying him as a bucket of seawater cascaded down his back.

Below decks, in the darkness of the little cabin she shared with Matz, First Mate Eyeless' eleven year old son, more cupboard than anything else, she rolled into the upper bunk and tried not to think about what Tacker had gone through.

Spirits blast it!

Long after it'd all fallen quiet, she went back up on deck and looked around. First Mate Eyeless held the wheel. His hands rose and fell in sweeps of description as he taught the finer points of helm work to Matz. Leveen stood at the taffrail gazing at the swell as she did most days before her watch at the wheel. Her tulwar was strapped to her shoulder harness as usual, though none of the other crew wore anything but knives on deck. A couple of crewmen mended some ropes. There was no sign of Tacker or Captain Pike.

Katleya joined Leveen at the rail and picked the mould off her bread, flicking the bits into the sea. Wrapping the bread around the lump of cheese, she stared at the passing land while she chewed. A stretch of shore known as Murak's Reef to which the Assacar gave a wide berth. It looked much the same as it had the day before and the day before that. Nothing but uninhabited and treacherous black cliffs and precipitous rocky islands filled with a cacophony of sea birds. Beyond them, the Ruel Mountains loomed and somewhere in there, almost due west of where they now sailed, lay Mureck, home of the blasted blood-priests.

'There will be times at sea when you will crave to eat the green of the bread too, girl.'

Surprised, Katleya looked sideways at Leveen. The strange woman stayed silent most of the time. In fact, she couldn't remember the last time Leveen had said anything to her between first getting aboard and today.

'Right now I don't crave it.' Katleya turned to lean back against the rail and chewed slow hoping to form enough spit to swallow the rather dry bread and very hard cheese.

Leveen watched the passing shore again. Tacker came on deck and paused when he saw them. He scrutinized Katleya, cast a glance at Leveen, then turned and climbed the ratlines to the crows nest as lithe and agile as an alley cat with barely a wince for the pain his cuts must be giving him.

Something spiked the back of her hand.

'Ow. Blast it!' She snatched the hand to her mouth but Leveen grabbed her wrist mid-air. Her fingers like steel.

'What has happened, girl?' Leveen demanded.

'I don't know.' Katleya tugged, wondering why Leveen had her arm in a vice-like grip, but there was no give. A drop of blood welled up. 'Something stung or bit me I think.'

'Let me stop the bleed, girl.' Leveen pressed her thumb against the blood. A small smile appeared on her lips but, with her eyes hidden behind the veil, Katleya couldn't make a guess at her thoughts. 'Doubtless it is the bite of one of the large fleas carried aboard this ship by the rats.'

'Rats! I hate those blasted rats and their blasted fleas!' Katleya pulled her hand away, this time the woman let her go. 'They infest the ship and everyone on it. Spirits know how many of the filthy vermin I've killed already.'

'It is most certain you are the best ship's cat we have ever had, girl.'

'Huh.' Katleya tried to work out if the woman had just made a joke, but Leveen's face remained as unreadable as ever. She rubbed at her hand and scowled at the shadows.

'Do you enjoy life aboard this ship, girl?'

'What?' From the corner of her eye Katleya glimpsed Leveen lift her thumb to her mouth. The woman's nostrils flared and she remembered how they had done the same on her first day aboard. Katleya felt edgy and she wondered, not for the first time, why the woman felt wrong. She snorted annoyed at herself for being foolish, again. But something about the whole situation felt strange, like an itch she couldn't find to scratch, an itch she'd lived with since she'd joined the Assacar. So it couldn't be Leveen, could it? 'Apart from the rats, human and otherwise, awful food and stupid whippings, I don't have any complaints. I won't be on this stinking tub much longer anyway. I'll be leaving soon as we reach Dal Abar.'

Katleya turned and looked down into the waves. A pod of dolphins took turns leaping through the air in arcing cascades of seawater.

'You think to leave, girl?' asked Leveen. She turned to stare at Katleya.

'Blasted right I do. Captain Pike said it's the last port he'll visit before turning south again.' Katleya gazed at the passing shore and wondered how she'd stay sane till they reached the next port, let along Dal Abar. Captain Pike told her on her second day aboard that it took around two tendays of sailing to reach Deorc's Cape from Black Rock and a further five days to Selassi. Always supposing they didn't get caught in the storms that roared round the Cape. The seaman vied to tell the most horrific stories about the sail-ripping winds and the ship-breaking waves of the Sutherne Sea storms. Then a further two tendays sailing to Ras Sul, with Dal Abar another three days after that, if the winds held.

A desperation to feel solid land under her feet again swept over her. How good it would be to get away from this stinking ship, the farting crew with their lice, and the pissing rats with their fleas.

'I'll find another ship from Dal Abar. Keep going north and west.'

'Captain Pike said you could leave the ship at Dal Abar did he, girl?'

'Yes, and...'

'Sail ho!' shouted Tacker from the nest.

'Where away?' cried Eyeless, his one eye glaring up at Tacker.

'Off the starboard bow,' Tacker called down from the crow's nest. 'Two points off south.'

Leveen sprang away from the taffrail and took the wheel from Eyeless. The first mate scuttled down to the main deck and leaped up the gangway to the foredeck. More crew scrambled up on deck and scanned the horizon shoving at each other eager to be the first to spot the ship.

Captain Pike came on deck and swept the seas just east of their heading with his spyglass. He stopped to linger on a single spot.

'Lower the top sails!' he bellowed.

'Aye, Captain.' Eyeless turned and shouted to the men already halfway up the ratlines. 'Away aloft! Lower the top sails!'

As the crew started to leap up the rigging, Katleya stuffed the last of the bread into her mouth and hurried to the mizzenmast.

With more sail loosed the Assacar knifed through the waves and Leveen steered her towards the distant ship. From the upper yardarm, Katleya soon spotted the clumsy looking trader. It had turned her stern to them and had crowded her masts with sail, but the Assacar was slimmer and had more speed. It sliced through the water while the trader's heavy belly dragged through the swell.

More shouted orders got the rest of the crew readied and armed with crossbows, bailing hooks and ropes. They lined the rails all eager for blood like sharks scenting a wounded whale. The Assacar came alongside the trader and arrows began to foul the sails. A flurry of darts came back in reply.

'Furl the top-sails.' Eyeless' shout sent sailors back up the lines.

'Hooks at the ready!'

Then a shuddering crack had Katleya grabbing hold of the yardarm. Shouts, yells and chilling shrieks accompanied flung boat hooks that snagged at the trader's rails. The Assacar's men hauled the ropes, tied them off, leaped over the rails and the fighting started on the trader's deck. Captain Pike, carrying a pair of scimitars, screamed and leaped over to the trader, nimble as a tumbler. He swung his blades, sliced through one man's sword arm above the elbow and slashed another's shoulder.

'No, no, no,' Katleya whispered. The screams echoed in her head despite her hands being clamped over her ears.

Eyeless took a man in the neck with a bill-hook, ripping out his throat and leaving the head to flop to one side as the body folded to the deck. Grinning, Leveen gutted three men in a row, leaving them to die painful, slow deaths, every one of them trying to stop their innards spilling on to the deck. Laughing, the woman chopped another man's arms off and left him to run about spurting blood from his shoulders till he fell into the sea. Another lost both legs from the knees down. It was foul. Did she pull the legs of beetles when she was a child?

Katleya couldn't watch any more, her body shook and she felt sick. She had seen enough awful things in Black Rock, and had hoped never to again. She screwed up her eyes, curled up hard against the mast and tried not to hear.

Howls of pain, screeched curses, the wet thuds of arrows and the clash of metal filled the air for what seemed like hours. Though bloody, it turned out to be a short raid, over before evening fell.

'Take those slaves below,' Captain Pike roared. 'Mind them captives now. They'll be as valuable as the cargo I'll be bound. There's never much of worth on an old slug like this! Lift the hatches, let's inspect the merchandise.'

Cracking open her eyes, Katleya watched the Assacar's crew efficiently strip the valuables from the blood-spattered dead and near-dead then toss the bodies overboard, ignoring any protests. The waters boiled with enthusiastic sharks and dying screams.

'From the forge to the anvil! What have I got myself into?' Katleya muttered, her knuckles white from gripping the ropes. A slaver! Why hadn't she listened to her instincts when she'd first set foot on deck? But she'd have been no safer if she had stayed in the seething pit of Black Rock. Tacker's words in the dark below decks earlier suddenly made so much more sense.

With the trader's cargo stowed in the lower hold of the Assacar, Captain Pike peeled off a skeleton crew for the tub. The ropes were unlashed so the two ships parted company. The trader soon lagged behind the Assacar when Captain Pike ordered the sails unfurled and set course due south. Pleased with the day's gains he swaggered across the quarterdeck and disappeared into his cabin.

'Though I'm no gambling man, I wager I know what you're thinking, lass.' She hadn't noticed Tacker climbing up the mizzenmast. He settled down next to her.

Ignoring him Katleya leaned her forehead against a cleat as her guts heaved.

'Here, this'll help, lass.' Tacker slipped a hand under his shirt and pulled out a small silver flask.

'I'm...I'm fine.' Katleya closed her eyes.

'No you're not. You're in shock. Nothing strange about that, lass,' Tacker insisted, 'this being your first sea fight and a lot of blood being spilled. It was the same for me my first time.'

Katleya looked up at Tacker and saw nothing but sincerity in his eyes. Taking the flask, she twisted off the stopper.

'Drink it in small sips, lass.'

Ignoring his advice, she took a large swig. The liquid, warmed by Tacker's body, slid down her throat. Then burned like the white heat of a forge fire. Between coughs and wheezes Katleya had a hard time putting the stopper back. 'Well...that gives me...something else to...think about.'

'Selassian Water,' Tacker explained. He slid the flask back under his shirt. 'It's the best liquor there is. Distilled from honey and flavoured with gingiver.'

'It's nothing...like water.' Katleya spluttered and coughed some more.

'True enough.' He grinned.

'What you said before...you know...when you...' Katleya stuttered to a halt.

'When I kissed you, lass?' Tacker smirked and leered down at her. 'I'm sure to remember that special moment for the whole of my short blighted life.'

'You could've just told me, blast it!' Katleya coughed and felt her cheeks redden. Holding her hands to keep from smacking that look off his face, she said the rest in a rush. 'I need to get off this ship. If I'd known it was a damned slaver...well I'm not staying on it a spark's life longer then I blasted well have to!'

'Aye I understand your feelings, lass. But you'll have to stay a while more,' Tacker muttered, his eyes scanning the deck far below. 'When we've reached Selassi I'll help you off. Till then say and do nothing. The captain mustn't know you've realised the truth, my sweet, dull-brained but damned beautiful, lass.'

'Selassi? I suppose there's nowhere nearer is there?' Katleya paused and thought hard on what she'd learned from the captain's maps and crew on the voyage so far about the ports they headed for. 'But he won't put in there – not carrying slaves! Even in Black Rock we'd heard they'd freed all the slaves in that city. The Thief-taker guild went frantic.' Katleya paused, relishing the memory. 'And wasn't that a sight to see! The bastards shouldn't ever have sold folk to the slavers in the first place. Slavers like your blasted captain.'

'Captain Pike doesn't buy slaves, he only sells them. What you say is true enough though, but you've no idea how brash our *blasted* captain can be, though he'll not tie up dockside, that'd be too rash, even for him. No, he'll anchor the Assacar out in the bay a good distance from the port. Then he'll put out on the launch to one of the quiet creeks feeding into the bay, carrying some select goods to sell to a couple of merchants he knows well. That'll be our first chance to get you off the ship, lass.' Tacker glanced down at Katleya with a measuring look in his eyes. 'Besides, his next port of call is Ras Sul. It's where he'll sell the captives down below. There'd be no escape for you there. A beauty like you I'm betting will stand little chance of staying free.'

'How will we get away from the ship at Selassi if he's not going anywhere near the docks?'

'You leave the planning to me, lass.' A frown flitted across Tacker's face. It didn't suit him. 'We'll speak no more of it now.'

'Leave it to you? Why should I trust you after what you did?' Katleya demanded. 'You really think I'm that stupid?'

'Look, I've not a single reason to help you and you're probably right not to trust me, but we have what you'd call a meeting of needs.' Tacker took a sip of his Selassian Water, smacked his lips and put the bottle away under his jacket again. 'I've a need for a new kind of life and I need a bit of help to get off this ship and start that life off good and proper. You'll be helping me out. I can't tell you the whole plan now, but when we get closer to the time for leaving, you'll know it all.'

Katleya stared hard at Tacker, but he stared right back his blue eyes wide and innocent. It was impossible for her to guess at what he wasn't telling her. She wasn't sure what she felt about that, certainly not trust. Still, she could believe he wanted to leave the ship, who wouldn't after such a whipping? She chewed on her lip and looked down at the deck. 'Captain Pike means to sell me in Ras Sul too, doesn't he?' She scowled and her skin crawled at the thought of being a slave. Now Leveen's earlier remarks began to make sense. 'That pus-filled boil on a rat's arse...'

'Not Ras Sul, the slave market at Dal Abar is where he'll be meaning to sell you, lass,' Tacker interrupted. 'He'll get a much better price for a golden-haired, green-eyed virgin there.'

'What?' Katleya pulled a lock of hair forward and squinted at it. Still the darkest brown crushed walnut shells could make it.

'The roots are showing, lass.' Tacker shrugged.

'Blast it,' Katleya muttered. She should have kept her hat on every day no matter how hot it had got. She'd not had a single chance to dye her hair aboard ship. She scowled up at Tacker. 'If that greasy pirate thinks he's selling me off to some rat-faced, wart-bollocked, turd-head in Ras Sul or Dal Abar, whose throat I'd have to cut if he tried to lay a single, slimy finger...'

'It never ceases to amaze me, the way you have with words, lass.' Tacker shook his head, laughter lighting his eyes. 'Such imagination, such colour. Didn't think I'd ever learn anything off a lovely lass like you but...'

'Katleya! Captain wants you. There's tallying to be done on the new cargo,' Eyeless shouted from below.

Katleya invented more strings of elaborate oaths all the way down to the upper cargo hold as the sun dipped to the horizon.

Leaning against the starboard rail, Katleya gazed at the view. Stuck in Captain Pike's cabin sorting out ledgers when they weighed anchor that morning, this was her first proper sight of the city. It was a wonder. Selassi City piled its box-shaped houses in a multi-hued jumble of painted plaster. At random levels on its terraces, stood grander buildings of various types of marble, on top of which sat copper domes, spires or cupolas, some verdigris, some polished to gleam in the sun.

Above, farmed and forested slopes rose in broad steps and beyond them loomed the Selassian Massif, a natural wall of limestone sheltering the balmy Selassian lands from the Shafi Desert. A desert, Katleya had discovered, that stretched for hundreds of leagues north, east and south. It suffered forge-like days and freezing nights, scorpions, snakes, wyverns, ifrits, warring tribes and much, much more. At least, the books and maps in Captain Pike's cabin had described it that way. When Tacker had stopped laughing over her ignorance, he explained that ifrits were a type of spirit that some saw, some didn't and others didn't believe in at all.

Katleya seethed with frustration as she stared at the city. It spread along almost the entire shoreline of the great sickle-shaped bay. To both north and south, peninsulas of rock held tall, round watchtowers. The colourful Selassian flag flapped above both with a simple white pennant bearing the Lehotan sun sigil below each. The Assacar had anchored at the extreme edge of the harbour, just as Tacker had said it would, and swimming to the closest shore would be a challenge. She figured she could do it, but she'd have to watch out for sharks. There were always sharks.

She had spotted Tacker up in the crow's nest when she first came up on deck, but there was no sign of him now. She hadn't seen much of him, let alone discussed any plans since their talk up on the mizzen-mast after the battle. Leveen wasn't any better either. The one time Katleya had tried to ask the woman anything, in particular the plans Captain Pike might have for her, Leveen had just turned on her heel and walked away without a word.

Blasted woman.

A sultry wind wafted over the teeming city and across the bay. It carried the scent of cypress, tamarisk, cinnamon and a thousand other enticing aromas. Katleya flared her nostrils, aching to put her feet onto dry land and eat food that didn't taste of salt or had things with far too many legs crawling around in it.

The sun blazed its death throes in the scarlet sky. A few men played a lethargic game of Thrones, with a worn set of bone cubes, near the main mast. Using the spyglass she'd lifted from the Captain's cabin, Katleya watched the launch make its way up one of the creeks that spilled sluggish water into the bay. Once out of view from the docks and the towers, the launch beached on the rocky eastern bank. Captain Pike clambered out of the boat while four crewmen heaved two small crates up and followed him onto the flat rocks. A cluster of merchants waited further up the bank. There was a lot of gesticulating then one of the merchants lifted his arm and a squad of soldiers came running out of the trees.

Katleya perked up. Captain Pike motioned and his men opened the crates. The officer inspected the goods. He lifted a scroll out of one crate, unrolled and read it. He signalled and his soldiers surrounded the crew with drawn short-bows. There was more gesticulating then one of Captain Pike's men drew his sword. He jerked back and fell from the rocks an arrow jutting from his throat. A splash of foaming sea swallowed him.

'Now, what could possibly be happening over there? Why, it looks like our good old captain might be having a problem.'

Katleya jumped. Tacker's hand felt heavy on her shoulder. 'What?' Snapping the spyglass closed, she slipped it into her belt and turned.

'By the look of it, it seems his bribes no longer work in Selassi.' Tacker's grin was feral but he kept his voice low.

From the main mast, the rattle of the bone cubes sounded loud in the humid air. Eyeless and Matz fished on the port side, their backs to Katleya and the city. There was a gentle swell in the harbour as currents made a half-hearted effort to shift debris out to sea. The boards creaked as the Assacar swayed against the anchor chains. None of the crew had noticed a thing.

'Now our Captain Pike will have to extend his stay ashore, all unexpected like.' Katleya strained to hear Tacker above the slap of waves. 'We'll all be taking our chances and our leave tonight, lass.'

'What have you done?'

'Signalled the tower guard to give them warning some smuggling was abroad. See that merchant who raised his arm? One of the port guards in disguise. I wrote down a few pieces of information on that scroll the officer there read, and every word of it nothing but truth. The Captain will have a lot of awkward questions to answer for a good long while, I'd imagine.' He smirked and his dark eyes danced.

'How'd you signal the guard all the way over there?'

'Nice shiny bit of polished silver and a few flashes of reflected light.' Tacker's face stilled. 'An old favour's been repaid. More to the point, we'll have a chance to slip off in the cutter tonight.'

'You worked all this out by yourself, the whole plan?'

'What? You think I haven't the brain, lass?' Tacker shrugged, looking over his shoulder. Katleya turned too but all she saw was Eyeless and

Matz, still fishing.

'You didn't show a lot of brains when you tried for my virginity.' Katleya snorted. 'Anyway, Eyeless'll never let us take the cutter.' Katleya measured the distance to shore. 'It's not so far to the docks. I could swim that distance and find a place to hide in the city in no time. I've not seen any sharks for a while, I think I could chance it.'

'It's not so simple, lass.' Tacker pointed down at the swells. 'These waters look quiet and innocent don't they?' At Katleya's nod, he continued. 'You see that old log over there?'

'Yes. What about it?'

'Sea krokos.'

Katleya snapped open the spyglass. Where a muddy river opened out into the other side of the bay the reptiles, masquerading as craggy tree trunks up to ten or twelve feet long, lounged in the sun's last shafts. A small one slid off the sands and snapped up an unwary sea bird. 'Blast it, they're big.'

'And don't forget the sharks, you might not see them but they're about, the water's not so shallow as to dissuade them. But those krokos, why they'd snap a morsel like you in half and swallow each mouthful quick as a heartbeat. Damn, but they're fast.' Tacker stretched. 'Trust me, we'll use the cutter and stay in one piece. I'll meet you there second hour after midnight. Now I'm off for a sleep before my watch. It'd be best if you got some shut-eye too, lass.'

Tacker hawked and spat at the sea. A gull squawked and lumbered away from the piece of flotsam it had been investigating.

'Nice aim,' Katleya murmured.

'Practise.' Tacker strode off pausing for a word into Leveen's ear as she came up on deck. She nodded and walked over to the railing along from Eyeless without looking Katleya's way once.

Katleya woke with a start.

'Katleya, get yourself up on deck, lass.' Leveen's disembodied voiced hissed into her ear.

'What? Leveen?' Katleya yawned and rolled out of her bunk.

'Time to go. Tacker's getting the cutter ready.' Leveen said in her usual curt manner, and turned toward the companionway without waiting.

Time to go?

Leveen and Tacker? Who would have thought those two could ever work together? One all mouth, the other grim and talkative as a lump of rock. Katleya wondered what sort of relationship those two could possibly have. Also, if Tacker had Leveen helping him, what did he need her for? What was certain was that she couldn't really trust either of them. She wondered if she'd ever be able to trust anyone ever again. For now, though, she needed them to get off the Assacar.

Katleya stood quiet and listened. The ship was still apart from the slap of waves and creak of planks. She couldn't see anything much in the dark and heard nothing but the usual atonal snores coming from Matz in the other bunk. So all seemed well enough. But something had happened, for certain. Had Captain Pike found out about their leaving? Was Tacker dead? But then, why would Leveen just wake her and walk off assuming she'd follow? She tugged on her clothes and grabbed her bag, packed and ready.

In the main hold of the ship, more snores filled the rancid air. The whole of both watches slept and only Tacker and Leveen's hammocks were empty. That was what was wrong. What had those two done to achieve this?

Katleya stayed silent and headed to the gangway leading to the lower hold. She needed to do one thing before leaving the ship.

'There you are, lass.' Tacker swung the cutter over the railings while Leveen kept it still so it didn't scrape against the ship. 'We were almost set to go without you.'

'Well, I'm here now. So why are you leaving too, Leveen?'

Neither of them answered, Tacker looking awkward, Leveen ignoring her completely. Leveen slung her kit into the cutter, motioned for Katleya to do the same, then helped Tacker lower the boat to the water. Why was the woman *sneaking* off the Assacar? She could leave any time she liked couldn't she? Who'd stop her?

'Everyone's snoring below decks.' Katleya looked out toward Selassi. The city sparkled with thousands of tiny golden flames, their reflections dancing on the water. The breeze had picked up and the scents of spice and perfumes were heady. She turned back to Tacker. 'How did you manage that?'

'Aye, they are indeed. Looks like someone found a cask of rum open and just begging to be drunk.' Tacker grinned. 'And not one of them thought it tasted strange.'

'Fools, every one of them,' Leveen muttered.

'Someone found a bunch of keys lying around in the lower hold too.' Katleya smiled when she heard the quiet whisper of bare feet, a series of soft splashes against the sides of the ship soon followed, back where the anchor chains met the water. 'Just begging to be used.'

'You needn't have done that, lass.' Tacker shrugged. 'The authorities will be boarding this ship by morning and they'd have freed them. Now they'll have to take their chances with krokos and sharks.'

'Well, I was worried Captain Pike might make it back, or that Eyeless would wake up early and realise what'd happened,' Katleya insisted. 'It wouldn't be fair for me to escape and leave those poor men to suffer the slave blocks of Ras Sul. Besides, they knew about the krokos and, if they're keen to take their chances, who am I to stop them? I figure it's their choice.'

'The girl is right. We all make our own choices and take our own chances.' Leveen nodded down to the cutter. 'Get in the boat and sit aft, girl. You will work the tiller.'

Katleya looked hard at Leveen, but in the dark there was even less chance of reading the woman's face. She wondered what choices the woman had made to end up on this ship and what made her decide to leave. Another mystery for her to pick at like a scab. Katleya hoped she wouldn't mind seeing what lay underneath.

They clambered down into the little boat and slipped the ropes free. Katleya picked her way over the short stayed mast and sail to sit on the board at the back and slipped the tiller free of its rope.

Tacker and Leveen sat on the main thwart, took hold of a long oar each and slid them into the rag-wrapped oarlocks.

'Keep the rowing even, Tacker.'

'I've done it enough to have worked out the technique, Leveen.' Tacker shifted to point over to the northern end of the bay. 'Steer us well clear of the other ships, Katleya. We need to head to the left of the main docks, over to where the fishing smacks pull up onto the beach, see them?'

'Yes, right.'

They rowed away from the Assacar, swift and almost silent.

'So, how come you're with us, Leveen?' Katleya asked again, keeping her voice low.

'I have my reasons,' Leveen answered. 'You do not have a problem about my joining your escape?'

'No, no, not at all. I'd just not realised everything was worked out so well,' Katleya whispered. She turned to Tacker. 'Well, why are you both helping me?'

'Me and Leveen we got talking and we realised we'd both wanted to put one over on Captain Pike for a while. Stealing you and getting him beached works just fine for us both. We knew you needed to leave too and, as we needed a hand on the tiller, we thought we'd bring you along.' His teeth glinted in the moonlight. Diaphos peered over the Selassian Massif. Liatos dawdled as usual. 'Aye, it does feel good to have holed his ship at least once in his life.'

'The captain was good to you, boy. He could have had you whipped till you passed out for touching the girl, and none would have protested,' Leveen muttered.

'I think I might've protested!' Tacker protested.

'What'll you do in Selassi, Tacker?' Lifting up the spyglass, Katleya scanned the bay. She could make out a line of heads bobbing halfway to the nearer peninsula and its watchtower. They would make it, she was sure.

'I think I'll buy myself a small boat and become a fisherman.' Tacker chuckled. 'Now, how about that? Seems I've gone and got myself a little boat already. You care to join me, lass? I could do...'

'Tacker.' Leveen stopped him mid word.

Katleya looked from one to the other. 'Thanks for the offer, Tacker, but I'm going north. I should have gone there long ago but got stuck in Black Rock.' Katleya fell silent.

'Where do you head, girl?' Leveen asked.

'Storr.'

'Storr? You're going to the High-King's castle? You think you'll fit in with all the fine ladies of the court?' Tacker sighed. 'Aye, I'm thinking maybe you will. Yes, you'd look damned fine in one of those fancy dresses.'

'I'm not going to any court and I won't be wearing any stupid dress either. I've got far more important things to do.' Katleya glared at Tacker. 'Do you know Storr? Why don't you come with me? Wouldn't you want to get a lot farther away from Captain Pike and his cronies?'

'Tacker has other places to which he must go,' Leveen interrupted. 'Is that not so, Tacker?'

'Er, aye. Storr isn't the place for me, lass.' Tacker sounded curt all of a sudden. 'It's too damned cold and you'll be safer journeying through the desert, not sailing on a ship with the likelihood Captain Pike hears of it and takes you again, or gets one of his friends to pick you up. I hate the desert and I'll not lose this lovely little boat.' His voice softened. 'Don't worry about me, lass. There are plenty of fishing villages to be anonymous in along this coast.'

'I will travel with you, girl.' Leveen glanced at her then away.

'Oh.' Somehow, knowing Leveen would join her on the journey through the desert didn't comfort Katleya. They moved in silence over the moon-licked waters toward the sparkling city.

Chapter 12

They made it to Selassi's northern market area as grey light fingered the morning and stirred men and camels awake into an uproar of belching, groaning and shouts. Leveen took the lead, asking an outlying guard questions in a language that sounded flowery and long-winded to Katleya. For some reason she couldn't fathom Tacker tagged along.

'What are you saying?'

'I asked which caravan is going north today.'

'It took that many words?'

'It is the common trader tongue. It is polite in the extreme for good reason. It is so that everyone takes care of what they say and no one takes offence. Perhaps it would be wise for you to learn this language. It will save you much trouble.' Leveen took her bearing. 'This way.'

'Now you tell me?' Katleya had to stretch her legs to the extreme to keep up with her. She turned on Tacker. 'I could've been learning it all this time on the ship!'

'And give the game away?' Tacker laughed.

'Why are you still with us anyway? I thought you wanted to become a fisherman.'

'Just making sure you're well on your way to freedom.' Tacker grinned. He pulled on her arm slowing her a little and letting Leveen pull away. 'Don't trust that woman.'

'Leveen?' Katleya narrowed her eyes, and tilted her head. 'I don't. Why don't you?'

'She's been with Pike for years. Why leave now?' Tacker shrugged. 'I'm just wondering.'

'Well, don't worry about me. I can look after myself.'

Tacker raised an eyebrow and gave her a look.

'What?'

He looked like he was about to laugh, then shook his head and frowned. Stretching his legs he caught up with Leveen, leaving Katleya puzzling behind him.

The three of them wove through the chaos till they found the master of a caravan at the far edge of the site almost ready to leave.

The man seemed bad-tempered, his answer to Leveen's question on the short side for trader-tongue, but then it looked like getting a caravan going must be like herding chickens, Katleya thought, looking round at the disorder.

Leveen touched her forehead, mouth and heart, dipped her head, mirroring the merchant, then turned to Katleya. 'We must hurry. This is the only caravan headed north today. But we are in luck for it is going straight to the desert city of Rialt and there is a silk merchant that may be willing to take you aboard.' Leveen kept turning to stare one way then another, but never stopped as they trotted past wagons, strings of camels and teams of mules.

'Where's Rialt?' Katleya asked.

'A city to the north of the Shafi Desert,' Tacker answered. 'Leveen's homeland.'

Leveen had already marched ahead.

'Let me take it from here, Leveen.' Tacker strode on ahead as they reached a silk merchant half way down the line of wagons and carts.

'Very well.' Without any explanation, Leveen turned and walked off into the crowd.

Katleya watched her go, confused. 'Wasn't she travelling with me?'

The merchant was a slim, tall man, with a black beard curling right down to his waist. He looked rather amused as, using a rather fast patter of trader-tongue, Tacker asked him to take Katleya on board his vast articulated cart. By the look of the merchant's rising eyebrows, she was certain it was all some grand mixture of bluffing and outright lies. Silence met Tacker's last words. The merchant looked at her, expectance on his face.

'Throw a knife.' Tacker nodded at Katleya, then smiled at the merchant.

'What?'

'I've said you're good, show him how good. It'll help.' *Go on*, Tacker's eyes urged her.

She looked back at him a moment, measuring, then shrugged and slipped a blade into her hand. It thrummed against the baseboard of the cart before they'd seen it in her hand. A moment later, a second shivered right next to it.

The merchant said something. He and Tacker laughed.

'His name is Abyan bin Kholar al-Derin.' Tacker drew her away a yard or two. 'He's travelling with his two young sons. He says it'll be good to have a strong woman aboard. It seems the desert people admire strong women.'

'Now tell me what else you promised I could do.' Katleya folded her arms and gave him a hard look.

'I might have mentioned you could drive camels.'

'What? This is the first time I've even seen the blasted creatures and they don't look too friendly either.'

'You'll learn fast enough, you were quick to pick things up on the ship.'

'A ship is nothing like a camel.'

'There are two ways to get north from Rialt,' Tacker said quick and quiet under his breath, looking about him. 'West along the river to Dal Abar.'

'Dal Abar! That's the place I wanted to avoid, blast it!'

'Only as a potential slave, you'd be fine as a free woman.' Tacker huffed, irritated. He looked round again. 'The other way is over the mountains due north into Manom. Turn west at the first big river you reach. It'll take you to the Elyat Sea. Either way, you should find it easy enough to get aboard a ship going on to Storr.'

'I could have got a ship from here,' Katleya grumbled.

'Look, Pike is rich, he's probably bribed someone by now and is free again.' Tacker looked into Katleya's face. 'Do you really want him catching you again?'

'Well, if you put it that way.'

'I mean it, lass, you've got to get away from Selassi as soon as you can.'

'Don't worry about me, Tacker. Go fish.'

They said awkward goodbyes, wishing each other luck. Tacker walked off, muttering about getting back to the cutter quick in case someone took a fancy to it, before Katleya felt quite ready to see the last of him. She remembered she'd misjudged him at the beginning, but then, he'd been an idiot. He should have explained better what he was up to, even if he was hankering to get past her underclothes while he was at it. She paused her thoughts, feeling confused and hot all of a sudden. Anyway, why he'd still wanted to help her after she'd held a knife to his sacks she'd probably never know for certain. Was it really only to get one over Captain Pike? And what about Leveen? Why did she want to leave the Assacar when she enjoyed being a pirate so much? It didn't make sense.

At least she was learning to accept a bit of help now, just like Laru had told her to do. Laru, someone else Katleya would probably never see again. Black Rock seemed so very far away now, and long ago too.

Spirits! It is far away, rats' piss for brains!

Katleya rubbed at her eyes. She'd swapped salt water for sand and dust getting into them and making them water. So that was another chapter of her life closed and done with. When, she wondered, would she get a chance to draw breath? She looked at Tacker's fast-disappearing back. He stopped, seemed to be talking to someone. He held out his hand and accepted something. She squinted, trying to make it out, but Tacker shoved whatever he'd got into his shirt and turned into the crowds.

She was just thinking about following him to find out what that was all about, when Abyan called to her from the seat of his cart. Well, it didn't look like drawing breath was likely right now. And whatever Tacker was up to didn't really matter any more did it? Katleya climbed up and sat down next to Abyan, shoved her pack under the seat and grabbed hold of the backboard as the cart jolted into motion. She watched carefully how Abyan managed his camels.

The caravan entered the narrow pass leading through the Massif, heading toward the southern edge of the Shafi Desert, by the time the sun rose. Looking back at the narrowing view of Selassi, Katleya fretted. How was she going to learn trader-tongue and handle camels fast enough that the merchant wouldn't throw her off his cart? Life just never got any easier!

Tacker and his blasted exaggerations.

Now that he had gone Katleya almost missed him.

Just under two tendays into the journey, the caravan climbed over a low ridge of arid hills and the land levelled to an area of rock littered sand. On its northern edge lay the oasis of Eage al Shafi, almost the midway point between the Selassian Massif and Rialt. The crossing had seemed longer. Between the mountains and the oasis vast waves of dunes, as endless, changeable and unchanging as the sea, played the sand-cast anvil to the sun's furnace-hot hammer.

They reached the oasis as the sun spilled the last of its molten gold onto the dunes.

Katleya pulled the camels round to come next to the cart in front, swearing at them in fluent Shafian when they didn't turn tight enough and almost clipped the cart's front wheel against the other cart's tail.

'You have a fine hand with those camels and would be a true woman of the desert if not for your pale skin, gold hair and green eyes, Fair One.' Abyan bin Kholar al-Derin, the cart's owner, slid down from his high saddle as his camel knelt. He stretched the travel cricks out of his back, a smile flashing against his mahogany skin. 'By the Mother, you have learned fast and well. Have you thought again on marriage to one of my sons? We Derin appreciate strong women for they remind us of our Mother Goddess, Daru. The best Derin seers are all women, every one of them as strong-willed as the desert itself. You would make a fine wife to either one and a fine daughter to me. You may choose Aslam or Assan, I have no preference. They are young but that would make them all the more malleable, do you not think?'

'Er, it is with regret that I must say no, once more.' Katleya wished she'd died her hair again some while ago, but water was short in the desert, and then she'd never actually been told why she had to dye it in the first place so it just didn't seem important. She clamped her hat back on and repeated her small lie. 'I am promised to another.'

Abyan sighed. 'As you say, yet I still do not understand why this promised one of yours would let you cross the great Shafi Desert alone, Fair One. No matter how great a warrior you might be. But you do have your Shafian woman also, do you not. Though I have seen nothing of her since we left. Does she guard you from the shadows?' Abyan shook his head, but smiled. He turned and slapped his hands together. 'Aslam, Assan, time to raise the tent.' His two sons of fourteen and twelve tumbled out of the cart.

Katleya also wondered what had happened to Leveen in odd idle moments. But since she was happy enough with Abyan and heading in the right direction, she didn't much care. She helped Abyan and his sons raise the large multi-roomed tent inside the circle of carts, then went out to scout the land.

There wasn't much to see around the oasis itself. A few green pools of water, leaning groups of date palms and scrubby bushes with thorns the length of her thumbs. She wandered on and, over a ridge of wind-burned rock, Katleya found the pillars and broken walls of an ancient city.

She walked across sand-worn slabs of paved avenues, passed the stubs of limestone columns, the crumbling walls of enormous buildings, fallen domes and faded mosaic floors. Pottery shards and crumbled marble littered the spaces and the scent of jasmine and roses grown wild laced the air.

The sun, a half disc of dazzling ruby on the horizon, washed a rough circle of standing stones on the far side of the ruins with red. Two leaned like drunkards, one had fallen prone to the sand, the other nine remained more or less upright. The blue-grey, squat stones didn't fit with the red sands or the cream limestone of the city behind her. Their black shadow fingers clawed eastwards.

Katleya's skin prickled and hairs spiked up on her arms and the nape of her neck. She took her hat off and scrubbed at her hair, closing in on the nearest stone. The one facing due west. It towered over her. Close up she could see faint remains of carved designs. Circles and swirls, both moons in all their different phases and fine lines weaving through all the other shapes, making intricate patterns. Patterns that reminded her of Wefan matrices and lattices. The stone felt cold compared to the heat of the day's end. Too far away from the camp to hear the groaning of camels or men shouting, only the wind's whispers across the sands kept her company. She opened her Wealdan and touched the stone.

It tingled. She leaned in closer. Just under the surface, Katleya saw the flicker of Wefan but instead of the normal fixed matrix of stone, silver flashes pulsed by with no discernible patterns at all. On the edge of hearing, a thrum trembled the air. She studied the stone again. Normal matrices still picked out the stone's structure around its edges, it was only in the centre they had disappeared. She flattened her palm against the centre of the stone, gasping as her hand slid right through its surface. It felt like ice sliced through her flesh.

'Spirits!' Katleya yanked her hand out. It was fine. No blood and all in one piece, but cold. Icy cold. The thrumming sound was louder now and she reached out with her hand again.

No, not thrumming. Heavy drumming travelled through the ground. Katleya whipped round closing her Wealdan off so fast it hurt.

Twenty or thirty camels swept up out of the dunes. With no words, the riders made their mounts circle round the standing stones till they surrounded Katleya. In a cloud of sand and dust, they came to a sudden halt. Spitting the fine grit from her mouth and wiping it from her eyes she looked up at the camels. They stared down at her with the usual superior look in their long, narrow faces. She scowled back at them.

If any of you spit at me, I'll punch you in your blasted hairy faces!

The riders had the veils and turbans all Shafian warriors wore in the desert. The same as the Shafian guards working with the caravan. Leveen wore them too, but unlike her veil these fluttered in the wind and hung past their mouths. These camel riders also carried light spears and small rectangular shields covered in white hide with tribal marks painted on them in ochre and red. The spears' narrow blades flashed in the last of the sunlight as they pointed down toward Katleya.

'By the Great Atash, it *is* a female,' one said.

'I told you so,' said another. 'A desert doe.'

Katleya spun but couldn't make out which of the riders had spoken. She slammed her hat back on.

'It is not wise to touch these stones.' A woman's voice, to her left.

'What? Who are you?' Katleya demanded in trader-tongue. Abyan and his boys being fluent in Shafian had taught her the language so she understood well enough what these warriors said, but pretended not to. Uncle Yadoc had told her long ago that to be underestimated was a good survival tactic. It had worked in Black Rock so she decided it'd work here. She flicked her wrists so her knives dropped into her hands.

'Have a care. She is no doe, but a sand wolf. See those sharp little teeth of hers.'

'I am blessed! A glorious she-wolf. I relish a challenge and shall rise up to be equal to this one. I have never before seen such a female.' This was from a man. He raised his spear and tapped his camel with its butt. The camel spat, groaned and grunted, taking its time to obey. 'Green eyes like emeralds, hair golden as the sun. A rarity, a desert jewel. I believe I have yet to enjoy a woman with green eyes and golden hair.'

'You must wait yet a while to enjoy such a moment for you will not have this one.'

Katleya turned in surprise and saw Leveen push her way through the circle of camels and into the stone circle.

'Leveen el Meera al-Shafi.' The tribesman tapped his camel so it lurched back up onto its broad feet again. 'You have grown since last we met.'

Some of the other riders shifted and exchanged glances but said nothing. They all raised their spears.

'I swear by Atash, you are now taller even than your father. Yet still I would recognise you anywhere. Our time together was...how should I encapsulate those moments into words? Memorable? Unforgettable? Remarkable?' His voice was loaded with sarcasm. His lips twisted into a sneer. 'So woman, what is it that brings you back to the sand seas of Shafi? Tell me in truth, it is for yearning of me, is it not?'

'I must pity you, Tareef el Daefi al-Shafi.' Leveen grabbed hold of Katleya's arm just above the elbow. 'The heat of the desert sun must have addled what passes for your brain. What other explanation could there be? For we have never spent any memorable time together, you are eminently forgettable and I find it remarkable you still live.'

Leveen squeezed her arm hard when Katleya made to pull away. The warrior woman's meaning was clear and, for now, she would let Leveen take the lead. Anyway, it was all getting very interesting.

'I see you have not changed in the slightest. Tell me how you have survived so long away from the sands, woman.' Tareef pulled his veil down to flap round his neck and grinned. His skin was even darker than Leveen's and his teeth shone white against it. 'Did you not find the great wet seas to your liking? Or perhaps the wetlanders proved to be weak and you discovered they could never satisfy a true desert woman, no matter how hard they might try?'

'I liked the seas well enough.' Leveen stared at him, her eyes hard. 'You were not there.'

'Do you claim this green eyed one?' Tareef ignored the jibe and nodded towards Katleya his grin widening. 'Is she your slave? Sell her to me. I would give you a fair price, woman.'

'She is no slave.' Leveen shrugged dismissively. 'Just a skinny wretch who travels with the caravan.'

'Skinny wretch? I think not. That she is no slave is of interest, however.' Tareef's full attention was on Katleya again. 'By what name are you known, my she-wolf?'

Katleya looked at Leveen keeping up the pretence she had no idea what was going on.

'Girl!' Tareef repeated in trader-tongue. 'How are you called?'

'I'm Katleya.'

'And I, Katleya of the Emerald-eyes, am Tareef el Daefi al-Shafi, Fearless One of the Red Sands.' Tareef banged his shield with his spear so it thrummed like a drum skin. 'My name is spoken of with respect and fear from the great city of Selassi to the Amalla Heights and from Dal Abar, dark pearl of the western seas to the treacherous heights of the Ruel Mountains. In combat, I am unbeatable. Before our enemies, I am smoke. Grown men are like children when they come up against me. Women fall at my feet. Even the fierce Leveen el Meera al-Shafi, when she first came into her blood, begged me to bed her and it was her most memorable night. Do not believe her when she says otherwise. I will have an even better night with you.'

'Blasted bollocks to that! Touch me and bleed.' Katleya tensed and relaxed her muscles then rolled her shoulders and softened her knees. She was ready.

'But my lips beg for yours, my arms yearn to hold you, my shaft hungers to pierce your flower.' Tareef's grin became fiercer. 'I would sicken and die if I did not touch you. How could you be so cruel as to deny me my needs, Fair One?'

'What sand-blinded babble you speak, Tareef.' Leveen lips twisted as if she smelled something bad. 'The terror of the harems is not fit to eat the droppings of a camel!'

'I disagree.' One of the other riders laughed. A woman, the one who'd spoken before. She raised her spear up high then holstered it. 'He's welcome to the droppings of my camel any time he wishes. But if I were Tareef the Fearless I would remove my arse from this place while it still remains intact.'

A fierce grin sliced across Leveen's lips at the woman's words but she kept her eyes on Tareef. All the other riders raised their spears and holstered them.

'I do not run like some wetlander coward, woman.' Tareef squared his shoulders. He slitted his eyes and his lips thinned. 'I never run. I prefer to face each and every one of the choices I make in life. To meet them all, eye to eye. No matter what the consequences.'

'Tareef.' Leveen sneered. 'You have the heart of a rock rat and the brains of a dung beetle. The sands are immense. Go and hide in them.'

'Make me, wetlanders' doxy. Or are the rumours true, woman?' Tareef spat into the sand. 'Have you been weakened by the blood-priests and made into their plaything?'

Katleya whipped a look up at Leveen, her heart hammering.

Blood-priests plaything? What does Tareef blasted well mean?

'Get down from your overburdened camel, Tareef All-Talk. And match your tulwar to your mealy-mouthed words!' Leveen ordered. She pushed Katleya to one side.

She backed as far as the encircling camels allowed and eyed all the riders. The nearest camel snorted and a slap of foul wet air splattered against her neck. Katleya jumped out of the way, swearing under her breath about the unflattering ancestry of the beast. Its rider chuckled. She added more unflattering descriptions about him in trader-tongue for good measure. A couple of slices through the saddle straps and he'd be too busy spitting sand and grit to laugh at her. Turning to watch Leveen again, Katleya waited. Ready for anything, aware of everything.

Leveen slid her tulwar from the scabbard on her back and waited in the centre of the circle. Long legs a little apart, one a shade forward of the other, she rolled her shoulders and shifted her balance, watching Tareef order his camel to kneel.

'It would have been more sensible to do this after night has fallen, woman.' Tareef leaped from his saddle and drew his own tulwar. It shone red with the dying light. 'The sun still burns without mercy. It seems Atash, gave you little sense at your birth and that little you have lost on attaining womanhood. It saddens me in the extreme that the passing years have not returned the sense to your mazed head since.'

'Do not be afraid, Tareef All-Talk.' Disdain dripped from Leveen's lips like poison. 'This will be over before I have broken much sweat.'

Tareef scowled and screwed his lips back like a snarling dog. He shook himself and came in sideways moving slow and easy. He looked like he knew what he was doing as his tulwar patterned the dusty air. Leveen drifted over the sand, her own broad tulwar in one hand a curving dagger in the other. They circled each other, darted in for a slice at a throat or a belly, jumped back and circled again. The tulwars clashed and flashed in the last rays of the sun, accents in their dance. Blood flew like sparkling rubies to the sand that sucked them dry.

Leveen's greater reach and ferocity wore Tareef down. Soon, he bled from slices all over his body but he refused to give in. Leveen had less than half the cuts and breathed easy still. Dismay registered in Tareef's eyes. He began to lose his nimbleness and sweat glued his clothes to his lean body. He staggered against every blow and his breath rasped loud and uneven on the arid air. A heavy strike to his right shoulder took him to the sand and he sprawled on the ground coughing dust. Blood leaked from the deep wound.

'He has had enough, Leveen,' the woman rider said.

'Are you done, Tareef?' Leveen asked. She pressed the point of her tulwar against his groin.

Katleya wondered for a moment if she'd leave him legless, or gut him, like those poor men on the merchant ship. But that'd be unlikely what with all his friends about, wouldn't it?

'Keep the girl, Leveen.' Tareef gasped and tried to back away from the tulwar. 'Gods know what you want with her but I will not try for her again.' He pulled in a breath through clenched teeth too exhausted to move any further. 'When did you learn to fight so well?'

'Leveen. It is finished.' The woman rider had dismounted and stood a tulwar's length from Leveen.

Shrugging, Leveen raised her tulwar, turned and began scrubbing away the blood from its curving length with some clean sand.

Most of the riders turned and rode toward the oasis but two dismounted and came over to Tareef to help him sit up.

'Why did you leave the Shafi Desert, Leveen?' Tareef asked through gritted teeth, wincing as one of the riders cut away his sleeve, cleaned the wound with a dash of clear liquid and stitched the slice there and then. It impressed Katleya that he didn't make a sound. 'It was not just because of me, was it?'

Katleya walked over. She opened her Wealdan a touch and saw the tracery of Wefan running through the man's body. None of Tareef's wounds looked too bad. His arm might remain useless for a good while but he looked healthy so he'd mend and recover soon enough.

'No, Tareef, it was not you. You never had that much effect on my life. The need to leave was not of my choosing.' Leveen slid her tulwar back into its scabbard, her mouth twisted. 'As you well know.'

'Stay, Leveen. I invite you to food, water and the shade of our tents.' It was the woman who had spoken up earlier. She lifted her veil revealing almost black eyes, a lined face and short iron-grey hair. She didn't quite reach Leveen's shoulder but an air of gravity and wisdom made her seem more imposing.

'I thank you Orno el Daefi al-Shafi. I apologise for the insult to you and your clan but I must ride on. I have business that cannot wait.' Leveen paused then raised her voice. 'Perhaps we will meet again under better circumstances.'

'May your journey be uneventful and may Atash, His Flames burn eternal, and all the lesser gods watch over you.' Orno raised a hand in salute.

After a moment's hesitation Leveen echoed the salute. 'May Atash, His Flames burn eternal, and all the other lesser gods watch over you too.' She turned and strode back towards the caravan.

'Thanks for fighting for me but you needn't have.' Katleya sprang towards the woman. 'I can take care of myself.'

'Do you believe that, girl?' Leveen spun and Katleya almost crashed into her. The woman loomed over her and she could almost see the eyes under the veil. 'In truth?'

Katleya felt a sudden thrill of danger finger her spine. There was something unusual about those eyes. She knew it in her bones. Yet, the woman had just saved her from Tareef. He'd been good and Katleya knew she wouldn't have been able to take him in an upright fight. She'd have had to wait till a quiet moment alone to take him down and who knows what would've happened before that chance?

'Well, not all of them.' Katleya shrugged. 'But wouldn't the guards have done something about a bunch of tribesmen taking a member of the caravan?'

'They will keep well away unless the caravan is attacked.' Leveen turned and walked on. 'The loss of one girl is of no concern to them.'

Katleya absorbed that. It sounded like the truth, where the caravan master was concerned anyway. Though Abyan might have something to say about it, she couldn't imagine he'd be able to actually do anything. She sighed and hurried after Leveen, hoping to try a few more questions while the woman seemed minded to answer them. 'That was a good fight. Did you get trained to fight like that?'

'I did.'

Katleya tried another tack. 'What Tareef said got me thinking about a few things...'

'Of which I will tell you nothing, girl.' Leveen kept walking so fast Katleya had to trot to keep up.

'For a moment there I thought you'd come home. This is your home, isn't it?' Katleya persisted. If she fired enough questions at the woman, she just might get an answer to a few of them. 'That woman seemed to know you well. Why didn't you want to stay with them? And where have you been all this time anyway? I thought you wanted to travel with me on the caravan.'

'I had some errands to run. Now I am intent on reaching Rialt as soon as possible. We will be leaving the oasis long before the sun rises.'

'You're not staying with the caravan?'

'It is far too slow for my purpose.'

'You said we.' The caravan was in sight. Katleya thought about the slow journey across the leagues of desert to Rialt. Another tenday at least of eating the sand of over a dozen carts and a herd of camels. 'You want me to join you?'

'Are you not eager to reach your destination?' Leveen stopped and looked down at Katleya.

'Well, yes. And if you're travelling faster than the caravan, even more so,' Katleya said and she meant it, though she'd be keeping a close eye on the woman.

'We leave an hour before sunrise.' Leveen turned and strode off again. 'I will have a second camel. If you are not there I will leave without you.'

Chapter 13

It took another tenday of hard travel through the desert to reach the city-state of Rialt, a whole tenday faster than the caravan. An hour or so back, the trail became a hard packed road making the going easier. When it climbed a ridge, Katleya had a fine view northwards of the distant Amalla Heights, old mountains worn to nubs, nothing like the tall, dagger-sharp Ruel Mountains. On the other side of the ridge the road passed through a township of tents, palm frond shacks, corrals and mud-brick huts then cut up an almost sheer cliff to the southern gate of the city.

The city of Rialt stood on a low plateau, the wide point of a ridge of rock spearing westwards, deep into the Shafi Desert, from the north-south running spine of the Ruel Mountains. The jagged peaks hovered in the distant east, like a snow-capped mirage, pinked by the lowering sun. Sand-scoured copper domes and minarets of differing sizes and shapes, and myriad towers tiled in every colour, rose above the deep crenellations of the tall city walls. Water plunged in slender cataracts from channels cut into the base of the west-facing walls. A startling sight, like necklaces of pink crystals sparkling in the sunset. Katleya imagined what the cool, clear water would feel like running over her hot, grimy body. Irrigated fields and groves stretched along the banks of a wide and sluggish west-flowing river, on both north and south banks, for as far as she could see and around the base of the cliff where the water from the plateau pooled.

To Katleya's left, the sun dipped towards the great dunes of the Shafi heartlands and slathered the ancient walled city with molten gold. The moons were already up. Smaller Diaphos, full and silver, stood high above the distant Ruel Mountains and the larger, sickle-shaped Liatos, resting on their peaks, had her horns dyed pink by the setting sun.

'Liatos will be blood-horned tomorrow night.' Leveen guided her camel down the ridge. 'An ill omen for travellers. It is a good thing we have reached our destination today.'

'I didn't know you believed in omens, Leveen.' Katleya stared at the city high on its cliff. It was almost as beautiful as Selassi. She tapped at her camel's neck to get it moving.

'All those raised in the desert have a healthy respect for portents. In particular those offered by the moons,' Leveen replied, 'something you would do well to remember, girl.'

'What's that supposed to mean?' Katleya turned to Leveen, interested to learn yet another snippet about the secretive woman.

'I will speak no more of it.' Leveen urged her camel on faster, though she'd have to slow the beast as soon as they reached the tent town and its crowded streets.

She should have known by now how Leveen hated straight questions. Snorting, Katleya went back to studying the nearing city, knowing she wouldn't get any more from the woman for a while.

'I hope they've heard of baths here.' Katleya wiped the dust from her eyes. There was more of the damned stuff than ever, raised by the increased traffic on the road so near to the city.

Leveen looked over her shoulder. The veil over her eyes was so thick with dust, Katleya wondered how the woman saw anything at all through it. 'They have baths, girl.'

'Good. I'm positive I've sand in every crack and crevasse I own.' Katleya shifted in her saddle and sniffed. 'And I stink worse than the camels, a bit of a blasted achievement that.'

'The House of the Rose is within the eastern district of Rialt.' Leveen turned back. 'That is one of the richer quarters of the city. They draw their water from the aqueduct itself before it reaches the city proper.'

'Aqueduct?'

'It is a structure like a bridge.' Leveen tapped her stick and her camel barged through a crowd of people. She ignored their shouts and raised fists, raising her voice. 'It carries water to the city from a lake high up in the mountains and far to the east along the Draco's Neck.'

'Draco's Neck?' Katleya urged her camel into the gap behind Leveen's, awkward at causing the people on foot more problems, but anxious not to get stuck in the milling crowds and run the risk of losing the woman.

'The name given to this great spit of rock,' Leveen explained. 'An old myth tells how a great hero slew the dragon and built Rialt on its head. Some people still believe the myth. Some people are fools.'

Katleya studied the grey cliff with more interest. It stood stark against the red sands of the desert, but it looked like what it was. One great long lump of dark rock dwindling into the distant shimmer of heat and the floating Ruel Mountains.

The cataracts gathered in murky brown-green pools at the base of the cliff before flowing into the irrigation channels of the farmed lands. The road ascended in a long, steep slope away from the cataracts, hugging the undulations of the cliff-face, wide enough for four or more carts to drive abreast with room to spare. The cliff rose around three hundred feet from the desert sands. Caves pockmarked the rock all the way along the length of the road, housing taverns on the whole, selling food and drink, welcome stops for travellers along the league or so of unrelenting incline.

The walls of the city proper, made of great blocks of stone cut from the same dark rock as the plateau, soared thirty feet high and stood at least a hundred feet back from the plateau's edge. Twin towers stood twenty feet higher on either side of the gate. Beaten bronze covered its enormous wooden doors through which a long file of camels, mules, carts and people on foot carrying bundles of goods entered. Katleya followed Leveen through the fifteen-foot deep arch, the shadows cool and gloomy after the bright desert light.

Blinking in the brightness at the other end, Katleya looked round an enormous square full of animal pens and cages of varying sizes, and a hubbub of sellers and buyers of livestock. Leveen angled right to cross the square, taking as much notice of the people here as below. They stopped by a camel pen and made the animals sit. Slithering off the saddle, Katleya heaved a great sigh of relief. Ecstatic wouldn't cover it if she never had to ride a camel again, ever. Leveen began haggling with the camel trader. It didn't take long, not as long as the trader wanted judging by the scowl he gave the woman.

Katleya shouldered her bag with a groan and followed Leveen out of the square. Flat-roofed houses lined the narrower roads leading off the wide street they walked along. The whitewashed walls crumbled in patches revealing the dried red mud and dark-grey stone beneath. But every so often Katleya spied, through open doors or grilled archways, startling views of small but colourful courtyards tiled and filled with fountains, flowers and fruit trees. Sun-warmed scents layered the air and mingled with cooking aromas and the other more usual stinks of a crowded city.

Long, straight canals cut a grid through the city, wide enough to carry the two-way traffic of long, narrow boats, all crossed by high-arched bridges. The boatmen pushed their boats along with poles, skilfully dodging the occasional contents of chamber pots thrown from windows. Seeing the lumps slowly sink into the water, those cataracts falling down the cliffs didn't seem so appealing now to Katleya, but at the least the city streets stayed a deal cleaner than Black Rock because of them.

'Who are all these people?' Katleya asked as they negotiated a second huge square. This one was filled with stalls, peddlers and entertainers all yelling for attention and coin.

'Locals.' Leveen indicated women and men in long voluminous robes of colourful silks strolling round the stalls trailing servants and slaves wearing iron collars. 'Shafians.' This time she nodded toward a prowling group of dark skinned men and women, like Leveen and her desert friends, wearing baggy white clothes with curved knives hanging from belts and tulwars strapped to their backs.

'Miners from the foothills of the Ruel Mountains.' Leveen nodded toward a gang of short, broad men in narrow trousers, sleeveless jerkins and heavy wool shirts passing by. 'That one is plainsman from Manom.' She pointed at a tall, lone man wearing leather trousers and a suede tunic beaded with turquoise and silver. 'Those are from Ras Sul.'

Katleya watched the women swathed in shapeless black robes, wearing ornate leather masks, that flocked in groups behind men in more fitted black robes. They also had slaves, but these walked in pairs chained together.

Leveen named other groups and peoples but there were too many for Katleya to remember. At least a dozen different languages braided through the common trader-tongue and not one of them was her own. The whole seething clamour of the place after tendays spent in the quiet of the desert sent Katleya's senses into a spin.

So much to see, to hear, to smell. Why did Leveen rush through the city? Instead of chasing after the woman, Katleya paused to gaze at knives of every shape and size on a blade-smith's stall, she considered none of them as good as her own blades. On the next stall was an enormous selection of ground spices set out in tiny copper bowls, every one a different colour, a different scent. The stalls after that had heaps of lemons, dates, oranges, figs, limes, garlic, onions, beans, and a cornucopia of fruits and vegetables in strange shapes and colours she couldn't name at all. A gaggle of children bumped into her and she whipped out a hand snatching the wrist belonging to one boy who'd tried to feel for a pouch.

'No luck for you here, boy,' she muttered in trader-tongue, letting him go with a little shove.

The boys eyes widened, then he ran off, disappearing quickly into the crowds. Katleya looked about, noting three or four other groups of pick-pockets. She looked up at the top of the buildings, wondering if they had roof-toppers here too. Those flat-roofs had to be the easiest ever to cross.

'There you are, girl.' Leveen grabbed her arm and half dragged her away.

'There's so much to see, Leveen.' Katleya shrugged out of Leveen's hold. 'What's the blasted hurry anyway?'

'I have told you of the inn where I wish stay. I know it to be comfortable and clean, but the owner is particular and does not take custom after a certain hour.' Leveen slowed so Katleya could draw level with her. 'You need to rest before you make preparations for your long journey into the north. I am sure you would wish to bathe, eat and sleep in a safe place. For you, this is a strange city, one in which it is easy to lose oneself.'

'Well, maybe. The inn sounds good, but I've not got the coin for all that, Leveen.' What did the woman mean sleep in a *safe* place? This city didn't look so bad, nothing like Black Rock, apart from there being slaves and an Atash temple of course. But then there were temples to all the gods here. She'd lived in the pit of Black Rock for almost a year and survived for spirits' sake. After that, nothing could be any sort of a challenge.

'I know the inn keeper well and will drive a good bargain.' Leveen walked faster again. 'We will share a room. I shall bear the small extra cost.'

'All right then if you're sure?' At Leveen's nod, Katleya grinned. 'I'll repay you when I can.' Katleya lengthened her stride to keep up with Leveen. The lure of a bath and a full belly was too strong to ignore, but still she wondered at the woman's generosity. Was it a desert custom? A tribal tradition of some sort? The woman had done nothing to worry her the whole journey north, and had been generous with her food if not with her words, so she reasoned she'd nothing to fear from her.

'It is of no note, girl.'

Katleya flicked a glance sideways at Leveen. What did the woman want in return, if anything? She'd learned the hard way that no one gave you anything without wanting something in return. She supposed she'd find out soon enough.

They left the market behind and walked along a broad avenue, crossing a bridge over the widest canal yet, filled with long, flat boats full of fruit and vegetables. Some even had little stoves smoking away on which the traders cooked soup and other well-spiced smelling foods they sold to passers-by.

Squat, at three stories high, compared to the five or six of most of the other buildings in the area, the inn was otherwise similar to its neighbours. Square windows, covered with ornate grillwork, punctured the flat front wall of the inn in two even rows along the first and second floors. A simple carved wooden cup and a plate hung from a bracket to one side of the wide double front door on the ground floor. Set into the wall above the door was a huge carved rose painted deep red. Leveen pulled at an iron ring and a bell clanged inside. A small shutter opened and Katleya saw a pair of dark eyes peer out. It flapped shut again, bolts scraped and the door opened.

A whip-thin boy bowed them in then closed the heavy door behind them and shot the bolts with the scrape of heavy iron. His bare feet whispered away into the shadows.

Katleya looked around as they waited. The inn was very different inside. Pale blue-veined marble floors, small fountains standing between black marble columns and large, carved stone tubs holding ferns made the interior cool yet opulent. Opposite the entrance, an archway led to a large courtyard garden filled with almond trees in full blossom, lemon trees heavy with fruit and sweet scented roses. Balconies lined the inner walls at each level and the last of the sun pinked the light flooding through it and into the entrance hall.

A fat man appeared from the low doorway the boy had disappeared through. The man's skin looked lighter than Leveen's, somewhere between hers and the mahogany of Abyan and his sons. He bowed so low the long plait of his grey-streaked black hair swung over his shoulder and Katleya could see the bald patch on his crown. He was dressed in an eye-watering range of colours and each layer of his silk robes shimmered in the soft light.

'Welcome, welcome, my name is Mabyn el Shar al-Rialt. I am the most proud proprietor of this fine establishment. Please tell me of your requirements from the House of the Rose, most welcome and honoured guests,' he said in trader-tongue. His voice sounded high, like a young boy's. He stroked his belly and smiled. 'With the will of all the gods we shall fulfil your every need.'

'I will have less of your chatter for you know me, Mabyn. I require a third floor room with two beds, a bath and a meal for us both.' Leveen crossed her arms over her chest and looked down at Mabyn. 'Three silver sickles.'

'I do remember you, Leveen el Meera al-Shafi.' Mabyn bowed again. 'However, honoured lady, without question, though our charges are reasonable, as they have been time out of mind, to accept three silver sickles for a third floor room, and to include a bath for you both, and two meals, would bring the House of the Rose to the very brink of ruination. I regret to inform you that the cost has risen a great deal indeed since you last stayed in our fine establishment. It is much to our regret and disappointment that, while guests are fewer, the price of food and servants rises without cease. Desperate times as these require me to charge a gold crown. Each.' He shrugged his shoulders, making his belly wobble, and wiped a tear from his eye, before bowing for the third time. 'It is most sad but unquestionable that prices must rise in accordance with the laws of commerce. As I am sure you understand, wise and honoured lady.'

'I will not allow you to cheat me.' Leveen glowered down at the bobbing little man. 'Eight silver sickles, no more.'

'How would it be possible for me to cheat such an astute person as you, most wise and noble lady?' Mabyn raised his hands palm outward and lifted his shoulders in an extravagant shrug then bowed again. 'I am in awe of your indisputable incisiveness. It must be the will of all the Gods and especially the mightiest of the Gods, the Great Atash, and the Great Mother, Daru, who watches over us, that I should charge you the smallest of sums possible for your room and board. A mere six silver sickles and a single gold crown will suffice. I will even include a flagon of one of our finest chilled wines as a gift from the House of the Rose to you, honoured lady.'

'A single gold crown and I accept your gift of chilled wine.' Katleya could swear Leveen almost smiled as she fingered a single gold coin from her pouch. It flashed in the dimness of the hall as it spun into the air.

'The House of the Rose shall be ruined, ruined without the smallest of doubts. I can only hope that no one learns of this terrible munificence or they shall break down our doors for similar largesse.' Mabyn sighed and shook his head, wiping a tear from his other eye as he snatched the gold coin from the air. He secreted it somewhere inside his loose robes with a conjurer's speed. 'I shall have the finest of foods and the promised flavoursome wine sent up to you forthwith from the legendary kitchens and famed cellars of the House of the Rose. If the noble ladies would care to follow me, it is my honoured duty to show you to your sumptuous room. In my humble opinion, one of the best in the House of the Rose.'

Up two flights of stairs, Mabyn stopped outside a heavy, black-stained wood door with a long iron bolt. He took a large key from a ring hanging somewhere in the folds of his robe, slid it into the keyhole and opened the lock with a well-oiled click.

Two large beds, both with layered gauze hangings pulled back to the wall, stood on either side of the door. Crisp white linens, plump pillows and thick mattresses were an invitation for Katleya to take a flying leap and belly flop onto the nearest.

'What?' She grinned up at the frowning Mabyn, bounced a few more times for good measure, the metal joints of the bed so solid it didn't squeak, then swept her eyes over the rest of the room.

Two shuttered windows faced the door and a large chest of dark carved wood stood under each. An unlit brazier stood between the windows and a round table in the centre of the room surrounded by two chairs and a pair of palms in enormous red enamelled pots. Patterned blankets, tapestries and rugs coloured the otherwise stark white room. Mabyn lit the candles on the tables, filling the large room with a pleasant golden glow, bowed yet again and left the room.

'This'll do.' Katleya wandered to the windows and opened a shutter. Through the plain bars, very unlike the ornate grills at the front of the house, she saw the blank wall of the next building, a narrow alley's width away. Over the muted street sounds of Rialt, she heard the call of a night bird.

'Drink up your wine, girl.' Leveen sipped at her own glass.

Katleya sipped some more of the red liquid. It tasted strange, not that she liked wine much anyway, but this one was off. So much for the inn keeper giving them the best wine. Leveen didn't seem to notice the taste though, she took another large gulp then finished off the last of her fish.

Mabyn opened the door with barely a knock. 'Is all to your liking, most noble ladies?'

Leveen rose in one smooth move, blocking Mabyn's entry into the room and looming over the short, fat man. Katleya took the chance and poured her glassful into the potted palm next to the table.

'Yes. We are clean, we are fed. It is now time for us to sleep. Do not disturb us again.'

'Of course, noble lady. A thousand apologies for any distress I may have caused you,' Mabyn said smoothly, covering his initial jump backwards. 'I wish only to ascertain your comfort in the House of the Rose.'

'Now you have, you may go.' Leveen closed the door in Mabyn's face.

Katleya pretended to swallow the last of her wine. To be honest, she was feeling rather odd, dizzy even. Was the wine that strong?

'You are tired. It is time for bed.' Leveen came over and pulled her from the chair.

'What?' The room wobbled, then steadied, then started spinning. Katleya felt her legs collapse from under her. She felt Leveen pick her up and lay her on the bed.

'Now you are mine.' The last thing she remembered was Leveen's fuzzy face smiling down at her and a sharp pain inside the elbow of one arm.

Katleya woke with a jolt on the tail of a disturbing dream. It trailed flickers of silver on black, then faded away, leaving her with a sense of unease. Still groggy, she checked for her knives. They had gone. All of them gone, even the one she'd stolen from the table earlier. In Black Rock, she'd learned the hard way to keep her knives close. Now she panicked.

Blasted spirits!

What had happened? Her arm felt bruised. It was bandaged round the elbow and a small amount of blood stained the wrapping. She started shaking, looked round the room and over to the other bed. Leveen had gone. Only the sounds of the city filtering through the shutters disturbed the silence.

She crawled out of bed. At least Leveen hadn't stripped her. Katleya still wore the clothes she'd put on after her bath. She stopped short. A chain wrapped her waist, over her belt so she hadn't felt it. It was padlocked snug against her body and a length of chain looped round the top rail of the bed. The stupid bed made of good, strong wrought iron.

Blasted rat's piss for brains. You were even warned, turd-head!

The chain allowed her to reach the table. She gulped down a whole glass of water then sipped a second while nibbling at an apple. Eating slow kept her belly from rebelling. The food and water helped clear her head a bit. Tossing the apple core under the bed where it would encourage rats – petty she knew but it had to be done – she checked the door. It was locked. Katleya pressed her ear against the wood then peered through the keyhole. It was as quiet and as dark out there as in the room. She took her picks from their hidden pocket on the inside of her belt. A few moments later, the padlock gave a satisfying series of clicks. She slipped the chain off and laid it on the bed, being careful not to let the links clink.

Her pack lay inside the chest. So relieved she could almost cry, she found her precious knives inside. Leveen wanted her, she wasn't remotely interested in anything else it seemed. But what did the woman want her for? Slavery? Was a girl like her really worth that much? But where had the woman gone at this time of night? There wasn't any sign of her pack either.

Back at the door, she turned the handle but it wouldn't open. She was about to pick it too, when she remembered the bolt on the outside of the door. She had thought it strange when she'd first seen it, but it hadn't registered as important at the time. She'd noticed all the doors on this level had bolts on the outside.

'Blast it!' She frowned, thinking hard. She'd taken the chance earlier, while Leveen was bathing, to check the inn over. Another hard earned instinct learned from living in Black Rock. The place had looked secure and safe. There were only two doors. The front kept locked, the back leading straight into the busy kitchens. No doors to the sides of the building that she could find, all the windows were barred and only the windows of the third floor looked over the alleys on either side. Katleya loathed the feeling of being trapped . Nothing would stop her from finding a way out of this blasted room.

She walked over to the left-hand window and peered out between the bars down into the narrow alley. The light of full-bodied Diaphos and the waning sickle of Liatos reflected off the whitewashed walls and almost down to the ground. It looked to be a drop of at least thirty feet to the rippled sand below.

Tricky.

The bars looked strong, but what about their setting? She checked and found the wall had crumbled around the base of the right-most socket. Katleya began digging away with the table knife, ignoring the ache in her elbow. Uncle Yadoc would never forgive her if she used one of the blades he'd made her. It might even provoke him into charging out of Annufen to berate her. She almost laughed out loud at the thought.

Spirits! It's just the sort of thing he would *do.*

A few minutes later the bar was loose enough at both base and top to pull right out. She studied the gap it left. Katleya was sure she could squeeze through without ripping her last shirt or trousers, but perhaps not her coat. She bundled her coat, boots and hat into her pack, then put on her soft calfskin gloves and roof-topper boots.

Tying the strap of her pack round a bar, Katleya squeezed through the gap earning a few minor scrapes. She gripped one bar and, with her toes balanced on the narrow ledge, pulled her pack free. The alley was quiet as was the main street in front of the inn. The closest noise came from the inns and night markets in the last square they'd passed through on their way to The House of the Rose.

Above her, the wind-worn wall revealed brickwork and plenty of hand and toe holds. The top was just another five feet up, so she shrugged her pack onto her shoulders and picked a small stone out of the crumbling wall. She threw it up over the roof's edge. It skittered across the flat roof. Katleya waited. Nothing. An easy climb up and she slid over the top of the wall and onto the flat roof just below.

Sinking to a crouch Katleya looked round, every one of her senses alert. Apart from some washing lines, the inn's roof had ten little squat towers, with slatted vents on all four sides to funnel passing breezes down into the rooms below, dotting its sand covered surface. Katleya grinned. She hadn't had this much fun in a long time. Again, people had underestimated her. She liked having that edge. Everyone needed an edge.

She heard voices. Katleya slipped over to the nearest tower, knelt and pressed her ear to the venting.

'...called Katleya aef Laeft...'

Katleya hissed in a breath and stiffened.

'...can keep her here till my return, I would be grateful.' It was Leveen's voice rising up from the room below the tower. The vent funnelled her voice up to Katleya clear as a bell. The woman was speaking Shafian not the common trader-tongue. 'You will be recompensed for your trouble and your silence.'

'How very good of you,' a voice replied, one loaded with subtle sarcasm. 'Do you have any idea how long it might be before you return for her, Leveen?'

'On horseback, it should take me no more than two tendays if I leave now,' Leveen answered. 'Once I have my guarantee, and the proof they can do what I need to have done, I will return for her and the transaction will be completed.'

'It is a high price that you pay.'

Katleya could guess she was the *high* price to be paid. But who was she being paid to and for what?

Chapter 14

Leveen did not snarl at Taraq though she very much wanted to. He was weak but at this moment useful to her. 'Yet I will do it to be free of this curse. I wonder if Atash Himself brought her to me. You must believe me Taraq, as soon as I realised what she was, I had no choice but to use her.' Leveen let the raw need inside leak into her voice.

'Atash? That new god and his followers are far too controlling for my liking. His ways smack too much of Murak's and his blood-thirsting priesthood.' Taraq snorted softly. 'I will pray to the Mother for your success. After all, Daru is the most ancient and wisest of the gods.'

'She is dying and her followers become fewer with each passing year. Better we turn to the younger and stronger gods, such as Atash, for help.' And to whoever or whatever may give her what she both wanted and needed, Leveen thought to herself. Inside she sneered at Taraq's short-sightedness. The world was changing, could he not feel it?

'Atash? A new god it is true, but Murak is the stronger, or so it would seem,' Taraq retorted. 'Have you not heard of Kalebrod's fall to the Murecken and of the war on Rophet's borders?'

'Kalebrod was weak, full of fools worshipping paltry spirits or that peace-loving god Lehot. Rophet belongs to Atash, the Rophetans will prevail against Murak.' Leveen slammed her fist against the table standing between them with just the right amount of fervour to be believable. 'He must.'

'He must, you say. Yet you turned from Atash some years ago to follow the ancient Murak. Do you not think it is a trifle late for you to change allegiance once more?'

'It is true, I made the wrong choice when young and idealistic. But now I have been given the chance to turn my fate. There is a temple to Atash right next to Black Rock's castle. I went there some months ago.' Leveen's voice became passionate again, almost fierce. With every word it became easier to play the part, easier to lie, especially when she laced the lie with truth. 'It was His High-priest there who told me what I should do. He gave me this hope I now carry. Also, it was in Black Rock's Royal Square, just as I was leaving the Temple of

Atash, that I first saw the girl. Then my hope burned all the higher. I thought to have lost her, after a bungled attempt at capture by one of those Rophetan Thief-takers, but then she boarded my ship. It was then that I knew it was meant to be, that Atash had ordained this future for me.'

'Atash rises in Rophet as the fires of war close in. Lehot dies there but rises in Selassi overtaking all the other gods apart from the Mother. While Atash has barely a foothold in that fair city, he holds sway over some of the city-states of the Shafi Desert, and over many of your Shafian clans. But in Derin only the Mother Goddess, Daru, rules as She ought. She is yet strong in all of the other cities-states where her Temples stand, especially here in Rialt.'

'Why do you lecture me, Taraq?'

'Bear with me, Leveen, this is important. It was thought Murak and his religion died a thousand years ago, yet now the blood-god rises again in the Ruel Mountains and pushes eastward. How long before Rophet bows its head to Murak as Kalebrod now does? How long before the blood-priests turn their eyes westwards? Not long I believe for they are hungry for land and for power. They have grown tired of their small and poor mountain state.' Taraq paused, perhaps expecting a response from Leveen. She gave him none. 'Gods are like the seasons, they rise and fall along with their followers. Except for Daru. The Mother, is eternal, like the rock and earth of our world. She will outlast them all and...'

'Spare me your religious history lesson, Taraq.' Leveen broke in. How was it that this man could irritate her so, almost beyond reason? 'I have no interest in it. Every person has their own beliefs and mine belong to Atash once more. I should never have left Him. I know this now as do you.'

'Yet your people left the Mother only half a lifetime ago.' Taraq's voice was quiet but insistent. 'Your parents still worshipped Daru when you were a babe.'

'What is it you are saying? You try to lure me into worship of Daru? It will not work.' Leveen worked hard to keep the sneer from her face. He might irritate her but she needed him. For now at least. 'The Mother is too weak for me now, she cannot help me. I need the God of Fire.'

'Daru's strength is more subtle than that of the other gods, it is

115

true, yet it endures.' Taraq sighed.

'Endures? That is not enough for me!' Leveen spat out the words. 'I need change now, I cannot endure any longer.'

'Leveen, do you truly believe you do the right thing?'

'You think I should feel remorse? That a second wrong cannot make the first right?' Leveen hissed and threw the wine glass she held across the room. The sound of it smashing felt good. 'I will do anything. Anything to be free again!' Leveen hated the loss of control the rites had thrust on her. If she had known, she would never have undertaken the first steps to become a blood-priest. But they had promised her power, and she liked power, had wanted power over others more than anything else, having had enough of her powerless to other people's wants. But the blood-priests had lied. The power was theirs over her.

'I understand, Leveen.'

'Do you? You have seen my eyes, my scalp, you know how I ache for blood. I cannot live this way any longer, not when there is hope I might be fully human again. When I first pierced the girl's hand to taste her blood back on the ship, do you know how hard it was not to take it all? I yearned to drink her dry, to eat her flesh, her heart, her liver. I yearn still. And the yearning is fearsome with every such Wealdan-bearer I meet. It claws at me, this hunger for the potency of Wealdan-blood. Nothing slakes it, not wine, nor fresh meat, nor even the sensual pleasures.' Leveen saw the shocked look in Taraq's eyes and hid her smile. She know how he felt about her. The rutting lust she could elicit at will from men such as him was useful. Perhaps she might mount him on her return from Elucame. She turned away to hide her sneer from him.

'Yes, I have tried and failed many times with men and women both. The relief is fleeting. I fight this curse with every fibre of my being, yet still I crave her blood. See?' Leveen turned back to him, holding out her arms. 'I shake at the mere memory of its taste. If I do not free myself from the blood-priests soon I shall lose all control. I have seen those who undertook the full blood-rite to become bloodhunter-priests, their madness, their pain. I am half way there. '

'I had no idea that it was so bad for you, Leveen.' Taraq shuddered and looked away.

'Do you wish to retract your support now that you do know?' Leveen clenched her jaw, holding in the violence she felt rising inside, reminding herself of her need for him. She softened her voice. 'Remember, you swore to help me, Taraq.'

'I did so swear, and I keep my word. I hope beyond all bounds that you succeed. May the Mother be willing and your Atash too. I mean that with all sincerity, Leveen. However, your guilt is your own to bear.' Taraq pointed to the spreading puddle of red liquid. 'And that was a waste of good wine.'

'You will soon have plenty of gold to buy more!'

'Do not try to pass your culpability onto me, it will not stick,' Taraq responded. 'When you fled Elucame's halls half way through the rituals, who was it that found and succoured you?'

Silence fell for a moment between them and the raucous sounds of the night market filled the air.

'I am sorry, Taraq. May Atash forgive me for those words. You have been a good friend these last few years when I had neither family nor friend left.' Leveen lowered her voice again, lacing it with the right amount of sincerity and sadness. 'It is the fear of returning to Mureck that makes me speak words I do not mean. Since being chosen to be raised to Murak's priesthood, since those rituals, the terror has never left me.'

'Remember that, Leveen.' Taraq rose and poured more wine into his own glass. He did not offer Leveen any. 'I hope that you will survive your journey. If Daru the Mother wills it, it will be so. I do hope you find success, for it will mean much if their blood-rituals are reversible. For you, the cost is the girl. But such knowledge would be valuable indeed, to some.'

'Always with an eye to profit, Taraq the gem dealer.' It was true that Leveen wanted the blood-ritual reversed, as had been promised the day she had left Elucame to become the Murecken's agent in the wider world, but she cared nothing for the others. Running messages between Atash's priesthood and Murak's had been lucrative, but she wanted done with the blood-lust, the blood-madness that took control from her, that made her their creature. Finally finding one with enough potency in her blood to fulfil the needs of the ritual, as dictated by the Murecken priesthood, was all that mattered.

'I would fight the rise of the Murecken and this new Priest-king of theirs, Leveen.' Taraq clenched his jaw and Leveen saw true anger flare in his eyes. 'I do not speak of coin.'

'No, no, forgive me, please do not rush to anger at my words. You are a good man, Taraq. May Atash, and your Mother Goddess, watch ever over you and yours.' Leveen made for the door, hoping Taraq would not require contact. He had a trace of potency in his blood that made her want him, and she needed him alive. For now. 'I will start at once for Elucame. Do they still keep the best horses in the northern corrals?'

'Yes, they still keep the most fleet-footed of Selassian horses there.' Taraq brightened. Leveen remembered he dealt in horses as well as gems and always found the best stock for Derin and Selassi. 'A new string arrived this morning brought by one of the larger desert clans. Your people I believe.'

'I see.' Her people no longer, Leveen thought, at least not until she had returned to herself, expunged the lacert-taint from her flesh. Those Murecken priests must reverse the rites. If they did not, she would have to kill them. 'Watch over the girl while I am gone. Here is some more of the papaeg tincture. She drank some earlier and I doubt she will wake before morning but she has strength, that one, so take care.'

'I will. I pray you have a safe journey, Leveen el Meera al-Shafi. May you receive all that you hope for and may Daru the Mother and Atash be with you.'

'May Atash, His Flames burn eternal, and Daru the Mother be with you also, Taraq el Meera al-Derin. My gratitude you will have to the end of my days.' Leveen forced a smile onto her face as she touched her fingers to her forehead, lips and heart and made a bow to echo Taraq's. She turned and left, relief juddering through her body. The journey to Elucame was a long one but, with the new-dug tunnels through the Ruel Mountains she had heard of, it would be far shorter than the first time she had travelled there.

Chapter 15

Silent, Katleya backed away to the edge of the roof while the sound of boot steps on the marble floors below faded away. She shivered. The desert might be hot as a furnace during the day but the temperature plummeted at night. She sat up and put her head on her knees, her arms wrapped round them. She had to leave Rialt tonight. Now.

Deep down, Katleya had known she should never have trusted Leveen. One day she'd pay attention to her hunches and not get into so much blasted trouble. At least she hadn't drunk much of the wine, no matter how much Leveen had insisted. Now she understood why it had tasted odd. She knew about the tincture made from the red-flowers' seed pods, had even given some to Uncle Yadoc during his last few days. Expensive stuff but useful. It had dulled the pain and let the old man sleep.

Leveen, a blasted Murecken priest!

A memory of Leveen licking blood from her thumb flashed into Katleya's head. She pulled the bandage off her arm and saw the shallow cut the woman had made inside her elbow. No doubt Leveen had needed a large quantity of blood to prove to the blood-priests she had a worthwhile payment for the ritual. To think Leveen had discovered her back in the Royal Square in Black Rock.

Then I went and walked right onto her blasted ship. Spirits!

And Tacker! Had he been paid by Leveen to help? Back in Selassi, where the caravans mustered, she'd seen him being given something. Could it have been a purse full of Murecken gold and the giver one Leveen el Meera al-Shafi? But he'd warned her about Leveen, Katleya couldn't deny that.

Biting down hard on a scream of frustration, Katleya stopped the shaking in her body by clenching every muscle. Nails biting into her palms, she wrenched her wits back and stood up to look over the outer edge of the roof above the left side alley. The roof across the alley was two stories higher. Pity, it would've been so much easier to jump roof to roof. Katleya strapped her pack over her shoulders, crouched and held onto the edge of the wall then swung her legs over

119

and climbed down. There was the odd hairy moment when the mud bricks crumbled under fingers or toes, but then she reached the granite blocks of the lower level and she landed on the ground in one piece.

After climbing up onto the flat roof of the neighbouring building, Katleya paused to take her bearings then headed north-west. With its many narrow alleys and flat roofs, the city was easy enough to traverse from the eastern quarter to the northern wall. She had to drop to a crawl twice to cross over canal bridges and felt eyes on her both times, but it wouldn't matter as she'd be out of the city soon enough. She thanked Leveen's dear friend, Taraq, for his kind directions to the horse corrals.

Safe from the glances of any casual observers in the darkness of the small hours, Katleya climbed a tall building with a bakery on its ground floor. The smell of baking bread made her mouth water. From the ridge of the pitched roof, she skimmed up to the top of the city wall with ease. She clung to the inner parapet while a pair of guards walked past, then flitted across the walkway and clambered over the outer parapet and down the other side of the wall.

The wiry desert horses greeted Katleya with soft whinnies when she slipped into one of the corrals far below the northern gate. Tents huddled on one side of the open-ended quadrangle, a pair of smaller corrals to the other. In the centre of the circle of tents was a communal fire surrounded by a group of desert people all wearing the usual pale, loose robes. They looked like a gathering of flame-painted ghosts in the darkness.

One of the horses nuzzled her and she scratched his forehead. Ropes hung in coils from some of the fence posts. Taking three, Katleya fashioned a halter from one and slipped it over the head of the young stallion that had first welcomed her. It had straight legs, good bone, sloping shoulders and a deep girth. Though young, it looked like it had the stamina for a long journey. Speed too. There was a butt full of water in a corner of the pen. She pulled the waterskins, given to her by Abyan, from her pack and filled them. Looping the second length of rope round the horse's neck and belly in a make-shift harness, she then tied a water skin to each side for balance.

Slow and silent, she slipped enough fence rails off their posts to create a wide opening then leaped onto the stallion's back. Kneeing the horse so it skirted around the back of the herd, Katleya hissed and whacked a few hindquarters with the end of the third rope. It didn't take long to make the horses stampede out of the corral.

With the thundering of hooves in her ears, Katleya guided the stallion to the outer edge of the speeding herd and slid down to hang along the stallion's flank with one leg hooked over its back, her arms wrapped round its neck. Hidden in a crowd of horseflesh and billowing dust, she heard, above the neighs and thundering hooves, the yells and shouts of the tribesmen. It wouldn't take long for them to mount up and give chase. For now though, she could get a good lead and, with luck, get far enough into the desert to give them the slip. They should be happy enough when they got most of their horses back not to bother chasing her any further, she hoped.

Katleya pulled herself up onto the stallion's back after the last of the tents faded into the darkness. She let him run on for a while longer trusting in his sure-footedness to find his way safe over the stony desert ground. A while later, blowing and sweating, he slowed to a walk and she angled him due north. A few of the other horses had followed but these stopped by one of the narrow irrigation channels to drink and eat the fruit in a pomegranate orchard.

As the moons set, Katleya reached the River Rial. She'd forgotten about the river. It looked like rains had fallen in the Ruel Mountains as, between the steep banks, the water ran fast and deep. Maybe it always flowed this strong. To the north, the land looked as black and unknowable as the river.

Katleya realised then she'd no idea where any water holes might be between the river and the Amalla Heights, or how far the mountains were, or how she would get across them, or if there was even a bridge or a ford over the river. She pulled the stallion up and let him graze on the grasses growing in clumps along the bank.

'Hah, that's your brilliant plan broken to bits like iron made brittle by too quick a quenching,' she muttered.

And now I'm blasted well talking to myself too. Spirits!

Katleya dismounted and stretched her aching legs. Her arse was numb. Riding bareback was no laughing matter. She laughed anyway till tears leaked from her eyes and her legs felt weak.

Westwards, the river should widen and there she'd find a ford, or perhaps a bridge, she could only hope. Back up on the stallion, she turned downriver.

The sun began to grey the sky to the east above the Ruel Mountains when Katleya spotted the lanterns on the river. A ferry? A barge? She heeled the stallion into a ground-eating lope.

Chapter 16

Coryn rubbed his neck. It still felt strange not wearing an iron collar. The welts had long healed and even the pink ridges had faded. He squinted through the evening's haze at the two moons hovering on the horizon. Eager as ever, full-bodied Diaphos had cleared the sands, while larger Liatos idled on the distant mountains, her silver horns stained deep red. Beneath lay the city it had taken him four tendays to reach, or looked at another way, nine years, three months and a tenday. It felt longer.

Almost as big as the great city of Selassi, Rialt contained temples to just about every god known to man and palaces for every sheik and merchant prince who could afford one. They jostled for space with myriad inns, taverns, squares and market halls. The inhabitants proclaimed Rialt to be the most cosmopolitan of the desert cities. Coryn reckoned it was true, to an extent. But it had slaves so, to him, Selassi was best.

Nothing had changed since he'd last ridden in as a slave almost a year ago. The River Rial, lined with palms, irrigated fields and groves looked the same. Barges sailed downriver, bearing gold and copper from the mines east of the city, and lines of camels towed them back upriver, bearing exotic goods from south of the Sutherne Sea and north from the Storratian Empire, just as they'd always done.

Rialt, being one of the largest city-states in the Shafi Desert, was a magnet for merchants from every land. Even here, in the stock pens below the western walls of the city, Coryn could hear its clamour, no different to before. He had been impressed when he'd first seen the place as a boy. This time he couldn't wait to leave.

Frowning, he turned back to rubbing down his horse. Its coat shone like burnished copper, the sweat and dust of hard travel long gone. But there was no point doing a job unless you did it well, or so Da had always said.

He turned his horse loose in the corral. It inspected, scraped then rolled on the sand, once, twice and then again. So much for the grooming. The dog copied the horse, twisting and wriggling in an orgy of scrubbing, then it leaped up and slipped under the railed fence and followed its nose off toward the wide, sluggish waters of the river. Coryn watched till it disappeared through a grove of date palms. Sliding the wooden rail back in place Coryn turned and almost stepped on a dagger snake. He froze as it rippled through the shadow of his raised boot. Two feet long and lethal, its undulating ruby line glowed bright along its blade-shaped black body. One bite and he would've died in a single agonising day.

He felt and smelled the Derin seer's presence in the shifting air as he lowered his foot.

'An ill omen.' Yaltos' voice cracked and hissed like sand over stone. She flung out an arm, her robes spreading more clove-heavy aroma through the air. 'To have a demon-snake cross your path on the night of a blood-horned moon. I would not travel till Liatos reaches her fullness were I you. Once she is whole again you will be safe enough.'

'It's only if you believe in omens that they've power over you. And I don't.' Coryn looked down at the old woman's time-tracked face. The multitude of long, thin braids seemed to twist with a life of their own under the thin silk of her headdress. It was unnerving and he was glad she'd stayed in her curtained palanquin for almost the entire journey. Though he'd felt her eyes on him often enough, she'd not spoken to him more than twice. The first time to ask his name and birthplace, the second to ask what he carried in his pouch. He'd not answered the second and had avoided her since then. It was easy enough in a caravan of this size.

'Omens care not if you do or do not believe in them.' Yaltos hawked and spat. The sand sucked her spittle dry almost as soon as it landed. Her four black-clothed Derin guards stood near, still and silent, hands resting on the ornate hilts of their scimitars, faces grim. 'Ignore this one at your peril, boy. You will not fulfil the grievous tasks lying ahead if you are dead.'

Grievous tasks? Spirits!

Coryn lifted a hand to touch the pouch hanging from his neck. The reassuring shape of the amulet steadied him. The knowledge of the protection it gave him made him strong. What did this old woman know about him? Nothing. Even so, he felt uncomfortable under her glare. A shout gave him an excuse to turn away.

'You are sure you will not ride with us on the return journey, effendi?' The caravan master smiled as he neared, revealing a wealth of solid gold teeth and caught him in a bear hug. He pressed his cheek to each of Coryn's then held him by the shoulders. 'You are a good man to have on the desert crossing, with a sense for danger better than any I have known before. You have proved to be a worthy man, one that I can depend on. By the gods, such men are rare.'

Yaltos scowled and lifted her scarf to cover the lower half of her face but remained silent.

'It's been good working for you, but I'll not return to Selassi, Master Barus. I'm heading further north. I hear Master Ameal's looking for guards.' Coryn cleared his throat, embarrassed at Barus' effusiveness and stepped back as soon as the man let go. He nodded toward a long line of grunting camels squatting well to the west of the pens. Nearby, men were loading up some of the long articulated carts the camel teams would pull. 'He's heading to Dal Abar in the morning.'

'Fool boy. To ignore advice given is to die with nothing but regrets.' Yaltos spat into the sands again. 'Every one futile.'

'Even so, I mean to sign on with that caravan.'

'Your acolytes await your arrival, High-Seer Yaltos al-Derin.' Barus waved an arm toward a group of white-robed women. 'I believe you are staying at the great Temple of Daru, in the eastern district? If you go now you may reach it before dark falls.' He flourished his arm, touched his forehead, lips and chest and then bent at the waist with his hand held out, palm up. 'It has been an honour to escort you safe and well to your destination, High-Seer Yaltos al-Derin. May the many gods watch over you.'

'Daru the Mother, the Ancient All-knowing One, is the one and only god I care for, Barus el Selas al-Sian,' Yaltos croaked. She glowered at Coryn. 'You must come to the Omphalos, at the Great Shrine in the Temple of Daru, for a true seeing before you leave. There is darkness on your path and it would be wise for you to know the dangers that lie ahead.'

Yaltos grunted in disgust at Coryn's non-committal shrug then marched off towards her acolytes and her palanquin. Her Derin guards flowed seamlessly around and behind her.

'Perhaps you should go to the Seer, it is not often a man is offered a reading by a Derin priestess of such high standing, effendi,' Barus said as they watched Yaltos climb into her palanquin, now unlashed from the camel's back. Four large men in voluminous trousers and baggy shirts carried it off toward the city by a pair of poles pushed through thick leather loops fixed along each side. 'But then again many now turn from Daru. Perhaps her priestesses see too much. Perhaps they know too much as some are want to whisper. Better to worship Great Atash, His Flame burns eternal. The All-Seeing One is followed by more of the desert peoples with each passing year.'

Coryn held out both his hands palm up in the Selassi tradition. 'I've no time for any gods or their priests, Master Barus.'

'None of the gods? You are certain of this, effendi? Ah, it is the amulet I know you carry, is it not, effendi? It is said spirit-magik can be of help to some, but it is most mercurial. Is it not better for a man to have a god or two to watch over his dealings? It is a great sadness that we have bandits in the mountains, raider tribes on the sands and pirates on the seas. Indeed, we are surrounded by parasites whose aim it is to bleed honest merchants dry in every way. There are many times that one needs a god on one's side, effendi, and we have so many to choose from. One or other of them should suit you well enough, I am thinking.'

'I have my bow and sword on my side, Master Barus,' Coryn answered. He grinned. 'And you pay well to have *me* on your side.'

'Indeed, this is very true, effendi. The gods may watch over us, but they are a long way from our earthly cares and we merchants must always take extra measures to ensure success in all our endeavours, no matter the inconvenience.'

Coryn's smile widened.

'Why, effendi, I am honoured by your smile. It is a most rare sight.' The caravan master beamed back, then sighed and placed his deep brown arms down on Coryn's gold-tanned ones, forearm to forearm. They gripped each other below the elbows and acknowledged the bond made during the long crossing of the desert. 'I will write you a most glowing recommendation for Master Ameal, effendi. He and I are old and good friends. You will be staying at the Wrestlers Inn with the other guards for this one night?'

'I will, and my thanks, Master Barus. If I'm ever back this way...'

'I will keep both an ear and an eye alert for your most welcome arrival, effendi.' Barus grinned again and lifted the horsehair switch hanging from his wrist to flick at the relentless flies. 'I will most assuredly miss you and your sword, Coryn aef Arlean. May your journey be uneventful and may all the gods watch over you whether you follow them or not.'

'Guess I'll be watching my own way. It'll give the gods more time to watch over yours, Master Barus.' Coryn returned Barus' grin and nodded farewell. He'd ask the spirits to watch over him. They might or might not, they were a capricious lot, but at least they'd no interfering priesthoods snarling in their wake. Turning, he headed towards the cliff road. He looked forward to a having his first bath in a month, some good food and a real bed.

Chapter 17

Over the red bluffs of the gorge the sun boiled its way towards day's end. Half a dozen iridescent wyverns drifted on thermals, vibrant against the bleached blue sky. Wings of translucent skin, from one to three feet wide, flashed in the light with every lazy shift. Katleya had seen the tiny remnants of the legendary dracos often enough since entering the Amalla Heights, but they still fascinated her. She stood in the freckled shade of a sweet scented acacia and watched them weave through the hot air.

A sapphire and emerald female, narrow ruff lying flat against its neck, plummeted from the sky. It flamed the face of a gazelle sidling along the shaded side of the canyon then spun a tight circle and landed on the slender doe's shoulders almost before it could react. The wyvern snapped its jaws, its serrated teeth digging deep into the gazelle's neck. The doe staggered, grunted out a last regret for foraging before dusk and collapsed.

A ruby wyvern, with the broader, spiked ruff of a male, landed nearby. The two bickered over the half-roasted body. Though small, the gazelle was still too heavy for either to lift. Then the rest of the flight landed in a flurry of leathery wings. Squabbling like hawkers over a lucrative pitch, they shredded skin and excavated flesh, each vying to swallow the biggest gobbets of bloody meat.

Good thing they don't grow any bigger than house dogs.

Katleya left the shade and picked her way between scattered boulders and scrubby bushes down the steep bank. Turning north again, she walked along the edge of the dry riverbed, keeping to the scraps of shade under scattered, stubby trees with leathery leaves. The pale linen shawl draped over her head wasn't much protection from the forge-white disc of the sun. Better than nothing though. Wind slopped down the mountains in hot gusts doing nothing to cool the air. The earth smelled of burnt grass, scorched dust, and animals hiding from the sun like sensible creatures should.

She turned her head one way then another, leaned into the gritty wind and licked her lips. The cactus syrup still tasted strange, but it worked, healing her burned skin. She deciphered what her Wealdan-senses told her. Tracks were few and far between in the shifting sands making it difficult to see the residual signs left by mountain lions, desert wolves and the many other animals that had passed through the gorge as the heat haze shimmered and played tricks with air and Wefan alike. Katleya found it almost as hard as trying to read the Wefan over and across water. In the nights the desert was easier to read and tonight Liatos would be almost full, plenty of light to see by so she could scout ahead without making anyone suspicious. She paused to take a sip from her water skin. It was warm and tasted of leather but it was wet. She heard the approach of a camel and released her Wealdan.

'Why do you roam so far ahead of the caravan, Adherent Katleya?' One of the Shafian guards grinned down at her, his dark eyes glinting with a hungry look to them. Katleya guessed it was Asheed by the shape of his beard, a little longer and more pointed than his brother's. Both twins smiled too much and had far too many teeth for her liking. He rode his camel with his left leg crossed around the pommel of the saddle, the right stretched down, in the typical Shafian way. Leaning down a little, so she was sure to see the full glory of his handsome face, his smile widened. He twirled his long camel-stick between his fingers in intricate patterns. Still trying to charm her. Still wasting his time. 'What is it that you look for, Adherent?'

'Something I don't want to find.' Katleya squinted round the canyon. South, to the ridge she had just come over and where the wyverns' eyries pockmarked the eastern facing cliffs, then north to the twist of the gorge where it narrowed and rose toward the stubby peaks of the central ridge of the Amalla Heights. Nothing to see with normal sight but sand, rock, bushes and those ugly leathery-leafed trees known as leatherleaf.

Inspired name choice.

'Why do you not take your ease, Adherent Katleya? You should ride on the cart like the other Adherents, not walk in this heat. We may have left the great Shafi Desert behind, but these mountains, they are as hot and dry as the sands. You will thirst, and your fair skin, it will burn, which would be most regrettable. You may even suffer from the heat-stroke.' Asheed's trader-tongue had a strong accent and he had the strange nasal twang of the northern desert tribesmen. He had no idea Katleya could understand Shafian and she meant to keep it that way. There was something about him and his brother she didn't trust and she really needed to listen to her hunches.

Better late than never, as Uncle Yadoc liked to say.

Asheed shrugged at Katleya's non-committal murmur and tapped his camel, turning it back toward the trail. The two high-wheeled, camel-drawn carts and the other three camel riders had just reached the base of the ridge. He bowed in his saddle. 'We are safe on this trail, it is a trail little used by merchants and so it is not watched by bandits as many others are. There are none living among these rocks, of this we have made sure. In this you must trust myself and my brother.'

'I'd rather trust a blood-frenzied krokos,' Katleya muttered low enough for Asheed not to hear. She looked along the riverbed and frowned. Something was wrong.

Very wrong.

She opened her Wealdan again and read the signs further down the bank. A shiver of fear ran through her. Threading her way through brittle sagebrush to the riverbed, she found what she'd not wanted to find, but had somehow known she would.

In the lee of a rock where the wind hadn't managed to blow it away, she saw a human footprint. Clawed.

One print. It was enough. More than enough.

A trickle of sweat itched its way down her back. What were the Murecken fiends doing all the way out here in the desert?

Spirits, I'd hoped never to see writhen again!

Katleya leaned against a boulder and concentrated. The faltering traces of the writhen bruising the matrices of Wefan led to an outcrop of rock on the other side of the riverbed, where the gorge narrowed before it twisted northwards.

There!

At least she thought they were writhen. They looked similar to the ones she'd seen back in Rophet. One hunched at the base of the outcrop, another crouched near its summit. A third raised a bow.

Katleya spun and ran up to the carts. 'Ambush!' she screamed. The long robes got in her way. She lifted them high baring her pale knees, not something any self-respecting Lehotan Adherent would do.

Like I give a rat's fart.

Instinct made her dodge left.

Thrrrup.

Katleya felt a rush of air and an arrow skittered into the sand ahead of her. She leaped to the right. 'Blast it!' That was close. A second cracked against a rock near her feet but to her left, flight feathers jagged, the iron head oily with poison. Any sane fletcher would have burned them, but they could still maim or kill if they hit.

'Writhen!' she screamed.

The driver of the first cart turned its four camels and they scrambled up the bank in a shambling trot, pulling the long cart to where a rock fall shielded a narrow gully. The merchant, Manzar el Khadra al-Fazul, raised his crossbow and shot over Katleya's head. Screeches sounded behind her. Too close behind. She pushed on up the bank, fighting against patches of soft sand and shin-bashing rocks. The second cart began a slow turn.

Katleya reached the trail, sweat dripping like she'd worked the forge for Uncle Yadoc. She spotted one of the Shafian brothers, Aras, he leaned over from his camel and grabbed the harness of one of the leading camels pulling the second cart. He yanked it over back onto the track and whipped them all into the nearest thing to a gallop the lumbering animals could go. There was a lot of shouting but she couldn't quite make out through the cries of the writhen and the grunting protests of the camels.

Katleya wove on up the bank, gaining on the first cart. It wasn't making good time, cracking into rocks and tearing through tough thorn bushes.

What's Aras thinking, splitting up the group?

They'd be easy pickings all strung out. As Katleya reached the back of the first cart, it jolted to a halt with a tremendous crack. One of the front wheels broke from the chassis and the cart lurched down at an angle. Then Asheed spun his camel up to the cart and cut the camel team free, grabbed the nearest harness and followed his brother up the trail.

'What?' Shocked, she watched them disappear around the twist of the gorge. With a shout, Manzul, the merchant's son, whipped his camel in pursuit.

Manzar loaded and fired his crossbow while shouting for his son to stop. The broken cart groaned, one of the forks cracked as it sagged onto the rocks. An arrow whistled past Katleya's face. The writhen were still right behind her. She ducked and dived past the back of the cart, cursing and spitting sand and grit from her mouth. She'd been right not to trust those twin bastards.

Spirits! Please, tell me how I get into these blasted messes?

Chapter 18

Night had claimed the city of Rialt hours ago, but the ridged sand under Coryn's boots still held the sun's heat. The red grains whispered as he moved over them. Standing high in the heavens the two moons washed the ancient city with pink-tinged silver. The inns on the nearby Street of a Thousand Pleasures spilled laughter, shouts and music out into the night air.

'I didn't call her over.' Coryn kept his arms wide as the knife point dug into the small of his back. He kept talking as he eyed the high walls of the dead-end alley. That damned dog would be handy to have around right about now. 'I came in with a Selassian caravan at sunset. I've been travelling for three tendays and my mind was on food, a decent pot of kaffe and sleep. I wasn't looking for trouble.'

'Even so, you have found trouble, wetlander.' The man's strong Shafian dialect was hard to understand but the knife said all Coryn needed to know.

'She's her own woman, free to make her own choices, I'd say.' Coryn winced as the knife dug in a little harder but the words kept coming. 'As I see it, no one should own another. Man or woman.'

'You have outlandish ideas, wetlander, but then you are not desert bred.' Coryn could hear the sneer in his words. 'Not with that yellow hair and those demon-blue eyes.'

'True, but I'm desert-raised, near enough and no more a *demon* than you.'

'If you are truly desert-raised, and you speak Shafian well enough for it to be so, you should know our ways and should have known better.' Drink slurred the man's words. No doubt fuelled the man's temper too. 'No man touches another man's woman.'

'She's a fine looking woman, any man would've looked and it's hard not to touch a woman sitting on your knee.' Coryn measured a stack of wood in a corner. He might make the top of the wall from it if he got a good run up. For now, he just had to keep the man talking. The serving maid at the Wrestler's Inn had looked damned fine, though he'd not seen her till she'd sat her rump on his lap, eager for some fun. He'd liked the look and feel of her, he'd be lying if he said otherwise. But a bit of pleasure between the sheets wasn't worth a man's life. 'She came over, she sat on my knee, she did what she wanted. I'd not called her over and she said nothing about being taken.'

'Yet she *is* taken, wetlander,' the man snarled. 'And by Atash, His Flame burns eternal, and by all the other gods too, I will make you pay in blood for touching her.'

Bitter experience told Coryn he'd run out of time. He half-stepped forward, pivoted and swung his forearm round to smack against the man's wrist. The moon-caught blade flashed as the knife spun high before skittering down past the planks. He dove left and kicked out at a thick, corded leg. The man jumped back fast, caught hold of Coryn's boot and flung him backwards to crash against a wall. He moved fast for a heavy man.

'Don't want the woman…and…don't want this.' Coryn grimaced and scrambled back up. Winded, he raised his hands palms forward. He backed up a few steps, near to the end of the alley but keeping some space for movement. 'I'm done in Rialt. I'm leaving with the morning light. You'll not see me again.'

'You think to leave? That I cannot allow, wetlander.' The man smirked. 'You owe me much and that pouch, it looks heavy. Throw it over and that knife, it too.'

Coryn recognised the man as one of the pit-fighters from the Wrestlers Inn. Though short at around five and half feet, he was well muscled. He'd won a fair amount of coin on the wrestler. Ten silver crowns it'd hurt to lose.

'So, it's not the woman, then.' Coryn shifted. 'Truth is you're a common thief.'

'The truth is that your pretty face will not save you a single scream in Atash's demon-infested fiery hells.'

'Spirits piss on Atash's damned hells and his arse-faced demons!' Being a good foot taller might give him some advantage. Coryn watched the wrestler and was ready for the man's surge. Grasping a meaty arm, just above the wrist, he used the man's own momentum to pull him forward and spun out of the way as the wrestler flew past.

Somehow, the wrestler twisted and hooked his foot round the back of Coryn's thigh, forcing him back toward the blind end of the alley and into messy shoulder roll. But he was up again with his knife in his hand while the heavy man thudded hard against a wall and slid down to the sand. Pieces of mud brick and white render showered over him.

The short, flute-like notes of nightjars hunting moths sung above the sounds of a raucous night market beyond the end wall. The stink of the wrestler was strong in the cooling night air. Blood poured from the man's crooked nose. His unlaced jerkin revealed bare, oiled skin, patterned with clan tattoos. His muscles bunched. Leaping up, he swung a length of wood at Coryn's head.

Coryn swayed back then shifted his weight and closed. Whipping out his knife, he scored a red line across the brute's belly. Deep enough to hurt, not much more. The wrestler pig-screamed in anger and pain.

Coryn leaped back again. He hadn't much room to manoeuvre. That good night's sleep in a proper bed began to look a distant likelihood. He snarled. He'd paid for that bed and this idiot wouldn't stop him from sleeping in it. The mattress might be thin and filled with straw, but it was the height of comfort compared to a single blanket laid over rock and sand. He just had to get past this great fool. A fool built like the damned city wall.

Coryn realised he needed to go for the foundations.

Diving under the meaty arms trying to catch him in a wrestler's hug, Coryn rolled and kicked out at the back of the man's knee, grabbed hold of his sweat-soaked jerkin and swung him backwards to slam to the ground. There was a sound of breaking wood as the wrestler fell back into the pile of planks. He grunted once then lay still.

Too still.

Coryn frowned and leaned over him, touching his fingers to the thick neck. No pulse. He pulled the body over and was staggered to see an iron spike standing proud between the meaty shoulder blades. Spreading blood gleamed in the moonlight.

'Spirits.' Coryn pressed his hand against his chest, closed his fingers round the pouch hidden under his shirt. This changed everything, and just when things were looking up. He looked at the dead man. The wrestler's luck had run out on him worse though. His gods hadn't helped him, not even the *great* Atash.

Coryn cleaned his knife in the sand, hurried to the alley entrance and scanned the street. It was empty, but the wrestler was bound to have friends nearby. Word would reach them soon enough and no explanation would satisfy. No bed for him tonight. It was unfortunate the caravan to Dal Abar wouldn't be leaving soon enough but the wrestler's friends would've soon found out he'd signed on with the caravan headed that way. He'd head due north and cross the Amalla Heights into Manom instead. It'd take a deal longer, but it seemed the best choice at this moment.

It didn't take long for him to grab his saddle, packs and bedroll from the inn and get to the horse pens. The dog waited for him, an unfathomable grin on its face.

'Damned dog,' Coryn muttered as he saddled his horse, 'could've done with you back there.'

Chapter 19

As the sun reddened the eastern horizon, Coryn left behind the last of the twisted stands of spiked iron tree growing on the boundary of the desert and the irrigated farmlands. Between the iron trees and the Amalla Heights lay nothing but rock littered sands, scorched dunes, a few scattered water holes and a single oasis. He'd studied Barus' maps many times and remembered them well enough to find his way. Problem was, if the wrestler's friends figured he had gone north, they'd track him. But he knew how to cover his trail, and his horse carried extra skins of water, so he reckoned he'd a fair chance.

He looked back, nothing. Far to the south, the pink-stained city stood on its plateau, its higher domes aflame with the rising sun. To the west, the two moons lingered, fading into the brightening sky. They'd be rising later too, the nights staying dark till well after midnight. Coryn walked now to spare the animal as he angled westwards, heading for the empty quarter where the dunes towered in strange sinuous sculptures. It wasn't long before his mouth began to feel as arid as the sands.

When the glowering sun swelled over the horizon hot winds rose from the south driving rivers of sand to snake across the rippled ground ahead of him. Sudden gusts raised red grains to scrape at his skin and sting his eyes. He pulled the hood of his loose robes further forward, wrapped a length of cloth round it and his nose and mouth. The dog disappeared over a wind-whipped dune crest, looking for a good place to wait out the coming sandstorm. It always found somewhere. Coryn headed the same way.

He chanced to look back and saw two riders hunched over their camels, closing fast, loose robes billowing in the strengthening wind. Coryn leaped onto his horse and dug in his heels. Surging off the trail, he angled his horse up a ridge, but it struggled in the sliding sand and rock. An arrow bored into his thigh as he reached the crest and he ducked in time to hear a second whirr by his ear. He held onto the high pommel as the first waves of pain hit him and urged his horse down into a shallow dip, then up another rise. The animal wouldn't be able to keep this up for long.

Coryn looked back again. A great bank of churning sand, hundreds of feet high, rolled across the desert, coming up hard behind the riders. It fogged up the sun, blurring the distances. The riders disappeared behind swirling dust. He moved on down the rise and pushed the sweating horse along a gully.

Seeing a broken wall with gaping windows built against a low ridge of rock to his left, Coryn slid from the saddle. Limping, he pulled his snorting horse into the meagre shelter offered by the cave-like room of the long abandoned home to wait out the storm. A low growl told him the dog had got there first. Covering his horse's head with a dampened cloth, he sank to the ground, his leg all kinds of agony.

In the gloom, he tied his scarf tight round his upper thigh and lifted his leg so his foot rested up against the rock. By touch rather than sight, he shaved the fletching from the arrow with his knife. Biting on the leather reins, he slammed his leg down so the arrow pushed right through his leg. Coryn fought against the pain, caught hold of the arrow's head and pulled it all the way out. Darkness took him.

He came back to the sound of the wind still roaring. He held a crossbow bolt, not an arrow. Coryn washed out his wounds, poured some Selassian firewater into the holes and wrapped his scarf tight around his leg. He might have bought a crossbow, like the one that must have fired the bolt, if he could have afforded one. But they cost more and were inferior in many ways to a recurve.

He looked up at his saddle, where the case holding his bow hung. A recurve bow just like his Da's, the one he'd inherited from Grandda, made from the same rich, kaffe-coloured wood. Coryn had known he couldn't pass this bow by when he'd first laid eyes on it in Selassi's lower market. He'd bought it there and then from the Tashk weapons trader. He'd not regretted it.

With a shake, Coryn brought himself back to the present and listened. There was no telling how long the sandstorm would last, but it was a powerful one. There'd be no doubt the two men after him were sheltering too. He'd the time and no option but to rest. He leaned back and closed his eyes.

Chapter 20

Hunting wyverns soared in great loops in the warming air. Occasional squabbles broke out and emerald flames spurted. Rodents and reptiles scurried for cool burrows under rocks and withered roots. Some never made it. One scarlet wyvern darted down and snared a lean desert rat in its long maw, its needle-like teeth flashing, no more than three yards from Coryn's mount. The translucent membranes of its gold speckled wings shimmered in the morning light and he reckoned it was around three feet from nose to tail with a wingspan of five feet, one of the largest he'd ever seen. In less than three breaths, it'd flown back up and disappeared into one of the nesting caves that pockmarked the higher cliffs.

After nearly a tenday of tortuous travel across the desert, laying false trails, scouting out every waterhole, concealing his passing each step of the way, Coryn felt exhausted. Now, deep into the parched and harsh terrain of the Amalla Heights, an uneasiness rose inside him. He was more aware than usual of all the peculiar sounds brought to him on the hot wind. Squinting into the glare, Coryn searched for a broken branch, a disturbed rock or smoke in the distance. But there was nothing solid to confirm the gut feeling of trouble waiting. Flies buzzed about the bloodied bandage on his leg, he waved them off but in moments they returned. With friends.

The old, wind-worn red mountains seemed normal. Wary, he turned in the saddle, checking behind him. Summer burned leaves whirled in the sporadic currents. There was nothing in the pass, except for the ancient ruins of a long forgotten people. Most of the balconies, steps and pillars had crumbled from the cliff face and were almost indistinguishable from the sand and rocks of the valley floor. The friezes and carvings all blurred with erosion. Spirits like ifrits, jinn and the flesh-eating ghaddar favoured old, deserted habitats of men like these. He'd keep his distance. Deep within the rock, Coryn sensed a presence. Seemed one or other of the mercurial desert spirits called it home. It was dormant though and he pushed it to the back of his awareness. His hand strayed over the place where his pouch lay and he pressed against it. He turned back and stilled, listening.

Within the last hour of travelling the air had altered in some indefinable way. Coryn itched. Certain it wasn't the desert spirit making him feel uneasy, he pulled the stiffened edge of his hood lower, deepening the shadow over his face. He studied the area, he'd not get a second chance if he missed the sheen of a sword, or the glint of an arrowhead, hidden between the rocks, or the branches of bush or tree.

The intense heat made the air warp and shimmer over the land like a magiker's working. He touched his pouch, where the amulet felt solid and reassuring, and whispered a word to the spirits. You never knew when they listened, or when they might feel the urge to help. He wrapped his hand about the hide-bound hilt of the short sword hanging at his side, eased the weapon half way out of its black leather scabbard to clear it then settled it back down again. The weight of the pattern-welded steel felt comforting. A rock snake undulated across the track to the shade under a sage and he remembered Yaltos, the Derin High-Seer, and her warning.

He rubbed at his face and frowned. Two, three days worth of stubble prickled his chin. Light on sleep and heavy on dust, he felt it'd be just about time for more problems to come his way. Coryn had ridden out through the last of the wind driven sands and screened by the eddying haze that lingered he'd managed to lose the wrestler's friends. He'd not seen evidence of them since. Still, a hunch told him someone followed. Sucking in hot air through his teeth, he heeled his horse on to climb further up into the mountains.

He'd broken camp at the first signs of a paling horizon around an hour ago and reckoned he'd almost reached the half way mark of this high pass over the mountains. Though it was little used, he'd paralleled it rather than followed it the whole way, still wary of those camel riders. Now he hesitated on a rock and thorn-bush covered ridge. The pass ran over its crest and he followed it on a parallel course, staying well below the ridge-line to avoid being silhouetted against the sky. By his reckoning, this pass would reach Manom around a league upriver of Roesette, where it nestled in the foothills on the northern side of the mountains. Though far smaller than Rialt, it was a busy enough trader town, the Roes River it straddled being a major trade route. Thirty leagues downriver lay the huge seaport of Manar, fifteen leagues upriver stood Castle Drogue.

He turned at the scrape of claws on rock. The dog worked its way up through scrubby sage and desert pea-bushes. After marking the last bush it sat on its haunches, focusing on the trail ahead, evidence enough for Coryn no one was coming up behind them. It raked a hind paw through the dust-coloured, wiry fur of its neck, flicked a look up at Coryn and yawned, showing off its yellowed arsenal of teeth.

Once rested, the dog trotted past the horse and wove upslope through the thorn bushes, boulders and twisted ironwood trees. Five yards from the ridge-top it froze. Coryn watched it for a few moments, then swung down, wincing at a sharp pain from the wound. He pulled the leather quiver from behind his saddle, hooked it to his belt, then took his bow from its case and slung it over his shoulder. He checked the arrows and started up the uneven slope.

His baggy trousers and knee-length robes blended into the desert and stayed noiseless as he moved. Up ahead, the dog had a scent but the wind kept it confused. It quartered the slope, turning and stretching its nose into the air then turning again and sniffing the ground. Coryn continued climbing.

The dog had disappeared by the time Coryn eased over the crest of the ridge. The pain stabbed a staccato rhythm up his leg and into his hip that he tried his best to ignore. He listened for a long time lying motionless in a patch of dried sage-brush, his scent smothered by the strong aroma of its crushed leaves. The wind dropped and a hush fell as the morning sun burned into him. Still cautious, he crawled forward till he looked over a wide gorge. At the bottom, a dry riverbed twisted, bordered by stunted leatherleaf trees. More scattered leatherleaf, ironwood and acacias grew higher up the banks nearer to the cliffs on either side.

The thrum of a short spear speeding through the air sounded loud in the heat and hush. It thumped into wood. A louder, sharper crack followed as something heavy glanced off a rock. It drew Coryn's eye. Magik tingled through the air, setting his teeth on edge. A momentary flash of light swelled and flamed the rock with red fire.

The Wealdan for sure, not blood-magik. Still good enough reason to leave. Curiosity kept Coryn from moving, surprised that anyone else used this trail. He looked along the ridge line to where the trail crossed over its lowest point. He saw where carts had cut deep into the softer ground of the saddle, the tracks not yet blurred by wind. Some merchants paid magikers to accompany their caravans on the more dangerous journeys, but it was uncommon. Magikers didn't come cheap.

He pulled a slender brass spyglass from the small leather case hanging from his belt, one of the best things he'd ever won in a game of crowns, and scanned the area. Squinting through the glass, he scrutinised the folds of the gorge till he spotted the faint smoke of a fire drifting in the air. It came from beyond a bend in the cliff-face to his right. After a while of searching along the gorge itself, he saw the granite-coloured creature who'd thrown the spear. Coryn cleared his throat and spat into the dust.

Writhen. It looked too much like one not to be. The twisted, poi-soned creatures inhabited the deep caves and tunnels underneath the snow-capped Ruel Mountains, over a hundred leagues to the east. Used by the Murecken as hunters and foot soldiers, they were the same creatures that'd attacked his farm in Kalebrod all those years ago. These were much darker and he could only believe they must have been bred specially for the desert conditions. As a rule they avoided full sun.

What in all Murak's flaming hells are they doing here in the desert?

Moments later, he had marked the positions of ten writhen hiding in pockets of shade cast by rocks, bushes and trees. He frowned. So many? He didn't like what it had to mean. Then he spotted their quarry a few yards above the trail where it ran parallel to the riverbed on the eastern side of the gorge. A long, heavy cart with splintered forks, stood nose down against a rock fall blocking most of the mouth of a gully. The gully led to a deep fold in the face of the gorge wall. A wide sand-wheel, broken from its axle, was jammed in the gap between the back end of the cart and the cliff wall. An overhang sheltered the long triangular space between the cart, rock fall and cliff. Sage, acacia and purple-flowering grasses grew in the space between, bathing in the slanting rays of the morning sun.

Further down the slope, not far from the wheel, a man lay face down, a short spear rising from his bloodstained back. The single red bands on the sleeves of his loose, pale yellow robes marked him out as a Rialtan spice merchant. His head-cloth was missing and his long, black hair coiled across the sand. A single camel lay in a twisted heap just above the trail. There wasn't any sign of the any other camels or desert mules that must have pulled the cart. Maybe they'd torn loose and run free after the cart had crashed, maybe survivors had used them to escape, maybe writhen had stolen them to eat. The shattered pieces of water barrels suggested the lives of any remaining behind the cart would be short.

The ambush had happened the day before by the look of the man and the camel. Another two days and the survivors would start getting delirious from heat and thirst, then fear would eat at their reason. Coryn couldn't see any other carts. It was rare for merchants to travel with less than three or four carts plus extra camels or mules. Had the others escaped?

Between rock falls, bandits and spirits knew what else, crossing the Amalla Heights was difficult and dangerous, and only two of the passes had Manom guards policing them. This was not one of them. With Roesette one of the only cities of any size in Manom you could reach any faster direct from Rialt, most merchants headed downriver, by road or water, to the port of Dal Abar and the safer sea routes.

A shape moved in the shadows behind the broken wheel. It disappeared before he could focus on it. Coryn sighed, shifting his aching leg. Whoever hid at the base of that cliff carried a good weapon though. He guessed they had one of those new crossbows. The distance between the cart and the rock indicated something with ample pull for a heavy quarrel. It wouldn't matter. It looked like the magiker had enough Wealdan to make flames. Enough to keep the writhen from swarming over the cart. No more than that. The quarrels would run out soon enough and their prospects were non-existent. Whoever survived would know that by now. The best they could hope for was not to be taken alive.

He scanned the piled boulders lying further along the cliff wall. Three writhen stood behind them, all the same dark grey, and like the others, all wearing some sort of animal-skin hood with loose skin flapping down over their necks and shoulders. A fourth climbed the rocks, no doubt trying for a spear throw from higher up.

Coryn focused the spyglass on this one. Various animal skins hung from its belt reaching just past its knees. Its belt also carried bunches of fetishes and charms, the usual feathers, bones and holed pebbles worn for courage, strength and wards against magik. Its bare feet were clawed and almost black, like its taloned hands. It wore a wyvern's head for a hat and the emerald green neck-skin flapped around its shoulders. Lumps and bulges stretched the scaled and ridged skin of its body in odd places. It stood around five foot in height, with skinny arms and legs, much the height of writhen back home. It also had the same short, yellowed tusks jutting from the lower jaw. It confirmed Coryn's doubts about the old tale that writhen bore any relation to humans.

It wasn't his place to get involved in this business. He didn't want to give the man hiding behind the cart empty hope. Coryn began to pull back when he saw another writhen, a sneering grin on its snout-shaped face, move to stand on the trail in clear view of the survivor. It dragged the dead Rialtan further down the slope, took its knife out and sawed one arm off, daring the survivor behind the cart to do something. The rest of the pack cackled and croaked with derision as the writhen tore at the flesh and smacked his lips with relish as it chewed. Coryn waited for a quarrel to fly, waited for the writhen to lurch backwards its chest feathered. Nothing happened.

He couldn't understand why the magiker didn't kill it. Too petrified with terror? No more quarrels? He scanned the space behind the cart and boulders again. Nothing. Closing up his spyglass, he slid it away and rose. Half crouched, Coryn limped down the ridge to a stack of wind-shaped boulders and a lone iron-tree. He squatted behind them, tightened the bloody bandages on his thigh, then pulled the bow off his back. He braced the bow, looped the string into place and notched an arrow.

Levering himself up, Coryn leaned against a waist-high boulder. The stone felt hot against his hip. With the sinew snug against his thumb ring, he pulled back till the fletching tickled his ear. He guessed the range at one hundred yards and sighted a fraction high. No wind for the moment, the charcoal shade of the leaves motionless, he aimed straight. The writhen stood on top of the boulders now, making a show of sighting its spear on the cart. The arrow's release was smooth and sure. No recoil, no sound to speak of except for a soft *thwump* as the sinew slammed forward. A moment later, his second arrow flew toward the writhen holding the merchant's arm.

For a fleeting moment he glimpsed the arrows arcing through the bright morning sunlight then they faded into the shadows of the cliff. The writhen on the rocks flew backward. Its head smashed against rocks. Dark orange blood spattered to the ground. The other writhen clawed at the shaft in its throat as it crumpled to the ground.

The three remaining writhen dropped down to crouch against

the cliff, searching for the archer. Coryn lay tense, ready to shift at a moment's notice, but it looked like they'd no idea where the arrows came from. He remembered writhen having poor sight. A moment later the remaining writhen lunged from the rocks, grabbed their pack-mate's bodies and dragged them down the gravelled slope towards the riverbed. Yet more writhen came out from behind rocks and bushes to help them. Not knowing where the arrow came from might keep them from closing on the cart again. For a short while at least.

Coryn studied the area again. The writhen stayed lower to the ground and hugged the shadows more. He moved the circle of glass over the cart and the boulders again. A face appeared out of the shadows. A pale, old woman's face. She stared straight at him from the gap between the boulder and the wheel as if she could see right into his eyes. Then she was gone. Astonished, he searched the cart, rocks, cliff and gully for some time but she didn't reappear and he saw no one else.

It burned where he lay. Flies buzzed over his crusted bandages and his mouth was parched. Coryn knew he'd need water soon. He'd lost a lot of blood and the wound still seeped when he used his leg over-much. But he lingered, thinking on the face he'd seen. Had he hallucinated? That face just didn't fit in a Rialtan caravan. He shook his head.

It didn't take him much longer to make up his mind to pull out. He'd done all he could for whoever remained by the cliff. He'd bought them precious time and it was up to them to do with it what they could. Coryn was sorry there was a woman involved though – if there was a woman – but there wasn't a single rational thing he could do to save them. One man against that many fully-armed writhen wouldn't stand a chance. He'd just be dying with them.

Besides, he'd his sister, Lera, to find, and a message to deliver. Both delayed years too long. No doubt delivering the message was pointless now, but Birog had saved his life all those years ago and he'd given her an oath. Coryn meant to see it through. That she'd said it didn't matter how long it took was a good thing in every respect. Most important to Coryn was that the man the message was for knew whether and where Lera lived, so Birog had promised. And Lera was the most important thing in the world to him.

Coryn moved back down the slope.

The horse was where he'd left it. A well-trained beast, desert coloured and of good Selassian stock, not tall but strong, lithe and sure-footed over sand and rock. It had cost him a fair part of his earnings from his year of soldiering in the Selassi City guard. Like the bow and the sword, the animal was worth it to the last copper dock.

Coryn finished strapping the recurve and quiver to the saddle and stood awhile listening for danger. He sipped from a waterskin. He was running low. Like those folk trapped behind the cart. He hesitated. Torn. Should he turn around? Was there a way to help them after all? No. It'd be senseless. He mounted his horse and heeled it back onto the uncertain goat track that stayed below the ridge. He remained deep in thought.

Chapter 21

Coryn rode for a while longer, checking every so often for signs of pursuit from men, and now writhen too, when a cut between two low ridges opened up. Half-way down the tapering valley, he found a second cart, near some shrubby leatherleaf. Seemed one at least had broken through the ambush. They'd done well getting this far before being overtaken. Scattered along the cart's path lay five dead writhen. He rode past them one by one. Each had a hole bored through its torso or head. Fine grey ash surrounded each round cavity.

From these dead writhen he sensed traces of the Wealdan. His muscles tensed, his skin prickled and the hairs on his neck stiffened. A metallic tang hung in air spiked with blood-magik. It came from somewhere up ahead. Swinging his bow from his shoulder, Coryn nocked an arrow and drew. The dog trotted forward, he heeled his horse to follow in a slow walk.

Like the narrow valley Coryn had passed earlier, this one bore the blurred remains of some ancient civilization in the cliffs at its far end. The balconies and windows were now nesting places for small, dusty-brown birds with white bellies, sandpipers. They flitted after insects and filled the air with musical chatter.

After a short while, the dog returned and flopped down on the trail. Soaked, the animal grinned up at him smug as a Selassian administrator. Coryn tightened the bandage on his leg again and swung down. He worked his way down the slope setting his feet down with care on the uneven ground. He wasn't of a mind to fall.

Looked like the Rialtan died around sunrise. Coryn looked closer. Young, not yet a man, with more sand on his face than whiskers. He lay stretched on the sand, bitten, slashed and clawed over just about every square inch of his mahogany skin. Both legs were gone. He hoped the writhen hadn't begun feeding till after the boy died.

The second man wasn't much older than Coryn. Tied spread-eagled against a sloping rock, his pale skin looked obscene in the brilliant sun. Burns, blisters and deep cuts in bizarre patterns covered the flesh of his arms legs and torso, apart from where a yellow-fletched arrow jutted from his neck, he could see no blood. Every drop drained from his body, taken along with the main organs. It meant only one thing.

A damned blood-priest!

Coryn scanned the valley. Nothing. He knew the work of a Murecken blood-priest when he saw it, though he hadn't seen any since he'd been a boy back in Kalebrod. The Murecken blood-priests hunted those with the Wealdan, they needed its power for their blood-magik. Controlling so many writhen would require plenty of power. The blood-priest would've had to hurry though, as the man must have been near dead with that arrow in his neck before the rites started.

Spirits!

Coryn hawked and spat. He hated being right. In this at least. The blood-priests were the reason he'd ended up in this damned desert and he'd hoped never to meet them again. He gripped his pouch with one hand and reached out toward the body with the other. Spikes of blood-magik repelled Coryn, but as he pushed closer they splintered and died away. He cut the man down and covered him with what remained of his robe. A stylized sun embroidered the collar.

Damn. That explains a deal.

A Lehotan Adherent. One of those who believed the Wealdan came from Lehot, their god of light. Desperate enough to use his Wealdan to kill, drilling holes in the writhen, despite the Lehotan Order advocating non-violence. But it hadn't been enough.

He covered the Rialtan too. The sleeves of his shredded robes bore the patterned bands of an apprentice to a spice merchant. Rialtan merchants should've known better. Maybe they thought having both a Lehotan and a Wealdan magiker made them safe. They might have been but for the blood-priest.

The flames the magiker created and these strange holes punched into the writhen by the Lehotan should have been enough to see off any ordinary attack. This was anything but ordinary. The Lehotan would have drawn the blood-priest like a vulture to carrion. Coryn just hoped there weren't any bloodhunter-priests about too. He couldn't sense or smell their distinctive stink anywhere, but that meant nothing. Although his amulet had kept him safe up to this point, he'd rather not put it to such a test. Better to rely on good old-fashioned caution, as his Da often said.

Coryn took out a small, folding spade from his pack and began digging.

Further down the valley a trickle of water squeezed out from a crack low in the east facing cliff wall. It spilled over a lip and plunked out a tune as it fell into a wide basin worn into the rock below. Coryn took a long drink and filled his two waterskins. The horse drank its fill and began pulling on the tussocks of grass growing round the basin.

After soaking his head, Coryn took a while over washing his hands then cleaned his wounds and the bandaging. The flesh, still swollen and tender to the touch on both sides of his thigh, looked too red. He smeared on some goldflower ointment. It stung like Murak's flaming hells, so he knew it was doing some good. He bandaged his leg again with dry strips of cloth, leaving the damp ones to dry on a bush, then limped over to the cart.

Two camels were still hitched to it. The long shafts allowed them to sit, but not much more. They chewed on sage and leatherleaf, stoic as only such animals can be. In the cart he found lengths of rope, jars containing spices and oils, sacks of millet and oats, and boxes of herbs. Then he smelled the unmistakeable aroma of kaffe. Excited, he rummaged around till he found a small sack of the rich, dark beans. He'd not had a drink of kaffe since the night he'd left Rialt.

Here, nearer to the ruins, he felt a presence deep inside the cliff. An ifrit, one of the most dangerous of the desert spirits. A trapped one with its power blocked in some way. Coryn could almost feel its anger and hunger for revenge this close to its prison. He wondered what it guarded. A treasure trove or a king's tomb? And for how long? He sighed and shook his head, sorry for whatever was trapped down there. He unhitched and unharnessed the camels. They grunted and wandered off to the drip-pool.

He mounted and rode back down the valley, through the narrow neck and back toward the gorge and its trapped woman. The dog, loping ahead of him, stopped. It growled deep in its throat, facing to the east of the way they'd come that morning.

Then Coryn heard distant screams setting his teeth on edge. He knew what they meant the moment he heard them. He urged his horse down a narrow path leading toward the bend of the cliff where he'd seen the smoke that morning. He placed a hand on his horse's neck to keep it quiet. The screams belonged to a woman. That much closer he could hear the agony and terror in them. The screams kept coming.

'Damned blood-priests.' Slipping off the horse, he led it behind a stack of large rocks in a spinney of acacia trees some way back from the track. Next to the path marking the turn off, he stacked some stones where he'd spot them in a hurry. The woman screamed again. Coryn slogged lop-sided but soft footed down the ridge in the direction of the sound.

He scrutinized the camp with his spyglass. In the centre of the short gully were a couple of large cook fires, spears and staves leaned against the far wall and a group of writhen sat near one of the fires eating. Coryn didn't care to look close at what they might be chewing on and swung the glass further along the gully. He spotted a second group of writhen standing under a fair-sized desert oak. Some held burning torches. The source of the screaming hung from the branches.

A woman, neither young nor particularly old. She'd patterns cut into every inch of her skin, just like the Lehotan man. It meant she had the Wealdan too. Another Lehotan? Her blood dripped into a large, shallow bowl that smoked with oily blood-magik. It spiked the air and Coryn's senses, strong, unnerving. A cloaked figure stood close to the woman, face hidden in the shadows of a hood. The long, dull black knife in one hand glistened. The Murecken blood-priest.

'Spirits take him.' Coryn clamped his mouth shut. Scowling, he pressed a hand against his chest, finding comfort in the hardness of the amulet inside its pouch.

The blood-priest sliced deep into her belly. Coryn winced, turning away as the intestines spilled down her legs. The woman screamed again and the writhen croaked their approval. The priest said something too low for Coryn to hear and all the writhen crowded together to drink from the bowl, lapping at the blood like dogs.

Coryn waited till the woman stopped thrashing for a moment then put an arrow through her throat. The writhen stared in surprise at the corpse, silent and still, not certain what had happened. A second arrow readied, he aimed for the blood-priest's throat. The man flew backwards, his chest sprouting an arrow a shade below the collarbone. His hood fell away revealing a pale face and a bald, rutted head.

As he notched a third arrow, Coryn scanned the campsite again. Above the leaning spears and staves, a tree clung to the cliff wall just below a ledge. One of its branches hung loose. An arrow sent it crashing into the weapons and they clattered and rolled across the ground. All the writhen ran toward the ledge, croaking and grunting, looking for the archer. Coryn spun and started running, the pain in his leg flaring as his feet pounded.

He almost crashed over the stack of stones on the path. Sliding to a stop, he turned and found the rocks, the acacias and his horse. The noise of its hooves was loud, but Coryn urged his horse as fast as he dared across the uneven ground. He went along the gorge in the opposite direction from the old woman. The screeching and guttural croaks from the writhen camp bounced off the cliffs and just about covered the sounds he made. They would find him soon enough if he tried to hide so he kept moving. Then the dog was with him again. They raced together up onto the trail along the crest of the ridge and down the other side.

The moons were sliding down the sky by the time he got back to the drip-pool valley. He saw no sign of the camels, seemed someone had taken them. A distant crack of rock on rock then a faint cough got him reining his horse in. Sliding out of the saddle, he lead his horse and limped in amongst the nearest stand of leatherleaf. He crouched down to watch motioning for the dog to do the same. It wasn't long before someone came to the pool.

A Shafian.

What in all of Murak's flaming hells is a Shafian doing here?

Coryn didn't like the obvious reason that came to mind.

The man seemed to be there an age, using up the precious liquid to fill his waterskins. A drip fed pool like this one would take a while to refill. Finished, the Shafian started back up the trail.

Coryn followed him. The Shafian led him to a narrow dead-end gully with clumps of grass and sagebrush making an effective corral. A number of camels, likely unsettled by the stink of writhen, snatched mouthfuls of leaves and paced the gully. A ledge hung over the gully and a small fire burned there. The Shafian joined another. Just the two of them then. Coryn shook his head and returned to the drip-pool. There was no sign of the dog.

Taking his scarf from his neck, he soaked up the remaining moisture in the basin and rubbed it over his face. It felt good. Coryn looped the cool, damp cotton round his neck. He found himself a place in the bushes where he could sit downwind of the drip-pool and still have a clear aim at anything that approached. Starlight glimmered on the water dripping down to refill the basin.

An arrow nocked, he settled down to wait. A band of skinny wild pigs with wiry hair trotted down to the pool. He was aiming at a fat-looking sow when he heard an antelope snort. He waited. Antelope steak would be even better than pork. The small desert buck, grey against the night, stepped into view, scenting the air. Its curling horns glimmered in the faint light. Coryn dropped it at twenty-five yards.

Dragging it back into the bushes, he skinned and butchered it, then wrapped the choicest cuts and organs in the antelope's own hide. He used sand to clean his knife and his arms, rubbing it in well till all the blood had gone. He'd no idea where the dog had got to. It would've enjoyed the fresh meat. Perhaps it had run off to follow someone else like the unreliable mutt it was. He cleared his throat, ashamed. It was a good dog.

Midnight passed and the two moons rose as Coryn made camp a league from the drip-pool valley. He hobbled the horse, unsaddled it and rubbed it down with a square of sheepskin. Then he unrolled his blanket on the ground and lay down in the cooling hush and stared at the moons. The thin crescent of Diaphos hadn't pulled so far ahead of Liatos. The larger moon, now a pale pink, waxed almost full.

As he watched the stars wheel past, distant and indifferent, Coryn knew he couldn't have saved those people. He'd only die along with them. He was free after years of slavery and able to complete his oath and find his sister again. It'd be stupid to throw that all away.

Spirits! It'd be more than damned stupid. It'd be madness!

Knowing all that still didn't make him feel any better.

Chapter 22

Mureen tried to meditate in the deeper darkness between the cliff and the cart for over two hours. Sweat trickled beneath her robes and she chafed with the ubiquitous sand. The itching distracted her, the stars that dusted the midnight skies distracted her, the moons rose and their beauty distracted her. She sighed.

Diaphos, now the thinnest sliver of a crescent, was followed as ever by Liatos, fast closing the distance between them and brimming with pink luminescence.

She pulled her eyes away, trying to ignore the hunger and thirst chewing away at her belly and throat. Taking a deep breath, Mureen gripped the focus crystal till its sharp angles dug into her hands. Each facet cut by her own hands over one long year of careful crafting. She had finished it forty-seven winters ago, and had then taken her solemn vows as a full initiate into the Lehotan Order. It had been her eighteenth name day. As she looked into the crystal's pale lavender light the memories of that day flooded in as clear as if it were yesterday.

Snow had fallen hard over the Isle of Ostorr in the Elyat Sea, and the small, ancient castle nestled deep in its valley, the principal Haven for women of the Lehotan Order in the Storratian Empire. It had been both school and home for her during the five long years of her novitiate period of training. Her mother and two younger brothers had looked so cold and alone standing in the square shaking in their winter cloaks as they bade her a last farewell. Mureen in contrast had felt warm inside, happy and at peace. It was as if Lehot's Light had risen in her belly on becoming an Adherent and dwelled there still, filling her with warmth.

She had known by then, beyond all doubt, that her Wealdan and the Wefan were both created and gifted by Lehot and that the God of Light was the God above all other gods in truth. It awed her still. Mureen also knew then that Lehot had granted her the Wealdan so that she might use it for good. It had been that simple for her and the feeling of peace and warmth had never left her. Even now with the shadows of death so near, the calm dwelt within her.

Even so, she was troubled. She rubbed the crystal between her fingers the way she always did when she searched for answers to problems. Moreover, on this night in this place darker than any she had ever known, she had a very great problem to solve. Mureen was not concerned for her own life. She was ready to drag her aching bones off to join Lehot and rest in the eternal embrace of His Halls of Light. Her concerns were simple and were for the others. She had two this night. She had been going over them in different ways again and again trying to see a way out of their predicament.

Mureen also felt the need to petition Lehot once more for Dame Alaya and the youngster Thoma. The poor boy raised to a full Adherent in the Lehotan Order just three days before they journeyed to Selassi, now lost to life. She must not forget apprentice Manzul, the eldest son of Manzar bin Khadra al-Fazul, or the spice merchant himself, who lay dead just to the other side of the cart she knelt behind. She glanced out into the darkness of the gorge.

With the mind-link in place, Mureen had felt Alaya's fear. Such terrible fear and agony. The shock when it ceased with such abruptness still pained her. She still could not tell the others, for Dame Alaya, Thoma and Manzul were their single hope. She knew they envisaged the three of them hurrying towards Roesette and help in the surviving cart along with the two Shafian brothers. She thought on the Shafians, hoping they lived still, unable to believe, as young Katleya had insisted, that the brothers had betrayed them. As long as she did not have to lie, Mureen would not, could not, destroy the hope the others bore.

She closed her eyes again and meditated on the spirits of Alaya, Thoma, Manzul and Manzar. She hoped that they might find peace in Lehot's Light and that, if Thoma and Manzul still lived, they reached safety soon. She knew Alaya well, knew that her spirit would not have been broken. She was far too strong and too stubborn for that.

In the hope that it would help, Mureen had focused her Wealdan and sent a little of her own energy down their shared mind-link before it broke. A link they had formed long ago, soon after the younger woman first arrived at Ostorr Haven. It was not the sort of link as of old, one through which Adherents could speak to each other no matter the distance. Their link conveyed only their emotions and some few impressions of what they experienced, no more.

They had become the firmest of friends in a short time, she the young Adherent teacher and Alaya the noviciate, and one of the most promising entrants the Haven had received in many years. Thoma she did not know so very well, not enough for a linking. Mureen knew him as half boy, half man and filled with the energy and enthusiasm of youth but far from having gained the wisdom that came with age.

She felt weak now and so very alone. Alaya had been like a true sister to her. The hole where she used to reside within Mureen's heart gaped wide and raw. She wished her Wealdan were stronger. She wished the others possessed more potency too. She wished the numbers of girls and boys coming into the Havens in possession of any Wealdan at all were not shrinking. Why it was no one knew, unless there was a direct link to the rise of Murak and his priesthood as some said. She wished it were not so. She wished...

But, wishing is of little use. I must meditate.

Mureen brought her mind back to her present needs. Straightening her small body till all the joints creaked, she squeezed the crystal between the palms of her hands.

'Lehot,' she whispered, 'I do not ask this of myself for I am willing to die in this place if that is my fate but...' She shuddered as if a hand had touched her. 'Lehot, make the Wefan-winged call I sent to that man work. Let him return and deliver the others from this terrible place.'

At a sound she turned. It was Wetham. The boy sat down and leaned against her, silent as ever. She placed an arm round his bony shoulders and squeezed. Mureen had to try again for this small child and for all the others. She would try to reach the man once more, then she would meditate and place her trust in Lehot. It was night and sleep with its time of dreaming often lowered the walls of the mind. It was a fragile hope.

She opened her Wealdan and funnelled it through her crystal with an ease years of practice had given her. The crystal's matrix enhanced her ability to focus and also strengthen her Wealdan enough that Mureen could both sense and draw on the fine matrices of energy that patterned through everything both animate and inanimate within the world of Dumnon. This incredible energy, the Wefan, was as pure now as when first created by Lehot. The patterning of its filaments glistened in the plants, rocks and air that surrounded her filling her Wealdan-sight with light. It astounded her each time she opened herself up to it. The Wefan was beautiful, more so on this desert night than ever.

Mureen drew on a few of the finer matrices of Wefan from a small rock. She did not like to draw from plants as they became limp and could die. Each Wealdan-bearer drew on the Wefan in a unique manner. Some drew it from particular rocks, others only from certain plants. Very few had the dexterity to snatch it from air or water.

She gathered all she could manage to both hold and shape. The threads tingled like a multitude tiny sparks against her skin and within her flesh. Mureen wove them into an ellipse-shaped matrix, braiding into it her need. A simple thought: *Help us.* Yet the meaning within was complex. A mind-to-mind cry in the dark to a man she had seen but once. A man, she had felt from her fleeting mind-touch, who was of great strength.

She worried that she was too weak, that the distance would be too far and that he would not be receptive. After all, Mureen had not been able to read him in full when he had been mere yards away. That had never happened to her before. Never. The man must be very strong indeed to have such barriers. She buried her fears and sent the ellipse spinning out between the hot layers of the night air. She pushed it northwards the direction instinct told her he had taken.

A sudden, shocking burst of energy surged through her, strengthening the push and driving her summons to its mark. More Wefan than she had ever drawn before poured through every fibre of her body. She gloried in the pure, intense force of it. Just as she began to thank Lehot for answering her, she fell unconscious into the sands.

Chapter 23

With a cry, Coryn shot bolt upright. The dog came up close and stared into his face. Drenched with sweat despite the cold and looking about bewildered and dazed, he stood up. The vast, inky heavens flamed with stars and the land spread quiet in all directions sluiced with moonlight. Apart from the whine of night insects and whispers of sand disturbed by small nocturnal animals, silence reigned.

He'd not yelled like that since he was a child. His heart hammered with alarm. Confused, Coryn pulled his blanket round his shoulders and tried to work out why. The dog sat down, watching him, its head cocked to one side, curiosity filling its almond eyes.

He remembered dreaming. A vivid dream, something to do with the old woman hiding behind the cart. He'd seen her face again, surrounded by utter darkness. She'd called out to him and Coryn had howled with the pain of her cry slamming into him. Hard on its heels, another pain spiked, rearing up from deep inside. One that felt like it had been trapped there all his life.

Coryn shivered. He beckoned to the dog. No comfort there, the animal stayed put and stared at him, its fur raised from neck to tail, a continuous rumble deep in its throat. He took out his amulet and rubbed his thumb over its surface, feeling the usual comfort in its round shape and the crack holding the sliver of crystal, and thought hard.

It was some hours after midnight when Coryn rose to saddle his horse. He tried to stay alert to his surroundings but his mind kept drifting back to the old woman. He mounted but didn't urge his horse on. He thought on the dream, his reaction and what he was about to do. He felt so chilled, the sweat tracking down his skin seemed hot.

Spirits! It just doesn't make a damn bit of sense.

He urged his horse back towards the gorge and the writhen. And the blood-priest.

High on a ridge, snug against a thin, wind-shaped spire of rock, Coryn worked the spyglass over the landscape. He searched for a campfire, a lantern lit tent, anything that would mean other travellers and help. After half an hour, he still couldn't find anything in the shadowed expanse of crevassed rock. He put the spyglass away and listened to the distant howling of desert wolves out on a night's hunt. Closer by, he heard the dog join in, then he saw its silhouette against a patch of moon-washed rocks. He clambered back through the rocks to his horse and rode down the ridge. Slow and careful, he headed back toward the old woman.

Sun must've boiled away what little brains I had!

An hour or so later, the sun rose to gild the very top edges of the east facing cliffs with red-gold. He'd circled the gorge area and now stood scanning the ravines and ridges southwards with his spyglass again. There seemed no way of reaching the cart alive. In the shadowed gorge, nine writhen stood on the trail, five more near the rocks by the broken forks of the cart and six just back from the wheel blocking the gap between the back of the cart and the cliff. Grown madder or plain crazier, every one of them in full view. No sign of the Murecken blood-priest, but Coryn knew he hadn't killed the bastard.

Two writhen, lurching about as if they'd been drinking Selassian firewater, staggered out in front of the cart. They turned and slapped their deformed backsides. The crossbow snapped again and the two scrambled for cover behind a rock. At the quarrel's concussion sparks spat and flames erupted against the red sandstone, dying quick to leave behind large sooty marks. Coryn's skin prickled as he sensed the use of the Wealdan. He shook his head.

How'd he miss that shot?

Moments later, the writhen lobbed a salvo of stones. Some slammed against the cart, others hurtled into the sand of the gully beyond. They croaked and screeched taunts too guttural to understand. This wasn't going to last much longer, they'd soon get drunk on enough alcohol to brave an attack on the cart. The fear of the Wealdan made them cautious, but quarrels and small flames wouldn't hold the writhen back much longer. Not if a Murecken blood-priest whipped them on. Then he'd have the woman and the magiker. But not if Coryn could do anything about it.

Damn.

Trouble was, he'd no plan. Then he remembered the pillared ruins, the ones in the drip-pool valley. It gave Coryn an odd idea. One that might just work if the spirits held with him. At least one spirit in particular. He touched a hand to his pouch, then put the spyglass back in its case.

Coryn rode his horse through branches of scrub oak and leatherleaf. Just below the ridge crest overlooking the gorge, he stopped. Dropping the reins, he searched for writhen. They'd moved past the rocks and leaped about on the trail, croaking and barking in their garbled language, intoxicated and erratic. Others joined them and he saw one swigging from an unmistakeable blue clay jug with a yellow stripe round its middle. One of the better brands of Selassian firewater. The drunkenness was a sure sign the Murecken blood-priest was injured enough to have lost some of his control over them, that they stood there at all, a sign he still lived.

Coryn picked the closest writhen. He guessed the distance to be around two hundred yards, very close to the bow's maximum range. The broadheads he preferred to use wouldn't hit with enough impact to kill, so he chose a bodkin tipped arrow. A chance shot that might give him away but he needed time. Those behind the cart needed time.

Coryn nocked, drew and aimed a good half-inch above the head of the writhen, hoping to catch him in the lung. The writhen screeched, flying back against another, the blue jug spiralled away and crashed to the ground. The shot was on the low side, taking the writhen in the stomach. It'd die, but it'd be a long, painful death. Unless the other writhen finished him off, and that'd depend on how hungry they were.

Coryn turned and kicked the horse into a trot.

Chapter 24

He left his horse in a thick copse of acacia, hard against the rock face. It nibbled on sage leaves and dry grasses, happy to rest in the deep shade. A few yards further on Coryn found and climbed a steep path cut into the cliff. A while later, he reached a ten-foot tall triangular opening. Worn to illegibility, words inscribed its two long sides. It led to a smooth-walled tunnel of the same shape that twisted into the darkness. Dust, smelling of things long decayed, stirred against the scorched air of the desert. He felt the malignant presence of the ifrit.

Aware, it waited for him.

He hesitated for a moment. Was he mad to contemplate this? Had the constant travel in the desert's heat affected his mind?

No, this felt right. He'd a hunch on it. Taking a deep breath, Coryn stepped through the entrance and sent more dust into the air. His eyes became accustomed to the darkness as he walked further down the tunnel. The temperature plummeted and he shivered.

After a while the tunnel split. Working on another hunch, he chose the left branch. It twisted and he slowed his pace as the light and heat from the entrance failed. Reaching out his arms, he touched the cold, dry sides of the tunnel. Coryn arrived at a second branching, again he chose the left turn. Three more splits and three more left turns led him downwards on a coiling journey deep into the cliff, till he guessed he now travelled well below the gorge floor. Then he lost touch with the tunnel walls and stepped into a vast space. He felt the ground becoming uneven. Whatever it was he walked on cracked, snapped or rolled from under his boots. The sounds echoed off distant walls. He stopped. Somewhere ahead, he felt the ifrit stir.

'I smell you, human.' The voice whispered like dust sliding from bone. 'I see you, human.'

'It'd be a fine thing to see you too.' Coryn's hand stole up to grasp his amulet, seeing its shape, its crack with its sliver of crystal in his mind's eye, gave him strength. His heart hammered fast as he worked out how close he was to the ifrit. He stepped back a pace. 'I'd very much like to speak with you.'

'What makes you think I would wish to hear you speak, you, a mere human?' The darkness chuckled. 'You sense me and you hear me. Yet you cannot see me. Why don't you come closer, human?'

'I think I'll not, if it's all the same to you.'

'Do you feel – vulnerable?'

'In this dark? A little, if I'm honest. I figure if I stay right here I'll be just fine.' Coryn tried to sound like he knew what he was doing. 'I reckon I don't need to see who I'm talking to.'

'You do not?' A long sigh, a moment's silence, then clink of chain. 'But I believe you should. So see me now and we shall see if you can still talk at all, human.'

Light blazed. Coryn twisted away from the inferno of white heat and grabbed his amulet where it hung heavy against his chest and kind of *pushed* against the magik. The fire didn't burn him.

Spirits!

It worked. The relief made his knees weak.

When the light became bearable, Coryn dropped his arms again. All around him scorched bones covered the ground. He stood on the blackened and broken skulls of all the people who had come before. If this worked, if he didn't join this ossiary, he would thank Birog for the gift of her amulet. He owed the woman everything. Always supposing he ever saw her again. He looked up. In the flickering light, ranks of pillars faded into the distance of an immense hall and stretched up to a ceiling lost in darkness.

Coryn turned, ready for another test. He'd listened to the stories of how ifrit worked. The games they liked to play on humans. He'd even met a few, but never alone. He stepped back a pace when he saw her. A female ifrit. He didn't know why it shocked him. Maybe because he'd never seen them take on anything other than a male form before. If he were honest though, his shock would be because of the blatant, sensuous nakedness of her.

'You do not burn, human.' She sounded curious and Coryn saw it reflected in her eyes.

'No,' Coryn agreed as he took in the sight of her. He felt heat rise in him. She looked wondrous. Every luscious curve and swell outlined in tiny ever-rippling flames. Her slanted eyes glinted like sun-caught emeralds.

The ifrit stretched over an ancient stone sarcophagus, luxuriating in his stare. 'How very unusual. All the others burned. Why is it that you do not? Are you not human? You smell human, you look human, all my senses tell me you are human.'

Coryn ignored the question. 'I've come with a proposal.' He tried to keep his eyes on her face. He wasn't quite successful.

'A proposal? How interesting.' One ruby fingernail stroked the line of her thigh, brushed over her hip and travelled up to circle a breast. Behind it, a line of flames licked higher in response. 'Come closer and tell me of this proposal, human.'

Coryn pulled himself up just short of a full step. 'You'll hear me well enough if I stay right here.'

She chuckled again deep in her throat. Then she flung her long flame-red hair back from her shoulder. It coiled and snaked over the stone with a life of its own. A round collar of black, pitted iron spoiled the golden column of her throat. A long, heavy chain of the same metal led from the collar to an immense iron ring attached to the base of the sarcophagus. He could both see and sense the blood-magik bleed from every inch of the iron like oily red smoke. It spiked out at the air all around. Still strong, even with the passing of maybe hundreds of years since it was embedded into the metal. He gritted his teeth, blocking out the feeling. It faded from his mind.

'Very well, human. Stay where you are, stand among the bones of your predecessors.' The ifrit's voice was low and laced with bitterness. 'But know that I am cursed to protect all that lies within this tomb – treasure and stone, jewel and bone – until the centuries crumble and the aeons expire. Till I am left solitary, isolated and insane. What proposal would you have that could be of any possible interest to me, human?'

'I don't want any treasure.' He gave her his best smile. A smile full of promise that had always worked well for him. 'I've come for you.'

'For me? For me, human? And what would you have of me? An ifrit, as near to madness as it is possible to be, is a dangerous creature. Know yourself warned.' She threw her head back and chuckled deep in her throat, louder and louder, till he slapped his hands over his ears. With a shriek, it cut off and she stared at him again, her eyes burning emerald fire. 'Now, would you still ask something of me, human?'

'First, I want to free you.' Coryn filled his mind with the tortured woman and the two young men, the face of the old woman at the cart. Anything to stop himself thinking of touching the ifrit. Of kissing that golden skin. Of losing himself in flames that held such wild promises. He stopped a groan from escaping his throat and gritted his teeth.

'Free,' the ifrit whispered. 'FREE,' she roared. 'HA!'

Flames shot up to billow against the arched ceiling a hundred feet high. She leaped toward Coryn making him stumble back and fall, scattering and breaking the brittle, charred bones. The ifrit came to an abrupt stop a bare three yards from where he lay. She leaned forward, pulling against the collar till it dug deep into her throat, dulling the gold flesh of her neck even more. Her arms reached toward him and her eyes blazed with hunger. But he saw the vast pain that filled them.

'Free?' she moaned. The flames skittered over her skin fast and frenzied.

'Yes.' Coryn's heart raced. He struggled back to his feet and faced her square on. 'Yes,' he said again, firm and quiet this time. 'I want to free you first, before I'll ask anything of you.'

She laughed, screeched again, then whirled into the air, till Coryn worried she'd gone as insane as she'd promised. Brought short by the chain, she spun and sprawled back onto the sarcophagus. 'How can you, a mere human, free me from this place? From these chains, from the blood-magik within them? Can you not see it, seeping from the iron, soaking into my skin, clawing at my very inner being, as it has done for aeons?' She snarled and her emerald eyes glowed. 'I sense nothing of a magiker about you. Do not toy with me, human.'

'I've no intention of toying with you.' Coryn clenched his fists then relaxed them and stepped closer. 'But I've got to get close, I've got to touch you. Will you let me?'

Her eyes became even more dangerous. Then they brimmed with seduction. She stared at him for a long moment. 'You are a pretty man, perhaps I shall let you put your hands upon me.' A curving smile sculpted her perfect lips. 'Tell me true, where do you wish to touch me, pretty man?'

'The collar round your neck. I think I can take it off.' Coryn was unsure if it would work. Unsure if it would kill him to try. It was a slim chance but he'd take it. He couldn't back down now.

Spirits! To trap anyone like this, human or not, is just plain wrong.

'This collar, human?' She reached up one finger. A breath before it touched the iron a crack of black lightning struck out. It flung her arm back and killed the flames on the skin of her hand. She raised her

163

blackened fingers. The flames crept with agonising sluggishness up her palm and back over her fingers. One fingertip remained black. 'It senses even the intent to touch. Yet you would make the attempt?'

Coryn felt the sickening spike of the strong blood-magik scrape against his senses again. He wouldn't back down. He pressed his hand against the pouch containing his amulet and pushed the blood-magik away.

'Yes.' He nodded. He tried to look confident, tried not to think of the bones lying under his feet. 'I know what it is to be a slave.' He bared his own neck, showed her the scars from his own iron collar, the rough pink ridges. Showed her the brand by his collarbone too. 'I know what it's like to be freed.'

'Even so.' The ifrit gazed at him for a long, long while. 'Yet I see you are uncertain still. I taste your hesitance. The stink of fear weeps from your skin.' She widened her nostrils, her lips parted and she sucked in a slow breath. 'You know you might perish but still you would make the attempt, pretty man?'

'I'm wondering if the desert's heat has boiled the wits from my head, but yes.' Coryn nodded. 'I'll still try and free you.'

'Could it be possible that this intolerable existence is at an end?' The ifrit shook her head. She frowned, slid off the sarcophagus and walked around it once, twice, then back again. She looked around the chamber and put her head in her hands. 'It is absurd even to think of it, to hope for it is, in itself, dangerous.' She looked back up at Coryn and he saw something else in her eyes. Hope. 'This is no trifling cantrip that holds the collar about my neck, pretty man.'

'I know.' Coryn shrugged and loosened his shoulders.

'Now you are more assured or you have managed to disguise your fear with more effectiveness.' The ifrit looked at Coryn sideways, her slanted eyes burning into him. 'Do you realise, pretty man, once free, I could do anything? I could snuff out the paltry essence that flickers within you. Or keep you close and amuse myself with you through eternity.' Her lascivious smile sent shock waves down his spine. 'Be assured – it is not a trifling temptation.'

'I think you will not.' He hoped she would not.

There was another silence. It stretched for quite a while and Coryn struggled to stay still. He kept his eyes on hers.

'So,' she said at last, her voice low. A faint tremor betrayed her eagerness. 'Do you still wish to free me?'

'Yes.' He opened his palms to her and smiled, hiding his fear behind a calm face.

'I feel your desire for something, pretty man. A question trembles on your tongue just behind that beguiling smile.' She stared at him, like she could see deep into his soul, and licked at her blackened finger. 'Why do you not ask your question?'

'I don't want you to think I'd chain or trap you again.' Coryn lifted his hands, arms wider, trying to convey the truth of what he said. 'I want you to know you're free before I'd ask anything of you.'

Her smile was glorious and she chuckled deep in her throat again. A sound that made him catch his breath. 'Then come, pretty man.' Her voice was warm like a smouldering fire, a slow burn of logs in a cosy hearth. She lay on the sarcophagus with a sigh, arched her back and tilted her head to expose the length of her neck. Her half-closed eyes sparked with erratic emerald flames.

He moved forward, careful, watching her the whole way. She didn't move. Each step crunched through bone and sent fine ash to drift in the still air. Then Coryn was within touching distance. The heat rolled from her but still it didn't burn him. He studied her neck. The collar was all one piece with the first link of the chain. How could it open? Here, so close to her, he was surprised at how slender the black iron was. Would it break?

Coryn raised his hand, hesitated. The blood-magik's spikes multiplied, almost as if it knew his intent, trying to repel him. Was it sentient in some way? That thought worried him. He could sense now how it held and twisted the Wefan using both stolen Wealdan and blood-magik. The whole melded together with pain and terror, making of the iron something that wasn't meant to be – a foul poisoned trap for this spirit.

'I am ready.' The words sighed from the ifrit's lips. 'I am done with this tedious existence. Long centuries have already passed into nothingness. Aeons more lie ahead into enervating eternity. I would end it one way or another. Are you ready, pretty man?'

'I'm ready.' Coryn took the amulet Birog had given him from its pouch and studied as if he'd never seen it before. It seemed such a simple stone, holed like every other warding amulet he'd ever seen, the only difference the tiny crack leading out from that hole, within which a sliver of crystal glinted.

'An unusual amulet you have there, pretty man.'

'What do you mean? It's just a normal protective amulet is all, nothing unusual about that.' Coryn looked up at her, then back at his amulet.

'I have seen many, very many amulets in this prison, and not one of them protected their bearers from me.' The ifrit leaned forward, staring at Coryn, then at his amulet.

'This one is special, made for me by a woman with the Wealdan. A Lehotan.' Again Coryn thought of Birog, standing in front of that monolith, the babe swaddled against her chest, his sister Lera clutching onto her back. He saw her stepping through that stone and how the lacert hadn't been able to, how she'd closed the opening against the lacert and the blood-priest. The strength of her Wealdan must've been vast.

'True. I sense no webbing of spirit energy within it like all the others. Only the matrices of a Wealdan-weaving, strengthened at its heart by a sliver of a focus-crystal. Interesting.'

'The important thing is it works.' Coryn closed his fist tight around it.

'Yes, that would be most important, pretty man. But it does not work in quite the way you believe.' She laughed in that deep, throaty way, but there was a catch in it. A shiver of uncertainty, he thought.

He shook his head, almost too distracted. 'Got to get to it.'

'I await you, pretty man.' The ifrit lay back and stretched out her neck again.

The amulet gave him the strength he needed, a certainty of protection. The woman may never have come to find him or freed him from years of slavery, but she'd saved Lera from slavery and given him this one thing of value. He'd felt magik many times over his life as a slave and a freed man, each time he'd been able to repulse it, and it was all down to this small stone with its tiny crystal splinter. It had kept him safe and alive. It wouldn't fail him now. He hoped.

Spirits, give me strength.

He held the amulet tight and looked into the ifrit's eyes. He saw a momentary flash of fear in them. The same fear seared through him.

'My name is Subrahima ibn Rashinabel.' The ifrit's voice was a whisper.

'I thank you for the gift of your name.' Coryn was surprised. She'd given him power over her telling him her name. No light undertaking for a spirit from any land. 'I'm Coryn aef Arlean.'

Subrahima smiled at him. He gave her a fierce grin and grasped hold of the collar before he lost his nerve.

Rust spat from the pitted iron and red-tinged black lightening lashed out. Writhing ropes of agony laced up his arm and burrowed into his skin. He pushed at them, willing them away with all his strength. Subrahima's screams merged with his, then an almighty explosion hammered through his body and into his brain.

Coryn blacked out.

'Coryn aef Arlean, wake up.' Her voice sent exquisite tingles along his nerves and he opened his eyes. Subrahima leaned over him. Her light had dulled, a few flames flickered over her tawny skin and a vast pain lurked in her darkened eyes, now the colour of old jade. Past the ragged edges of her burnt hair he could see the triangular door.

'What?' he muttered. His hand burned and he flexed his fingers to make sure he could. The ifrit's finger hovered over his cheek, but she did not touch him, he felt the tingle of her magik, so different from either the Wealdan or blood-magik. More like the touch of the tiniest sparks from wood popping on a fire, or the prickle of a downy thistle against his skin. Pure spirit magik.

'I ask again, pretty human.' Subrahima drew her hand back. 'What is it that you wish of me?'

Chapter 25

The effect worked as Coryn had hoped. It seemed ifrits terrified writhen, and Subrahima was magnificent. She swooped down on the writhen again and again using their unreasoning fear against them. Though weakened by the blood-magik's backlash and centuries of imprisonment in the dark, she laughed with the sheer freedom and thrill of the hunt. He watched her chase them all away from the carts, but she was unable to do much more than scorch the slower ones. The writhen screeched in pain as sparks caught in their furs, turning to devouring flames in moments. They panicked, crashed into each other and got nowhere fast.

A fierce grin on his face, Coryn shouldered his bow and moved his horse out in a slow canter down into the gorge. The pain in his leg hadn't eased and the wound began to bleed again. The deep burns under the rough bandaging on his hand throbbed, but he felt exultant. He stopped midway down the slope where an iron-tree thicket gave him some cover and watched the ifrit chase the last of the writhen from the gorge.

Subrahima flew over the banks of the dry riverbed, following the panicked writhen toward the far cliff. As the writhen disappeared around the sharp bend, the ifrit turned and soared straight up the cliff face. She flew high above the cart, next to where a pillar of rock jutted up above the gorge. Exhausted, she didn't quite make it, but clipped a stack of rocks and spun over an overhang. There was a pop of displaced air and Coryn knew she'd gone.

He hit the open stretch between the thicket and the cart at a dead gallop, allowing his horse to find its own path through the rocks and up the slope from the trail. The horse surged its hooves churning sand and grit, charging for a gap between the cart and the cliff.

'I'm a friend, don't loose,' he yelled as his horse leaped over the wagon wheel. Then he was safe behind the cart and the piled leavings of the rock fall. Flinging himself off the horse, he sprawled on his belly breathing hard. He crawled over to the gap, levered himself up by the rock fall, whipped his bow off his shoulder and had an arrow nocked and ready in moments. He thought it unlikely he'd see any writhen for a while, but he'd be ready for them anyway.

Out of the side of one eye, he saw what appeared to be a shadow move behind the cart. Coryn turned his head and looked. Though he'd half expected it, he was still stunned.

Spirits take me. Another Lehotan Adherent.

Little, old and worn-looking, the woman knelt. She held a large crystal attached to a fine gold chain circling her neck, much like Birog's. But this crystal glowed with soft golden light. Her eyes stayed fixed on the gap between the cart and the cliff through the spokes of the wheel. Her deep grey robe, with a full sun motif embroidered on the bodice, was red with dust. A sturdy re-curve crossbow, sinew slack, was in her other hand. Next to her lay a quiver, still half full of heavy quarrels. He scanned the shallow gully but there was no one else. His horse had already found something to eat and had its nose deep in a scraggy white sage bush.

'Are you all right?' But the old woman didn't answer and Coryn looked back out into the gorge. 'You need to get ready. We're going to have to get out of here, now.'

A moment later the pain hit and he slid down to the ground and sat with his back against a rock. He gritted his teeth against the moan, his hand burned and he dropped both arrow and bow.

The old woman crawled over to kneel beside him. The paleness of her wrinkled face, reddened with patches of sunburn, told him she'd spent a deal of her life indoors. Meditating and reading in a Lehotan Haven, he'd guess. Her braided pale grey hair coiled round her head like a crown.

Coryn looked over the rocks. The gorge still looked empty.

Though Subrahima had disappeared, the writhen hadn't got the courage to return. In the bright sunlight the gorge was quiet but for insects and the riverbed and trail remained empty. If Coryn moved now, he'd be able to get the old woman on the horse, get the magiker to follow, and head north-west. If the old woman was the magiker too it would simplify things. They could get to one of the better-used trails and reach Roesette in three or four days, depending on the going.

As Coryn got to his feet, the blood-priest stepped out from behind the bend and strode down to the riverbed. Showing no sign of his wound, the blood-priest wore the usual deep red tunic and trousers under his long black cloak. He stood a good foot and a half taller than the twisted writhen he herded with a heavy staff almost as tall as himself. The staff's iron-shod haft crackled with blood-magik every time it thumped into the ground and leaked oily red-black smoke from its entire length that whipped out at intervals to lash the writhen. The writhen screeched at every stroke.

Even at a hundred yards, Coryn could feel the blood-priest's rage.

Coryn rose to stand against the cart's duckboard, nocked an arrow, drew and...

'No.'

...the arrow flew, feathering the blood-priest's chest, a little lower than before. Coryn glanced at the old woman, surprised and angry. She gazed at him with intense blue eyes, her thin, fine features bore a strange look of calm authority.

Uncomfortable, he turned back to the gorge. The priest had disappeared, but again Coryn was sure he hadn't killed him. Blood-priests were damned difficult to kill. The writhen now hovered around the rocks on the slope down along riverbed, wary and alert. It'd be more difficult to get out now.

'Bloody bastard,' he whispered. Killing the priest would've sent the writhen running never to return. He picked a writhen at random and dropped him with an arrow straight into its throat. Coryn heard the old woman suck in her breath, but he kept his eyes on the writhen as they all scurried for cover, looking more to the sky than the cart.

Neither of them spoke for a while. The old woman watched him and Coryn watched the rocks and riverbed. He felt her eyes on him and his voice came low and harsh. 'We can't get out of here without killing some of them. Not with a Murecken blood-priest controlling them.'

There was a hiss of indrawn breath. 'That was a Murecken blood-priest? How do you know this?'

'Seen them before. And yesterday morning I found another cart, like this one, and a man around my age, a Lehotan like you, with Murecken blood-runes cut into his skin. Blood-priests need to keep their victims alive all the way through the rite, right till just about the last drop of blood is drained from their bodies. He'd have taken a while to die if not for the arrow to his throat. The Rialtan boy was tortured by these writhen and probably still alive when they began eating him, but he'd have died a lot faster than the Lehotan. Do you want that for yourself. Being a magiker, you'd get the slow ritual.'

Brutal words, Coryn knew, but the old woman had to understand the truth of her situation.

'Magiker? I am no magiker.'

'I know when magik's been used. And you've used it. Call it what you like, the Wealdan, Light of Lehot, blood-magik of Murak, fire of Atash, even Daru's gift to the Derin of farseeing, it's all magiking.' He looked at her and realised this little, old woman had both fired the crossbow and created the flames. 'Look, the blood-priest's controlling those writhen with his blood-magik, powered by a Wealdan-bearer's blood.'

'A blood-priest from Mureck. So far west of the Ruel Mountains.' The old woman looked at him and Coryn saw sadness fill her eyes. She looked away. 'This is hard to believe.'

'What do you think they're doing here?' Coryn ground on. 'They're spying out the western lands, they'll be coming down from the mountains to invade the cities in the Shafi Desert soon enough. Or buying them with their red gold, more like.'

'But why do they invade?'

'You tell me.'

She looked at Coryn a long time before replying, then nodded. 'Some say they now use the Ascian in the old way, as they did centuries ago when Baelur Macule ruled all the lands east and west of the Ruel Mountains. Some say they never stopped down in the bowels of Elucame, their ancient city. We heard rumours some time ago that they raised a descendent of Macule to be their new Priest-king. A man intent on renewing the power of their god, Murak, and spreading their religion across the lands they ruled long ago. But many say it is just rumour. '

'Have those people not heard about the war on the other side of the Ruel Mountains?' Coryn shook his head. 'They been living under rocks?'

The old woman looked at him for a long while. 'Perhaps. Perhaps they just fear the truth. We have been studying the Murecken recently, due to their incursions against Kalebrod and Rophet. I know for instance, that for their Ascian, their blood-magik, they need blood with potency, as you say. These blood-priests seek such blood and those, such as I, who have the Wealdan are their favourite prey, this I know too.'

'Like I said, and exactly what that blood-priest out there's doing.

His power is all the stronger for the blood he's just drained. Last night I killed a woman in their camp. They'd hung her up over a bowl to catch her blood and the blood-priest was cutting her like he'd cut your other Lehotan friend, the man. And the more Wealdan those two had in their blood, the more powerful his blood-magik will be. He'll be all the harder to damned well kill.' Coryn stared at her again, trying to push the message home. 'I feathered him in their camp and I've feathered him again just now. But tell me, where is he now? He isn't lying out there dead like he ought to be.'

'Even so, I am sure that Lehot did not send you to kill.' Her voice sounded firm, but Coryn heard some hesitance. A tremor. He had got to her, he was sure of it.

'Lehot? What's Lehot to me? Anyhow, no god sent me, I just came.' Coryn squinted against the bright sunlight and scanned the gorge. 'And if we don't kill some of them, especially that damned blood-priest, they'll kill us, sure as the sun burns.'

'Lehot sent you.' Her tone was matter of fact. 'Even though a demon aided you, Lehot called and you answered.'

Spirits, a devout Lehotan, that's all I need.

That at least explained why the shots from the crossbow had never done any damage, even though she had the Wealdan.

'She's no demon. She's an ifrit, one of the desert spirits.' Coryn shook his head. That was the problem with people who worshipped gods, they got all irrational about spirits. 'Without her I'd never have reached you. She's less demon than that damned blood-priest.'

The old woman looked at Coryn for a moment then nodded. 'Do you have water?' she asked, tucking her crystal under the neckline of her loose robe.

'In the waterskins.' He nodded to his horse. 'Fresh meat too, but don't drink too much as we're going to be running hard. I'll send the horse out first, it'll follow the river bed and draw the writhen, then we'll go the other way.'

'The others cannot run.' The old woman went to the horse and untied one of the waterskins.

Her words crashed down on Coryn. He looked hard at the old woman as she swung the waterskin over her shoulder.

'Others?'

She turned without answering and hurried towards the cliff, disappearing where the gully narrowed to a fold in the rockface. Coryn loaded the re-curve crossbow, using the ratchet to pull the waxed hemp-string back. It was much more powerful than his bow but too heavy for horseback use. He spotted the head of a writhen, its earflaps studded with iron rings, standing proud of some rocks down-slope of him. He aimed a little high. The big quarrel sent rock fragments flying and the head whipped back with the satisfying sound of a death screech. A chorus of croaks, howls and hisses followed.

Deciding the threat would hold them for a while, Coryn sidled to the fold in the rock. He found a cleft in the mountain just wide enough to let him through. Beyond, it was almost pitch dark and silent.

'Who's in there?' Coryn called.

There was no answer. After waiting a few moments, he squeezed through the crevice. Coryn was relieved when after a few yards he began to hear voices ahead. Then he was in a narrow chamber maybe ten by two yards wide. High above, faint light filtered in through the tapering cleft and some scrubby leatherleaf. A fat candle burned on top of a shelf of rock near the back, its light dancing with the shadows against the walls revealing many shapes in the room.

'Who's in here?' It was cool and Coryn breathed great lungfuls of air.

'I, Adherents Katleya and Maisie, and the children.' The old woman's voice came out from somewhere in the blackness.

'Children? How many?'

'Five.'

Coryn slid down the wall with a thump. He stayed there without saying anything for a while, his energy drained. He listened to the grateful sounds of children drinking. From the small animal-like noises they made they'd needed water for a while.

'Don't give them too much at first.' His face set, Coryn rose and sidled back out to the gully to sort things out in his mind.

After the cool shadows of the cleft, Coryn found the air outside hard to breathe. The sun laboured towards noon and blazed into the gorge. After taking the saddle off his horse and rubbing it down, he poured some water into his cooking pot and let it drink. Coryn sat down against the wall of the cliff under a scrubby acacia where he could see through the gaps on both sides of the cart, and reloaded the crossbow. The horse nibbled at some tough yellow grass growing close to the fold in the cliff where an overhang shaded a splinter of sandy ground. Sweat ran into Coryn's eyes and he wound a broad strip of cloth round his head in the Shafian way.

He had come back here to save one woman and one magiker, assuming they'd be the sole survivors. He'd been relieved finding the lone woman, thinking her the magiker. Now what in all Murak's flaming hells was he going to do with three women and five children? He'd never get all eight of them out of this hemmed in bit of dust without the writhen knowing. And if he somehow did, they'd be discovered on the trail for sure, with the children crying and clattering, falling down and unable to keep up.

Coryn laid the heavy crossbow down and picked up his bow. He ran an oiled rag over the wood, his eyes scanning the shortening shadows beyond the carts as he worked. His wound seemed in no hurry to mend and ached like misery. He didn't even want to think about his hand. He shook his head to clear it and let his mind run over the facts for a while, thinking up various escape scenarios. He shook his head again. Whichever way he looked at it, he couldn't see any way of getting out of this trap with all of them.

Coryn hated feeling cornered. He rubbed a hand along the ridges round his neck and closed his eyes for a moment. He'd lived trapped for most of his life and here he was again. Trapped.

Chapter 26

He'd gambled and it'd gone wrong. Coryn could almost hear Ma's voice warning him against crawling too far along an untested branch, his father telling him to check each handhold before trusting his weight to it when climbing cliffs. Worked out he'd not done either this time. He pressed his hand to his amulet, felt its hard shape push against his chest and wished it could head him in the right direction.

Coryn pulled the leather cord from his hair, ran his hands through the tangles, listened for the sound of his parents in his memory. He heard nothing but the wind. They remained, as always, shadowy presences in his thoughts. Still, he half remembered a few things and he felt they'd have approved of what he'd done. Da would've come for the old woman. He might have done things differently, but he'd have come. He tied his hair again.

Coryn heard a noise to his right and whirled, bringing the crossbow up cocked and levelled at the old woman's head. She stared at him for a moment then put the emptied water skin down by his saddle and packs.

'That is what weapons do.' Her words hung in the air for a while.

'What?' Coryn turned back to scanning the rocks and the riverbed. 'What do weapons do?'

'They make you afraid.' She stood up, took hold of a second water skin and walked over to him. 'I am Dame Mureen. A Lehotan High-adherent trained in the art of herb and Wealdan-healing. I see you are wounded, Sire. I will tend to you. Be assured, my ability with healing far outstrips that of making flames.'

He looked up at her again. What was the crazy old woman doing? 'Keep down or you'll be dead. The blood-priest controls the writhen still, he'll push them and they'll try for another attack. Fear of the ifrit and the crossbow won't stop them forever.'

'Perhaps.' She knelt, easing a large leather satchel from her shoulder. 'I know I shall die when Lehot has ordained that it is time for me to die.'

'They've just been waiting. They could've taken you by now.'

'Have they? Could they?'

'They don't want you dead, just weak enough for them to walk in and take you alive.' Coryn flicked a look at the old woman then went back to staring out to the gorge. 'The writhen have been taunting you, waiting till you're all too weak to fight back. Like I said, the Murecken blood-priest wants you alive to get the Wealdan from your blood.'

'Yes, I see that now. It makes sense,' she said after a pause. 'Now let us start with your leg.'

'It's fine. It's just a hole. You don't know much about Murak, the Murecken or their blood-magik do you?'

'It seems not, not as they are now. Let me see your leg, please.' She put the satchel down on the sand, undid the straps and unfolded it revealing pockets of various sizes filled with packets, bottles and pots. 'I will then tend to your hand and your shoulder.'

Coryn stared out at the gorge through the gaps between the cart and the cliff walls. The wind rose, moaning through holes in the rocks, sounding like distant horns. A mournful song. Spirals of sand danced to the dirge. Dame Mureen gathered some small sticks into a pile. She touched a hand to the crystal hanging from her neck, it glowed gold as she made a gesture, and the kindling burst into flame. She put some larger sticks on the fire.

'Those quarrels you shot. You did that to them too.' Coryn watched the flames.

'Indeed. What little Wealdan Lehot granted me I use when I must in the ways that I can.' Dame Mureen placed a shallow bowl over the flames and poured a little water into it, then a crushed leaf from one pouch and powder from another. 'Now, from the amount of blood I can see on that bandage, it is more than just a hole. The children will need you healthy and strong, that way you can help them with some hope of a successful outcome.'

Coryn realised Dame Mureen wasn't going to leave him alone till she was done. He stretched his leg out. The wound was oozing again. She took a small clamp with a long handle from her satchel and used it to take the bowl off the flames, then added some more water to the liquid and stirred. Pouring some into a silver cup, she held it out to him.

'Here, drink this.'

He took the cup and sniffed at it.

'Meadowsweet, for the pain.'

He sipped a little. He remembered his mother making this and drank some more. The bitter juices flooded over his tongue. Moments later his head swam a little. He looked up at Dame Mureen and raised a brow. She frowned, impatient, so he drank the rest down.

'It also contains comfrey to knit bone breaks and fractures, feverfew to keep fever at bay and valerian to help you sleep,' she said when he was done.

'Sleep? I can't sleep now!'

Ignoring him, she unwrapped the cloth on his hand and inspected it. 'It is fortunate this is a clean burn and fresh. I think it will be best to deal with this first then the leg.' Dame Mureen paused as Coryn winced when she pulled his hand forward

Dame Mureen laid her hands over his burned one, one on each side, then bent her head low. Coryn felt his skin prickle. He felt the fire and ice of Wealdan in his flesh and pushed it away. The old woman yelped and fell back on her rump. Guilty, Coryn looked at her.

'Are you all right?'

'I...yes.' Dame Mureen stared at him for some moments, then shook herself and knelt by him again. 'It seems you have the...most unusual ability to block, or repulse, the Wealdan. I must admit, I have only ever read of such an ability in some of Ostorr Haven's most ancient records. Yet, you still need healing.' She lifted her hands again, a determined look on her face.

'Wait.' Coryn lifted his hand to his pouch. He looked into the old woman's eyes, tried to read them. He sensed nothing but good. It was still hard to take the pouch from his neck, hard to put it down on the sand and hard to let it go. Dame Mureen looked at him but said nothing. He nodded, ready. 'Now.'

Coryn cried out again as the Wealdan froze and flamed through his flesh. But he was prepared this time and he held onto his will, not even thinking of pushing the magik away. Not that he could without the amulet. The pain disappeared as fast as it came.

'I have done what I can but the flesh is delicate and must be poulticed.' Her gaze did not waver. 'Or, the skin might split and become infected.'

Coryn leaned against the cliff as he watched Dame Mureen fold a large square of cloth in half, filled it with a selection of herbs and powders, wet them with the boiled water, then wrapped it round his hand. 'There, I believe that within a few hours you will feel this hand to be almost as good as new.'

'I doubt it,' Coryn growled. 'I feel awful.'

'I am afraid that is to be expected. Wealdan-healing uses the energy that resides in the patient's own body as well as the Wealdan-bearer's. Now, let me deal with your leg.'

'Your leg looks like it has had time to fester. It will be much harder to heal and it will take more from you also. Prepare yourself.' She smiled at him and laid a gentle hand on his shoulder. 'Be assured that you will feel much better in the morning.'

She unwound the filthy bandages and, taking a pair of small shears from her satchel, she cut a wide slit in his linen trousers. The arrow had hit bone and though he'd broken the shaft and pulled it out, the wound was swollen, ugly and dirty. He hadn't managed to clean it well over the last tenday, or often enough, and the raised skin around it looked dirty and purpled. Coryn watched the Dame Mureen's thin, delicate hands as she worked. Though old and mottled with liver spots, they stayed steady. She'd dealt with such wounds before.

'What is your plan?' She kept her eyes down, cleaning the hole with more of the boiled water cooled to a bearable heat.

Coryn sat staring at the wound and her dexterous fingers. 'I don't know.' Would he have come, if he'd known about the other women and the children?

Dame Mureen looked up at his face. 'You would have.'

Coryn jumped. 'What?'

'You were thinking you would not have helped if you had known there were so many of us.' She waited a second, still staring into his face. 'You still would have.' Her voice was matter-of-fact.

He looked into her eyes, surprised she'd guessed his thoughts. 'Another gift from Lehot?'

'All gifts are from Lehot.' She smiled. 'Do not fear, I did not read your mind, it is your face that is an easy study.'

Hooding his eyes, he shrugged. He'd always had few choices in his life. Slaves didn't have any as a rule. But he'd more choices this last year or so and nothing could take that from him, let alone an old woman and her god. Coryn pulled his eyes away from hers and shook his head, squinting back into the brilliant sunlight bouncing off the gorge walls beyond the cart. Sweat ran down his neck, prickling its way down his back and chest.

'It's unusual. Such a small caravan travelling through these mountains so light on guards.'

'Is that so?' The old woman's voice was flat.

'Yes. Every caravan I've ever ridden with was at least three times bigger, and I've travelled with many.' Coryn snapped a look at Dame Mureen, then looked back over the gorge. 'Why just the two carts, and where are all the guards?'

'I do not know. The Rialtan merchant seemed sure all would be well as did the Shafian guards. I assume they did not expect the writhen or a blood-priest. I have never seen writhen or a follower of Murak before now.'

'How many guards did you have?'

'Two Shafian desert men, twin brothers. They were quite charming. They helped Dame Alaya escape.' Dame Mureen paused to rub her eyes. 'I presume that they too are now dead.'

'Looks like they charmed you all well and good.' Coryn cleared his throat and made to spit. With a glance to Dame Mureen, he thought better of it.

'What is that supposed to mean?'

'They're alive and well not far from here. I saw one of them come for water and followed him to the place where they're holding the camels. I'm thinking their pouches are heavy with Murecken gold too.' Coryn paused as Dame Mureen stared at him. 'Murak's priesthood is rich, the mountains around Mureck are thick with gold and silver. They can afford to buy information and people.'

There was a long silence as Dame Mureen looked down at her hands cleaning his wound.

'I see. That is unexpected and it saddens me.' She stopped working for a moment and looked into his eyes again. 'This will hurt. Before I start, I want to thank you for saving the children. They were close to death.'

'How long have they been without water?'

'Almost two days.' Dame Mureen kept her eyes on his. 'However, the shortage of water was not the whole problem. It was the fear.'

Coryn didn't quite understand. 'So what's changed?'

'They know Lehot sent you to save them. They have hope.'

The words slapped into him. Dame Mureen placed her hands around the edges of the wound and Coryn saw a momentary sparkle of pinprick lights.

'Do I have your permission to continue?'

'Yes, but listen, Dame...' Coryn started to say, before the pain slammed into him and he fell unconscious.

Chapter 27

The last light of the sun leeched from the sky when Coryn woke. The ache in his leg was awful and lethargy dragged at his mind and body. Bandages, made from some ripped clothing, bound his thigh. When he could get his eyes to focus, he saw a young woman's heart-shaped face peering at him. He gaped.

She had the ifrit's eyes. He stared into them. No, they were a softer green. More like the new leaves of spring in Kalebrod with a gentle sun shining through them. She knelt in front of him and looked concerned but wary. He guessed her to be around sixteen or seventeen. Dark with sweat, the curls of her hair struggled to escape a scarf.

'Hello, I'm Adherent Katleya. Would you like some water?' He shook his head. She turned and called. 'Dame Mureen, he's awake.'

Dame Mureen came over. 'Good. Lehot would never have forgiven me if you had died.' Her eyes laughed and she smiled.

'Why do I feel so damned awful?' Coryn fought back a moan.

'Wealdan-healing results in weakness, the extent of which depends on the healing done.' Dame Mureen waited but, when Coryn just looked at her, she went on. 'As I have said, my Wealdan allows me to begin and spur your own healing process to a far greater speed than is normal. However, much of the energy, the Wefan, within your own body is used to facilitate that healing, not only that which is funnelled into your body by the Wealdan-healer. This drains you and will continue to do so until your wounds fully heal. There is always a price for what Lehot grants us.' Resting a hand against his forehead, she nodded. She looked haggard herself. Seemed using the Wealdan drained Dame Mureen as much as it had him. 'The leg wound was filled with dirt. Poisons infected the flesh and the bolt's head grazed the bone. Of your wounds, it was the harder to work on and would have drained you the most.' She walked back towards a small campfire of burning sticks in the centre of the gully. 'You are healing well and will soon regain your strength.'

Coryn watched the flickering light of the campfire for a while, thinking about what Dame Mureen had said, before he realised what bothered him.

'For spirits sake, put that fire out!' he yelled rolling towards the fire pit.

The two women caught him by the shoulders stopping him with more ease than he liked. He hated feeling so weak.

'Do not struggle like that.' Dame Mureen knelt and looked into his eyes. 'You will hurt yourself and slow the healing. And you will scare the children.'

'Scare the children, by all of Murak's flaming hells.' His voice was rising. 'You're going to get yourself and them killed with that fire.'

'I insist you do not swear in front of the children.' Dame Mureen rose and turned back to the fire. 'They have to eat as do you. As soon as the meal is finished, I will put the fire out. Thank you for your concern.'

Coryn couldn't believe it. Had the heat worked on the old woman's mind and broken it? That would explain a great deal. Adherent Katleya still supported him. As he started to pull away, pain tore through his leg and he caught himself with a grunt.

'Are you all right?' Adherent Katleya's face creased with concern. She frowned as he shook her off.

'I'm fine,' he mumbled crawling back to the cliff wall.

It took Coryn a while to regain his bearings. Adherent Katleya continued to watch him till he returned her stare. She bit her lip and turned away shaking her head. He picked up the crossbow, ignoring the way his hands shook, and scanned the grey contours of the gorge. His leg drove him mad with pain and he felt tired beyond belief, but he forced himself to think on the writhen as he peered past the cart.

Coryn couldn't see anything out of the ordinary but it didn't mean anything, not with his eyes fire-blinded and the gloom filling the gorge. Writhen might have spawned over generations in the cold mountains of Ruel, but he'd guess they'd be as dangerous down here in the desert. Creeping up in the dark, lying in ambush behind rock or shrub, waiting for the signs those they'd trapped behind the carts had become weak enough to take.

The sounds of cooking distracted him. The smell of roasting antelope wafted over and his mouth watered. It surprised him to realise just how ravenous he felt.

Coryn heard scuffling noises behind him. He turned to see the children crawl out of the cleft, one after the other. Katleya sat them down where they could lean against the cliff near the fire. Painted by the firelight, they looked small, hunched and forlorn. There was a larger shadow at the end of the line. He watched it till he realised it was the third Adherent, a woman a few years older than Adherent Katleya. She had a rounder face and reddish hair.

'Ah, Adherent Maisie, children, there you are.' Dame Mureen smiled and her teeth flashed in the firelight. 'Is it not wonderful to be out in the fresh air?' Her voice was light as if they were on an outing. 'Children, I would like you to meet the man who has come to take you out of here.'

Coryn shot her an angry glance but she wasn't looking at him.

'I am sorry.' She leaned over a large pot and stirred the stew. 'But I am afraid I do not know your name, Sire.'

Coryn waited a few moments. 'Coryn.' He turned his head back towards the gorge and the desert sounds. 'Coryn aef Arlean.'

'Coryn aef Arlean.' Dame Mureen sounded happy. 'A good, strong name. Children come and say hello to Sire Coryn. Sica, you first.'

'Hello, Sire Coryn.'

Coryn watched the shadowed gorge a while longer but the innocence of the voice tugged at him and he turned. What he saw in the flickering firelight disturbed him. Sica was small, maybe nine summers old. Thin and dirty, she wore nothing but a ragged dress. Her dark hair fell in two plaits to her waist.

'Hello, Sica.' He glanced over at Dame Mureen. She smiled encouragement.

A gangly girl neared. No more than thirteen summers, the age his sister Lera would be around now. Under the dirt, she even had the same honey coloured curls. She wore a filthy linen dress, it stretched over a belly swollen with child.

'Tell Sire Coryn your name,' Dame Mureen said, but the girl didn't speak.

Awkward, she stood half holding, half covering her stomach with both hands. Her eyes stayed on the ground. Coryn felt anger simmer inside.

'That is fine, do not worry, my dear.' Dame Mureen came forward and placed a hand on her shoulder. 'Sire Coryn, we do not know this lovely child's name yet, but we have dubbed her Eilem until we do.'

'I'm Neima and this is Pella.' Two girls of anywhere between six and eight summers old, came to stand in the firelight. They gripped

183

hands, looking about them as if lost, their eyes wide and anxious. As dirty and ragged as the others, their starved condition made it hard to be sure of their ages. The last child wouldn't leave the cliff till Dame Mureen brought him forward.

'And this, Sire Coryn.' Dame Mureen had her arm around the boy's skinny shoulders, giving him a squeeze of pride. 'Is the man of our party, Wetham.'

The boy was in the worst shape of all of them. He was around the same age as Sica and rake thin. Just under his jaw-line, two slave brands marred his neck. Coryn recognised the slave marks as Dal Abarian, though it should have been a single one and lower, near the collar-bone. A sloppy job, and to be burned twice, that smacked of sadism.

'It's good to meet you, Wetham.'

Wetham stared at the ground, a great dark mop of hair half covering his face. He bit his lip and kicked at the sand. Adherent Katleya came up and took hold of one grubby hand and bent to give the boy a hug. Coryn glanced at her. Tall and slender, she'd taken off her scarf and her short hair was the rich, warm colour of hazelnuts under all the dust and sand. She looked down at him with those green eyes of hers and he realised he'd stared at her for far too long. He turned, scanning the sand and rocks beyond the cart again.

The Lehotan robe Adherent Katleya wore didn't quite hide the shape of her. Coryn shifted round some more, clearing his throat with a short cough, awkward and annoyed.

Damn. Why'd she make me think of the ifrit?

Dame Mureen gave the last child a plate of food then threw dirt on the fire. Stillness fell on the gully. Coryn listened to the desert and to children eating, amazed the writhen hadn't loosed some arrows or thrown a spear while the gully was full of people and firelight. But it was silent out there. The temperature began to drop and the moons had yet to climb high enough to fill the gorge with silver. Somewhere off in the distance an owl let out a soft hoot. Once, then twice more. A mountain wolf howled somewhere to the south.

In silence, Maisie brought him a plate of mixed beans with millet and big chunks of meat. She smiled at him and he forced himself to smile back. There was also a half cup of water. Coryn ate and thought about the children, the two Adherents and Dame Mureen. But his thoughts muddled together, his eyes blurred and before he'd finished eating he fell asleep.

Chapter 28

The cleft smelled of dried herbs and almost felt cool.

Thank the spirits!

Katleya flicked a quick glance at Dame Mureen. The old woman had taken her in and she wanted to be respectful of her beliefs, she really did. At least this Lehot seemed better than Atash. So far as she knew at this point anyway. She looked to the area of the cleft brushed by breezes funnelling through the entrance and up the tapering chimney. She'd had a look earlier, but it was far too narrow a crack for even little Pella to climb. The children slept on blankets, snuggled together like puppies on the soft, sandy floor.

For the first night since she'd known them, not one of them cried, shook in fear, or called out in their sleep. Katleya thanked the spirits for that too, or rather, Coryn and his water. The candle, stuck to a rock near the back wall of the cleft, flickered gold over the children's faces and softened their gauntness. They looked peaceful, as if they weren't scared or even worried, at least to anyone who didn't know them. She wished she wasn't scared.

Katleya scowled and got on with scrubbing the pan clean with sand. Her mind wandered back to Coryn. Sire Coryn, Dame Mureen called him. Did she think trying to make his name sound noble, he'd come over all noble? At over six feet, slim but well muscled, with dark-blonde hair and sky-blue eyes, he looked the part. A fine looking man. No doubt about it, a fine...

What's the matter with me?

She snorted in disgust and rubbed harder at the pan.

Maisie sat cross-legged nearby sewing a pair of trousers for Wetham out of an old cloak she'd cut up. A second candle burned next to her. She paused and gazed at the children, her eyes filled with love. 'Was he not wonderful to come? He is a true and good man, a man of Lehot, to risk his life for theirs in such manner.' She turned to Katleya, her brown eyes serious and earnest. 'Do you think he might be of noble blood?'

'Being *noble* hasn't anything much to do with being *a noble*. And, believe me, I really do know what I'm talking about.' Katleya dumped the sand out of the pan and reached for a plate, avoiding Maisie's astonished look. She rolled her eyes at the plate and wondered how the girl could be so naïve. 'I'm sorry, but I don't know if he's a good man, he's not a man of Lehot though. He's wearing a pouch, it'll have an amulet in it and that makes him a believer in the spirits. He swears by them often enough too, I've heard him. Most of the people from Kalebrod believe in the spirits rather than any gods. Used to be most people in Rophet did too before Atash came along.' She supposed the Kalebrodians would now be made to bow to Murak and the Murecken Priest-king, those who'd survived anyway. She wondered if it'd be better to be dead.

Katleya had been amazed on discovering the burned out barge and Dame Mureen arguing with another barge captain and getting him to ferry them all across the river if he insisted on refusing to carry them downriver. A Lehotan, with a bunch of other Lehotans, all from Storr and Ostorr Haven, the very place she'd been heading for. She'd thought her luck had finally turned. Yet another big mistake on her part.

Dame Alaya and Dame Mureen had tested her as soon as they dis-covered she could see the Wefan. They'd said she had great potency and would learn to do great things with the Wealdan and she'd felt wonderful, a dream finally looked like coming true for her. If only, she'd thought, Uncle Yadoc could be there too. But the dream had turned into a blasted nightmare just a tenday or so later. From the forge flames straight onto the anvil for a hammering, as Uncle Yadoc had liked to say.

Nearly every day Dame Mureen told Katleya not to use her Wealdan again. Not till they reached Ostorr Haven. Like Uncle Yadoc, the old woman insisted she needed to be taught to use it and to be patient till then. Besides, she'd said, one person using the Wealdan is dangerous enough out in the wilds.

Blast it! I just want to learn how to use it!

She had to be patient, that was all. But patience just wasn't her strong point. And right now flames would be blasted useful against the writhen. And she'd bet those light globes Dame Alaya could create, could be thrown. And Thoma's little fire-balls could've proved useful too.

Hah, they'd create havoc amongst the writhen.

Katleya sighed, Dame Mureen was right. With no moving water to hide it, actually drawing on the Wefan was dangerous, it'd be sensed by those with the ability who'd likely be after her blood within moments. Writhen meant blood-priests, like smoke meant fire.

Spirits though! To heal, to cure someone, that'd be something blasted special.

She'd sneaked out and caught Dame Mureen working on Coryn. She'd used her Wealdan-sight to watch the old woman manipulate the Wefan in his body, just as she'd watched Laru all those months ago. She'd seen Dame Mureen mend and make the energy flow along the right paths again so his body could heal his wounds. She'd realised then that Laru was stronger in the Wealdan. That'd been something to think about. She'd told Dame Mureen about Laru, and that'd got the old woman excited. Said she'd send word as soon as she could and maybe they'd send a group of Lehotans over to Rophet to find her and any others that might have the Wealdan. It'd be good to save them from Atash's priesthood.

'We don't know why he came,' she muttered.

'He came to save these children.' Maisie's voice stayed soft but now there was a worried edge to them. She didn't stop stitching, but let out a heavy sigh. 'Why else would he have come to us, past all those horrible creatures?'

'I don't honestly know. He's been a soldier, or a hired guard, maybe even a mercenary. A man who'd sell his sword to anyone for a price, is a man who can't be trusted.' Katleya had known men like that, all three types in fact. Had avoided them every day in Black Rock. Had to, to blasted well survive. It'd take time to forget what she'd learned to survive on the streets. Fighting for scraps, stealing for food and medicine, kicking a man in the forks because he didn't like the word no. It'd taught her to have faith in no one, to know she'd only herself to trust in.

She looked over at Dame Mureen again. The old woman sat in the deeper shadows of the cleft, propped against the red stone wall with her eyes closed. It was her way of trying to hide her exhaustion and fear. Katleya knew she could trust Dame Mureen. 'It's what I think, for what it's worth.'

'Oh.' Maisie covered her mouth with a hand. 'Oh dear.'

'I'm sorry, Maisie.' Katleya softened her voice. 'But I've learned the hard way, there are a lot of people out there who aren't anything like they seem.'

'I suppose it is true you would know of such things. You have known more of that side of life than I.' Maisie put her hand on Katleya's shoulder, patted it. 'And I am sorry for it, for your sake.'

Katleya grunted. What could she say to something like that? Life would've been a deal easier if she could've read people's minds like she could the Wefan, but at least she could read Maisie like a book. She imagined anyone could as Maisie hadn't a false bone in her body.

'Dame Mureen says he's killed a lot of men, not just writhen. I'm sorry Maisie, but I wouldn't rely on him staying to save anyone. I don't think he realised there were so many of us. I doubt he'd have come if he'd known. It'd be easy enough to save one or two of us, but eight? And five of them these poor, sick children?' Frowning Katleya worked over the plate far longer than it took to clean it.

Maisie didn't answer and Katleya looked up to see tears in her eyes. They shivered in the candlelight for a moment before she rubbed them away. Perhaps she'd said too much. She'd a tendency to blurt out the truth as she saw it without thinking. This time she was sorry. She gave Maisie's hand a squeeze.

'He joined us when he needn't have. He has come to save the children.' Dame Mureen's voice drifted from the shadows, gentle but firm. 'This he will do, I am sure of it in my heart. We must not question Lehot's gifts, Adherents.'

'Yes, Dame Mureen,' they replied together.

Katleya wanted to believe. To have faith in a god, like Dame Mureen and Maisie had in Lehot, would make life so much easier. But Uncle Yadoc taught her to distrust the religions of gods, specially their priesthoods. Since then, she'd seen a whole lot of terrible things done by priests for their gods. Both the blood-priests for Murak and the red priests for Atash. She scowled.

A horde of rats can piss on the blasted lot of them.

For Dame Mureen's sake, though, she'd respect Lehot. For now. 'I won't question it any more. Anyway, he's probably just the kind of man we need.'

'That is just what I was thinking.' Maisie smiled and gave Katleya's hand a squeeze. 'In all truth, he is the kind of man who might be able to save us.'

Katleya didn't answer. She didn't want to wait around to be saved. Never had, not since long before Uncle Yadoc died. Uncle Yadoc. It felt an age since he'd left her, even longer since she'd felt anything near as safe as when she was with him, before Black Rock at least. She'd not felt truly safe since they'd left home.

Spirits, I miss Laeft.

The cool mists on her face, the smell of green things growing, not itching head to toe with sand and dust or having thirst as a constant companion. She leaned back against the rock and closed her eyes, wallowing in the flood of memories.

Chapter 29

Both moons beamed into the gorge and the sky shimmered with stars by the time Coryn woke. Someone sat near him and he tensed. Realising it was Dame Mureen, he relaxed. Still, he moved his hand around till he felt the comforting solidity of his sword, his knife, his bow, one after the other. His hand and his leg felt better but the ache in his entire body was still bone deep. He lay quiet, peering through the spaces between the cart and the silver-gilded cliffs, probing the familiar sounds of the desert.

'The desert night is beautiful, is it not?' Dame Mureen's words flowed across the space between them.

Coryn pulled himself into a sitting position. He flicked his eyes to her then back to the gorge. 'Tell me about the children.'

'There is not much to tell, Sire Coryn.' Her face turned at the sound of the horse snorting in the darkness on the far side of the gully, her fine hair all silver strands of moonlight. 'We were travelling by barge from Rialt toward Dal Abar when we came into sight of another barge. Burned, holed and taking on water, it was close to sinking altogether. On board were ten children, all in terrible condition. They had a terrible story to tell. Pirates had taken their ship off the coast of Mureck and enslaved all who survived that boarding. Most of them were refugees fleeing Kalebrod and Rophet. They were taken to Dal Abar and sold to slavers. Ten of the children were then taken aboard the barge to be sold in Rialt.'

'I am from Kalebrod.'

'You are?'

'What happened to the slavers on the barge?'

'There was no sign of them and none of the children had any idea of what might have happened to them all. From what we could gather, first a fire raged on deck, then a sand storm hit the river.' Dame Mureen touched a hand to where her focus crystal lay. 'By the time we arrived, none of the slavers remained.'

'Slavers.' Coryn hawked and spat into the sand beside him. 'Let's hope they all drowned and now burn in Murak's flaming hells.'

'I would appreciate it if you did not spit in my presence.'

Coryn cleared his throat again, then swallowed, embarrassed.

After a short pause Dame Mureen went on. 'We knew we had to take them with us on our journey home. We could not take them back to Dal Abar however, as you can well imagine. Also the barge master would not take on the children. A superstitious man, he thought they were cursed, poor things. So, we decided to travel north over the Amalla Heights to Manom instead. The barge master did ferry us over to the north side of the river to a small farming village. We thought ourselves fortunate indeed to find a caravan there heading to Manom the very next day.'

'Fortunate?'

'It is unfortunate that my Wealdan does not extend to foretelling the future.' Dame Mureen sighed. 'Very few indeed are born with that gift.'

'So, why just these children?'

'One died during that same night of his injuries. Four more died as we journeyed to these mountains.' She took in a deep breath and let it out in a long sigh. 'The last one lost the struggle for life not long after we left the dunes behind. There was nothing I could do. Mistreatment, malnourishment, burns but most of all, loss of hope had weakened them beyond even my Wealdan-healing.'

Coryn studied Dame Mureen's face and saw a deep sadness there.

'Perhaps we should have turned back to Rialt, but the children needed to know they headed toward their families with all possible speed, away from the deserts that held only pain and slavery for them. They talked of cousins, of aunts and uncles who had long ago left the eastern countries and headed toward Losan, Albane or Faran and other countries within the Storratian Empire. One girl, Eilem, had hidden her condition under a cloak for days, poor, terrified child, never allowing any to touch her. Like Wetham, the only surviving boy, trauma has stilled her tongue.'

Coryn didn't speak for a while thinking about the children huddled back in the shadowed cleft. Then he thought of Maisie and Katleya sitting with them and felt better. He heard the crack of a rock fall against another out in the muggy air. A little later, another fell. Small sounds, neither was natural. He twisted his body and lifted the crossbow to his knee. He couldn't see any movement yet. He turned his head one way then another to pick up any other sounds.

He peered into the deeper darkness under the cart's back end. He could see it now. A piece of shadow grew from nothing near the broken wheel. Fluid as water, the shadow moved under the cart, then rose and trotted into moon and star light. The dog sat down a few yards away from them and stared northwards, like he could see all the way through the mountains to the grasslands of Manom. He looked rested and fit. Coryn was pleased to see him, but the scare made him angry.

'Dame Mureen, you'd better tell the children not to touch that animal.' He kept his voice low. 'He could tear an arm off soon as look at you. He can't be trusted.'

The dog continued to peer out into the distance ignoring them both.

'What is his name?' She studied the dog.

'I don't know.' He shrugged.

'What do you call him?'

'Dog.'

'Then that must be his name.'

Coryn and Dame Mureen sat together in silence for a while longer. Now the dog was near, Coryn felt easier. He rolled out his blanket and lay back on the sand. Gazing at the endless constellations, he felt the urge to talk.

'What's your full name Dame Mureen?'

'Dame Mureen aef Callan,' her voice sounded as if from far away.

'How did you end up being a Lehotan Adherent?'

'Ah, now that was all too easy for me to manage.' She chuckled. 'I woke up one morning in my home in southern Darafen and discovered I had the Wealdan within me and that I could touch the Wefan. That was it. I was packed off to Ostorr within a moon.'

She had a young laugh, which seemed odd in a woman of her years. In fact, much about her was unusual. She was a brave woman though, there was no denying that.

'I was fourteen summers old when I joined the Lehotan Order in Ostorr Haven. When my father discovered I was to become a Dame ten summers later, he became furious.' Coryn heard a trace of sadness in Dame Mureen's voice. 'He told me I would lose the chance forever to marry and have children. I told him it was too late anyway as I had already married Lehot.'

'He didn't like it?' Coryn wondered if Birog had had much the same experience in Ostorr. Now remembering the time he'd been with her, seeing her face and eyes again in his memory, he realised how lonely she'd been, something he'd not appreciated being a boy at the time.

'No, he did not like it at all.' She smiled again, leaning back on her hands to look up at the stars and the moons. The higher ridges of the cliffs, etched with dark and light, scraped against the sky. 'It is stark yet I find it beautiful here in the desert.'

He said nothing.

'And you, Sire Coryn, you came from Kalebrod?'

'Yes...originally.'

'How did you come so far?'

He told her. It seemed easy to tell her everything after she'd told him her story, but he kept the names to himself, names had power and Birog had not seemed to want to be known.

'The brevity of your tale does not hide what you must have suffered. And now you find yourself trapped with us here in these mountains. I understand how hard this must be for you. The day you were freed from slavery must have been wondrous for you though, as it must have been for all the other slaves in Selassi.'

'You know anything about how it all happened?' Coryn shifted, opening and closing his hands a few times, still amazed at how quickly it'd healed.

'I do indeed. It was the Selassian Queen's younger sister, Shezar, an Adherent herself, who managed to bring Lehot to that desert city. One of our Lehotan High-adherents discovered Shezar had the Wealdan when the princess turned fifteen, five years before. Dame Ciara persuaded Princess Shezar's parents to let her enter Ostorr Haven. When she returned for her sister's coronation, Princess Shezar persuaded her to let Lehot into her life. The rest is history. Lehot works in wondrous ways indeed.' Dame Mureen sighed into the heavy air.

They didn't talk for a long time then. Coryn watched the shadowed gorge, Dame Mureen the flickering skies.

'Might I see this amulet of yours? The children say they each had one, their parents too, but they were taken by the slavers and thrown into the sea. ' Dame Mureen paused, glanced toward the cleft, then back at Coryn. 'I wondered if they might be different from the ones we have in the Storratian Empire.'

'I suppose.' Coryn opened the pouch and spilled his amulet into his hand, taking care not to let the roll of vellum fall out too. 'Not sure why the slavers let me keep mine, they never seemed to notice it for some reason.'

Dame Mureen leaned forward and he felt the delicate spiking that meant she'd opened her Wealdan. 'It is cracked, is that unusual?'

'I can't honestly tell you. I've not met many with amulets in the desert and we don't usually show them to anyone.' Coryn's hand curled round his amulet. Hearing about the children losing theirs made him wonder again how he'd managed to keep hold of his all the years he'd been a slave. 'My first wasn't cracked, the one my mother made me for my first nameday. Neither was my brother's.

'I shall not touch it, Sire Coryn, do not fear.'

Coryn uncurled his fingers till his amulet lay exposed to the moonlight. The crystal splinter glimmered like a tiny star deep inside the crack.

'I cannot tell if it is spirit blessed, but then I have never studied such magik and do not know what to look for.' Dame Mureen reached out her fingers to hover over the amulet and her voice dropped. 'I do sense a Wealdan weaving within and around the stone. Can that be a piece of focus crystal within the crack?'

'Yes, I think it was a part of the Lehotan woman's focus-crystal.' Coryn stared at his cracked amulet again, wondering. 'It's the same colour as her crystal anyway.'

'The same colour, hmm. I wish I could see more clearly her weaving of the Wefan, but my Wealdan is not strong enough. Perhaps it is a pattern of disguise or dissembling, to hide your amulet from others. It is clever and means she had great potency in the Wealdan, far greater than mine.' Dame Mureen looked up at his face, studying it. 'That she struck a piece, however small, from her focus-crystal for you tells me that you were of great importance to her.'

Coryn shifted, awkward. Important to Birog? He'd been a slave for years, yet the woman had never come and found him or freed him. Either she was dead or she'd forgotten about him. He shook himself and put the amulet back in its pouch. Trying to reach under the bandages to scratch at the itching of his mending hand, he changed the subject. 'Where's Ostorr?'

'It is an isle joined to the Isle of Storr by a narrow causeway as Storr itself is joined to Losan. Leave the bandages alone, your wound still heals.'

Coryn stopped scratching and looked at the small, thin shape of

Dame Mureen sitting beside him, her pale hair catching the starlight. 'You come from Storr? That's an awful long way, isn't it? How'd you get here?'

'By ship, by beast, by foot.' There was laughter in her voice. 'But I have been living in Fara, the capital of Faran for the last ten years. It is on the eastern coast of the Elyat Sea. I have a position within the Duke's castle as Wealdan-healer and truth-seeker.'

'Truth-seeker?'

'I told you I have a small ability to Wealdan-read minds.' Dame Mureen smiled. 'That is why I know you to be so unusual.'

Coryn shifted, awkward, and stared at the cliff tops. From this angle the pillar of rock loomed against the smaller moon, Diaphos. He wondered where the ifrit, Subrahima, had gone after she'd plummeted past that pillar. Did she live? And how had anyone managed to lure Subrahima into that trap in the first place? She'd seemed so clever. 'What will you do with the children if you can't find their families?'

'We shall keep them together, somehow.' Dame Mureen looked back at the stars. 'How could we split them apart if all they have is each other?'

Coryn looked right at her. 'I'm betting you'd want to keep any Wealdan-bearers. They'd be important to you lot.'

'*You lot?*' She smiled. 'All children are important, are they not? How could we choose who to keep and who to let go? You have seen them. Could you choose? Wealdan or no, we Lehotan will take care of them all if their families cannot be found. I shall see to it myself if need be. Indeed, I feel they would find happiness in Fara.' Dame Mureen was smiling now, her small even teeth a row of pearls in the moonlight. 'You do not smile enough, Sire Coryn.'

Coryn grunted in reply. He pressed his hand against the pouch, felt the hard lump of his amulet. None of these people had amulets to protect them, not even the children. What if any of them did have the Wealdan in their blood? 'You know writhen and blood-priests are twisted, blood-thirsty monsters, so why stop me from killing them?'

'Where there is sentience, there is hope for redemption.'

'I saw what they did to your two Lehotan friends and the boy. They'd do the same to you and your two adherents. They're dangerous and evil. Nothing you say will change my mind. You've got too little of the Wealdan to protect yourself let alone all the others. Even the

Lehotan man couldn't keep them away with his Wealdan-fire. Though he killed a few with it, they still got him in the end.'

'What do you mean?'

'I counted five dead writhen along the trail of the other cart. Every one of them had a neat hole burned clean through its body.' Coryn rubbed at his head. It was beginning to ache. 'There's one Lehotan who didn't mind killing writhen. I only wish he'd got the blood-priest too.'

'Do not make the mistake of believing he would not have minded. Yet you are right, ignorance and evil hound us.' Dame Mureen stood up and moved towards the far side of the gully as if the conversation had pushed her away. She looked back at him. 'At this moment in time, I must think of the children and the two young women still in my care.'

'And do you think you'll all make it?'

'I hope that we do, I ask Lehot for it with each passing hour.'

'How often does that work?'

The first hint of annoyance flickered at the corners of her eyes. Then she smiled. 'He brought you to us.' She turned and walked away.

Coryn shook his head and watched the gorge again. Dame Mureen had stopped beyond some rocks where he couldn't see her, but he knew she was busy meditating again. He scowled when he heard her say his name. He shifted about, checked the crossbow and the bolt, again.

The dog slept under the acacias. Coryn picked up his half-finished meal and walked over to the animal. He squatted down and looked at it, all stretched out, its head on its paws.

'Good job.' He placed the plate on the ground near the dog. The animal whipped up and snatched a mouthful. Its paws either side of the plate, it pulled its lips back in a vicious snarl. Coryn stepped back. 'You ungrateful, Murak spawned…'

'Sire Coryn!' Dame Mureen interrupted in a bright voice. She came over to where he stood. 'Dog seems rather upset.' She watched as the animal wolfed the food in hungry gulps.

Coryn felt hot. 'The damned dog's always like this with food. He's a cantankerous, evil-tempered animal. I should've feathered him long ago.'

'Why have you not?'

Coryn looked at her surprised. 'Because he's the best dog I've ever come across. He's stuck by me for six or seven years now. That's got to mean something.'

Dame Mureen crossed her arms over her chest. 'That explains why you keep him but what I cannot understand is why he keeps you.'

'He might hate people, but he hates me the least I suppose.' Coryn frowned down at the dog. He didn't even have any idea of the dog's age. Why had the creature stuck by him all these years? He guessed he would never know the answer. But he must be a pretty old dog by now so maybe it was just habit.

He walked back to his blanket and sat with his back against the rock again. He realised then his thigh didn't hurt anymore, he'd not even limped. Dame Mureen had healed him well. He still had to think of a way out of this hole but at least he'd be able act on any workable plan he came up with. He got thinking about the Wealdan. Maybe these women could do more with what they had than they thought. Like that Lehotan using his to kill the writhen. What could the other two adherents, Maisie and Katleya, do with theirs?

He wondered then how strong Birog had been. Stronger than any of these Lehotans, that was for sure. He remembered the night he'd met her all those years ago and how she'd seemed to know everything.

Chapter 30

Mureen studied the silhouette of the young man sitting a few yards away. She had no doubt he was one of Lehot's mysteries. Coryn had not told him the name of the Lehotan Adherent who had helped him, but knowing the unusual colour of her crystal, a rich blue-green, and feeling the particular texture of the Wealdan-weaving on the amulet, made her fairly sure the woman was Birog Llawgoch, former Moder of Ostorr Haven. Birog Llawgoch had disappeared without trace or warning almost twenty years ago.

How strange the quirks of time were to lead him here to this place and time just when Mureen needed him, a man protected by her old Moder. Lehot worked in wondrous ways indeed.

She had seen enough wounds to know that the thin scar running the length of Coryn's jaw was due to a knife and the hole in his leg was an arrow wound. He had killed. He had done it with such ease, such reflex that Mureen knew he had done so many times before. He swore a great deal and had a roughness about him that showed his poor upbringing. He seemed to have little respect for Lehot or any other god. Yet all of this was understandable in the circumstances. His life had been hard. More than hard. And he was so young still.

He had a good heart, this she knew. He had buried poor Thoma and Manzul's mutilated bodies. A burning would have been far better but perhaps not wise given the circumstances. Mureen glanced to where she had last felt Alaya, to where her body must lie, with no rites said over it, no flames to help send her spirit to Lehot. Then there was Manzar's body, lying just yards from the cart, part eaten. There was nothing she could do about him and for that she was sorry too. She shuddered and turned back to look at Coryn.

Mureen wondered again why she could not read Coryn's thoughts, not even the ones that lay to the forefront of his mind. Her delicate probes slipped past his mind like rain drops on glass. It was disconcerting. Was her meagre Wealdan failing her now just when she needed it most? Perhaps her sending had not reached him and he had come of his own volition as he had said. She shook her head, she had felt a surge of the Wefan. One so strong it had taken her senses with it.

What could it have been but Lehot using her as a vessel of His will? He wanted these children saved as much as she.

She pulled her crystal out by its silver chain and held it cupped in her hands. 'Lehot.' She kept her voice soft so her words became lost in the sigh of the soft wind through acacia leaves, 'I have never questioned Your wisdom. I know it was with Your help I sent my call to Coryn aef Arlean, but now he is here how should I deal with him?' Mureen stared into her crystal knowing she would receive no answers and that it was all up to her. Lehot gave her strength and it was up to her to do what she must with that strength. That she must help Coryn in some way as Moder Birog had done was obvious. But how?

She knew she had done the right thing in gathering up these children. It was true that the Havens tried to find and gather in those who showed any signs of the Wealdan and any one amongst these poor youngsters might well be a bearer. They were too young to show any of the signs yet, except for Eilem. It usually came to girls at their first bleeding, but was possible the pregnancy masked any Wealdan she might bear. She looked toward the cleft where they lay sleeping and sighed. Wealdan-bearers or not, all the children were worth saving.

Her own abilities in the Wealdan were modest. Like her, Adherent Maisie could Wealdan-heal too but it was weaker than Mureen's so she had to use it in unison with herbcraft, and then just on minor wounds and illnesses. Alaya could create a light-matrix, creating globes of light. Thoma could create small balls of fire, which it seemed he had adapted to use as a weapon against the writhen. Even though she knew that Thoma would have used it only as a last resort, the thought that he had killed with his Lehot-given Wealdan sent a stabbing pain into Mureen's heart. It was almost untenable for anyone to use the Wealdan in such a manner.

As for young Katleya, her potency in the Wealdan was astonishing. There was a great deal more to her than Mureen had cared to tell, even to the girl herself. Time would tell what she was truly capable of doing. Great things, Mureen and Alaya had hoped. Great things as in times of old. To think that those with the Wealdan once raised great buildings, saved blighted crops, healed herds of sickening livestock, brought rain and ended it, cured plagues, and so much more. Did it feel for them as it felt for her when she sent her mind-message out to Coryn? She shivered at the memory of the Wefan-energies that had coursed through her.

Why have we faded so?

Even the rise of the Lehotan Order in Selassi had not much in-creased the numbers of those found bearing the Wealdan. It was sad to contemplate how the Havens had dwindled. Perhaps the vow of chastity some of the Lehotans took did not help, but so few did so, it could not have any bearing on the lack of children born with potency. Perhaps it was due to lack of effort in finding children bearing the Wealdan. Katleya had mentioned a girl who Wealdan-healed in distant Rophet. That the Lehotan Haven had fallen and Rophet now worshipped Atash was a great sadness. That the Atash priesthood had turned the Rophetans against the Wealdan, lumping it together with all other magiks as evil, was truly horrifying. That they burned to death all those accused of magik was almost too terrible to believe. She worried about the Atash priesthood in Manom busy converting people to their religion.

Mureen and Alaya had decided a party from Storr and Ostorr must be organised to go to Rophet to discover any Wealdan bearers remaining undiscovered by the Atash priesthood as soon as possible. It should have been done long ago, but Rophet and Kalebrod were distant lands almost entirely cut off from the Storratian Empire, one reason for the fall of the Lehotan Haven in Black Rock. And how long had these Murecken blood-priests been hunting Wealdan-bear-ers? Was the rise of Murak and the Murecken blood-priesthood the cause of this fall in Wealdan numbers? Did they secretly hunt in the Storratian Empire too?

The Havens had been far too inward-looking for decades and it was beyond time that they went out into the world again. The previous Moder had been right. Birog Llawgoch should have been listened to all those years ago. Perhaps it was frustration that had made her leave. Mureen remembered her as a prickly woman, cold and hard to like, but fiercely intelligent and with a potency in the Wealdan that would be sorely missed in the difficult times ahead.

She looked up from her crystal and back towards young Coryn. She had heard him speak of the spirits, swear by them even. Was that what blocked her from his mind? Spirit magik? It made her curious and would bear more study. The new Moder of Ostorr Haven, young Brianna Shon Catti would be much interested in him. She had gone well beyond Mureen's training in the art of Wealdan-reading. Mureen sighed and closed her eyes to meditate again.

Chapter 31

More bone-weary than he'd ever imagined he could feel, Coryn sat propped against the rock wall of the mountain staring without seeing into the darkness of the gorge. Dame Mureen slept curled up on a blanket a few yards away. Though night cooled the desert, Coryn was drenched with sweat and thirsty, but felt far too tired to move. He wasn't desperate enough to wake the old woman though.

Let her sleep in peace, it might be her last.

He looked away from the sleeping woman back out into the night. He gripped the crossbow in his lap and felt tense. The dog had disappeared into the night not long after Dame Mureen fell asleep. It still hadn't returned when he drifted into a fitful sleep.

Coryn almost screamed when he woke with something pressing against his lips. He shoved it away and raised his crossbow in one swift movement. The boy lay sprawled in the dirt, wide-eyed, holding one of the waterskins to his chest.

'Wetham. That was dangerous, boy.' Coryn's heart hammered. 'You could've been killed.'

Wetham struggled up without spilling any of the precious water, then hesitated, embarrassed and unsure what to do. He turned back towards the cleft. Then Coryn realised he still held the cocked crossbow on the boy. He put it on the ground beside him.

'I could use that water.' He spoke loud enough for Wetham to hear but not so loud he'd wake Dame Mureen. The boy turned and walked back. He offered Coryn the waterskin with both hands.

Coryn forced himself to keep his eyes steady on the child's face. The branding looked bad. Scar tissue marred his skin from under his left jaw to his collarbone. All too easy to see in the double wash of moonlight. He wondered if the boy had seen himself in a mirror yet. He hoped not. Anger welled in his chest against the sort of people who could do this to a child. He'd met such men.

Coryn pretended to take a long drink from the waterskin, then offered it to the boy. Wetham didn't move.

'Thanks.' Coryn corked the skin. He waited a few seconds to see if the boy would speak. When he didn't, Coryn put the waterskin back in the boy's hands. Wetham started back towards the cleft.

'I need help to keep an eye on things out here.' Coryn kept his eyes on the child's skinny back. 'Someone to take turns on watch with me. Are you willing?'

The boy stopped where he was and sat down. He stared straight ahead, out towards the gorge.

'That's good.' Coryn nodded, knowing the boy would see the movement from the corner of his eye. He flicked his eyes up to the sky then back out to the gorge. The bright moons didn't lighten his mood.

They sat a while without talking and Coryn drifted back into sleep. When he woke again around an hour or so later, the boy still sat there staring out at the night, but now he held Coryn's knife in his hand. Surprised, Coryn reached down and felt his empty sheath.

'When did you take my knife?' he asked, feeling groggy. The boy didn't answer. 'That knife's too big for you, Wetham. I've another that'd suit you better.' Coryn fished in the pack lying next to him and brought out a folding-knife with a bone handle. He tossed it over. It landed next to the boy's leg. 'This one I bought in Selassi on my first day as a freed man. It's like the one I had as a boy. You're welcome to use it.'

The boy said nothing and didn't look at the knife. Quite still, the child stared out into the darkness. When Coryn was almost convinced Wetham was deaf, he saw the boy's small hand reach out and pick the knife out of the sand. He laid it in his lap next to the other one.

'Don't let Dame Mureen catch you with either one of those or she'll switch both our backsides. It'd be better if you gave me the big one back.' Coryn held his hand out towards the boy. Wetham curled his hand round both knives. Without looking at Coryn, he rose, walked over and dropped the larger knife near Coryn's leg. Then he sat back next to the waterskin.

'Where are you from, Wetham? Are you from Kalebrod like me?' He waited a few minutes to let the questions sink in, watching the boy's face for some expression. He got the smallest of nods. Coryn picked up his knife and slid it back in its sheath.

'They branded me in Dal Abar too. Right here.' Coryn opened his shirt to reveal the silvered brand on his left shoulder, just above his collarbone.

But the boy didn't turn. Coryn wondered if the blood-priests and their writhen had wiped out Wetham's family too. Something heavy filled his chest as his mind pitched back to the day the writhen burned his own home. He seldom allowed himself to think on it. At times like this, it was hard to keep the images from his mind.

The night before the writhen came was the last time Ma had ever held him in her arms and told him she loved him. He'd tried to say he loved her too, but he hadn't managed to get the words out. He was sorry for that.

He forced himself away from the old memories and glanced at Wetham sitting so quiet. For all that passed between them, the boy could've been sitting a thousand leagues away. But Coryn understood.

'I was on my own too, when I wasn't much older than you.' Coryn thought Wetham's head moved again, but he wasn't certain. 'But we've both got friends now, haven't we? We aren't alone now.' Coryn sighed and looked out into the night. Where was that dog?

We all need friends.

The desert wind moved up the gorge, its desiccating breath scented with the sharp smell of acacias, desert pea-bush and flowering shepherd trees. It gusted over and between the cart and the rocks. Dame Mureen tossed under its touch but continued to sleep. The boy stayed put, his back straight, staring ahead, though Coryn saw his small body wobble a few times.

Coryn wished the dog had returned. He whistled for it again, but it still didn't come back. The long days of strain, the wounds, the Wealdan-healing, the lack of sleep and shortage of water, all wore him down and it would've been good to have had the dog nearby. He reasoned at best, if he made no mistakes, he would make it through the next day with strength enough to fight. After that with no real rest and too little water, he didn't think he'd function so well. He glanced at the boy again. None of them would.

Coryn concentrated his thoughts on plans for escaping so he couldn't let sleep take him again just yet. He didn't want his life to end here, not like this. Nor those of the children or the women. The children had never even had a proper chance at life. So much for that all-powerful god of theirs.

Maybe I'd better work harder on a plan.

He rubbed his hand through his hair and at his temples where it throbbed like Murak's flaming hells. If he died the children and the women wouldn't have a hope. Not that any of them had much of one anyway. Was this it for him? Were his dreams of a life after years of slavery nothing? Would he never see Lera again? Sadness filled his heart as he watched the boy's slow tilt down onto the sand. Unable to stay awake a moment longer, Coryn stopped struggling with his thoughts and felt better. Then he too drifted back into fitful sleep.

Chapter 32

Deep in the bowels of Elucame, Leveen stood waiting outside the door of High-priest Dracil's offices. Down here the round corridors, created by wyrms in times of antiquity, were smoothed with age, the floors flattened by the footfall of generations. They connected the natural caves and caverns beneath the Ruel Mountains that honeycombed the subterranean lands of Mureck.

The weight of all that rock made Leveen feel trapped used as she was to the wide skies of desert and sea, and she fretted at the wait. She had travelled leagues in less than two tendays, riding to the ground two of the three horses she had bought in Rialt. All that kept her standing was her need to be free from what the blood-rites had made of her, a freedom she could almost taste. Her hand strayed over a pocket of her coat. In it hid a glass phial, well wrapped in thick silk and nestled in an ebony box. It held the proof of Wealdan-potency that would win her that freedom. The blood of Katleya aef Laeft.

The door opened and one of Dracil's skinny acolytes bowed Leveen in. The second most powerful man in Mureck, and the most hated, stood over a low stone plinth not far from the fireplace. Lying on the plinth, was another acolyte. This one was naked and his back was patterned with blood-rite sigils. The linen strips that had tied his wrists and ankles to the bronze rings at each corner of the plinth were red with blood. Leveen remembered all too well the same treatment being meted out to her when she became an acolyte. Dracil slapped the boy's face, waking him from his stupor.

'You may leave now.' Dracil stroked the ill-formed lump of red rock hanging from a gold chain about his neck, his Blodstan, a full Murecken priest's link to his Priest-king. 'And take your blood with you. See that it is given to the wyrm young that need to be imprinted.'

'Yes, Master.' The boy struggled to his feet and wobbled over to Dracil's stone-crafted desk to pick up a shallow scrying bowl full of blood so fresh it still steamed. The second acolyte helped him out of the room and the door closed with a soft click behind them.

Leveen remembered how the blood-letting took its toll. Her scars itched at the memories. The pain of the cutting and the fear of possible death strengthened the potency of the blood making the scrying clearer. She wondered what truths or futures Dracil had been searching for. The truth she had discovered by drawing the blood from the arm of Katleya as the girl lay drugged in the House of the Rose, was that neither pain nor fear was necessary to enhance its potency. At least not in Katleya's case. Leveen had bled the girl of only a cupful. The phial contained a fraction of that. Enough for her purpose.

'Leveen el Meera al-Shafi, it has been a long time since I have seen you within the walls of Elucame.' Dracil sat at his desk on a chair made of Selassian cedarwood and silk brocade cushions. His desk was made of the same wood, carved with the sigils of blood-rites. He pressed the fingers of his hands together, tip to tip, and stared at her with cold, sharp eyes. He did not offer her a seat. 'You have been an excellent spy in the outer-world. What is it that brings you here? Do you finally wish to complete the bloodhunter-priest rituals and come into your true power?'

Fear shivered through her. This man was the most dangerous she knew and now she must tell him that she wanted to cut her ties to him. Was the girl she had found payment enough? Giving herself a moment to calm, she looked about his room, pretending nonchalance. It was sumptuous, the pillars carved to mimic ivy-covered tree boles, the rugs of deep red wool, the wood furnishings all of precious timbers, the heavy and intricate tapestries hiding most of the polished rock walls of the mountain. The hot waters of the red lake, pumped through pipes to all the levels of Elucame, also warmed these upper caverns where Dracil's rooms lay. They tainted the blood-laced air with a faint sulphurous stink.

'I have found something – someone – you might find of interest.' Leveen prowled forward and sat in the chair opposite the desk unasked. An act of confidence would give her actual confidence. Ignoring the smell of blood, no doubt deliberately spilled to distract her and put her at a disadvantage, she stared down at him, making her height, even sitting, an asset. 'I wish to trade.'

'Trade? And what, Leveen, do you wish to trade?'

'I do not wish to become a full bloodhunter-priest.' She narrowed her eyes. 'I demand a reversal of the blood-rites already done on my body.'

Dracil's thin lips stretched in a caricature of a smile. 'And who told you such a reversal is possible?'

'Your own spymaster priest, Reantor.' Leveen kept a steely hold on her temper, though it was hard with her blood-lust roiling at the stink of fresh blood. 'He said that it was both possible and that you would be willing to authorise the reversal given the right incentive.'

'I shall have words with Reantor. It is not within his authority to tell you such things. Perhaps it is time for him to move to other duties.' Dracil tapped his fingertips together with a regular beat. 'It surprises me that you should want to reverse your status. Do you not wish to rise in the priesthood of Murak? Have you not found it lucrative, powerful?'

'Exactly the words with which you priests first tricked me into joining your ranks.' Leveen sneered. 'Power? I only became a powerful tool for you Murecken.'

'For Murak, may His Shadow enfold us in Eternity.' Dracil's face hardened. 'We know where you have travelled. We know where you have deposited your coin. We know with whom you have consorted. Do not believe for a moment, Leveen al Meera el-Shafi, blood-priest to Murak, that anything you do is unknown to us.'

'I want to be free.' The words felt weak to Leveen's own ears. Where had her need gone? Her anger? Her heart stuttered and began to pulse to the beat of Dracil's tapping fingers. As his tapping quickened, her heart beat faster...*tap...beat...tapbeat...tapbeat tapbeat tapbeat...*

Do you have this *incentive* with you now?' Dracil smiled and his Blodstan glowed like an ember in a pit of shadows.

Leveen staggered to her feet, trying to wrest control of her heartbeat from the High-priest, but her fingers crept to the pocket holding the phial of their own accord.

What blood-magik did he use that he could so easily slide under her defences? It seemed Dracil had timed Leveen's appointment so that she would arrive just after a blood-letting when his Ascian would be at its most powerful. But she would show him how much stronger she had become since Dracil had first taken her blood.

Leveen allowed her blood-lust to rise a fraction, just enough for its power to aid her in wresting back control. She had drunk some of Katleya's blood in preparation for this meeting. An intuitive precaution, which worked as well as she had hoped. Her barriers rose and her heart slowed to normal. She turned back to Dracil in time to see the fleeting shock registering in his eyes.

'I do.' Sliding her hand into her pocket, Leveen withdrew the wrapped phial. She placed it on the desk in front of Dracil. 'Look for yourself.'

Dracil frowned, it was obvious he was greatly disturbed by the failure of his Ascian over Leveen. But he picked up the package and unwrapped the cloth. The phial rolled into his palm and his frown deepened. He levered the cork from the neck and sniffed at the contents. Leveen smiled in triumph at his gasp. His lack of control told her everything she needed to know.

'Who does this belong to? Where is this person? Is...?'

'She is in safe keeping and only I know where she is.'

'*She?*'

Leveen settled back into the chair and, still smiling, stretched out her long legs. 'Now shall we trade?'

Chapter 33

Morning stole over the cliffs of the gorge. Another oppressive day was on its way, one more in a long, unbroken line of burning days. Coryn stood and stretched, surprised at how much better he felt.

Light filled the gully, empty apart from his horse, standing listless under the acacias. He poured some water into his cook pot and held it for the horse to drink from. Dame Mureen must have taken the boy inside during the night.

Coryn had told her it would be best if she kept them all inside as much as possible. The last of the candles would soon burn out and he knew they might cry in the dark, but the cooler air would stop them losing so much water. He needed them strong for a day or so more. Tonight, they could have one slim chance to get out of the gorge. Then there would be the journey north out of the mountains. It would take everything they'd got and more and would be hardest on the children.

He took his time walking round the gully, working out the problems. As soon as the writhen discovered they'd all gone the blood-priest would have them out hunting their trail. In the open Coryn wouldn't have any way to defend the women and children. This was the problem he hadn't been able to solve since he arrived. He continued to walk in wide, slow circles, dog-tired and hungry. He steadied himself with a hand on the cart.

Coryn looked down and saw it.

The dog lay on its side close to the rocks and half under the cart-wheel. Its eyes were shut tight. It could have been asleep, but its mouth hung open and its tongue lay dry and cracked in the dirt. Dried blood caked its shoulder and side. Coryn squatted down next to the dog and saw the blood trail where it'd dragged its body through the sand and up the slope from the riverbed. He choked, realising it'd tried to answer his whistles.

'Dog.' He willed a response. The animal didn't move. Coryn reached out and touched the side of its head. In the best of times the dog was dangerous. Now it was hurt it might tear his hand off. It didn't stir.

He stroked the animal's head once, then again. When it still didn't move he began to run his eyes and hands over its body. An arrow pierced one leg, its jagged flint-head chopping through bone. Another arrow feathered its ribs. A third drilled its hip. Then they'd let it go. The blood-priest knew it would die, and he'd also known it would struggle to reach Coryn, had wanted the dog to reach him.

He ran his hands over the rough fur, down the long, bony legs, over the blood-soaked side. Then he felt the faint pulsing of an artery. Coryn closed his eyes for a moment as the lump grew in his throat. He couldn't believe the dog was still alive.

Coryn carried the limp body into the dappled shade of the acacias. He spread his saddle blanket out, moved the dog onto it and grabbed the half-emptied waterskin. He sat down, propped the dog's head on his thigh and dripped water into its mouth. It took a couple of times before the animal swallowed and tried to move its swollen tongue. He kept giving the dog water till he judged it'd drunk enough, then gathered the animal up into his lap and sat cross-legged, holding it like a too-big child in his arms. He stared out into the brightening morning and rocked to and fro.

'We'll have a good life up north, you and me. Up there the land's green with meadows and forests, much like Kalebrod in some places, so I've heard.' He could see the place in his mind's eye. 'Good life for a man and a dog both.'

The dog's head twisted and it took Coryn's hand in its mouth and held it for a moment. It let go and ran its swollen tongue over the back of his hand. Then it went limp. He told the dog things he'd never told it during all the long nights and days they'd spent together over the years. And he wondered why. Why hadn't he shared something more with it, other than his food and water, in all that time? He didn't know. The dog had always been a good listener, had done what had been asked of it, was clever enough to know when to avoid danger, when to attack. It had never spared itself for him. Yet neither of them could show or know affection. Would it take death to bring them together?

Wetham came out of the cleft and spotted the dog. He walked over and sat in the sand as close as he could without touching. By the time Dame Mureen came out, Wetham had huddled close to Coryn and held of one of the dog's paws. They both stared out into the brightening light of the gorge.

Coryn could feel the old woman standing there looking down at them. She came over, studied the dog and knelt down in front of Coryn.

'He is still alive, Sire Coryn. Let me heal him if I can.'

Coryn lifted his head. 'Look at what they did to him, Dame Mureen. How can you heal this?'

'I will try.'

The two other women came out. They looked over at Coryn and saw the dog. Katleya spoke to Maisie and they began to prepare breakfast, taking the last of the meat from its bag and re-lighting the fire.

'I can't let him go, don't ask me to let him go.' Coryn looked up at Dame Mureen and blinked.

She paused and looked him in the eyes, her face softening. 'I can heal him where he lies. You hold him while I work.'

He held the dog for what seemed like hours, talking to it every so often as Dame Mureen put her hands to one wound after another. Wetham helped her, snapping shafts and drawing the arrows out when she asked. When it was all done he stayed close by, holding a paw again.

'The rest is up to him, Sire Coryn.' Dame Mureen sat back on the sand, lines of exhaustion etched into her face. 'If he wakes, he will need to drink.'

'If he wakes?' Coryn didn't take his eyes off the dog. He could see the wounds had closed, but it breathed too shallow. He couldn't see its sides move.

Dame Mureen sighed but didn't say anything else. Rising she left him to join the others by the fire. Coryn longed for just one campfire night with the dog alive and lying nearby listening to him and the wind in the trees. Just one, no more. He wasn't a greedy man. He'd tell it things then. Tell it what it'd never known. He would tell the dog it was his only friend. He felt something dying inside him as he held the dog, but was afraid to admit it.

Chapter 34

The sun was creeping over the gorge walls by the time the children finished their breakfast of fried antelope. They sat quiet, resting in the deep band of shade under the cliff. Katleya and Maisie watched over them while Dame Mureen had disappeared into the cleft. The horse dozed under the tree, its tail flicking at persistent flies and the back of Coryn's head. The dog lay on the blanket next to him. Wetham dozed on its other side, his small hand still holding the dog's paw.

He spotted a small flightless wyvern, red as the desert, no taller than the length of his hand. It'd squeezed its narrow body between a rock and a clump of sagebrush. It stood still and tall on its hind legs, the long fingers of its forelegs gripping a branch as it peered out from its shadowed hiding place. It waited for insects, small rodents and birds to come within range of its flame. Coryn leaned against the same large rock in the dappled shade of the acacia, the crossbow across his lap.

Coryn scanned the trail below then looked over at the children. They seemed tired, listless and hot. Their eyes dull, their faces burned. He knew their throats must be as parched as his own. The water he'd brought was running low. The children should go back into the cleft, he thought the heat would soon become brutal.

He glanced down at the sand and began to pick up and examine pebbles. Some he kept. Some he tossed away. Then he whipped out a hand and grabbed the leggy wyvern out of the bush. He pulled his scarf from his neck and laid it over the hand holding the wyvern.

The girl Sica was closest to him. 'Sica? Why don't you come take a look at this.'

The girl looked at him, then stood and helped the little ones, Neima and Pella, to their feet. Pregnant Eilem, her dulled eyes gazing into middle distance stayed where she was. The three little girls stood close, inside the shade cast by the acacia, the little ones holding each of Sica's hands.

'What've you got there?' Pella twined one finger in her matted fair hair. Round and round then round and round again.

Katleya wandered over and stood nearby, but looked out at the gorge. He knew she listened. He was convinced she didn't approve of him.

'I've got an imp-demon under my scarf. One of the tiniest of the demons, one that's travelled here all the way from the fiery caves of Murak. Bent on doing some mischief hereabouts and no doubt about it,' he whispered to the girls and winked. Wetham sat up and watched, silent as ever. 'But it didn't take care and got too close to me. So now I've caught it, do you want to see it?'

'Never.' Sica snorted, raised her chin and slitted her grey eyes. 'There's no such thing as an imp, everybody knows that.'

'But there must be otherwise how could I've caught one?' Coryn asked, his eyes wide. He lifted his hand a little. 'It's right under my scarf. Go ahead, take a peek and see for yourself? Go on, it's just a little imp-demon, it can't do you any harm while I'm holding it.'

Sica dropped Pella's hand and reached out towards the scarf. She jerked back with a gasp when the cloth moved and ran on the tips of her toes for a few moments, her plaits flying off her shoulders. The others shrieked with the thrill of it, then grabbed Sica's dress and pulled her forward again.

'If you've got an imp-demon for real, what's it look like?' Sica demanded. She stood close again legs flexed and fists tight, ready to flee at a moment's notice.

'Now this one here's got a fan of spikes on its head, a tail like a whip and is redder than blood,' Coryn answered, grinning. 'And when it gets real angry it spouts a flame that's green as emeralds.'

The children squealed and laughed. Katleya stared at him her arms folded below her breasts. She rolled her eyes. He ignored her.

'Why's it so small then? Ain't all demons supposed to be big as – as – bigger than trees, anyway?' Neima folded her skinny arms across her chest in an unconscious mimic of Katleya. Her lower lip jutted and she nudged Pella for confirmation. Pella nodded at her in agreement and Neima turned back, triumphant. 'Big and dangerous, like them genies an' ifrits.'

'Imps, genies an' ifrits aren't real.' Sica rolled her eyes at Coryn. 'They're just old desert stories told to frighten little desert babies.'

'They too are real!' Pella's brows came down in a scowl. 'They're real, aren't they, Sire Coryn? Jus' like spirits back home?' She turned to look at him, enormous blue eyes imploring.

'Of course they're real, I've seen them myself. In fact, an ifrit helped me get to you just yesterday,' Coryn asserted. 'She scared those writhen off, burning their bottoms so they screamed and ran away like frightened little rabbits.'

Now Katleya bit her lip and turned away. She coughed, shaking her head till her scarf fell from her head freeing her nut-brown hair. She made an impatient sound as she adjusted it. The girls giggled and clapped their hands with glee.

'Writhen with burned bottoms!' Sica sniggered. 'Ha! Served them right it did!'

'Burned bottoms, burned bottoms!' Neima echoed, giggling.

Katleya hunched and coughed again, her shoulders heaving. Perhaps it was the dust, Coryn thought, perhaps not. He smiled.

'A real ifrit, honest?' Pella stepped forward and Coryn wondered if her eyes could get any bigger. 'What was it like?'

'All made of golden fire with eyes as green as this imp-demon's flame.' Coryn thought they were as green as Katleya's eyes too. 'The writhen were terrified they'd be cooked and gobbled up right where they stood.'

'Why didn't it kill them all then, so we could get away proper?' Sica put her fists on her hips, her grey eyes slitted with suspicion again.

'She'd been trapped and chained in the dark for hundreds, maybe thousands of years. She was very, very tired and getting freed from that trap hurt her real bad.' Coryn shook his head. 'She did what she could.'

'Oh a *lady* ifrit. Trapped for hundreds and thousands of years and years. That's terrible. Is she all right now?' Sica's whole demeanour changed in a blink. 'Was she beautiful? Did you free her like you're going to free us?'

'I helped her, yes. And she was very beautiful.' Coryn slanted a look up at Katleya. Her back stiffened. She would be biting her lip round about now. 'I'll do my best for all of you too.' He looked back at the little girls. Then he dropped his eyes to the sand, chewing on the inside of his cheek. 'I think she's all right. I hope so.'

'Me too! But what about them demons then,' Sica demanded. 'How come the one you've got there's so small?'

'Like spirits, demons come in all shapes and sizes and some are more dangerous than others. It's true, cross my heart and hope to die,' he insisted, seeing Sica's mouth open with more protests. 'This one here under my scarf is a real live imp-demon. It must've escaped from one of Murak's fiery hells. Come up right through the caves under Mureck, the land of the blood-priests in the Ruel Mountains, then travelled all the way west along these old mountains here.

'These are the Amalla Heights.' Pella nodded in agreement with herself. 'The Rialtan merchant said so. He said they go all the way west to a neck of sea 'tween the Sutherne Ocean an' the Elyat Sea.'

'A neck? How can a sea have a neck?' Neima jutted out her lip again, her grey eyes scornful. She shook her head, her dark, curls bobbing about her dirty face. 'That's just silly!'

'No, Pella's right. It's a narrow stretch of sea between Manom and Losan.' Coryn nodded. He smiled at Pella and she grinned back. 'Before I show this little imp-demon to you I want you each to take one of these pebbles and put it under your tongue and keep it there.'

'Why?' Pella peered at the pebbles in Coryn's hand. She was small and far too skinny but she was smart and some of the dullness had left her eyes letting them sparkle like the blue lakes of Kalebrod in summer. Her white-blond hair curled about her head and, though filled with sand and dirt, it made her tanned, dusty skin look all the darker.

'Because it'll make you feel better. These are magik pebbles you see.' Coryn held his hand flat and let each girl select a pebble, he handed the last to Wetham. To his surprise, the boy took it. They all put the pebbles in their mouths. 'Good. Now let me count to five. One, two, three, four...and five. There. Feel better?'

They all nodded. He knew they would. Their eyes widened with wonder. It was an old trick he'd learned soon after arriving in the desert. The small stones helped to fight the thirst by drawing saliva into the mouths.

'Now, who wants to be the first to see this little imp-demon all the way from the fiery hells below Mureck?'

'Me,' Pella stated firming her jaw. She looked scared but she grabbed the scarf and yanked it off. As she did, Coryn shoved the little wyvern at her and growled.

The wyvern's spiked neck-ruff shot erect, sparking with gold in the sunlight and its tail whipped the air. All the girls jumped backwards, shrieked and ran in circles for the pure joy of it. Wetham stayed put, his dark eyes huge with fascination.

'Sire Coryn, the children have little enough energy left. Don't wear

216

what's left out of them.' Katleya banged and brushed at the cloth of her robe raising puffs of red dust that swirled in the heat for a few moments before settling back onto the grey material. Tiny beads of moisture sparkled on her upper lip. Her eyes, though sunken, remained beautiful, a fresh leaf green. They reminded him of spring leaves drenched in sunlight more than Subrahima's eyes. 'And stop filling their heads with nonsense.'

Coryn grinned at her and that seemed to annoy her even more. His smile widened as he showed Wetham how to stroke the little wyvern's belly with his finger. 'I was just trying to give them some fun. They don't look like they've had much for a long while.'

'Well, that's true enough.' Katleya had turned away before Coryn looked up.

The three girls came back giggling and all too ready to run again.

'Let us see him again,' they pleaded.

'Please!' Pella wrapped her arms around herself, almost bursting with glee.

Coryn held the wyvern out for them and one by one, they touched its knobbly back, its ruff and the tail wrapped round his wrist. He kept a finger against the gland in its throat so it couldn't flame.

'You said he could make fire,' Sica gasped out between fits of giggles.

'Emerald green fire, like an ifrit's eyes!' added Pella.

Katleya tilted her head to one side, a single sardonic eyebrow raised. Coryn looked over to make sure she was watching. 'I did, and it can. Stand well back now.'

When they had cleared a pathway in front of him, Coryn pointed the wyvern's head towards the open area and released its throat. Opening its jaws wide it spurted a thin line of bright green flame two yards into the air. The fire licked against a stone. It didn't last long, but the children's eyes grew huge and their jaws dropped to the floor. Pella ran across and stooped to study the sooty stone.

'It's been burned! It's real fire! It is, it is!' She squeaked and hugged her little body trying and failing to hold in her excitement so she ran over to Katleya and hugged her instead. 'It is an imp-demon, right from the fires of Murak's hells! It is, it is!'

'Now, watch how it runs.' Coryn released the wyvern and it ran on its hind legs, out past the cart, its toes in the air to avoid the hot sand, its arms held close to its sides and its neck-ruff wide.

The children scattered squealing, then ran about copying the wyvern's gait, then back to the shade under the cliff laughing and fighting to tell Eilem all about it.

Around half an hour later, Pella came back and stood in front of Coryn holding something behind her back. Her huge blue eyes crinkled at the corners.

'I've got something for you, Sire Coryn.' She hesitated, then held out three purple spikes of desert pea-bush grasped in her bony little hand, looking as serious as she could. The crushed leaves and petals sent out a strong fragrance on the searing air. 'They're to thank you with.'

'Ah, Pella, they're very nice but you didn't have to thank me.' Coryn smiled up at her. 'I'd as much fun with the imp-demon as you.'

'But that's not why I'm thanking you.'

'No? Why then?'

She seemed surprised. 'Because you came to save us, silly. I thanked Lehot just the way Dame Mureen said, but I gotta thank you too. My mamma always told me I should thank them what helps us.'

Coryn cleared his throat and swallowed, then nodded. 'You must miss your mamma a lot.'

'Yes, the pirates, they...they...' She trailed to a stop, unable to deal with the memory. 'You'll get us safe outta here won't you. You won't let them writhen get us will you?' She gazed at his face, her eyes full of trust. He dropped his eyes to the dog. 'Won't you?'

'No, I'll not let the writhen get you.'

Coryn sat staring at the aromatic flowers in his hand as the little girl walked back to the others. Her innocent words seemed to pound like small skinny fists into his head. He still hadn't quite got hold of an idea of how he'd get five children and three women out of this flaming Murak damned hell-hole. Even if he could, writhen would chase and catch them before they'd got as far as they could spit.

Chapter 35

As the sun reached high enough to shrink the shadow at the bottom of the cliff, the writhen began to screech from the shadows where they hid. A cacophony of hooting and mangled catcalls. Dame Mureen rose and spoke to the children about inconsequential things as she ushered them back into the cleft. But Coryn saw Pella's hands trembling and a few seconds later Neima began to cry. They all whimpered as they disappeared one by one into the cleft. Katleya fetched Wetham. He didn't want to go, but she gave him a hug then took him by the hand and stroked his hair, murmuring something soft, as she led him to the cleft.

Coryn looked, back out to the rocks where the writhen hid, grabbed the crossbow and moved forward. Crouched down by the gap between the cart and the rock fall, where the shadows remained deep, he pulled the heavy butt of the crossbow in tight against his shoulder and watched. At a movement, he fired into the rocks.

A screech, then a writhen stumbled away from the boulders below. Coryn grabbed his own bow, nocked and aimed just high of another writhen's neck as it looked where its fellow had fallen. The arrow whispered through the air and the writhen fell to the ground, feathered through the mouth, right between the tusks. Working fast he reloaded the crossbow. Another writhen rose readying a spear. The crossbow thrummed and the writhen somersaulted and lay still, the spear still clutched in its hand. No more showed themselves. The screeching stopped.

As silence descended on the gorge Dame Mureen came out from the cleft. Her gaze lingered long and unfathomable on his face. Silent, Wetham followed her out and crouched back in the shade of the acacias again, close to the dog. He watched Coryn too. The boy's face was as unreadable as Dame Mureen's.

From inside the cleft came the sound of Katleya and Maisie's voices. They carried on a conversation with the children, talking about all the wonderful clothes the girls would have, the toys, the food and other delights waiting for them. Maisie talked about Faran and a Haven in the royal city of Fara, then about the one on Ostorr. The vast forests and rolling farmlands of Losan and Usar. The gentle shores of the inland Sea of Elyat, of the Isle of Storr with its magnificent castle, the royal seat of the High-king Nicoln II, Emperor of the Storratian Empire. How they'd be kicking autumn leaves soon after they had got there, as summer would be almost through by the time they reached Faran. Then winter with its snows would make a wonderland for them to play in.

Coryn listened, keeping his eyes on the trail, the riverbed and the rocks.

How long since I last saw snow?

Wetham rocked back and forth for some time, staring up at the mountain like his very life depended on something lying deep inside it. He ignored the words coming through the cleft mouth, except when Maisie said Lehot loved them all. He raised his eyes and stared into Dame Mureen's face then, searching. But it was hard to tell what he looked for. Coryn forced himself to look away from the scarred neck and back out at the gorge. He thought again on his escape plans, of his long delayed errand to Storr, of Lera, and of Birog.

A short while later, after Katleya had carried Wetham back into the cleft to sleep with the others, Dame Mureen came over to Coryn. She stood beside him for a few moments, staring out at the gorge. The sun blazed down and the air shimmered in its light. A swirl of sand rose and twisted, glittering. Two wyverns, one lapis lazuli, the other sapphire, helixed along the dry riverbed.

'I know I have said it before, but it is beautiful, do you not think?' Dame Mureen asked.

'Things have looked better to me.' Coryn didn't raise his head. 'On occasion.'

She sat down next to him. 'We are almost out of water again and run low on food, Sire Coryn.'

'I know.' Coryn sighed into the stifling air. Had he known there were so many he'd have brought along more of the meat. He couldn't have done anything about the water though.

'How long can the children last without it?' Dame Mureen straightened out her robe and patted at the red dust, her lips drawn into a thin, tight smile.

'Without water, if they stay in the cleft, another two, maybe three days.'

She smiled. 'That is a long time. Perhaps the writhen will get tired of waiting and leave.'

To another woman he'd have lied. 'Not with that blood-priest controlling them.' He sat staring at the boulders in the gorge mulling over his thoughts. 'We had blood-priests in Kalebrod using writhen and men they'd captured the same way. Men with minds so twisted by blood-magik they near became writhen themselves. What would you think of your own kin attacking you, not knowing you. From what I've been told, it took them less than a year to conquer the whole of Kalebrod, from the mountains to the sea.' He and Birog had managed to stay only a bare step ahead of them the whole way to Rophet. Not even that at times. 'Can't imagine how Rophet's holding them off.'

'This I now know, Sire Coryn.' Dame Mureen's voice was soft.

'And now it begins here. There'll be these small raids at first, testing defences, taking slaves, taking those with the Wealdan, like you, back to Mureck if not sacrificing you here.'

'Why did this blood-priest sacrifice both Dame Alana and Adherent Thoma?' Dame Mureen took a breath, steeling herself. 'Why did he not take them to Mureck?'

'I guess he needed their blood to tie these writhen here to him,' Coryn answered. 'Adherent Thoma likely died before the ritual finished, there was an arrow in his neck, so his Wealdan would have fled the body along with his spirit. That's why he needed to sacrifice Dame Alana. Otherwise, he'd have brought her back to Mureck for sure.'

'It will not happen in the Storratian Empire.' Mureen clenched her jaw. 'Faran has its own standing army and the Duke is a wise man, he will stop any efforts at an invasion.' Dame Mureen paused in thought. 'High-king Nicoln will gather all the princes and dukes of the other lands in his realm. Each will send companies of soldiers to Faran and Manom.'

'Kalebrod had an army. As does Rophet.'

'Rophet has not fallen yet.'

'Maybe, but it can't last on its own for much longer, and neither will these desert lands.' Coryn glanced down at Dame Mureen, then back out into the gorge. 'There's nothing here but city-states, each with their own small militias. Not good for much more than guarding walls and watching out for roving Shafian war-bands. They'll not stand a chance against the Murecken army with its writhen and slave-soldiers full of filthy blood-magik. Likelihood is that they'll sell out to the Murecken, like those Shafian guards of yours. Bend to the winds of war now, then plot to overthrow the Murecken priests when they grow complacent.'

'Yes, you have told me of these thoughts before. '

'I think it's the most likely outcome. I know the desert well enough.'

'Perhaps what you say will be, but at this moment these children and the two Adherents that live are of more concern to me.' Dame Mureen drew a finger through the sand. 'Do you think it at all possible someone else will come down the trail? Another merchant's caravan, perhaps?'

'No. I didn't see a merchant train making ready to go north when I left Rialt, and none would come through this pass anyhow. It's not the normal trail to Roesette.'

'We are not on a well used trail?'

'No.'

'I see.' She tried again. 'Then perhaps it will rain.'

'Dame Mureen, that won't happen either. Look around you. It rains so little hereabouts that on the few occasions it does people stop what they're doing and dance in the streets.'

'Can we not just sneak past the writhen in the dark of the night?'

'Their eyesight might be bad but they've an excellent sense of smell.' Coryn shook his head. 'They'd sniff us out and follow our trail if they missed our leaving. And it wouldn't be long before they realised we'd gone, then they'd be after us faster than we could run. It's the one thing I've not worked out how to overcome.'

She didn't respond right away. 'Sire Coryn, I do not believe you understand how fortunate you are.'

Coryn stared at her. 'Fortunate? Stuck in a trap of rock, sand and heat with three women, five children, no water and no way out isn't fortunate, Dame Mureen.' Coryn felt sorry as soon as he'd said it. Frowning, he looked away again to scan the sand, rocks, beaten down trees and shrubs, looking and listening for any changes.

'Lehot chose you to rescue these children.' Dame Mureen looked at her hands for a moment. 'I do not understand why He selected you but the fact remains, Lehot chose you. That makes you one of the most fortunate people in the world. Few are chosen, Sire Coryn.' She stood and walked over to the cleft. 'You will find a way, you will save the children.'

'I wasn't chosen.' Coryn leaned his head back against the rock, glanced at the dog and thought. With his wounds all healed and the bone ache fading, he had to admit at this point he was glad Dame Mureen had the Wealdan talent for healing, and he was as ready as he could be to get out of this trap. Not far from where the dog sprawled on the blanket, Pella's three spikes of desert pea-bush lay wilting on the sand. He smiled and began to put a solution together.

Chapter 36

It was close to sunset when Katleya followed Dame Mureen from the cleft again and out into the furnace of the gorge. The children weakened with every passing hour. There just wasn't enough water. Even in the cleft their faces flushed with the heat and it could only get worse. In the dappled shade of the acacias, she saw Wetham sitting next to Coryn's dog, one skinny little hand on its shoulder. Coryn sat nearby with his hand resting on the dog's side. In the other he held the crossbow.

'Dame Mureen.' Katleya reached out to touch the old woman's shoulder.

'Yes, Adherent Katleya?'

'You don't need to keep up the pretence when we're alone you know. I'm no Adherent yet and at this rate I don't know if I'll ever be one.'

'It would be best until we reach the safety of Ostorr, Adherent Katleya. And you should have more hope, you will become an Adherent soon, I am sure.'

Katleya bit her lip then nodded. She turned and looked back at Coryn again. 'How's he lasted so long out here in the heat? Shouldn't we have asked him into the cleft?' Hunger and thirst got her feeling dizzy and sick, but she wouldn't blasted well let it stop her from doing what was needed. She turned to Dame Mureen. 'The children won't last much longer. We've got to get out of here. We can't sit around waiting for this man to do something any more.'

Dame Mureen turned and stared out past the cart into the shimmering heat of the gorge. She didn't turn back when she spoke. Her voice was calm as always but filled with a deep sadness. 'Adherent Katleya, I do not know...' Her voice trailed off like she'd got lost in her thoughts. 'He grieves for his dog.'

'Has the dog died then, Dame Mureen?' Katleya looked into the old woman's face and bit her lip. She turned to look at Coryn again. Even hurt, she'd seen him move, all smooth and powerful, almost graceful. She closed her eyes and took a deep breath. 'Well then, he should bury it and tell us how he'll save the children.'

'I do not think it is dead. Not quite yet.' Dame Mureen looked over at Coryn.

Katleya hoped he hadn't heard her. He looked empty, all his strength drained out of him. The dog lay still. It looked dead enough. She opened her Wealdan and looked again. No, it still lived, if only just. Weak threads of Wefan pulsed and flickered in its body. She still thought they should escape now, while strong enough to have a chance. Not sit around waiting for a dog to die. She shook her head, was it wrong to think like that? The children. She had to think of them, they were more important than a dog, blast it. 'We should've left last night.'

'He was wounded, Adherent Katleya. He could not have done anything.' Dame Mureen gave her one of those looks that filled her with guilt. The old woman swayed and Katleya caught her round the waist. With a nod Dame Mureen straightened her back and stepped out of Katleya's hold. 'In truth, I do not know that he could have done anything in any case.'

'But they shouldn't have to die,' Katleya insisted. She felt her eyes water with stupid tears and got angry. How she had enough water in her to waste on crying she'd no idea. She turned her back on Coryn. She straightened and looked up at the cliff. She could climb it if she got rid of the stupid robes. But the children couldn't, not weak as they were. The same problem faced them if they tried to escape along the gorge. The children would slow them, then the writhen would overtake them, and then...

There was half a skin of water left. Katleya trickled a quarter of it into the empty waterskin and left it in the shade next to the cart before following Dame Mureen back into the cleft. They made their way down the line of exhausted children. At each one, they stopped and poured out the same measure of water into a small silver cup, about three swallows worth. The children gulped it down, their eyes searching the women's faces. When done, Katleya offered the small amount remaining to the other women. Neither would accept it. She poured it into the cup and gave it to Eilem. The pregnant girl would need it the most.

Katleya knelt by the children. She looked at all their faces surprised and touched by how at peace they were. Far more than she'd ever be in their position.

'Children.' Dame Mureen's voice was firm but a little cracked. It sounded loud in the silence of the cave. 'I know you are all hot and tired. So sleep now and know the Light and Love of Lehot keeps you safe.'

A little later, Katleya and Maisie sat side by side in the cave near the entrance. Maisie looked anxious as her eyes probed the shadows of the folded walls. Katleya drew idle patterns in the sand with a finger. They'd managed to form one new candle with scraped up wax melted into a small bowl and a short length of dipped string for a wick.

'I hope he is all right,' Maisie whispered.

'I know how much you believed in him,' Katleya murmured back. 'I'm sorry.' She agreed with Dame Mureen, how could he ever have saved them? One man against all those writhen and a blood-priest. There'd never been any hope.

'I do not believe he has given up. Once he has finished mourning his dog, he will take us out.' Maisie's voice wobbled.

'The dog's not quite dead yet, Maisie.' Katleya smiled and reached for her hand. Maisie trembled. Katleya moved closer, putting an arm about the Adherent's shoulders. 'And I don't know if there's any time left for mourning.'

'I wonder what it is like to die the way Dame Alaya died.' Maisie sobbed now.

'Plenty of people have suffered more than we have. Back east, it's not just writhen and Murecken blood-priests who are after anyone with the Wealdan. Everyone there is suspicious of all kinds of magik, no matter who's got it or what they do with it.' Katleya summoned the courage into her voice that she didn't feel and tried to give Maisie some comfort. 'It's like Dame Mureen would tell you. Lehot will help us accept the pain when the time comes and we'll enter into His glory arm in arm.'

Then kick him hard in the bollocks for letting all this happen.

They hugged each other for a long while.

'I still believe what Dame Mureen said when he first came to us.' Maisie pulled back and smiled through her tears. Pursing up her lips like Dame Mureen did before she said something she felt was important, she drew in a deep breath. 'He was sent to save the children and save them he will. He will come back to himself quite soon. I feel it here inside me.' She pressed her hand to her chest. 'Right here in my heart.'

'I hope you're right, I really do.' Katleya listened to their whispers drift away and die in the sultry air. 'But we'd better be prepared for it if he doesn't.'

But could she ever be ready for death? Even when it had stared her in the face, she hadn't been prepared or accepting.

No, I'd tell it to blasted well burn, then stick it full of knives.

Katleya sighed again.

Chapter 37

While the children and the two young women slept, Mureen stood, with difficulty, and left the cleft again. The high desert had changed its colours again. The landscape of red sand, rusty cliffs and dun-coloured vegetation began to soften into shades of pink and blue as evening edged closer. But the heat did not change. It clung to the stones and drifted in the air. Oppressive and unrelenting.

Mureen paused, thinking of the two young women. Adherent Maisie had come to these desert lands because of her. As had Dame Alaya and Adherent Thoma. They had trusted her and had trusted that it was Lehot's Will to save the children. Katleya, now she was another matter. Something about her bothered Mureen. For some reason she could not determine the girl was as unreadable as Coryn. Though stubborn and prone to anger, Katleya was honest, fierce and loyal. These things she could see with great ease, but the child's mind was closed to her. She took her crystal in her hand and delved its depths.

The thought crossed Mureen's mind that she wished Coryn was sent by Lehot only to deliver her from the burden of the children's suffering. The possibility she was so selfish was numbing and she could not continue that line of thought. All her life she had fought against her own headstrong will, had tried to humble herself before Lehot. Had she now, in her time of most pressing need, the moment she had lived and prepared for most of her life, failed the Lord of Light? Had the dark gods, Murak foremost among them, preyed on her frailties, her love for the children and the Adherents, made of them a wedge to drive between her and Lehot? 'Please, let it not be so.'

Picking up the waterskin from where Katleya had placed it by the cart, she walked over to the young man and the dog.

He had sat in the heat for the entire day. Most men would be half delirious from dehydration by now. Nevertheless she knew in her heart that young Coryn was not like most men. When he looked up at her, there was such hope struggling with such loss in his summer blue eyes that she had to drop her own gaze. He looked back down at the dog.

Mureen knelt, placing a hand on the dog's shoulder. 'He lives still,

Sire Coryn.' She waited for him to focus his thoughts.

Nothing but the normal sounds of the desert disturbed the silence for a long while.

'Sire Coryn, I need to speak with you. We have given the last of the water to the children and they will begin to leave us soon on their journey to Lehot's Halls of Light. By the time the sun rises again at least one will be gone, maybe more.' Mureen paused, waiting for some indication he listened. His eyes did not waver. He looked as if he peered through some terrible hole in this world and saw all of Murak's hells lying below, one after another to the very pits of oblivion.

Her parched throat hurt her to talk, but Mureen had to continue. 'We have saved you a quarter of a skin of water. It is not enough to keep the children alive any longer, but it will keep you alive till you reach fresh water yourself.'

Mureen waited again. Still nothing in his face indicated that he had heard her. 'You did your best for us. However, there is no reason for you to die here. I – I have a reason, the children. Moreover, we have a place to go, we will return to the Light of Lehot from which all have come. However, you are not ready, Sire Coryn. You have things to do, to reach out for and to resolve. This I know though you have kept the details from me. You cannot save us now and you never could have. I realise that now. It was unfair of me to have put that burden on you. Please forgive me.'

She set the waterskin down on the sand in front of him, then reached out and touched his hand. 'You are a brave man, Sire Coryn. Take the water and go, while you still can.' Mureen watched his face for a few moments but his thoughts were so far from the surface that she was unable to read him. Plucking at the Wefan, she sent out a tendril of thought, a comfort for the man who had lost so much of what little he had. 'I ask that you take Adherents Katleya and Maisie with you. They at least have the strength to go on. I shall remain with the children.'

Coryn twitched and Mureen thought he would turn his head. He did not.

'Sometimes it is far easier to die, Sire Coryn, than it is to live.'

She stood up. Her head whirled and she realised that she had plumbed the depths of her own strength. She stood a moment to gather herself. White desert owls wheeled down the gorge. Dusk made the pale, gliding birds spectral. Mureen saw Coryn motion at

229

her with his hand. Fighting the dizziness, she bent down close to his face to hear his response.

Chapter 38

'The sun's setting.' His voice came out like a croak. 'It's time to get going.'

Mustering his strength, Coryn laid a hand on the dog's shoulder for a moment then stood up. He picked up the waterskin and shuffled to the end of the cart. Though there wasn't any pain he was still damned tired and stiff. He uncorked the waterskin and took a small sip of the water. It tasted hot but wonderful on his parched lips and swollen tongue. When he finished half the water in the skin, he re-corked it and put it in the cart. Then he waited. His body began to respond. His mind swam less and he turned to Dame Mureen.

'Get the children ready. I'm taking them out of here.' Coryn kept his eyes on the old woman.

Her feelings written large across her face, Dame Mureen overcame her struggle. She took a deep breath. 'Sire Coryn, I appreciate your courage. But do you truly believe there is any chance of success now? What with so many writhen and so little water. Moreover, what of the Murecken blood-priest? They can go to Lehot in peace right here.' She motioned out beyond the carts. 'Out there they face pain and terror.'

Coryn half listened while he scanned the gorge a while longer, then turned back and looked down at her. 'Dame Mureen please get them ready,' he repeated.

Four of the children could stand without help. They formed a hesitant line in the shadows near the cleft. Adherents Maisie and Katleya rubbed their legs and tried to cheer them. The two littlest ones, Pella and Neima, whimpered. The others stayed silent and dazed. Dame Mureen stared down at the sand.

'Do you have any dark grey cloaks?' Coryn asked her.

She looked up at his face, her eyes filled with confusion.

'Dame Mureen, the cloaks. Do you have any?'

She gazed into his face for a long while without speaking. Then she turned and looked at the children. 'Our cloaks are in the cave. Adherent Katleya, can you help Sire Coryn please?'

Adherent Katleya looked at Dame Mureen and Coryn her face

231

unreadable. She went into the cave, returning with four cloaks, one partly cut up for Wetham's short trousers. Coryn took out his knife and began slicing into them.

Finished, he stepped back and looked at the children, nodding. Each now wore a piece of grey material from neck to ankle. If they stuck to the deeper shadows of the gorge, the cloth would help keep them hidden. Always supposing they didn't walk right into any writhen. Coryn's head whirled. There were lots of ifs. If the children didn't cry, if he could get to the camels before the writhen discovered him, if the drip pool had water, if the second cart remained in the valley, if...

He stopped himself from chewing over the possibilities and focused on doing. The desert pea-bush flowers next. 'Pella, will you show me where you found the flowers you gave me.' He pulled the wilted but still pungent stems from his shirt and held them out to her.

Pella looked at them then staggered to the far side of the gully. Coryn followed. In a crack of the wall, hidden by an old rock fall, grew a fair sized shrub covered with fragrant flowers and leaves. There might just be enough for them all. Cutting off every leaf and flower he could find, he brought them to the women.

'Rub them over their clothes and skin, don't forget their feet. The scent will stop the writhen tracking us.' Coryn passed bunches of the fragrant flower stems to the women and began rubbing one over his own clothes and skin. Then the horse.

'You too,' he told Katleya. 'And don't forget your own feet.'

He turned to Dame Mureen. 'It'll be the darkest part of the night soon. We have to finish moving the children before the moons clear the top of the gorge.'

'Sire Coryn, are you sure?' she whispered. 'I would not have them die frightened.'

'Neither would I, Dame Mureen.' Coryn looked into her eyes and saw the conflict there. He softened. 'Don't assume failure, don't assume death. Hope and know that I'll do my best.' He quirked a small smile. 'You should have trust in your god, Lehot.'

She looked a little stunned. He went back to the cart, pulled out his spyglass and scanned the trail. Dame Mureen trailed behind as if she might argue again, but she didn't speak. Coryn picked up the crossbow and handed it to her.

'I am not Adherent Thoma. I mean...I do not think I could recourse to killing.' Dame Mureen lifted her chin.

'I never thought you would. Just hold it and shoot at the rocks as you've done before. Your fire trick will keep them back a while longer. You stay here with Adherent Maisie, Wetham and the dog. I'll take the rest out. Then I'll come back for you. The two of you should make some noise. Maybe argue a little. It'll be enough keep the writhen watching the cart, listening to you and thinking we're all still here, while we slip away.'

Dame Mureen looked at him a long time before nodding and taking the crossbow.

Chapter 39

Katleya looked out into the night. With the sun long gone behind the mountains and the moons yet to rise, it was as dark as it would ever be. If Coryn thought to leave, now would be a good time. Then he stood next to her, motioning at her to follow him. He took her behind a cart and made her drink the last of the water. She refused at first wanting to give it to the children.

'If you don't drink it you'll never make it to the top of the gorge with a child on your back. If you don't make it, then the child won't make it.' Coryn sounded harsh, but she realised he was desperate to get the message across.

Katleya nodded and drank. She helped Coryn tie layers of pea-bush scented cloth round the horse's hooves. The poor creature suffered as much from lack of water as everyone else. She watched as Coryn knelt by the dog and placed his hand on its shoulder.

'I'll come back for you,' he whispered.

Embarrassed at overhearing, Katleya moved down to where the children stood to give him privacy. He was a good man. A sight better than she'd thought. It felt good to be doing something.

'We'll be fine.' She hugged Maisie goodbye. 'Stick close to Dame Mureen.'

'And you stay close to Sire Coryn,' Maisie retorted with a small, brave smile.

'I will. And you were right about him Maisie.' Katleya smiled. 'I'll always trust that heart of yours. '

Maisie hugged her back, no words getting past her sobs.

With Dame Mureen's persuasion, Eilem allowed Coryn to hoist her up onto the horse. He then put Sica up behind her. The lighter of the two small girls, Pella, he lifted up onto Katleya's back. She could feel the girl's heart racing inside her skinny little body. Neima, wide eyed and frightened, he swung onto his own back.

'Pella,' she whispered. 'We're leaving now. Sire Coryn is getting you out just like he promised. You'll be brave and quiet won't you?'

'Uh huh.' Pella tightened her hold round Katleya's neck and she felt the girl's nod.

'Wetham, you'll look after these two women till I come back?' Solemn, the boy nodded. Coryn looked at Dame Mureen. 'Make a noise but not so much they crawl up to investigate. Just keep them listening, believing we're all still here.'

The old woman nodded, her face sad but resigned. Wetham put his hand in hers and she smiled down at him. Maisie stood close to her, staring at the children. Starlight silvered her tears but she raised her chin and her lips stayed firm. Katleya wanted to hug her again.

'Go with Lehot.' Dame Mureen laid a hand on Coryn's arm.

Coryn glanced down at her, shaking his head as if he disagreed with the old woman's meaning, but Katleya saw a slow smile crawling up the side of his face.

'Have just a little faith, Sire Coryn.' Dame Mureen's eyes twinkled. A spark remained somewhere deep inside the old woman, contradicting the strain on her face. Katleya bit back her own smile. 'And I will nurse my hope.'

Coryn nodded his smile gone. 'I'll come back for you. Believe me.'

'I do.'

Now Katleya began to believe this Coryn wasn't like any other man she had known. Now he reminded her of Uncle Yadoc. Her heart dropped. She turned away to look out at the night.

Coryn turned and started toward the northern gap between the cart and the cliffs, leading the horse out, its well-padded hooves almost silent on the rocks. Eilem gasped at the animal's first steps, then clenched her jaw and held tight to the pommel. Katleya followed with Pella clutching her back. She staggered across the soft sand and unstable rocks. Coryn stopped and allowed her to come up beside him.

'Look, you've got to keep up. We've got to move out of here like one creature,' Coryn whispered. He looked concerned. 'Are you scared?'

'I should say no, shouldn't I?'

'Why?'

She shook her head. 'For the sake of the children perhaps?'

'Are you or aren't you?' he asked.

'Yes.' She bit her lip but she kept her eyes on his. 'Be blasted daft if I weren't, wouldn't I?'

'Me too.'

That surprised her. Coryn smiled, still staring down at her. She looked away, hoping it was too dark for him to see her blush.

They moved past the cart and Katleya knew the next hundred yards were the most dangerous. At any moment, one of the writhen could turn from watching the cart and see them on the open trail.

About thirty feet from the gully, Coryn picked up a rock and tossed it back over the cart. They heard Dame Mureen say something loud and Maisie's nervous laugh. He started off again, leading the horse on at a fast walk. Fifty yards further on he stopped again, letting the horse rest for a few moments. Katleya's legs shook and her arms ached where she held Pella's legs close to her sides. It'd be hard, having such short rests, but she'd rather get across this exposed area fast.

She looked back to see a fire flare up behind the cart. A dramatic gesture from Dame Mureen to keep writhen eyes on her. Katleya turned and saw Coryn nod, then he moved them on again. After an age of prickling fear, they crossed the last of the open area between the trail and the cliff.

Threading their way through iron tree, leatherleaf and thorn bush, they made it past the bend in the gorge. The desert silence seemed to magnify each thud of a hoof, each rasping breath of Coryn's and her own, each child's soft whimper. Katleya half expecting a shout or an arrow at any moment, twitched at every sound. Head pounding, she used her Wealdan to trace all the glimmering matrices of Wefan webbing the gorge. It took a lot of concentration to hold both normal and Wealdan-sight together but it'd give her some warning of recent movements and possible ambushes.

Coryn let them rest again when they'd got another hundred yards or so past the bend of the gorge. They stopped at the base of a small goat trail weaving up from the riverbed to the ridge. They began moving up the steep slope weaving between rocks and sagebrush. A stone clattered from beneath the horse's hoof. Freezing, they squeezed against a stack of rocks where the trail switched back on itself. No writhen appeared.

'There's nothing coming,' Katleya breathed into his ear. 'I can tell. Trust me.'

Coryn looked at her for a moment, then nodded. He started them moving again. Katleya heard Eilem gasp and stepped closer. The girl held her swollen belly with one hand, the other clutched at the pommel for support. Her eyes filled with terror.

Coryn stopped the horse and Katleya put a hand on her thin forearm.

'Be strong, Eilem. Breathe as slow and deep as you can all right? If you get a big pain, take short, little breaths till it's over. Whatever you do, don't push. Do you understand, do you think you can do that?'

Eilem nodded once.

'Is she near her time?' Coryn whispered.

'No, but with what she's been through,' Katleya whispered back and shrugged. 'Who knows?'

'Is there anything you can do for her? Something you've got with you to give her?'

'Not that I can give her without boiling up some water.' She'd use her Wealdan if she could, untrained as she was, but it'd call the blood-priest right to them, like a stinking rat to offal. No rushing river here to hide her manipulation of the Wefan. Thank the spirits seeing the Wefan wasn't the same as using it. 'I'm sorry.'

He nodded. 'Let's get moving again.' Was he trying to sound more confident than he felt? Katleya wouldn't blame him if so. 'She'll be fine on the horse. It's a good animal and will look after her.'

Katleya bit her lip and reached up to lay a hand on Eilem's belly. Deep inside, she could see the delicate matrices of Wefan belonging to the baby. Eilem's belly got hard and the poor girl whimpered. A contraction. It had started. She looked up into Eilem's wide eyes. The poor girl was terrified. It wasn't surprising. Spirits knew what she'd been through already. It put her own troubles into perspective. She whispered to the girl and tried to sound calm and cool like Dame Mureen would. 'Short, fast breaths now, Eilem, like I said. Every time you feel your belly getting hard like this.'

Katleya hated not being able to help more. The heat made thinking difficult and she was so tired now she couldn't even keep open her Wealdan. It slipped away entirely then and the cobwebs of Wefan faded from her sight. The night seemed all the darker.

Spirits blast it!

Why was she always getting into such awful messes? Her snort was soft in the night. She'd lost count of how many times she'd asked herself that particular question. Katleya hoped she'd get the chance to ask it many times more.

Chapter 40

The stars swathed the inked skies with glittering rivers and the moons seemed tardy in their rising this night. Did they linger behind the mountains in sympathy for those escaping? Mureen pulled her eyes from the rim of the gorge and watched Maisie feed the fire with the last few pieces of wood.

Mureen walked a full circle about the gully for the fifth time and came to a halt where the dog lay on Coryn's blanket. Without bending down, she could not be sure if it even breathed any more. It saddened her more than she could say to think it would die. It was just an animal but she knew that it was all Coryn had.

There was a small sound and Wetham put his skinny hand in hers. He gave her hand a little tug and knelt by the dog. Then he looked up at her with those huge dark eyes.

'A last word for Dog?' Mureen smiled and knelt beside Wetham. She placed her hand on the dog's shoulder.

Wetham laid his hand on top and looked up at her again. Mureen had the strangest feeling that the child could look right into her soul. She shook her head at the silliness of the notion and looked back down at the dog.

'Do you think it would serve Lehot's purpose to use a small measure of the Wefan to ease his last moments?' Mureen asked.

Though she had posed the question of herself, she saw from the corner of her eye, Wetham give a tiny nod. He kept his eyes on her face.

'Then what ease that is possible I shall give him, child.' If not for the decades of practice, Mureen would have found it difficult to draw on the Wefan, being so very tired and thirsty, but she held her crystal tight and managed to pull a few strands from the matrices in a rock nearby. She wove them into a healing pattern and guided it into the dog. With her Wealdan-sight, she saw the Wefan pattern flow deep into the dog, meshing with the matrices within its flesh, blood and bones. She hoped it fed the animal a little energy and soothed some of the pain. She did not think it would help much for the dog lay too near the brink of death. But how could she refuse Wetham? There could be no harm in it and she would not begrudge him or this dog the effort.

Wefan-energies burst into her, deluged her senses, stormed through her mind and body, before spurting out through her hands and into the dog powering the pattern she had made with a phenomenal amount of force. Just as she remembered how it had happened before, she lost consciousness.

Chapter 41

Coryn felt light headed, his mouth dust dry, his legs like lead. He took comfort in the fact the children should be starting to feel better by now. He had left them and Katleya hidden behind some rocks, under an overhang of the cliff wall, not far from the valley where he'd found the second cart, while he went ahead. For a wonder, the drip-filled pool contained enough cloudy water to fill the skins. He'd brought them straight to Katleya and the children. She understood enough about thirst to allow them just small sips, while the horse had sucked at the water he had held in his cupped hands. He barely did more than wet his own mouth. He couldn't afford to get any cramps during the next part of the night.

Now Coryn moved in silence, sliding between tall bushes and short trees, looking and listening for the camels in the shallow gully. He knew he was close. He'd taken a length of rope from the cart, along with a bag of oats, which now hung from his belt.

A few yards away in the dark, he heard a camel grunt, another groaned, then he heard the animals shuffle around in their corral. Relieved the Shafian had stayed put, but wondering on the reason he'd stayed when he'd all these camels and his job had been done, Coryn closed the distance.

Up on a ledge, well above the gully floor, the Shafian squatted by a small fire. Flames flickered against the sandstone walls of the bluff behind him as he looked into the flames. His worst mistake. He'd blinded his eyes to the night. The man spoke and something moved on the other side of the fire. A second man lay there, covered by a blanket. Coryn hoped the fire crackled enough to cover any small sounds he might make.

Waiting a while to be sure they were alone, he took his chance. Selecting two small stones, he threw one to rattle against the rocks further down the gully from where he hid amongst the branches of an acacia. The first Shafian rose to search the darkness, his hand darting to the hilt of his curved sword. Coryn threw the second stone into the same rocks, a little closer. The Shafian said something to his friend, then came to investigate.

Slipping his long knife into his hand, Coryn waited. The man was wary, but not wary enough. As the Shafian passed, Coryn clamped his hand over the man's mouth and pulled his head back to slit his throat in one quick move. Holding the body close he stepped back under the branches and let it slide down to a noiseless heap on the ground.

Coryn crouched, crabbed out from under the acacias, along a shelf and down a small outcropping of rocks to the camels. Moving slow to let them get accustomed to him, he rose and stepped in amongst the animals. Two still wore their harnesses, for which he was both glad and sorry. They'd be sore, but it'd be easier to hitch them to the cart in a hurry. Reaching out a hand, he let them sniff the pea-bush scent of his skin and gave them each a handful of the oats. He worked his way to the end of the gully. The remaining Shafian lay quiet, oblivious to the night.

Sliding his fingers into a fissure, Coryn began to climb, slow and careful. He reached the ledge well away from the man and drew himself up. Crouching in the dark, he pulled out his knife again. The man hadn't moved. Curious, Coryn closed the distance.

The man lay quite still and Coryn couldn't feel a pulse at his neck. He'd probably died as Coryn had slit his friend's throat. He tugged the blanket down from the Shafian's chest. Though his chest was wrapped in bandages, there was no blood. Curious, he pulled the bandages down. A neat, round hole had bored right through the ribs, close to his heart. Leaning against the rock ledge was a quiver full of yellow-fletched arrows. Distinctive, the same type of arrow that had feathered the Lehotan man's neck. These Shafian guards *had* sold out Dame Mureen to the Murecken blood-priests.

A pouch, heavy with coin, lay next to the dead man's body. He reckoned the old woman could put it to good use, buying new clothes for the children for a start. Satisfied with the night's work so far, Coryn shoved the pouch down his shirt, picked up the waterskins lying nearby, and climbed back down.

Taking care to make as little sound as possible, he pulled open a gap in the scrub oak and brushwood blocking the mouth of the narrow gully. The luck of the spirits held, as the six camels followed him through the opening without protest. When Coryn decided it was safe he got one of the camels to kneel, mounted it and, leading the other five, trotted them back to the drip-pool valley.

Chapter 42

Katleya had just settled the girls in a huddle under the overhang. They'd been crying, more with relief at not being thirsty any more than anything else. Now the little ones drifted in and out of sleep. Eilem's labour hadn't changed much, but at least it hadn't moved forward and the baby wasn't any nearer to coming out.

Thank the spirits.

She heard the whisper of falling sand and looked up. Coryn was back. Katleya couldn't help smiling at him.

'Spirits, Coryn. You're a blasted welcome sight.' Katleya dried her eyes with the back of her hand.

'Thanks,' Coryn mumbled. 'I've hitched a pair of camels to the cart.'

'Where'd you find them?'

'Your Shafian guards had them corralled not far from here.' He looked her straight in the eyes. 'They'll not need them any more.'

'Good.' She was glad they were dead.

The rat-faced bastards.

Now that Coryn had found the camels, it looked like they'd stand more than a spark's chance of getting out of this dust-hole.

'How's Eilem doing?' Coryn's eyes searched the trail and the rocks beyond, then he looked back at Katleya and grinned. She grinned right back at him.

'She's doing all right, the baby's well too. It's started but it'll be a while yet.' Katleya brushed the hair back from Eilem's forehead. The girl's sweat glistened in the starlight. 'And you will be just fine, Eilem. Soon you'll have a squalling little brat annoying you even worse than those three over there.'

She studied the girl's face, pleased to see the ghost of a smile flit over it.

'Let's get them to the cart then.'

She glanced up. 'Yes, but there's no way Eilem will be able to ride.'

Coryn nodded then lifted the three sleepy-headed girls up onto the horse's back. 'You lead the horse, I'll carry Eilem.'

Eilem shrank from him as he came near her and something got heavy and hard in Katleya's chest. She squeezed the girl's shoulders.

242

'Trust him, Eilem. He'll get us out,' she whispered. 'You'll not get hurt ever again. Soon as you're able, I'll teach you how to handle the knives. Would you like that?'

Eilem almost smiled. She looked from her to Coryn, bit her lip, then gave the tiniest of nods.

Coryn moved forward with determination. 'It's all right, Eilem. We'll get you to safety.' Gritting his teeth, Coryn picked her up from the ground.

He looked surprised at how easy it was. Katleya could have told him the girl was much lighter than she should have been. Everything she had was going to the baby.

'You've no idea how glad I am you made it back,' Katleya whispered, hoping he realised she meant every word.

Coryn nodded at her. 'Thanks, but anyone would think you didn't expect me to return.'

She studied his face a moment, chewing on her bottom lip. 'I didn't know what to expect. Thanks for everything, Coryn.' Katleya let her eyes linger on him for a few moments longer. She smiled again. She felt exhausted, that's why she was starting to like this man more than she wanted to, it was obvious. 'Thanks for coming to save the children.'

Coryn nodded. He looked about to say something then, without another word, strode past her. Scowling, she led the horse out from under the overhang.

I'm an idiot, not a blasted spark's doubt about it.

Not much further along the trail, in a wider valley filled with the sound of dripping water, she saw the cart. Coryn had backed it off the trail, hiding it under some scrawny trees.

'I suppose it could've been found without much effort, but it's the best I could do here.' Coryn looked back at her.

In the moonlight, Katleya could make out his earnest face. The man risked his life to save them, had got them out of that gorge, right out from under the noses of the writhen and a blasted blood-priest, and he felt the need to *apologise* for not hiding the cart well enough? She almost laughed out loud. Instead she nodded.

Beyond him, a smudge of light showed on the eastern horizon. The moons would be up soon. That meant Coryn had no more than half an hour or so left to get back to Dame Mureen, Maisie and Wetham.

Moments later, he handed the children up to Katleya in the back of the cart.

'This time expect me to return.' Coryn grinned. Katleya smiled back. If felt good to smile. 'Keep as quiet as you can while I'm gone.'

'I will. Keep safe yourself.'

He nodded, shouldered two waterskins, and walked away into the darkness.

Chapter 43

Wetham saw him first when he crawled into the gully. Coryn motioned him over. The two women slept under the acacia. After Wetham had taken a drink, he crawled over and woke Dame Mureen.

'You made it,' she rasped. She looked haggard, though she brightened when she saw the waterskins. 'Are the children safe?'

Coryn watched her drink from the waterskin, pulling it away when she'd had enough. 'Eilem's baby is coming but the others are fine. They're all waiting for you in the cart.'

Dame Mureen clasped her focus crystal and closed her eyes. He woke Adherent Maisie and gave her a small drink. Then he went back to Wetham and got down on his hands and knees. 'Crawl up.'

And Wetham did.

Coryn's heart lurched when he felt a tongue rasp against his hand. Thinking he'd lost his mind, he turned and looked into the almond eyes of the dog. 'Murak's demon-infested hells!' he breathed.

'Sire Coryn, what have I said about your cursing?' There wasn't a shred of anger in Dame Mureen's voice.

'Spirits. Am I dreaming?' There weren't any more words in him. He reached out his hand and placed it, feather-light, on the dog's shoulder. It leaned in against him, yawning so close to his face that Coryn could smell the antelope meat on its breath. It then limped up to the gap between the cart and the cliff wall and turned back to face him. Come on then, it seemed to say, time to move.

They made it to the top of the ridge just as Diaphos peered over the sandstone buttresses, splashing the gorge with silver. Once again, Coryn marvelled at the old woman's luck. They scurried on like grey dreams a shade below the rim. This time they reached the cart without mishap. The women spent longer than he liked hugging one another and the children.

'We're not safe yet.' He checked the camels' harnesses one last time. 'Time to leave.'

Coryn helped Maisie up into the bed of the cart. She sat by Eilem and eased the girl over so that Eilem leaned against her. He then lifted

Dame Mureen onto the cart. The old woman moved to Eilem and ran her hands over the girl's belly.

Little gasps of pain worked their way out of Eilem between stretches of rapid breaths. Coryn had seen enough births, in the slave tents on caravans and in the slave quarters of his late master's home, to know she'd have a babe in her arms before another night passed. Katleya was already on the driver's seat holding the reins. He nodded at her then led the camels in a half circle to get them pointed down the pass towards Roesette.

'Don't worry about resting the animals. The pass out of the mountains is nearly all down hill from here and there are two of them to share the weight. They're a deal stronger than they look. Just keep them moving. You know how to use the cart's brake, don't you?' Coryn asked.

'I do.' Katleya nodded, though she stared straight ahead, her lips pressed together.

'There's a big water hole about three leagues further down the trail. You'll hit it about dawn. Don't worry about missing it. You'll never get these animals to go past it.' Coryn looked up at Katleya and grinned. 'You're sure you can drive one of these things?'

'I'm no stranger to driving blasted carts, believe me, Coryn.' Katleya met his gaze with her large green eyes, but this time she didn't smile back. 'You're not going with us are you?'

He had nothing to say to that.

Dame Mureen lifted her head from the back of the cart and turned towards him. For the first time since he'd met her she looked furious. 'So this is it. This is how you get the children out without the writhen catching us? You sacrifice yourself.' She stared hard into his eyes. 'Why did you not ask me?'

'I'll keep them listening to my singing till just before morning. That should half kill them. Then I'll slip out in the pre-dawn dark. It's no problem. It'll give you a whole night's lead.' Coryn shrugged and tried to look casual about it. 'By then, they won't even try to catch you, you'll be too close to Roesette and the border guards will spot you long before then. Besides, I'll have the dog with me.'

'You should have asked me.' Dame Mureen turned away to glare into the darkness. 'The dog is still weak.'

Coryn turned to see tears running down Katleya's cheeks.

'Spirits keep you safe, Coryn. I'll expect you to return to us. You've done it before, you can blasted well do it again.' Katleya turned to the camels and slapped the reins against their sides. They groaned as they moved off.

He stared at her. *Spirits keep you safe?* Again she'd said it. She was no Lehotan Adherent.

Shaking his head, Coryn walked along the length of the cart, raising his hand to run his fingers through Wetham's hair as he passed. He mounted his horse as the cart moved down the trail toward the end of the pass, followed by the four loose camels. Maisie and the children watched him. Not Wetham though, he stared at his feet where they hung off the end of the cart. Dame Mureen didn't turn round, concentrating on Eilem. Katleya looked back over her shoulder at him once.

Coryn raised an arm in farewell.

Chapter 44

As Coryn rode along the rim of the gorge, a vague, gnawing thought formed in his mind. If he failed, if he died and the writhen caught up with the cart, there'd have been no point to it all. All their effort would be wasted.

The dog walked close. Sometimes, it looked up at Coryn. He reined in above the gorge and studied the dry riverbed. It was quiet. The writhen shifted about behind the rocks, nothing more. None had moved even though the fire had burned out. He dismounted, turned the horse back toward the drip-pool valley and smacked its rump, its hooves, still covered with wadded cloth, padded across the hard ground. It was a sensible horse, it would head back to the water.

He didn't watch it go, but slipped down the trail surprising a writhen in the shadows near the riverbed. The writhen took a half-hearted shot with its bow then scurried away without the dog having raised a growl. Strange how they seemed so afraid of him. Coryn didn't know why and didn't much care as long as it stayed that way.

He and the dog ghosted past the cart and into the gully without incident. Spirits knew how.

Coryn kneaded the lump of scar tissue in his thigh, it didn't ache and that felt odd. He didn't think he'd ever get used to being Wealdan-healed. A tongue rasped at his fingers. It was the dog. They had feathered it enough to send it to its death yet now it moved well, almost as good as before. He'd Wealdan-healing to thank for that too. The dog had changed though, changed a great deal. He smiled inside.

Maybe he had too.

Coryn broke off some acacia branches and restarted the fire. Moving away from the flames, he sat down hard in the sand, beyond bone weary. Liatos now peered over the mountains and Diaphos shone bright enough to silver every shape and blacken the shadows. Then exhaustion pounced and he lost consciousness for a few moments.

He woke with a start at the dog's growl and forced himself to stand. There was some movement out in the night, but nothing to alarm him. He listened for a while to make sure, then took the shovel off the side of the cart and banged it a couple of times on the wheels. He drank from the waterskin, poured some more into his cooking pot for the dog and stretched back against the rocks under the acacia. The dog stretched out next to him and Coryn scratched it behind the ear.

He caught himself, amazed. The dog actually let him treat it like a normal dog. It made him feel good. Perhaps the best he'd felt in a long time. Coryn wondered why. Feathered, burned, almost dead from thirst, and trapped in this sand-burned hell-hole. Why did he feel good? It seemed the dog did too and it'd been through as much if not more.

He laughed out loud. Both the moons poured silver over the rocks, Diaphos floated high above the mountains and even Liatos had dragged her arse above the worn peaks. The women and children would've been on the trail for a good while. Soon they'd start the downward slope into the foothills, then they would see the distant grasslands of Manom lit by the rising sun. By mid-morning, they would reach the next waterhole and be a good twenty leagues away from here. By noon, they'd be too far away for the writhen to follow.

Coryn clung to that thought. But the writhen wouldn't even think to look if they thought the women and children were all still trapped in this gully. He stood, picked up the shovel and banged it on the wheel again.

Sitting a little way from the fire again, Coryn wondered about getting to Storr, if it was still possible. All he had to do was leave in the last hour before sunrise, sneak past the writhen again and go north through the mountains. Then west along the Roes River to Manar Port and the Elyat Sea. A berth on a ship should get him to the Isle of Storr by the festival of Mabon. To think, at thirteen summers old Lera would be big enough to dance with him at the Summer's end festival. Could she dance? Who would have taught her? He'd missed so much.

Coryn hadn't seen a Mabon festival for years. For far too long he'd not thrown kernels of corn into the fire with the other boys just to watch the adults jump when they popped, or eaten apples layered with molten sugar, or drunk filched cider and mead till he was sick. He hoped they'd the same celebrations in the west as they did in Kalebrod, that'd be something.

They didn't celebrate harvests, or sowings, or any of the other seasonal festivals in the desert lands. He supposed it was because the desert never changed, so had no seasons to speak of. They had various celebrations all through the year, colourful, noisy, celebrations for one or other of their numerous gods, or kings ancient and new, or battles won. Each celebration was very different from the next, but still, none were as good as those he remembered from home.

He let his thoughts drift to Dame Mureen. If Eilem's baby had arrived, the old woman would be singing like a mountain wheatear to that bunch of waifs. It felt good knowing the women and children had escaped. He hoped Dame Mureen's anger was long gone. Coryn didn't think she was the sort of woman to hold onto anger and he didn't like to think of her being upset with him. And then there was Katleya. Katleya who haunted his mind.

Smiling, he pulled the crossbow close beside him and rested his sword across his lap.

Chapter 45

Coryn couldn't believe his eyes when he woke. Was he dreaming still? But he knew he wasn't. Dame Mureen sat in the sand in front of him, smiling that smile of hers that raised an automatic response within him. He grinned back.

'What're you doing here?' Various scenarios rose to Coryn's mind and his grin fell away. 'Did Katleya lose control of the camels? Are the children all right? Did writhen attack you?'

'You worry too much.' Dame Mureen's smile broadened. 'Everyone is fine. Eilem has not had her baby, the children are well, and we saw no sign of any writhen. Adherent Katleya is very capable. She manages the camels with ease and Adherent Maisie is a capable healer and cook.'

'Then why in all of Murak's flaming hells are you here?' Coryn demanded.

'Because I have never before met anyone sent by Lehot.'

'Spirits! Don't twist me about, Dame Mureen. I risk my...'

'I do not *twist you about*, I would never do that,' Dame Mureen interrupted. 'I am quite serious. You were sent by Lehot to save the children. I know this in my heart. There is no doubt.'

'I was not. I might have got the children out of this dust-hole, but that's all.' Coryn scowled out into the gorge past Dame Mureen's shoulder.

'Oh no, young man, it is not.' She shook her head so the loose braids flared out catching the moonlight. 'First I asked Lehot for you to come to us. Then, after I saw you, I sent out a call and that very night you came back to us.'

'Chance.' Coryn shrugged.

'That was not chance. How many men would have looked at what was happening in this gorge, seen death waiting to strike us, and ridden into it? You even knew that a Murecken blood-priest was behind the writhen and still you came. I believe that very few men would have done what you did, Sire Coryn.' Dame Mureen paused a moment, her back straight, her eyes like steel. 'And of those few, how many would have had the courage to sacrifice themselves as you meant to do? No, it was not chance, Sire Coryn. I cannot believe other than that Lehot sent you. You must understand that this is true.'

When he spoke, all the feeling of relief that'd flooded over him before had vanished leaving behind nothing but annoyance. 'Why's this so damned important to you?'

'Because it is the most important thing that will ever happen in your life. Just as it is the most important thing that has ever happened in mine.' She stood and stepped a little closer. 'Sire Coryn, you have been touched by Lehot and I cannot let you die here alone.'

'I never planned to die here, you should know that. I told you I'd get out.' Coryn took a drink of water from the waterskin. 'Anyway, if Lehot had bothered to send me to save the children, why would he let me die here? That doesn't sound very fair.'

'It is not our place to judge Lehot.'

'No. You're not going to get off that easy.' Coryn slammed the cork back into the waterskin's neck. 'You're telling me that after I went ahead and messed up my life and all my plans to do what Lehot wanted me to do, I'm now going to die here? And you think because you've come down here to die with me that makes it all right, that evens things out? Or did Lehot send you here to die with me?'

'I do not know,' she said.

'Why not? If you're so certain I was sent here, why don't you know if you were sent here?'

'Because it does not work that way, Sire Coryn. Believe me.'

'Why should I believe someone who isn't certain of a damn thing?'

'I do not know. I suppose that either you have faith or not.' Dame Mureen settled herself down on the sand again, turning her face to the moons. 'I want you to know something else.' She lowered her voice. 'In this place, I had almost lost my own faith. It is because of you that it has returned.'

He stared at the ground between them, drawing a finger through the sand. 'Why'd you almost lose it?'

'When I first saw the children, it broke my heart to see what had been done to them. It was hard to hold on to my belief in the goodness and greatness of Lehot then. After we became trapped here with writhen eating the flesh of Manzur right in front of us all, when I realised I could not save the children myself, I doubted Lehot again. Nevertheless, I began to do the one thing I knew how to do. I asked Lehot for help. It was then that you came.' She turned to Coryn again.

'I saw you and that night I called to you. I know that the call reached you because He sent a great surge of His own Wefan-energy through me. I had never before felt such power. It flowed through me with such force that I fell unconscious. That has never happened to me before either, Sire Coryn. It was then that I knew again that He existed. That everything is all right within Lehot's Light.' She was smiling at him again. 'I can assure you, Sire Coryn, that it is a wonderful feeling. I wish you could feel it too.'

He half smiled. 'I'll take your word for it. And if everything's all right with Lehot, then maybe things aren't so bad after all. But now you must understand why I'm no follower of any god myself.'

'I can understand, but you must understand why I believe in Lehot. A second surge of His Wefan-energy flowed through me again when I laid my hand on your dog to comfort it.' Dame Mureen looked down and laid a hand on the dog's shoulder. 'I know that He did that for you. A gift for a gift.'

They didn't talk for a while after that. Coryn sat against the rocks with the crossbow leaning next to him while Dame Mureen fed more sticks into the fire. Every few minutes she looked up at him and smiled. He didn't return the smiles. He was trying to deal with the problem she had caused by returning. Without her, he would have taken his chances. Now he had to worry about her. He realised then, it was when he'd other people to worry about that death seemed to hold any sort of power over him.

After a while, Dame Mureen came and sat next to him. 'Do you play Thrones, Sire Coryn?'

The question surprised him. He watched as she searched through the contents of the bag hanging from her belt. 'Yes, I do.'

'Good.' She sat up straight holding a worn set of bones and a slim silver flask. She opened it and he smelled the unmistakeable scent of brandy. 'Losan's finest.'

'Spirits! I'll be damned by Murak himself.' Coryn took a sip and relished the taste and feel of the fine spirit run over his tongue and down his throat.

Dame Mureen smoothed an area of sand. She rattled the seven bone cubes in her hands, blew into the gap between her thumbs, and tumbled the cubes onto the sand with a practised flick of her wrist.

'You've played before.'

'Three nights a week at Ostorr. More often in Faran where I was less likely to get caught.'

'Did you have brandy in the Havens too?

'Mostly mead in Ostorr. I took up the brandy when I moved to Faran. Why, do you think it is a sin in Lehot's eyes to take a drink?' Dame Mureen's eyes twinkled with amusement.

'Never thought about it, I suppose. Never thought drinking a sin myself.'

'Nor do I, in moderation. Would you put more wood on the fire so that we can see the bones?'

Since he wanted all the writhen to keep their eyes on the gully, Coryn roped a small thorn bush and heaved. It came out of the ground on his fourth try. Dragging it over to the fire, he chopped it up with his sword and flicked a couple of branches onto the flames. His sergeant in the Selassian Guard would've been aghast at his using the sword for chopping wood, but needs must. He'd get out his whet-stone and make it good and sharp again later.

Picking up the crossbow, he stood next to the cart and studied the light and shadow beyond. He could sense the writhen were close, but he had a strong feeling they weren't going to try an attack any time soon. It was strange. Perhaps he'd wounded the blood-priest more than he had thought.

Before he turned back, Coryn thought he saw something move far down the trail. He watched it for a moment longer but couldn't be certain. The dog sat next to him and looked out into the darkness.

'See anything, Dog?' Coryn was certain it wasn't a writhen. None would leave themselves exposed on a moonlit slope like that. Not when a man had a crossbow trained on the night.

'Sire Coryn, are you delaying the game?'

Coryn glanced at Dame Mureen then back at the trail. The shadow had gone.

They played for hours. They played for black beans. They drank brandy. They argued. They laughed. By the time they finished the last of the brandy, she had all the beans.

Coryn leaned back on his rolled up blanket. 'I think you won fair.'

'You know I did.' Dame Mureen smiled and put the bones away.

'I suppose I should keep my shirt, though.'

'I think it might be a little large for me in any case.'

'Is there any more of that Losan brandy?' Coryn asked.

'I'm afraid that flask was all I had.' She drew a tired hand across her face. 'There was some Selassian fire water in the cart Dame Alaya and Adherent Thoma escaped on.'

'Ah, it did some good there.'

'How so?'

'It slowed the writhen, they were too drunk to attack when they downed it yesterday,' Coryn said. 'And, after that, they'll have had some damned terrible headaches to deal with. We can hope alcohol works on them the same as us anyway.'

Dame Mureen chuckled into the night.

They both sat without speaking for a few moments. She looked out towards the gorge while he watched the stars overhead.

'You know, you remind me of my grandmother even though I never really knew her.' Coryn paused, uncertain. 'Maybe, what I mean is, I'd like you to remind me of my grandmother. Does that make sense?'

'It does. And I would be proud to remind you of her.'

Much later he woke and discovered the second surprise of the night. Coryn had half expected it.

Wetham sat in the sand near the cart and stared out at the gorge. Coryn walked over and sat down next to him. He handed him a waterskin. 'Wetham, what happened? Are the others all right?'

Although it was almost imperceptible, he thought Wetham nodded his head. He was filthy from crawling through bushes and between rocks.

Coryn watched him drink and felt a strange change take place inside him. He felt as trapped as ever, but this time he didn't feel so alone. It wasn't even a near thing. He raised a hand and curled his fingers round the pouch lying over his heart, squeezing hard till it hurt. Maybe things weren't quite finished. There might yet be a way out of here after all, even with these two to protect. The night remained silver and black, velveted in silence. For some reason, the writhen still didn't attack. He'd sleep now and give it some serious thought in the morning.

Chapter 46

As dawn fingered its way into the gorge, Coryn woke almost too stiff to stand. But he was happy again. As happy as he'd ever been. Wetham slept curled up in the sand a few feet in front of him. The dog sat next to him staring out into the brightening gorge. Dame Mureen cooked breakfast over a small fire.

Coryn stretched out the kinks and walked over to the cart. He pulled out his spyglass to check over the trail and the slope leading down to the river. For a brief moment, he saw a quick movement between the rocks of the dry riverbed, then all went still again. He saw nothing else. But he knew what the movement meant. He picked up the crossbow and watched the gorge with it cradled in his arm. Dame Mureen glanced over at him once or twice but said nothing and continued to cook. Wetham slept on, exhaustion in every line of his skinny body and face.

Coryn studied the riverbed a moment longer, then drew the crossbow to his shoulder and fired. The explosion as the heavy quarrel hit a rock created a concussion of air that smashed into the far wall of the gorge and rebounded off the cliffs behind him. Dame Mureen shot up as if slapped by the sound. Wetham bounced to his feet.

Coryn had fired at an exposed foot. It was gone now. He didn't know if he had hit anything but it didn't matter. As ever, the shot alone would keep them cautious. He smelled the aroma of meat frying. Astonished, he walked over to the fire.

Dame Mureen watched him as he approached. He looked at the length of meat coiled round a stick over the fire. Snake. 'Where'd you get that from?'

'Lehot provided.' She knelt down next to the fire and shook the skillet. 'In truth, your dog brought the snake in. Does it not smell good, do you think it will taste as delicious?'

'I do.' Coryn grinned. He walked over to a point where he was well out from under the overhang of the mountain and stared up at the rugged rock face rising hundreds of feet above. It was steep and dangerous-looking. He looked back at Dame Mureen. She seemed small and worn out, hunched over the fire. Wetham sat beside her, even smaller and scrawnier.

Dame Mureen handed the boy a plate of steaming beans and shreds of snake meat. He ate it up, shovelling it into his mouth though the heat of it must have burned his lips.

'Would you like some breakfast too?' Dame Mureen looked over at Coryn.

'Please.' He squatted down next to Wetham, looking into the boy's sleep-filled eyes. 'How are you doing?' Wetham didn't respond. Unsurprised, Coryn watched him for a few moments, then turned to Dame Mureen. 'Do you suppose he'll ever speak again?'

She ran her fingers through the boy's hair, trying to smooth it out but having little success. 'Wetham is as clever as anybody. He is just a very quiet one, that is all, who will speak only when he is good and ready.' She smiled at the boy. 'I like that in a man.'

Finished with eating, they all sat back against the rocks. The dusty smoke rising from the campfire hung on the air. A wind rose, chasing streamers of sand that rose to veil the gorge. Wetham sat between Dame Mureen and Coryn under the dappled shade of the acacia.

Coryn shot out an arm and snatched a lobed lizard off a rock. The lizard turned its head and stared at him with its bulbous eyes. He put it on Wetham's shirt and its skin turned a dark, dusky blue. Then he picked it up and set it down on the orange sand. The boy watched. In moments, the lizard had turned orange. Coryn set it on Wetham's lap and stood up. He walked over to the cart and motioned for Dame Mureen to join him.

'They're in the rocks well above the river now.'

'I do not see them.'

'I can smell them. Take a good sniff, they're as ripe as ancient goat's cheese mixed with stale piss. They've been creeping closer all day.'

Dame Mureen chuckled, then realised he was serious. 'Will they rush us soon, do you think?'

'Not while the sun's up. If anything, they seem to be more afraid of us than they were. But they'll come tonight. The blood-priest will have used blood-magik to heal his wound by now. He'll be angry and he'll force them to move on us.'

'Could we not hide in the cleft? Such a narrow entrance would be easy to defend.'

'Easy to block you mean. They'd pull us out when we'd got too weak to fight.' Coryn shook his head. 'Not a way I'd like to die if it's all the same to you.'

'What then?'

'We don't have many choices.' He looked up the cliff face to the skies above. 'Not now.'

She nodded toward the northern end of the gully. 'If they are on the rocks above the river can we still get out that way? As we did before?'

'No, that's one of the choices we don't have any more. They're no more than a few yards down the slope. They've sealed us off. I've got an idea though, but it'll be hard.' Coryn studied the river rocks. 'I was thinking we could go over the mountain. They'll not expect it and we won't leave a trail.'

Dame Mureen's eyes widened. 'Up this cliff?' She put a hand on the cart's side and tilted her head back to look up at the cliff face. 'It must be two hundred feet straight up.'

Coryn nodded and turned to her, smiling. 'About that, perhaps some more. Have a little faith, Dame Mureen.'

She laughed.

Chapter 47

Coryn chose to leave the gully in the brilliant sun of late afternoon, the most difficult time for man or writhen to see past its harsh rays. When the sun moved over the rim this side of the gorge and slanted into rocks and riverbed, the effect increased. And a writhen's eyes were poorer by far than any man's in daylight. By the time the sun stood at noon, they had reached getting on for around a hundred and fifty feet up, by way of narrow cracks and slender ledges. It was exhausting and dangerous work. The sweat didn't make it any easier.

Coryn stopped on a faint path, stitching over the uncertain and crumbling sandstone. Wetham clung to his back, his arms wrapped into the cloth of his burnoose. Dame Mureen struggled a few feet below them, her skirts tied up into her belt. The dog had gone on ahead. Somehow, the animal had found paths up the cliff they could all follow.

Here the rock face sloped more and Coryn looked up. The stubby crown split into three giant pillars of stone, one much taller than the other two. The very one that Subrahima the ifrit had spun over. It was a maze of cracked cliffs and terraces. Above it, sunlight exploded out of the vast, arching blue sky flooding the mountains all around. It was breathtaking in its beauty and enormity.

The thought of climbing higher worried him. He looked down at Dame Mureen again. She'd reached the top of a large rock and sat, resting. She leaned back, saw him and nodded. Coryn raised a finger as a signal to wait then turned to the rock again. Past the shallower slope, the cliff became vertical again. He found small clefts and cracks in the worn stone and inserted his feet and hands.

He was panting by the time he reached the top. Once there, Coryn set Wetham down and beckoned Dame Mureen to follow. She moved faster than he expected and she soon sat on the ledge next to Wetham, staring across the vast expanse of desert. She breathed hard, but smiled too.

'What's funny?'

'No, not funny, it is not funny at all. It is magnificent. The starkness and the simplicity of the desert are as beautiful as anything I have ever seen. I have told you so before, have I not?' She didn't turn towards him. 'The view from here is wondrous. Do you know, as I was climbing, Sire Coryn, I had the feeling Lehot was looking over us and that the world was brimmed with His Light? Did you feel that too?'

'I can't say I did.'

Dame Mureen sat thinking for a few moments, then gazed off across the land again. Her eyebrows rose. 'Could that be rain on its way?'

Coryn glanced at the tall clouds massing over the eastern horizon. Like sculpted stone, the granite and slate colours seemed stark against the aching blue vault of the sky. 'It's nothing but a false promise. Clouds drift over the desert from time to time, but don't drop their rain. The riverbeds stay dry this time of year.'

'That is a shame.' Dame Mureen gazed at the clouds for a while longer.

Coryn stood and helped Wetham crawl up on his back again. 'We'd better climb higher. I've a strange feeling about this place.'

'A strange feeling?'

'It's an itch I can't explain.'

Dame Mureen frowned not quite understanding.

'I reckon we'll see when we get there.'

When the faint track veered left, Coryn turned right and edged along a ledge half a foot wide that led round the base of the huge sandstone pillars. He had guessed right. The dog had stopped and looked back at him as it leaned against the stone wall.

He was close to finding the place that made his skin itch. The pillars grew out of the slope and a small ledge of stone, a foot or so wide, traced a ribbon round the rock to whatever was on the other side. There wasn't any sign of the dog. Coryn studied the pillars and the ledge and stretched his sore muscles.

'Stand facing the wall, like this, and follow me nice and slow.' He looked toward Dame Mureen, then back the way he'd be moving. 'Don't look down or lean back.'

Coryn put a foot out on the ledge and pushed down, transferring his weight onto the narrow strip. It held. He inched forward, heel to heel. Now both his feet were on the ledge and he was committed. If it gave way, nothing lay between him and the broken rocks far below.

Spirits! Please make sure the ledge holds us all.

His arms spread wide, he pressed his sweating palms against the stone, then he slid his feet along, his heart beating fast. Soon the ledge widened a fraction and cracks in the rock face gave him finger holds. It wasn't long before he'd shuffled round the pillars. He stepped out onto a flat plateau, his clothes drenched in sweat. The dog panted nearby watching him, it's tongue lolling. Wetham slithered down from Coryn's back and joined the dog.

The plateau was circular in shape and a good fifty feet across. At the far end a deep cave cut into the hillside, its entrance a perfect circle seven foot in diameter and quite smooth. Curious, Coryn walked across the plateau. Past the short entrance tunnel, the cave's roof reached an arm's span higher than his head and stretched maybe twenty feet or so wide. The rear hung thick with shadows and for a few moments he could see nothing.

When his eyes got accustomed to the dark he saw silver, gold and copper dishes and small vessels sitting on deep shelves carved out of the cave wall to either side of the entrance. Jewels filled the bowls, some rough, some faceted. Painted decorations of plants, birds and beasts covered the smoothed walls. He'd never seen designs like them. As far as Coryn knew this wasn't Shafian, Rialtan or any other desert people's work.

As he turned, his eye caught a face in the shadows and a strange sense of awe filled him.

He had an answer to his itch.

At the back of the cave, lying on a high stone ledge, still as a sculpture, slept Subrahima ibn Rashinabel. The ifrit's skin was whole, the burns on the soft gold of her throat and hands all gone, her flame red hair hair, re-grown, flowed over the edge of the ledge. Between her parted lips, her teeth gleamed pearl white. But not a single flame licked over her body. And it didn't look like she breathed. Did ifrits breathe? Coryn hoped she wasn't dead.

Coryn stood staring for a long time, wondering. The insistent prickling of his skin told him some type of strong magik worked here. Not the Wealdan or blood-magik though, not even the spirit-magik he remembered from his childhood. Another kind, one that used the flows of Wefan in a way he'd never encountered before.

Carved into the ledge below the ifrit, were strange patterns or maybe words he couldn't read. Just as Coryn started forward to take a closer look, a lick on his hand from the dog brought him out of his thoughts. Then Dame Mureen called out to him.

'In here,' he called back.

Chapter 48

The three of them stood in the cool shadows of the cave, staring at the ifrit. Wetham seemed as touched by her as Dame Mureen and Coryn. The place felt sad like they stood in a sacred temple. The dog padded in and flopped down on the sandy floor.

'She helped me get to you.' Coryn chewed the inside of his cheek, remembering what she'd made him feel.

'It is hard to believe something so beautiful is a demon.' Dame Mureen patted her dress. A puff of dust rose and settled to the cave floor.

'She's no more evil than a mountain lion or a wolf.' Coryn stared back at Subrahima. 'Ifrits are a type of spirit, a wild creature of nature, made of the Wefan itself.'

'I see, much like writhen when left to their own devices, perhaps?' Dame Mureen looked up at Coryn, eyebrow raised, her lips pressed into a tight half smile. She walked forward but bounced to a stop a few feet short of the ledge. The air shimmered in ripples from where she stood, like a stone thrown into a still pond. 'How clever, an invisible shield protects the end of the cave. I sense some sort of magik, but it is very strange. Neither Wealdan, nor Ascian, but whatever it is, it has still made use of the Wefan.'

'Ascian?' Coryn asked, but then he remembered she'd mentioned it before.

'The old name for blood-magik before it came to be used the way it is now.'

'It was used differently once?' He couldn't believe it could ever have been used in any good way. It needed blood didn't it? So someone had to die to give it to the magiker.

'In ancient times they spilled their own blood to quicken their Ascian. In a way, the Wealdan is much the same, it is in our blood, but we do not need to actually spill it to access the power. The difference is that we can use the Wealdan to draw on the Wefan and manipulate it to our needs.' Dame Mureen pressed a hand against the shield. It rippled again but nothing more happened. 'I would very much like to study this. I should tell the Moder at Ostorr Haven too. It would be of great interest to her and also to the Fader of Storr Haven. They might well send someone back to study the phenomenon.'

'Spirits.' Coryn rubbed at his neck as the itching intensified. 'I'd prefer it if they left her alone. She's been through enough.'

Dame Mureen didn't answer but placed her palms on the shield and moved them about. He felt the itch turn to a prickle as she opened her Wealdan. 'It is cool and slick to the touch. It seems to cover this entire back section of the cave. It is made of Wefan, but it is something other also.'

Wetham also seemed fascinated by the barrier that protected the ifrit. He stroked the surface again and again with his bony fingers, stretching to reach as high as he could and moving from one end to the other. The surface shimmered and the hairs on Coryn's neck rose.

A rock protruded from the wall a few inches from where the barrier met the cave wall and Wetham put his ear to it for a short while. Then he wrapped both hands round it and pulled.

'What is it?' Coryn asked. Wetham didn't reply, but redoubled his efforts to pull the rock from the cave wall.

Shrugging, he joined the boy. Wetham stood back as Coryn wrapped his hands round the rock, giving it a good hard tug. The stone slid out with a grating noise and sand cascaded to the floor. Gushing, crystal clear water followed.

'Spirits! I'll be...well done, Wetham.' Coryn shook his head in amazement. The water flowed into a stone bowl cut into the sloping wall. The deep bowl soon filled and the water poured over a wide lip, rushed along a channel cutting across the cave, pushing aside drifted sand and other wind-blown debris, then disappeared through a round hole in the far wall. Cupping his hands, Coryn drank long and deep. 'It's good.' He nodded to Wetham, smiling. 'Very good.'

Wetham almost smiled back. Dropping his head, he knelt by the flow and sucked up great mouthfuls, then dunked his whole head under. Shaking it like a dog, he turned and stuck his feet and hands into the flow, as fascinated by the water as he'd been by the barrier. The dog came and lapped up great long tongues of coolness. After a while, Coryn pushed the rock back in its hole and the flow became a dribble.

'Someone else might need it someday. Other fools like us, maybe.'

After Dame Mureen and Wetham wandered out of the cave, Coryn moved back to where the ifrit lay sleeping. He reached out to touch the barrier as Dame Mureen had. It didn't ripple. It sparked and fractures ran out from his fingertips like forked lightening. He snatched his hand back, worried he'd damaged it in some way. Subrahima opened her eyes and smiled at him. She gave him a slow wink, licked her lips and stretched with wild sensuousness. Then she faded from sight with a flicker of light. In a blink, the barrier dropped away to disappear into the rock at his feet. His itch disappeared too.

'Do you think you have seen the last of me, pretty man?' Subrahima's whisper stroked against his ears.

After a shocked moment, he laughed. Shaking his head, he walked out of the cave.

'It's a dead end,' Coryn murmured.

Dame Mureen looked up at him.

'There's no way off this plateau for us except the way we came,' he explained. 'I'm sorry.'

'You tried, Sire Coryn.' Dame Mureen sighed. 'For that we are all grateful. I shall meditate and hope Lehot sends me inspiration and if that is not forthcoming, for a peaceful ending.'

'I'm not giving up yet, Dame Mureen.' Coryn grunted. 'Don't be so willing to die and go to those halls of light or wherever it is you're aiming for.'

The boy wandered over to the far edge of the ledge and stood staring out across the ridged mountains where the stacked clouds glowered red in the sunset. Wondering why he didn't feel despair at the futility of it all, at being trapped yet again, Coryn walked over to join him. He stopped with a start before reaching Wetham and crouched down fast.

'Wetham, come back here.'

The boy backed up and Coryn crawled forward to peer over the edge. Their stone perch was right above the cart and, even though they were high up, a writhen happening to look their way would catch any movement. Coryn reached down to pull his spyglass from his belt. He focused it on the desert below. He counted ten writhen hiding in the riverbed, all watching the cart. Could they be all that remained? He doubted it. They just couldn't be that lucky. He slid back. Wetham now sat by the cave entrance, next to the sprawling dog. He played with the folding-knife, opening and shutting the blade.

'There are writhen down there, Wetham, best to stay back where you are now,' Coryn said. As usual, the boy didn't respond.

Far off in the distance, the wall of clouds bumped against the worn serrations of the mountains and broken arrows of lightning split the brooding ramparts. Coryn counted time till he heard the deep roll of the thunder. A good fifteen leagues away yet. More lightning speared down, edging each rock and cliff with mercury.

He looked over at Dame Mureen. 'Looks like someone will get some rain after all. Be good if it came down the gorge and washed those damned writhen away.'

Wetham looked up at him, then over toward where the lightning fingered the worn mountains.

The thunderstorm was beautiful, wild but brief. By the time it was over, the sun neared the horizon. The growing shadows etched the snaking trail far below with black ink. Coryn shivered as a chill wind rushed up like a wave over the rocks, damp with the smell of rain. He stepped over to the edge of the rock shelf and peered down again. Along the dry riverbed he could see the writhen. Some pointed up at the cliff. Cackles floated up to the ledge.

Frowning, Coryn looked down the face of the mountain. The blood-priest he'd feathered was working his way round the bulging rock, his clawed hands spread wide, digging into the soft sandstone. His staff was strapped to his back and bloody bandages wrapped his shoulder. He seemed to have healed well enough to climb the cliff face though. He looked up. Hatred leaped from his narrow face and his eyes burned as they fixed on Coryn. With feral ease, the blood-priest leaped onto the shelf and pulled the staff from his back.

'Come on then, you stinking heap of offal.' Coryn spat and cursed his luck while pulling his sword from its sheath.

'Where are the others?' The blood-priest looked about, obviously searching for the Adherents.

'Gone too far for you to have them.' Coryn bared his teeth and stepped forward.

'No,' Dame Mureen yelled, scrambling up and moving between Coryn and the blood-priest.

'Get out of the way.' Coryn felt a tingle and the hairs on his neck spiked. The old woman held her Wealdan ready.

'No, you cannot die this way, not now. I will not allow it.' Dame Mureen raised a hand and small blue flames danced about her fingers.

Wetham ran over and wrapped his skinny arms round her waist.

His eyes glazed over and Coryn worried fear would send the boy into shock. The blood-priest's eyes focused on Dame Mureen.

'You I will have.' He lifted his staff high and shot along the last of the ledge toward the plateau, snarling, his filed teeth bared. But before he could use his blood-magik, a spurt of blue fire pummelled the blood-priest's chest. With a long wailing screech, he fell. The sound stopped abruptly.

Coryn trembled in the backwash of magik, then a faint hum grew inside his skull. It wasn't over. Below, the writhen ran towards their master, their screeches wild. More Wefan swirled then shot past him like a torrent and he gasped, struggling for breath and stared at Dame Mureen. She stood frozen, her eyes blazed, her hand still raised. It shook and glowed bright blue for a long while, before fading.

The hum faded with the light, and Coryn shook his head, trying to rid it of the lingering spikes and prickles left by so much powerful magik.

A relentless grumble came from further up the gorge. It soon grew into to a steady rumbling roar. Louder and louder.

He looked down. What he saw made Coryn shudder.

A massive torrent of wild brown water exploded through the narrow gorge below freed from whatever natural dam had held it back. Dame Mureen's Wealdan sent blast of Wefan must have destroyed it. The water surged round and over trees and boulders, taking up the smaller ones like leaves on a wind. It rushed high up the cliff walls, its noise shattering the evening. Desperate, the writhen tried to scramble to higher ground. But the flood poured forward faster than a horse could gallop. Writhen screeched, ran, and died. Some were swept under the raging flood, others were smashed by the rocks and trees carried in the churning waters.

In moments the silence returned, the water disappearing as fast as it came. The gorge was left subdued and eerie. Nothing to see but wet sand, rocks and scattered pools. Coryn watched a single writhen pull itself up the far riverbank, its movements hesitant and weak. It collapsed after a few yards.

Chapter 49

Dame Mureen staggered, falling to her knees. She retched, heaving out her last meal, then retched again. Wetham crouched by her, patting her back with his skinny hand, his face creased with worry.

'Wetham, I think Dame Mureen could do with some water.' The boy rushed off to the cave glad to be doing something for the old woman. Coryn knelt down beside her. 'I didn't know you could do that.'

'Neither did I,' she managed to say, and wiped at her mouth with a corner of her robe. 'I did not intend to. I am ashamed to say that it was not under my control.'

'I think it's over.'

'I believe it must be. There cannot be more.' Dame Mureen shuddered. 'Dear Lehot, let there be no more.'

'I don't understand.' Coryn looked back at the shelf edge where the writhen leader had stood moments ago. 'I thought you said you didn't have enough Wealdan for that.'

'I do not. I believed it was Lehot's doing the last two times, as I told you.' She glanced up at him, her face pale and a worried look to her eyes. She glanced at the cave, then back at him. 'But now I think, perhaps not.'

Coryn thought on it for a while. 'No, it wasn't Lehot.' He'd felt the Wefan driving through the old woman. Her own Wealdan and another's.

'No, I know now that it was not Lehot.' Dame Mureen turned and looked toward the cave mouth. 'Lehot would not have done such a thing.'

Wetham. He turned to where the boy was coming back with one of the bowls from the cave. Water slopped from its edge. He froze when he saw Coryn and Dame Mureen staring at him. His eyes grew huge and shimmered. There was an imperceptible shake of his head then his jaw bulged.

'It's fine, Wetham.' Coryn motioned to the boy. 'Come on.'

Wetham stepped forward. Kneeling by Dame Mureen, he offered her the bowl.

'Thank you, Wetham.' She gave his shoulder a quick squeeze with one hand and sipped at the water. 'That is much better.'

'Now's the time to leave.' Coryn stood again. 'While there's still light enough to get down this wall and nothing down there to stop us reaching the cart.'

Dame Mureen nodded and stood. She trembled but waved Coryn's hand away. The dog was already trotting along the ledge.

Their luck held. The horse and a pair of camels grazed near the drip-pool. They were all soon mounted and travelling hard. Coryn touched his heels to the horse's sides, urging it into an easy loping canter, the kind it could keep up for leagues, but not fast enough to be dangerous on uneven footing. Wetham held on tight behind him. Dame Mureen rode one of the camels, Coryn's blanket folded for a saddle, and a rope halter for a bridle.

Coryn couldn't quite grasp all that had happened back at the gorge, but he wasn't taking any chances. There could be other writhen any-where in these mountains and more blood-priests too. So far, it looked like any survivors of the flood had disappeared into the desert. The dog looked unconcerned as it loped ahead, and that eased his mind. He hoped the writhen would be too scared to come near Dame Mureen again, ever.

Coryn flicked a glance at Dame Mureen when they slowed for a stretch. The horse and camel picked parallel ways through the trees and scrubby bushes. She looked shrivelled, dishevelled and exhausted. She took that moment to look over at Wetham. It seemed like she'd no idea where he'd come from or what he was. How must it feel for her, thinking Lehot had worked through her, only to discover it was a small boy come far too early into his Wealdan? And to have been used like that, to kill. That would be hard for a woman like her to get her mind around.

Shaking his head, Coryn realised he felt protective of her, something he'd not felt for anyone since Lera. For the first time since he was a child, he grasped that someone understood and cared about him. It was a good feeling.

Coryn rode on, looking forward to fulfilling his oaths to Birog and Lera. He breathed deep feeling the reality of survival sinking into his mind. Wetham clung to his back and he patted the boy's skinny arm.

'Well done, Wetham,' he said under his breath. 'You did good.'

For a moment, Wetham's arms tightened.

Chapter 50

Coryn pushed them hard till well after the last traces of sundown had left the mountains. He could tell Wetham was on the fringe of sleep behind him but through force of will, the boy still held tight. The night threw a tangle of shadows onto the sand making it hard to see what was underfoot, so he slowed the horse. He stopped on a stony rise to check their back trail, scanning the gorges, ridges and cliffs behind him with his spyglass. Nothing. He closed the glass and looked up. The moons hovered over the eastern horizon. Cleared of clouds, the skies shimmered with stars.

A few hundred yards from the water hole, Coryn left Dame Mureen and Wetham with the horse and camels in a gully. He took the crossbow and stared out across the darkening sands to scout for signs of tracks. The vegetation was thicker here. Acacias, iron trees, thorn bushes, aloes, and agaves grew in abundance. He could smell the silvery sweet foliage of sagebrush and pea-bush, which thrived on this side of the mountains too. He moved through the low branches listening and watching out for anything untoward. When a stick broke nearby, he folded up into a crouch. He heard nothing else.

Coryn eased himself into the side of a bush and readied his bow. He waited in silence, his eyes wide to take in the silvered outlines of the night. The massive spiral horns of a desert ram lifted from a sage to his left. He let his breath out in quiet relief and sent an arrow into the goat's eye, killing it.

Coryn butchered the animal, wrapping as much of the good meat as he could carry in its own skin, before moving off again. He studied the ground and found the tracks of the cart. He could see where Katleya had stopped in the bushes a hundred yards from the water and then got down and scouted the area on foot. She was clever. Surprised at how good he felt about that, he grinned.

Chapter 51

'Blast it!'

Katleya was angry. Spitting angry. It was all very well for Dame Mureen to have gone off, but she should've realised Wetham would follow. And why couldn't the old woman understand that Coryn could look after himself anyway? Katleya had seen that right from the start. She knew he had worked out how to get back to them when the time was right. That was often the problem with these old people. They never thought youngsters had brains enough to look after themselves. Well, she'd found the waterhole all right, and a safe place to hide the cart.

It wasn't long after Coryn had left them that Dame Mureen insisted on leaving too. Taking one of the camels, she'd disappeared into the night. Katleya knew better than to go after her, so she'd got the camels going at a fast walk again after that, only stopping the cart a while after dawn arrived. That's when they'd realised Wetham had gone off with the old woman and wasn't huddled up under the cloaks with the other children.

While they waited, she had rigged up an awning over the cart using a few branches and scarves. She'd taken off her skirt too and used that for an extra bit of shade. It wasn't ideal, but it worked well enough and she liked being back in her trousers. Katleya moved them on again after a few hours. They could put as much distance as possible between them and the madness they had left behind in the blasted gorge safe in the knowledge that Coryn would find them.

As dusk settled on the desert, they'd negotiated a long, steep path down to a scrubby area of rocks and sand hills and reached the water hole. It was just as Coryn had described. There were three pools of water reflecting the calm purpling sky. Katleya had stopped the cart and backed it into some trees before going on ahead to scout the area. Using her Wealdan, she'd found nothing had passed through for days apart from the normal desert animals. She'd then found this gully nearby and decided the best thing to do was wait through the last of the night and travel on again in the morning.

Maisie agreed, her mind more on Eilem and the coming baby than anything else. The girl's labour came and went as if the baby couldn't make up its mind whether to come out or not and the poor girl was worn out. At least they had plenty of food and water for her now.

Katleya dug a fire hole a few feet into the sandy wall near the gully's dead-end, close to the cart where the cliff jutted out creating an over-hang, so if anyone looked into the gully it'd be almost impossible to see the fire. That was one of the many things Uncle Yadoc had taught her. She paused her digging to rub at her eyes. Problem was, there was too much stupid dust in this blasted desert. She'd not stay here a spark's moment longer than she had to, that was for sure, and would never, ever come back.

Filling a cookpot with water, Katleya boiled up some beans and the last of the meat, now rather dry and chewy. She'd have to go out hunting, see if she could find and kill some animal or other with a knife throw. She might get lucky. Coryn had better hurry up with those bows.

It was full dark by the time she finished tucking the girls in using the cut up cloaks for blankets. With food in their bellies and uncountable hugs, they'd fallen asleep. A deep groan came from the ground near the end of the cart. Katleya got down and knelt next to Eilem. She opened her Wealdan and put a hand on the girl's swollen belly. Inside, the slow pulse of energies flowed through the lattices of her body, strong and regular. The faster pulse, belonging to the baby, seemed fine too. The baby had moved down and would soon be coming out.

Katleya and Maisie could really do with Dame Mureen coming back right now. The old woman should never have left.

'You're doing well, Eilem. Thanks for not screaming. I understand it hurts like all of Murak's flaming hells but you're strong. Strong as a...' words failed her.

'As a horse.' Maisie rose and walked a little way from Eilem, beck-oning for Katleya to follow. 'She's in pain still, but I can't give her any more of the tincture,' she whispered, rubbing sleep she hadn't had from her eyes. 'It might be dangerous.'

'Don't worry. It won't be long now, Maisie.' Katleya gave Maisie a hug. Somehow, though she was younger by a good two years than Maisie, she felt older. 'I'll gather up some wood and get more water. We'll need to keep the fire going.'

'I'll stay with her, don't worry.' Maisie still looked worried. 'I've seen this before. I know what to do. I think.'

'Good. I'll be right back.' Katleya grabbed the waterskins and left.

She knelt down by the larger pool, dipped her head right under and scrubbed. The cool water ran off her hair and face, taking some of the sand and grit with it. Squeezing and shaking her hair dry, she tied it back with a leather thong. It had grown a deal since she'd left Black Rock and hung past her shoulders. She'd have to cut it soon and dye it again. Long hair wasn't any use to her. It got in the way and was nothing but a headache of sand, sweat and tangles in this furnace of a desert.

She found it almost impossible to accept Laeft would now be shaking off the tail end of winter. That the snowmelt would be running through the foothills, the rivers threatening to burst their banks. Bears would've woken from their long sleep too and be lumbering about in search of food in forests of budding aspen and mountain ash. A wave of home-sickness almost overwhelmed her, but Katleya bit it back and washed out the cookpot and the bowls. She re-filled the waterskins at one of the smaller pools.

Stacking some wood a little way from the fire, Katleya put the pot, full of water again, on to boil. The girls still slept. Not Eilem though, she lay hot and uncomfortable on the cloaks looking every kind of miserable. The poor girl's contractions came fast now. Maisie kept her calm and encouraged her to breathe in the right way at the right times.

Then the dog turned up. It sauntered into the gully like it owned the place and lay down by the fire. Its almond eyes glowed in the night.

'They're coming.' Katleya surprised herself by how excited and relieved she felt. The last of her anger at Dame Mureen vanished like mist in the sun. 'I'll go see how close they are and hurry them up if I can.'

'Don't leave me on my own too long,' Maisie whispered. She looked a little more desperate. 'I'm not sure I can do this after all. Eilem is so young and so small. What if something goes wrong?'

'I'll be minutes. If they don't show up, I'll come right back. Promise.' Katleya gave Maisie another hug. 'Be strong.'

Walking out of the gully, she breathed in the delicate scent of the desert mistletoe's small greenish-yellow flowers growing on some ironwood. Across the valley floor, scattered clumps of bright yellow brittlebush flowers glistened with pale starlight.

Chapter 52

When Coryn returned, Dame Mureen was talking to Wetham. The child's head drooped and his hands hung slack between his knees. They sat together on the sand near the camel.

'They all made it.'

Dame Mureen's face lit up. 'That is the best news I could ever have.' Her smile was magnificent. 'You did it, Sire Coryn. You did what Lehot asked of you.'

He sighed but didn't answer.

Coryn began to feel they might be safe now. But he was a cautious man so he stood on the highest hillock, holding the crossbow in the crook of his arm while Wetham and Dame Mureen drank and washed their faces, scanning the darkness as if a thousand writhen chased them.

The three water holes were in a small depression filled with rock and banked by sandy hillocks studded with more rocks, scrubby sage and wind-twisted leatherleaf. Insect noises filled the air, owls called and a jackal yelped to its mate. Because of the rain, the night air was cooler. It was as beautiful a spot as he'd ever seen in these mountains. Coryn could smell desert lavender, pea-bush, acacias and sage. Within a day or two, the rain would've lured the desert flowers from hibernation and the arid land would sprout swathes of colour. That would amaze Dame Mureen and Katleya. He couldn't wait for them to see it.

At the mouth of a narrow gully, maybe three or four hundred yards further on, they found Katleya keeping watch half way up a desert oak. Coryn grinned to see her climb down like a monkey. He was surprised to see her in trousers, but they suited her and were a deal more practical than a dress.

'Come quick, Dame Mureen.' Katleya's voice was thick with relief. 'Eilem needs you.'

The other children were fast asleep, all arms and legs on the rumpled pieces of cloak in the back of the cart. Maisie now supported Eilem on a blanket spread over the ground nearby. There wasn't any sign of the baby and the poor child looked exhausted. Dame Mureen went straight to Eilem's side and placed her hands on the girl's belly.

'The head has engaged. The babe will come very soon now.' Dame Mureen's face frowned with concentration, her eyes closed as she moved her hands over the distended belly. 'Adherent Katleya, is there any willow bark left?'

'She's had a lot already, I didn't dare give her any more, Dame Mureen.' Maisie laid a hand on the girl's forehead.

Katleya opened the old woman's leather satchel and took out a small pot. 'There's not much left.'

'Very well. Steep some camomile and valerian. We will give her that for now.'

Katleya picked out the relevant packets and emptied the herbs in a bowl. She poured some of the boiling water over it. All the time she glanced at Dame Mureen as the old woman soothed Eilem's birthing pains with her Wealdan. Only once did she look up at Coryn with those startling green eyes of hers flashing in the light of the fire. They made his heart lurch and he stepped away to check on the camels and rub down his horse, listening all the while to the night and the women.

'Adherent Maisie kneel behind Eilem and hold her a little more upright. There, that is much better. Do you feel a little more comfortable Eilem?' Dame Mureen knelt between the girl's legs as the child nodded, her eyes wide with fear and pain. 'Have we any cloth left?'

Katleya took an underskirt from the cart, ripped it in half and soaked it in the boiling water, using a long stick to poke it down. Sweat ran down Eilem's face and she moaned low in her throat, her body trembling with exhaustion.

Feeling useless now he'd finished with the animals, Coryn walked the length of the gully up its entrance. He climbed up some rocks to scan the darkness with his spyglass. There was a cry and he scrambled back down the slope. In the firelight he saw a dark haired babe nestled against Eilem's skinny chest, suckling.

Katleya cooked over the fire as Dame Mureen and Maisie made the girl comfortable. The wonderful smell of roasting goat wafted into the warm desert night. The scent might carry for a few hundred yards, but it would be hard to locate, and the hot wind carried it northwards, away from any writhen left alive. The children, woken by the smell of food, scrambled off the cart. They gave Coryn tentative smiles, their eyes large in the darkness. The little girls gathered round Eilem, fussing over the new babe, till Dame Mureen chivvied them away to let the girl sleep.

After the meal, Coryn boiled more water and made kaffe, looking forward to sitting back and enjoying a strong, rich cup or two. Dame Mureen, Katleya and Maisie drank some too, all tired, sitting but not yet ready for sleep. He offered a cup to Wetham. The boy sniffed it, tasted it, then shook his head, his little nose scrunching up. The fire died to rosy embers, casting a warm glow against the bank and back onto them.

Dame Mureen looked at Coryn. 'Are you still determined to go to Storr?'

'I am, as you know. My sister is all I have left. To find her again... it'd be something. And I've my errand. An oath given is as strong on the day you die as the day it was made. That's what my Da always said, anyway.' He waited a moment or two, all too aware of Katleya's stare. 'What about you?' he asked Dame Mureen.

She smiled. 'I shall return to Fara with the children first. Then I will go to Darafen for a short time. It is my home and I feel the need to see my family. I have many nieces and nephews there apart from my younger siblings.'

'What about Wetham?'

'He must go on to Storr, to the Haven there. The Fader will know what to do with him.'

Katleya hissed in a breath and Coryn studied Dame Mureen's face to see if she was serious. It seemed she was. 'He's too young.'

She looked across at him. 'Yes, yet his Wealdan is both immense and wild and his ability to use it through others is...unusual. He needs all the help and training the Masters on Storr can give him or he'll be a danger to himself and others.'

'You can't send him there on his own, not after what he's been through.'

'I agree and, as you say, he is very young. He will need someone he knows and trusts to watch over him.' Dame Mureen looked straight at Coryn. 'I am glad you too think he should not be alone.'

Coryn didn't say anything for a long time. He stood up and stretched. 'I reckon, once we reach Roesette, we'll all take a river boat down to Manar. From there we can take one of those shore-hugger boats to take us up the Manom coast to Faran.'

'It is a long journey by road up the coast.' Dame Mureen sighed.

'But I feel the children might be happier staying on the land.'

'Fine, we'll swap these camels for a good team of four horses.' Coryn poured out the last of the kaffe into the proffered cups. 'It shouldn't take us as long to get to Faran then.'

'Yes, that sounds sensible.'

Coryn slung his bow over his shoulder, picked up the crossbow loaded it and walked away from the fire and past the cart. Millions of stars spiked the black velvet sky overhead. The moons were up too, Liatos at her fullest, while Diaphos' bowl swam with darkness. The camels chewed on grass and leaves just inside the mouth of the gully along with his horse. He stood in the shadows watching for a few moments.

So it was settled. It'd been a long journey, in more ways that one, but the end was in sight. He'd reach Storr soon, be able to discharge his oath and hopefully find his sister. He looked forward to reaching Manom in the next day or two. Coryn looked forward to seeing Katleya's leaf-green eyes sparkle in the vastness of the grasslands too. The thought made him grin into the night.

As one, all the animals lifted their heads. Snorting and nervous, the horse moved down the gully toward the cart, followed by the camels. Coryn slid into the acacias to the right of the gully mouth, threading his way to the edge of the rocks.

He smelled the stink of writhen. Whipping an arrow out of the quiver, he nocked it and eyed the darkness. Then he smelled something else.

Lacert. He froze. The round, red eyes glowed at him from the dark.

'Put your weapons on the ground.'

Coryn lowered the bows to the ground. Another blood-priest here, so close to Manom? Right now, though, the lacert was the real problem. Lacerts meant bloodhunter-priests. Was the man who had spoken one? Coryn hated not knowing what he faced.

Damned Mureckens.

Coryn turned, slow.

A wyrm? A damned wyrm too?

How had a creature that damned huge gotten so close without him hearing it?

The wyrm hissed and opened its maw wide so every row of its serrated teeth glistened in the moonlight promising terrible things. It's

277

jaws were large enough to take off his head and half his body with it.

'The sword too.' A bloodhunter-priest sat in a saddle on the wyrm's back, the lumpy, red gem hanging from his neck glowed like old embers, matching his eyes. He smiled but there wasn't any humour in it. He motioned with his levelled crossbow for Coryn to sit down in the sand. 'Most accommodating. Tie him up.'

A writhen ran forward from the darkness beyond the wyrm. It circled round to come up behind Coryn and tried to pull his arms behind his back. Coryn whirled round, grabbed a leathery arm and yanked hard. The writhen slammed into his shoulder just as the bloodhunter-priest's quarrel flew through the air. It thudded into the writhen's chest and the creature slid to the ground without a sound.

Coryn snatched up the crossbow and fired from a kneeling position. The quarrel whirred straight past the wyrm's teeth, hammered up through the roof of its mouth, drilling into the creature's brain. Roaring in agony, it reared and twisted its forelegs up in an effort to claw the pain away, gouging at its own face. The priest screamed, thrown from the saddle, he thudded into the sand with a grunt.

More writhen came for Coryn.

He whipped up his bow. Screams came from the camp, thin and high-pitched.

Spirits! The children. Katleya!

He took a wild shot at the nearest writhen, feathering its shoulder so it flew back against another, slung the crossbow and his bow over his shoulder and grabbed his sword. He sprinted back down the gully while buckling on his sword belt.

Maisie straddled the driver's seat of the cart, a long pole in her hands and a terrible grimace on her face. She swung it round with surprising dexterity to give one writhen a hefty crack on the skull. It fell back onto another writhen trying to scramble up onto the cart. Both crashed to the ground. Coryn feathered a third trying for the cart.

Katleya crouched at the back of the cart, holding a burning brand in each hand, thrusting them into the faces of any writhen getting too close. Coryn's skin prickled like a rash as he feathered another, and then a third. Dame Mureen stood by one of the wheels, her hands high, searing the night with great gouts of blue fire. Wetham held tight to her skirts.

Out of arrows, he dropped the bow and drew his sword. It was hopeless. He knew it as he leaped towards the cart, hacking at a spear-wielding writhen. Surprise was with him. The writhen fell, clutching at its blood-gushing stump, the rest of its arm falling to the ground, the spear still gripped in its hand. Something hammered into him from the right. He smashed to the dust with scrawny arms clinging to him, claws reaching for his eyes. He drove his knee up into the writhen's belly. It grunted, falling to one side as Coryn rolled. He was up again in one swift move. But where was that damned lacert?

As he pulled his sword from between another writhen's ribs, he heard the clash of weapons. Coryn took a moment to glance around. A desert warrior wielded a pair of scimitars, his pale burnoose swirling round him in the dark. A second fought a little further off, ghostlike but vicious.

Coryn swore under his breath, sure they were the pair who'd chased him through the desert from Rialt, intending to take him down for killing their wrestler friend. At least they were busy fighting off the writhen first. Their dark grey bodies lay scattered across the gully floor, feathered, chopped, sliced and gutted. Some twitched, some screeched, some sprawled on the ground unmoving.

He twisted and jabbed as a blood-priest fell on him. He leaped sideways, his knife slicing along Coryn's jaw. He grabbed the blood-priest's wrist, elbowing him in the face. Dark blood spurted from his crushed nose and he fell back with a gurgling cry. He finished the Murecken off with slice into the neck, deep enough to almost decapitate him. There wasn't a chance the damned blood-priest would get up from that wound.

Then the lacert came through the darkness, leaping for his throat. He yanked his sword from the blood-priest's neck, clouted the beast's long, narrow head with the hilt, and swivelled out of its way as it flew past. Flipping his sword and holding it with both hands, he hammered it down, but the lacert twisted away, coming back at him from the left. Throwing himself to the ground, Coryn rolled and came up to his knees, grabbing a writhen spear just as the beast leaped towards him again. The grounded spear pierced its chest but it kept coming. Its claws scraped gouges out of the ground as its drooling jaws reached for his face.

A bolt of blue fire battered into the lacert's ear. It howled as flames scorched its head and the stink of burning meat filled Coryn's nostrils.

The lacert sprawled to the ground writhing in agony, the spear's haft lashing the air with each movement.

Springing away, Coryn left the creature to its death throes. Dame Mureen stood a few yards off, her face unreadable. She held her arms crossed over her chest. Wetham's skinny arms hugged her waist.

'Never. Never again.' She levered Wetham's arms open. Holding his hand, she turned to walk towards the cart.

'I wouldn't be too sure about that,' Coryn muttered, shaking his head in disbelief. He would never understand the old woman. Scanning the gully, he saw no writhen left upright. The two strangers prodded at the grey bodies with their scimitars, finishing off any that responded.

A movement by the back of the cart caught his eye.

Chapter 53

'This one I will take.' The bloodhunter-priest's voice sounded like grating gravel, his stink made her want to vomit. 'The High-priest wants her and what he wants, he gets.'

'Bollocks to that. Get off me and fester in Murak's flaming hells.' They knew she had the Wealdan? All the way back in Mureck?

Leveen!

She must have told the blood-priests about her. But that didn't make sense, Leveen wouldn't have let the blood-priests know Katleya existed till she was good and ready to use her, would she? And the blasted woman said she'd take her to Elucame herself when the time was right.

The bloodhunter-priest held Katleya by the neck, his claws digging into her skin. It was hard to breathe past his grip, or to think. The tip of his knife pricked her throat and she felt a trickle of blood run down her neck, like a runnel of sweat. All her knives were still stuck in the bodies of various blasted writhen. She held on to the string of curses trying to burst through her gritted teeth.

Spirits! The bastard stinks!

She couldn't decide whether his hand or the rat's piss stench of him choked her more.

'She is young, strong. There is much Wealdan in her blood.'

He moved the knife and stroked his tongue against her neck, licking up some of her blood. 'It is as we have been told.'

'You're not getting another drop of my blood, arse-wipe!' Leveen *had* told them. She must've given this High-priest of theirs a taste of Katleya's blood and he'd found its potency strong enough to feel it worth his while to send out this blasted bloodhunter-priest to find her. Katleya's guts twisted. 'Leveen!' She spat out the name. They must've tracked her all the way from Rialt.

There's not a spark's chance in Murak's blasted hells this rotten piece of rat offal or any other shit-stinking Murecken is taking me anywhere!

'Ah, yes, our little desert woman and failed blood-priest. Desperate women make the finest hunters, as our High-priest says. In Leveen's case, he was right.' The bloodhunter-priest chuckled as he dragged Katleya backwards, towards the mouth of the gully.

Little? One thing Leveen wasn't was little.

It almost made Katleya laugh.

'Let her go!' Coryn took a step forward, his face thunderous. His lips twisted into a snarl. He looked like a man intent on bloody murder if ever Katleya had seen one and her heart leaped.

'I would not were I you,' the bloodhunter-priest grated. His hold on Katleya's throat tightened. She struggled, choked, and tried hard not to panic. 'You like this one, yes. I smell it in you.'

The terror rose higher in Katleya. In sickening detail, she remembered everything she'd overheard Coryn tell Dame Mureen about Adherent Thoma's and Dame Alana's deaths. 'Blast you! Get off me,' she managed to hiss past his grip.

'But we will have such times together, you and I.' The priest's laugh was a clatter of rocks. He pressed the knife deeper into her neck and she felt more blood flow. 'Perhaps I shall be slow to hand you over to the High-priest. The journey to Mureck is a long one.'

She bit back a sob.

This isn't the time for blasted crying!

She had to think. Fast.

Pella charged out from under the cart, a stone in her fist. 'Leave Kat alone! Get off her, yer big bully!' she yelled out, throwing the stone at the bloodhunter-priest. It bounced off his shoulder and he laughed again.

'Pella, no.' Katleya gasped as the blade dug deeper.

But the scrawny little girl charged at the bloodhunter-priest anyway. She grabbed and pulled at the arm holding the knife.

The bloodhunter-priest sliced down with casual ease, the knife a blur, then it was back again, digging into Katleya's neck before she could react. Pella crumpled to the ground, her neck open, her blood spilling into her cloud of blonde hair.

'NO!' Everything was happening too fast.

Do something, shit-for-brains!

Ignoring his knife, his scaled and clawed hands, his vile stink, Katleya opened her Wealdan uncaring if he sensed it. Not like it mattered now. Closing her eyes, she found the fine webbed matrices of Wefan inside the priest, pulsing through his skin, muscles, arteries and veins. Though wild and unstructured in the flow of his blood, they were like flexing cages around the pumping chambers of his heart.

Everywhere she felt the clinging, skin-crawling ooze of blood-magik wrapped round and feeding off stolen Wealdan. It twisted the Wefan within the very essence of his being, and there, deep inside his body and more twisted than any other part of him, was the mind and essence of a lacert. She recoiled, the malignance of the man and beast combined almost too much for her.

I can do this. I will do this!

She'd seen Laru heal the matrices in her arm back in Black Rock. Had watched Dame Mureen work her Wealdan-healing on Coryn. She could blasted well do the opposite in the bloodhunter-priest's body. But how? Could she unravel the matrices instead of knitting them together? And if she did, how would the blood-magik react? Could it attack her somehow through the link she'd have to form?

One way to find out.

Using her Wealdan to weave the Wefan into an approximation of a sharp blade, being more comfortable with the thought of a knife than anything else, Katleya began to slice through the matrices inside his heart.

It faltered. And her own heart soared.

Then his blood-magik closed in. Thick and oily. It yanked at the matrices, repairing them in moments. So fast the bloodhunter-priest didn't notice a thing.

Not enough. Not blasted enough! Stop pissing about girl! Get it right!

They'd almost taken her before and there was no way Katleya was going to let this rat-stinking, blood-sucking parasite take her now. He'd blasted well learn he'd made the biggest mistake of his entire putrid and disgusting life when he'd grabbed her.

Focusing harder, Katleya slashed through all the matrices in his heart. Again and again. Muscles clenched, arteries collapsed, blood stopped flowing. Faster. Faster.

The bloodhunter-priest's heart lurched and shuddered. He dropped the knife and clutched at his chest. Katleya twisted free. More blood-magik crackled and spat out from the lumpy red gem hanging from his neck. The rock glowed and oily reddish smoke coiled out from it, sinking into his flesh to fight off the attack.

It isn't going to blasted well work.

Panicking, Katleya grabbed the priest's hand, tried to keep the link. Somehow, she knew her Wealdan would have more impact if she touched him.

Then Coryn lurched forward and grabbed the red gem, his other hand clutching at the pouch Katleya knew contained his amulet. The smoke stuttered, failed. The blood-magik stalled. One last quake and the heart stopped. The bloodhunter-priest shuddered, gaped, spasmed and crumpled to the ground.

Dead.

Staggering, Katleya fell to her knees and vomited. Pulling herself together, she crawled over to Pella.

Coryn was there first. He traced the fingers of one hand against Pella's cheek, flicking a look at Katleya, his eyes hollowed and wet. Then he brushed the child's lids down over her eyes and gathered the little girl in his arms like a broken doll. His head sank into the white-blonde hair.

'How did you do that?' She stared at Coryn but he didn't look up. 'How did you stop the blood-magik? You've the Wealdan too?'

'Oh, my dear.' Dame Mureen rushed over. She put her arms around Katleya. 'My dear girl, what have we become?'

'Sometimes you've got to do things you don't like to survive, to protect those that need protecting. It doesn't mean you've changed.' Coryn rose, ignoring the blood soaking his shirt. 'War's coming west now and you and all the Lehotans will need to use the Wealdan to fight these blood-priests. If not for yourselves, to protect those like little Pella here.'

'It is not what Lehot would want.'

'How do you know what Lehot wants or doesn't want? Did he tell you himself? Or did some priest take it on himself to decide what your god wills?' Coryn turned on her. Katleya saw the rage flaring in his eyes, hot and wild. 'They would've taken Wetham, Katleya, Maisie, and killed all the other children too, if the Wealdan hadn't been used to defend them. Do you think Lehot would've wanted that?' He held Pella tight to his body, looking down at her. 'Do you think he'd have wanted this? Do you?'

'No I...I do not,' Dame Mureen blurted out, she shuddered, dropping her head into her hands. 'But it goes against all I have been taught, all I know. It is wrong to harm others.'

'I couldn't let him take me, I couldn't.' Katleya gulped. She tried, but couldn't stop the sobs from shuddering through her body. Dame

Mureen wrapped her arms around her again and rocked her. She leaned into the motion. She couldn't ever remember someone holding her like this, or crying so hard it hurt. She was exhausted and her head was fit to explode. 'I wish I'd used it earlier on the stench-ridden leech. I blasted well do. Then Pella wouldn't be – be dead.'

'I would not have let him take you,' Dame Mureen said.

Shocked, Katleya looked up and saw raw emotion fill the old woman's haggard face, an agitated mix of fear and regret.

'Lehot forgive me, I was ready to stop him.' Tears filled her eyes. 'I too am sorry I did not act sooner. I thought it was me they were after, but it seems I was mistaken.'

Katleya's head pounded and she could barely see straight, but her skull didn't feel like it was about to crack right open any more. She blinked then saw the two strangers that had helped fight off the writhen come forward.

'We have followed you far, Coryn aef Arlean,' one said, then they bowed to Coryn, Dame Mureen and Katleya in the desert fashion.

Coryn nodded in response but looked puzzled as he stared up at them. He still cradled Pella though he'd stopped his rocking. 'Who in all Murak's flaming hells are you?' Coryn blurted out.

'We are Derin, Honour Guards of the Temple of Daru in Rialt. I am Daras ibn Lasheef al-Derin,' the one who'd spoken before said.

'I am Rias ibn Lasheef al-Derin,' said the second. 'High-Seer Yaltos al-Derin sent us.'

'Why'd she do that?'

Katleya looked from one to the other. They looked like brothers, twins almost. Like those Shafian traitor brothers who'd dumped them in this mess. And they were not wearing the usual outfits of Derin Honour Guards either, they were dressed as Shafians. She narrowed her eyes.

'The High-Seer's exact words were: *That fool boy goes into great danger. He will need help if he is to succeed in his mission.*' Daras looked at Rias who nodded, then back at Coryn. 'You have made our task difficult. We have had to wear the garb of the Shafi dwellers to pass unmolested through their lands and these mountains crawl with writhen. Those we could not avoid, we killed, but that took time.'

'Then, also, you have used many tricks to hide your passage through the desert, doubling back and forward many times,' continued Rias.

'You are good at hiding your trail. Yet, still we found you.'

'By the Mother though, it took a longer time to reach you than we had anticipated,' finished Daras.

'But it was *in time*, do you not think, brother?' Rias looked at Daras.

'I would say it was *in perfect time*, brother,' agreed Daras, nodding at Rias.

Katleya couldn't stop the laughter bubbling up. She laughed so hard she had to sit or she would have fallen. Coryn stared at her, then at the brothers, and started laughing too.

'A Derin Seer?' Dame Mureen studied the brothers. 'Helping Coryn aef Arlean? Are you sure you have the right man? And do you have proof of your identity?'

'We have tracked him for three tendays now, all the way from the great city of Rialt,' Daras confirmed. 'We travelled in the same caravan across the Shafi Desert as he, and were there when High-Seer Yaltos spoke to him of the dagger snake in the shadow of his boot. We know we have the right man.'

Sobering, Coryn nodded.

Katleya stopped laughing too and looked up at the brothers. They were young, not much older than Coryn. Both lean and tough looking, with narrow curved swords hanging at their hips that were very different to the wide Shafian tulwars such as Leveen wore. They also carried unusually small crossbows on their backs. They looked back down at her, waiting. Though ready and determined, patient and watchful, she sensed they told the truth.

'Spirits! Whatever mission he's on can wait, don't you see we've got important things to worry about right now!' Coryn looked at her and Katleya stared right back at him. 'We have to give Pella a proper funeral. Then we've got to get the rest of the children out of these blasted mountains.'

'Indeed. You two gather some firewood, enough for a decent pyre.' Dame Mureen helped Katleya to her feet. She placed a hand on Pella's forehead and raised her eyes to the heavens in appeal. She turned to the two men. They hadn't moved. 'Firewood?'

They looked at each other and back at Dame Mureen, then shrugged and walked into the darkness. Moments later came the sound of branches dragging across the sand. Katleya walked off into the darkness too. She felt the shakes take her and another wave of pain crashed into her head then tried to battleaxe its way out of her skull. She vomited again.

Spirits! If using the Wealdan makes me feel like this every time, it's going to be no fun at all to use, blast it.

Her legs folded, dropping her to the ground. It had been close, so very close. She'd been in this blasted desert far, far too long. Katleya had to get out. Once she was out, everything would be fine.

Chapter 54

It took a while for the stack of wood to become sizeable enough to satisfy Dame Mureen. Maisie wrapped Pella's body in her bit of cloak and Coryn placed the child with infinite gentleness on top of the pyre. Everyone watched apart from Eilem. She stayed on the blanket in the cart, her baby attached to her breast. After saying the Lehotan words of the dead, Dame Mureen placed her hands against the wood and blue flames licked out.

Wetham wanted to join her but Katleya held tight to his hand. She felt the old woman had had enough of his help for now. Also, the fewer people who knew what he could do the better, Katleya thought. They might have helped, but the two Derin warriors were still strangers. She watched Dame Mureen move round the pyre, placing her hands on different places, till the flames licked high into the air.

One thing was certain, there weren't any more writhen or blood-priests in the region, or they'd have been on them in a moment.

The horizon hinted at dawn when they pulled into another narrow gully. Her headache fading fast, Katleya helped Maisie tuck the children in again where they snuggled next to Eilem and her baby. Everything felt odd, unreal, as if she wasn't in this desert with half a dune's sand itching under her clothes. Her body was doing all these things, but her mind was elsewhere.

She had killed a man using her Wealdan. Had stopped a his heart. And it terrified her.

Coryn built a fire and put the kaffe pot onto a stone at its edge to heat. He skewered some large pieces of goat meat and hung them over the fire to roast, then put a pot of water on to boil. He threw in some brown beans and some pinkish-green things, looked up and saw Katleya watching.

'Agave flower buds,' he explained. 'Both nutritious and delicious. There are plenty of the plants around hereabouts.'

Katleya sat close to the flames. For some reason, she felt very cold.

'You young men must be tired and hungry, just as we all are. We have plenty of fresh meat.' Dame Mureen put her hands on her hips, staring about her. Katleya could see the conflict warring inside her. 'You can clean yourselves up first, the meal should be ready by the time you return.'

The Derin brothers looked at each other, shrugging. Nodding at Coryn, they went to do her bidding. Dame Mureen could get anyone to do what she wanted when she gave them that look of hers. Katleya watched the men work sand into their arms and hands. Perhaps a look like that would be a good trick for her to learn.

'I have never seen a wyrm before. I had not realised they were so large.' Daras sat down.

'Blood-priests, bloodhunter-priests, lacerts, writhen and wyrms, all here in the Amalla Heights.' Rias sat beside his brother. 'The High-Seer must be informed. Word must be sent to Derin.'

'We wonder why Coryn aef Arlean lingers with you women,' Daras said. 'He should fulfil his oath.'

Dame Mureen stopped what she was doing and looked up at the men. 'Sire Coryn saved my life, saved the life of Wetham here and the lives of these other women and the four other children in the cart.' With almost perfect timing, there was a tiny cry in the darkness, soon muffled. 'One of the girls gave birth during this very night. If not for him, the babe would have died too. He risked his own life again and yet again to do it.' She turned back to the fire and turned the skewered meat. The juices spat and sizzled in the flames. 'This man has kept the Murecken from taking us for two days and two nights without rest.'

'That is impressive.' Daras gave Coryn another appraisal, then nodded.

'His hand was burned, there was a hole in his thigh from a quarrel, yet he freed us from a terrible trap back there in the mountains,' Dame Mureen continued, stabbing a skewer back toward the pass. 'We would not be here if it were not for him.'

'Did you see the two Rialtans who'd followed me out of the city?' Coryn sat down on the opposite side of the fire from the two Derin warriors.

'We were but moments behind those two,' said Daras.

'We persuaded them to give up their pursuit,' added Rias. 'Their friendship with the wrestler was not so very strong.'

Dame Mureen sighed. 'More deaths?'

'Not on this occasion. Our words were enough.' Daras beamed, flashing even, white teeth around the fire. 'It seems they had great respect for a Seer of Daru, the Mother Goddess, and also for her Derin Honour Guards.'

'The Derin do not kill in a wanton manner, Lady of Lehot,' Rias said.

'I am happy to hear that,' Dame Mureen said, 'but please call me Dame Mureen. I am but a High-adherent of the Lehotan Havens.

Katleya flicked a look up at Coryn but he stared at the two men, a wry smile on his face. The flames flicked orange and gold light over him.

'Is this the correct way to brew kaffe, Sire Coryn?' Dame Mureen looked up at Coryn, then spooned kaffe beans into the pot of boiling water. Coryn nodded. 'How do you two like your kaffe?'

'So strong it could stand on its hind legs and walk.' Rias grinned.

'So strong it could run rings around my brother.' Daras' laugh boomed across the gully.

'You say this High-Seer Yaltos sent you. That means Sire Coryn is important to her, correct?'

'That is most correct.' Daras shifted, looked over at Coryn then back at Dame Mureen. 'But we cannot tell you more.'

'High-Seer Yaltos takes no one into her confidence,' Rias added. 'No Seer of Daru tells any man everything he wishes to know.'

'This is true, as you would know if you had ever asked any Derin Seer a question,' Daras continued. 'We were commanded to follow Coryn aef Arlean and to help him traverse the Amalla Heights so that he might reach the Lehotan Haven on Storr. No more and no less than that.'

'With the aid of the Mother Goddess, Daru, High-Seer Yaltos saw your path. She saw that you would meet trouble.' Rias looked at Coryn, his dark eyes grave.

Coryn stared at the fire. To Katleya, he seemed as annoyed about a Derin Seer telling him his destiny in Daru's name as he was with Dame Mureen telling him Lehot had sent him. She could understand that. She liked being in charge of her own life too, not have it preordained in any way by some bloody god or other. Who would want to be that helpless to fate?

'And she saw true,' Daras added.

'The food is ready,' Dame Mureen announced.

The meal was delicious and Katleya's hunger surprised her. Probably needed to restock the energy that using the Wealdan had drained from her. Roasted rare, the wild goat's juices soaked into the red beans and rice Daras had given them. She'd not known what to expect, but the agave flower buds tasted sweet and the acacia pods were sweet and tart at the same time.

Coryn, Daras and his brother wolfed the food down, then looked apologetic, wiping their mouths with their sleeves. It was funny how alike the men all were, even though the two strangers were dark haired and had eyes the colour of kaffe beans. She looked into Coryn's eyes. The deep blue of them had darkened to stormy grey. He was still angry. She bent her head over her cup and breathed in the steaming aroma of kaffe.

'I have not had cooking such as this in a long time.' Daras gave a quiet burp and looked abashed. 'Thank you all.'

'You're welcome.' Coryn nodded.

Dame Mureen stood and turned to Coryn. He sat cross-legged on the sand his eyes flicking from one brother to the other, Wetham leaned against his side. The dog sat just behind him, its eyes catching the firelight. 'It is late and we are very tired. If you and these two good men could set some sort of watch for the last hour of the night, I would be most obliged.'

The night air was chill now. A soft breeze came from the north, bringing with it the faint scent of the rain-wet grasslands of Manom. The acacias rustled their dry leaves and wolves howled somewhere in the mountains making Dog prick up its ears. Katleya threw a few more sticks of wood onto the fire. Coryn looked up at Dame Mureen. It was obvious he was uncomfortable. He sighed, scratching at the growing stubble just under his chin.

'I'll take first watch.' Coryn rose.

'You are in need of rest, far more than we two.' Daras stood, his brother followed suit. 'We will watch till sunrise. Then we must leave these mountains.'

The silence stretched. The wind strengthened, twisting sand up from the ground. Then it died off and the quiet of the place rested on them all.

'I'm fine.' Coryn stared at the two men, quite calm.

'It is late.' Dame Mureen reached out a hand to Wetham. 'Come child, you must sleep now.'

Wetham shook his head. He didn't look up at Dame Mureen.

'You have gained the child's trust, Sire Coryn,' Dame Mureen said.

'Are you going to help me with first watch then?' Coryn looked down at the boy.

Wetham sat up straight, turned a little away from the fire and looked out into the night.

The two brothers looked at the boy.

'What happened to him,' Rias asked, 'and to the other children?'

'Pirates. Then slavers.' Dame Mureen sighed. 'It affected them badly. I hope they recover soon and I have faith, for children are nothing if not resilient.'

'Blasted bastards. I hope their bollocks putrefy and drop off.' Katleya blushed, the words had popped out of her mouth without her brain engaging.

'You use colourful language, Adherent Katleya. But as I have seen the child with my own eyes I must agree with the sentiment.' Daras smiled at her, his teeth bright against his dark skin, his dark eyes flashing with laughter.

Katleya had to smile back. With Coryn, Daras and Rias, she felt safe. A feeling she'd not had in a long time.

It made her nervous.

Chapter 55

Her blood still boiling with a rage hotter than the sun, Leveen tracked Katleya through the desert. Anger, shame and betrayal battled within her. Taraq had saved her years ago when she had first left the Murecken capital, Elucame, when she was near lost in the madness the blood-rites had inflicted on her. He had taught her how to control the Ascian using the ancient techniques he had learned within the Derin temple of Daru, the Mother Goddess. She would have forgiven him anything

But not this.

Taraq had failed Leveen in the most important task she had ever entrusted to him. He had allowed Katleya to escape from the room at the House of the Rose. He protested that he had not even seen her once, that the girl must have escaped right after Leveen had left the inn herself. It was nonsense, the bleatings of a man desperate with guilt and fear. The madness had roared and she had beheaded him there in his room. It was over in moments and she could not believe what she had done once she had calmed the beast within. But it was his fault, his failure, Leveen had reasoned.

His usefulness ended, she had taken from Taraq all that held any interest for her.

She could still taste Taraq's blood on her lips. His liver had been exceptionally fine. But it was Katleya's blood she wanted, needed, and she was determined to capture the girl again. With High-priest Dracil's seal on the trade, time was short. She could not allow another to take the girl, and there were many Murecken blood-priests in the desert lands now, searching for those with potency.

Leveen had to find Katleya before any other knew of her existence, before the High-priest discovered the girl had escaped and sent blood-hunter-priests after her, negating their agreement. It worried her that there might be bloodhunter-priests in the mountains already and that the High-priest would have contacted them through the Blodstans. She would have had one of the red gems herself had she gone through the last stage of the blood-rites.

The horse stumbled under her again and she swore, hitting it with her stick till it lurched into a faster gait. Not many yards further on, it fell to its knees, letting out a strangled groan. Leveen jumped off its back and mounted her second horse, leaving the first to die where it lay. She urged the horse into a ground-eating lope, on towards the Amalla Heights where they stretched across the northern horizon above a shimmering haze.

Somewhere in those stunted mountains, Katleya lived and breathed. Leveen could sense her, her blood, pumping through her veins as she moved ever north towards Manom. The blood-link Leveen had created between them back in Rialt allowed her to track Katleya with ease once the trail was found. The Murecken blood-rites she had undergone in the bowels of Elucame had given her the ability in the Ascian to do so.

She barked out a laugh at the irony.

The girl would pay for this chase. There were all sorts of ways Katleya could be made to pay for this trouble the girl was putting her through. Ways that did not lead to death but would give Leveen great pleasure.

Chapter 56

The sun rose and the heat would soon follow.

'Let's get this journey done.' Coryn itched to go. There could be more damned Murecken blood-priests in the mountains making their way down to Manom to snare themselves some Lehotans or other Wealdan-bearers. That they hunted Katleya specifically had worried him and he'd some thinking to do on that.

'You should go on ahead, Sire Coryn.'

'What?' He turned to Dame Mureen.

'You have saved us many times over, but now we no longer need you to help us. I know that you must be anxious to continue on your own journey, now you are so very close to fulfilling your oaths. Most especially finding your sister. We will travel far too slow for your needs. I believe that we can trust these two to see us all to Roesette safe enough.'

'We will.' Daras and his brother nodded. 'High-Seer Yaltos would want us to help the Lady of Lehot and her charges. I will accompany Dame Mureen to Fara itself.'

'Thank you Daras, that is very generous of you.' Dame Mureen turned and looked at Coryn for a while. 'I understand your need. Go, Sire Coryn, may Lehot go with you.'

He turned his horse north while the smell of kaffe was still strong on the morning air. Coryn paused and looked back toward the mountain heights, remembering Pella and the flowers she'd brought him. He jumped when Katleya approached and handed him a bag.

'I've put in some of the meat and the last of the kaffe beans.' Katleya looked deep into his eyes with her green ones, like she could see the fire deep down inside him that roared so high he thought it'd burn him right up.

Coryn looked away, cleared his throat, then looked back. 'Keep your knives close. Be safe.'

'I can look after myself, Coryn aef Arlean.' Her lopsided smile faded. 'We'll meet again soon enough. You and I need to talk.'

He looked away again. It was hard to leave, without saying anything, but he'd nothing to offer her. He was an ex-slave with no coin and little hope of ever being anything more than a soldier. She, an Adherent of the Lehotan Order, a Wealdan-bearer so strong that the High-priest of Murak sent bloodhunter-priests and wyrm riders to capture her. What would she want with him? She was special and he wasn't, it was as simple as that. Nodding his thanks, Coryn tied the bag to the saddle along with his bow and quiver. He looked down at Dame Mureen. She smiled up at him, her eyes glistening. He fought the same feeling.

'You sure you'll be all right?'

'Yes, Sire Coryn. These young men and I will get along just fine. They are good men and are sure to be good conversationalists.' She looked over at the brothers, tilting her head.

They nodded. Daras was far too enthusiastic for Coryn's peace of mind. He remembered the smiles the Derin had given Katleya the evening before, and again this morning and slitted his eyes.

Coryn looked around, he'd another goodbye to say. But the boy had disappeared. 'Where's Wetham?'

'Do not worry about the child. It is hard for him to say goodbye to you.' Dame Mureen laid a hand on his thigh. 'I will tell him that you asked for him. He will like that.'

'You take care now.'

'You do the same. And, Sire Coryn, you have that talk with Lehot. He will be looking forward to it.'

He had to clear his throat before he could speak. 'Maybe.'

Coryn looked at the brothers. 'Take good care of them all.' He turned his horse, putting his heels to its flanks, the dog following. At the top of the gully, he stopped and looked back. Dame Mureen still watched him, her old body ramrod straight while Katleya jabbed at the fire with a stick. He felt a pull on his trousers and looked down into Wetham's tear streaked face.

'Take me wiv you.' Shock at the boy's words ran through Coryn. Wetham raised both his skinny arms up.

Visions flooded in on him. Coryn could see little Pella again, his father, his brother and his sister. The boy stretched his arms harder. How could he help this one when he couldn't even help himself? He looked into Wetham's great, dark eyes. How could he not try?

Coryn caught a wrist and swung him up behind. Then he looked over at Dame Mureen. She smiled, nodding, but her shoulders dropped.

'Look after him, Sire Coryn. We will see each other again on Storr. Have faith.'

As they rode into the darkness, the horse picking its way out through the mouth of the gully, he heard her voice, firm and clear as a bell.

'So do you boys like to play Thrones, or Crowns perhaps? Good. Do you have any of that fine Selassian firewater? Excellent! This evening we will tell tall tales and throw the bones till our own bones ache for sleep. Does that sound like a good way to spend our time?'

'It does indeed. What do you think, brother?'

'I agree.'

Pinpricks of green punctured the desert in a million places where rain-fed plants forced their way to the sun. The air was warm and still, birds sang in the acacias near the trail Coryn rode along. Like Dame Mureen had said, the desert could be beautiful. He shook his head and heeled the horse into a gentle lope.

Wetham held on tight.

The next day, as the light faded, Coryn rode down out of the last of the foothills with Wetham still holding tight to his back. In the distance, the Roes River sparkled between the trees lining its banks and beyond, hazed with varied golds and greens, were Manom's grasslands. It was a sight to drink in for sure.

'We'll get a riverboat at Roesette.' Coryn glanced back at Wetham, but the boy was silent. He'd not spoken another word since the morning they had left Dame Mureen and Katleya. Turning back, he pointed down between pair of rounded hills ahead where something shone gold in the lowering sunlight. 'Look there, you can see the towers of the city now.'

Getting a boat was no problem, but getting the horse on board was, so Coryn sold it. It was hard to part with the beast. Using all the haggling skills learned from years working for and watching his old master, he sold the beast for an astonishing amount of coin. Gold and silver weighed heavy in his coin pouch. He'd never thought to have so much wealth in his life. Selassian bred horses were valued in the north. Perhaps, when all this business was finished he'd take up breeding, if he could get some land. He'd build a home and...Katleya's face swam into his mind. He shook his head.

Spirits! Stupid to think like that.

They had time to wander through the vast market, waterlogged from the recent rains. Spread round the crossroads just beyond the city's southern gates, it was frenetic in its last throes of business. The stalls were as numerous and varied as any he'd known.

Coryn bought Wetham a whole set of new clothes in colours of the boy's choosing. Blue, yellow, green, red, even orange. Perhaps he'd made a mistake to let Wetham pick for himself, but he could not begrudge the child his pleasure. The boy couldn't stop stroking the furred lining of his short cloak and the soft silk of the scarf tied about his neck, hiding his scars.

With the enthusiasm of any young boy, Wetham stamped in every puddle he could find in his new leather boots, fascinated by the spray and fall of droplets. Coryn didn't have the heart to stop him and listened out for a child's laugh. None came, but it was early days yet.

They had a private set of rooms in the finest inn Coryn could find, with a bathing house in the back and good food in its crowded common room. It was good to see Wetham so overwhelmed by the variety of flavours and generous quantities of food. He still hadn't spoken a word, but his eyes said everything, the hollows under them beginning to fade, the joy a child should have in life returning.

The dog was another story. I seemed he couldn't ever overwhelm the animal with any quantity of food. The strange thing was that it'd stayed close throughout their journey, still did even in the city. It had changed.

Coryn promised himself he would stay on the look out for that painful moment when it changed back.

Chapter 57

Seven days later, Storr sailed into sight. The high southern cliffs of the Isle of Storr rose sheer and rugged out of the deep blue waters of the Elyat Sea, like the prow of some vast ship. Its farther shores, like those of the nearest mainland, the coast of Losan, stayed lost in the sea mists of early morning. Four leagues wide by five long, big enough for many farms, two small towns, a scattering of villages and the city of Storr with its great castle, the island was vast. The castle towered on the cliffs high above the port.

'There it is, in all its glory, the Castle Storr, home of His Majesty High-king Nicoln, second of his name. It's the finest castle ever built, and finished so long ago no one can remember how it was done. None today can imagine how it could have been done.' Avarr had a broad, rolling accent that was easy to listen to. He leaned his meaty forearms on the forward railing and grinned at Coryn, his bluff, red face beaming, tufts of his bright red hair blowing about in the wind.

The man had turned out to be a good travel companion on the journey from Manar and across the Elyat Sea to Storr. He seemed to know a great deal about many places and Wetham had been fascinated by his stories. Coryn had mentioned a little about his time in the desert with Dame Mureen and had made up a story about wanting to see the Havens she'd mentioned. A fumbling excuse for coming to Storr, but he'd not really thought about one till Avarr had asked.

Avarr bit into his apple and nodded up to something behind Coryn, his chestnut eyes sparkling. 'A wonderful sight is it not? Something for your little lad to be boasting of to his friends back home.'

Coryn turned. 'Wetham! Get down from there. I didn't bring you all this way just to see you fall into the sea!' Wetham grinned and clambered down the ratline, free of fear as if he was born to it.

Coryn shook his head, hiding his smile and turned back to view the island. The spume of waves crashing against the rocks flickered with silver and gold. Storr Castle soared, many-towered, above the cliffs. Because it was made of the same stone as the red rock of the island, it was hard to see where the rugged cliffs ended and the rough, lower walls of the castle began. Slanting rays of gold made the red stone glow like rubies. Myriad thin metal bridges arced between the towers, shining in the sun like a mad spider's web. Coryn wondered what it would feel like to walk those bridges in high winds. From every tower pennants streamed in the stiff breeze.

'Storr is as old as time itself, so it is said. There are no records telling when it was built.' Avarr threw the core of his apple over to the dog. It snapped it out of the air and gulped it down. 'Each of the blocks you see is hundreds, even thousands of years old. Look close now, you'll not see any wear or damage, none at all. It's a mystery and a wonder, that it is.'

As he watched the seamen make the ship fast to the dock and lower the ramp, Coryn didn't know what to feel. Well over nine years it had taken him to reach this city. He was close to fulfilling an oath he'd carried for all those years for the woman who had saved his life as a boy. It crossed his mind to wonder if Daven still lived here, or lived at all.

What scared him most though was the thought of seeing Lera again. Deep inside, Coryn felt so close it hurt, even though there was little real likelihood she'd be on this island. But would she even know him? But would she forgive him for letting Birog take her all those years ago? What had her life been like? He could only hope it'd been nothing like his.

Wetham's tiny hand slipped into his. Coryn felt better looking at the looming cliffs with those bony little fingers cradled between his.

'Over yonder is the causeway. It runs all the way to the town of Keel in Losan.' Avarr pointed to a long, broad road of rock and sand, standing a yard or so higher than the sea and stretching out westwards from the island. It disappeared into the morning mists. 'It's almost a league long. Perhaps your lad would be interested to know there are hundreds of different types of crabs living all the way along it. You ever been crabbing boy?'

Wetham ducked his head and gave it a small shake.

'Maybe you'll like me to teach you, eh?'

The port town of Lower Storr lay in a triangle made by the long stone quayside and a deep fold in the base of the cliffs. Red-tiled houses, inns, warehouses and shops rose in steep, narrow terraces. Gulls screamed and dove down in flurries to steal from fisher boats mooring at the lower wooden jetties at the western end of the quay. Ships of all shapes and sizes filled the quiet waters inside the wide, sheltering arms of the harbour walls.

'You know a lot about Storr then?' Coryn asked, keen to learn as much as he could.

'Have I not mentioned my brother? He is a High-adherent in the Haven on Storr.' Avarr's eyebrows rose to hide under his bushy hair.

'No, you didn't.' Coryn cleared his throat. 'But, as it happens, I've business in the Haven.'

'I stay with him every year for the Festival of Mabon. You want me to introduce you to him? He knows everyone there. Is there someone in particular you want to be seeing in the Haven?'

'Ah, yes, I do. Thanks, that'd be good.' Coryn scratched at his neck and changed the subject. 'I can barely remember the last time I saw a Mabon festival.'

As soon as they disembarked, Avarr led them right through the middle of the town. They threaded through squares and streets packed with stalls. Near the quayside, the stalls were loaded with fish, shellfish and other seafood. Further up, it was fruit, grain and vegetables. Most of the doors and windows had been decorated with late summer flowers and sheaves of grain. Coryn remembered his Ma having done the same and a lump formed in his throat.

Men hung ropes strung with pennants of yellow, red and green, from poles jutting from the tall buildings. The ropes criss-crossed high above the streets. Acrobats, fire-eaters, jugglers and musicians showed off at every corner. Wetham's eyes couldn't have grown any larger. On a small stage in one large square, some players performed the yearly rise and fall of the harvest goddess, Mabon.

Avarr's tortuous, steep route along narrow cobbled roads and through crowded squares, eventually led them to an open area stretching along the base of the towering cliffs. At one end, a huge arch of carved stone framed a smooth-walled tunnel three wagons wide. Four soldiers stood guard scanning everyone going in and out of its entrance.

'This is where the road to the castle begins.' Avarr paused to point at the arch, then wove a path through the crowds toward the base of the cliff.

Coryn held Wetham close, aware it'd be all too easy to lose him in such a mass of people.

'We'll be hiring horses here. I know the stable master well.' Avarr stopped at a pair of wide doors built into the solid rock of the cliffs.

Windows, cut into the walls on either side of the doors, stood open to the salt air. The distinctive smell of horses wafted out. 'It's a long walk otherwise, you'll see. Or there's the basket. It'll be faster, though there's a wait for the contraption today by the look of the queue. You want to ascend the cliff that way?'

To the other side of the stables a large, square basket began to rise up the cliff face. Men and women in bright coloured clothes and hats covered with leaves and flowers squealed and laughed as it jolted up from its platform. Next to it was a pulley mechanism and a huge capstan where a pair of horses, harnessed to long shafts, plodded round on a circle of sand. High above, a second basket made a slow descent. A line of people waited their turn, some carried baskets of flowers, foods, wines or fruits. Others held musical instruments. Another pair of soldiers eyed the queue.

Avarr laughed at the look on Wetham's face as the boy craned his neck back to see up the folded and craggy face of the cliff. It must've been at least five hundred feet high.

'Do you want to go in the basket, Wetham?'

'No.' He shook his head.

'Horses it is then.' Coryn grinned. It was good to hear Wetham's voice. He still had few words to say.

'Does the lad need his own pony?'

'No, he'll ride with me.'

'That'll be fine. Soon as we find my brother, I'll get him to show you round the castle and the Haven both. The windows in the main hall of Storr Haven are exceptional and the carved ebon doors leading to the throne room are even more astounding. I never get tired of seeing it all, that I don't.'

Avarr disappeared through the stable doors while Coryn and Wetham waited. The dog followed its nose around the area in front of the stables. It stopped to sniff some debris to one side of the doors just as a black-headed gull flew past. It came in low holding a fish too large for its beak. Leaping up a full ten feet, the dog snatched the fish right out of the gull's beak.

'That is a remarkable leap.' Avarr appeared with another man. They led two sturdy, short-limbed horses out into the square. Coryn watched the dog bite the fish in half and gulp each glistening lump down. 'It is an unusual hound. Quiet, mannered, but dangerous when needs be. You've owned him a long time?'

'He's been with me a while.' Coryn smiled. Licking its lips, the dog came up to him and leaned against his leg. He reached down and scratched its head. He still marvelled at how the dog had changed since Dame Mureen's Wealdan-healing. 'But he's his own master. I've still to work out why he stays around as it is.'

The narrow, steep road stitched up the cliffs, in and out of tunnels and along wide, low-walled ledges. They passed groups of people taking a bite to eat and a drink as they rested on benches carved deep into the cliff face or in torch-lit caves along the tunnels. A few riders came the other way and a single cart.

Wetham clung tight to Coryn's back and every time they came out of a tunnel, he would gasp at the views. Sometimes he would point, sometimes he would even say a word or two. That made Coryn grin. Once, he was sure he heard the boy laugh. A fine sound.

The horses, dark with sweat, neighed when they reached the top. Answering neighs came from inside the city walls of Storr. The mid-morning sunshine bathed the Elyat Sea with clear, warm light that burned off the mists. Up here, the hazed shores of Losan were visible. Avarr, his face pleasant and open, spoke to the guards who waved them through the gate. They passed through the tunnel of the massive gatehouse and out into a large square.

Inside its walls, the castle was astonishing. The vast square, paved with multi-coloured stones in complex patterns, bustled with people rushing around putting up garlands of corn and flowers. Peddlers, with trays strapped to their shoulders, hawked goods to anyone who stopped long enough. A company of mounted soldiers clattered past and into the tunnel. Groups of musicians practised around a fountain in the square's centre that had three marble porpoises spouting water in different directions. Crystal drops sprayed and sparkled in the sun as they fell into the pool below. Around the square's edges, trees rustled in the breeze, the leaves beginning to turn gold.

'Permanent stalls are not allowed in this square.' Avarr waved at a wider arch to the left with tall, iron-grilled gates standing open. Beyond, Coryn could see blue sky and nothing else. 'A ramp runs down the cliff wall there and leads all the way down to the causeway. It is for the use of the High-king's staff and soldiers only, so this square is kept clear in case of emergencies. Not that anything of note has happened within the empire in countless years.'

Avarr led them to the stables by the arch and called out. A youngster appeared and took hold of the reins of their mounts. They crossed the square and entered a wide road leading up to the castle proper.

There were squares at every crossroads with trees and more fountains. Boxes of flowers decorated windows, ivies climbed up the red walls of tall houses and more trees peeped over garden walls. At the upper levels, thin metal walkways leaped in shallow arcs from house to house high above the roads, striping the ground with lacy shadows. The railings of each bridge had been wrought into different designs, intricate scroll work or feathery leaves, curling stems or stylised flowers. None looked like they could carry the weight of a full-grown man, yet Coryn saw many walk over them.

Higher up, they passed through the wide arches of the inner wall and into an upper ward. Here, gravelled paths meandered through grass lawns dotted with beds of flowers, trees and clipped shrubs. Mosaic framed, stone-mullioned windows looked down from buildings even taller than the ones in the lower levels of the city. On its mount, inside a third ring wall, the castle's square and round towers soared high. More bridges laced the air between the upper floors of these towers.

On the northeast edge of the outer castle wall stood Storr Haven. Carved into the grand, columned archway was the rayed-sun design of the Lehotan order. Coryn took a closer look. The carving of the rayed-sun was of a different stone to the rest of the arch, a later addition perhaps. They passed under it, following a cart through a short, wide passage. They stopped in a large courtyard surrounded by tall walls covered in carved wooden balconies and stairs. A long railed gallery ran round the entire square just under the eaves of the tiled roof.

'Avarr! Finally it is you! I expected you a week ago, that I did.' The full-throated bellowing voice reached them from one of the windows overlooking the quadrant. Coryn spotted a man as large as Avarr, with even redder hair, leaning out of a casement. 'You're only just in time for Mabon. Don't you move an inch, I'll be down in a moment, I will.'

'My brother, High-adherent Daven aef Kaerin. He is a member of the Assembly amongst many other important posts,' explained Avarr with obvious pride.

'Daven aef Kaerin?' Coryn felt his heart hammer. It had to be him, there couldn't be two men with that exact same name in Storr Haven, in the Lehotan Order, could there? He pressed his hand against his chest, feeling the lump of his pouch under his coat.

'You have heard of him? He is a good man to have risen so far. Got where he now is through honesty and hard work.' Avarr lowered his voice. 'Not like some. Mind your ears, he is rather loud at times, that he is.'

Daven thundered up to join them, puffing and red faced. Coryn looked him over and pulled Wetham close. Now he was down in the courtyard he could appreciate how large the Lehotan was. Grey robes, covered in gold stitched Lehotan symbols, stretched over broad shoulders and came down just short of his bare ankles. His hair, speckled with grey, bristled from head, chin and eyebrows and his chestnut eyes sparkled.

Could Birog have meant this man? He reminded Coryn of a mountain bear.

'Ah, Daven, you're always rushing about when walking would do just fine.' Avarr laughed. 'One day you'll be learning to slow down and be more dignified as befits your age and station. I hope it'll happen before you fall flat on your face, that I do.'

'Same old Avarr, you'll still be treating me as if you're my Da till we're both in our dotage.' Daven grinned and clapped his arm about his brother's shoulders giving him a sizeable hug. He glanced over at Coryn and a frown fleeted across his face fast hidden by another grin. 'So, you'll be introducing me to your friends?'

'Of course. This is Coryn aef Arlean and his lad, Wetham.' Avarr turned to Coryn. 'Let me introduce you to my brother Daven aef Kaerin, High-adherent of the Lehotan Order of Storr Haven, Master-scholar of Heah Danaan Studies and Ancient Lores, Member of the Assembly and Counsellor to the High-king.' He turned back to Daven. 'I've been telling them you'll give them a tour of the Haven when you have the chance, that I did.'

'I'd be delighted to show them round. This place is steeped in enough histories and mysteries to satisfy any and all enquiring minds.' Daven held his arms wide. 'You could not have a better guide.'

'Believe me when I tell you he speaks the truth.' Avarr turned serious. 'Tell me, brother, how fares the High-king and the Assembly?'

Daven's smile disappeared. 'Come, let us go to my apartments where we'll be able to talk in more comfort. I'll have some food sent up. I'm sure you'll all be hungry after your ride from the port.' He eyed the grinning dog sitting next to Wetham, its tongue lolling and its almond eyes keen. 'Your wolf is welcome too. It looks like it's starving.'

Coryn glanced down. 'It's no wolf. And it always looks like that.'

Not giving them a chance to say more, Daven strode off toward one of the many doors leading off the courtyard. His bulk and height created a slipstream through the crowds in which his brother and Coryn followed. Wetham's small hand gripped Coryn's hard, giving as much comfort as it received.

Chapter 58

The Haven was a warren of corridors and stairs. Running crowds of boys of all ages, wearing calf-length versions of the Lehotan robes, slowed as they passed Daven then sped up again. Open doorways showed them classrooms, libraries, workrooms, and offices. The air hummed with Wealdan. Coryn felt spikes and tingles all over his skin. Some as powerful as those he'd felt from Dame Mureen when she'd not had Wetham's boost. None anywhere near as powerful as the burst of Wefan that'd caused the desert gorge to flood.

Daven led them to a large, well-furnished room. Its floor to ceiling windows opened wide to let the sun and breeze flood in. Colourful woven rugs scattered the polished wood floor. Bookcases covered every spare piece of wall space, every shelf crammed with books, sheaves of paper and scrolls, more than Coryn had ever seen together in one place before. The large fireplace was laid with logs and kindling but remained unlit.

Coryn walked over to the windows looking north, inland. Green meadows, farmland and woods rolled up to sheep-bitten moors. Scattered tors and ridges of red rock thrust through the grass, heather and gorse of the wilder lands beyond. The air smelled sweet and vibrant, of earth and growing things, of sea and distant rain. Nothing like the desert. It reminded him of Kalebrod and that felt right. 'Looks a good place to live, what do you think?'

Wetham leaned against him and looked up. His eyes held that haunted look Coryn hated. He gave the boy's shoulder a squeeze. 'We'll stay together, Wetham. Here or anywhere else we go.'

The boy's face lit up and he pointed out at the moors.

'Yes, we'll take a walk up there soon as we can, Wetham.' Coryn looked up at the moors again. 'Do you think Katleya would like it here?'

'Yeth. Want Kat hugs 'gain.'

Coryn looked down at Wetham, amazed, but before he could say anything, someone knocked at the door.

'Ah, food!' Daven boomed.

Turning, Coryn saw two boys, a few years older and a lot bigger than Wetham, carry in large trays filled with covered platters. A third followed, carrying a tray with a silver carafe, plates, cups and a large basket of steaming bread. Quiet and fast, they loaded the large oak table in the centre of the room, and lifted the lids off the platters. The dishes held meats, cheeses, sauces and vegetables. Tantalising aromas wafted round the room. The boys left, closing the heavy door behind them with a quiet click.

'Sit, sit, let us not waste any time in partaking of this delicious food.' Daven sat and began piling his plate with everything. 'This cheese is fresh in from Ostan, it goes very well with this Losanian red.'

'Ah, this is as fine a wine as I've ever tasted.' Avarr smacked his lips and held out his cup for refilling. Daven obliged, his huge grin half hidden by his bush of a beard.

For a while the only sounds were of eating and smacking lips. Coryn put a little of everything on Wetham's plate so he could find out for himself what he liked best.

'Now, Coryn aef Arlean, tell us about your journey here. Avarr mentioned you'd met Dame Mureen on your travels,' Daven prompted. 'I'm sure you've an interesting story to tell us about that. And there's nothing like hearing an interesting tale while digesting a good meal.'

'That's the truth,' Avarr agreed, around a full mouth.

The truth, Coryn thought, how much to tell them? He decided he'd start from when he became a freed man. Neither of the men interrupted him as he spoke, though Avarr choked a bit when Subrahima came into the telling.

A long while later, Daven burped and patted his large stomach. 'That'll be doing it for me, except for some more of this fine wine.' He slopped more of the red wine from the carafe into his cup. 'It'll take time to digest this meal and that's a fact. Food and story together.'

'This is all very generous of you, er, Sire Daven.' Coryn pulled a last roll apart and breathed in the warm yeasty smell. Perhaps he could manage a little more. He took a lump of the creamy cheese and pushed it into the bread. 'But I'd like to know why you're treating two complete strangers so well. Not that I'm complaining, mind.'

'A tale such as yours is payment in plenty for a meal, that it is. But your question is excellent and it is in truth time for me to talk. Avarr, why don't you take the lad and the hound out into the gardens?' Daven beamed, his eyes almost disappearing under his eyebrows. 'I'm sure after all this food they could do with some exercise. And exploration is always good for boys and hounds alike, that it is.'

Coryn nodded to Wetham and the boy rose from the table. 'Go with him Dog.' He motioned to the animal.

It stood, following Wetham out, a sheep's leg bone clamped between its jaws. The door closed behind them. The quiet filled with bird song.

'So, Coryn aef Arlean, you want to know what's going on and that's a good thing, as I said. Curiosity leads to learning as long as it is done with the right guidance.' Daven leaned back in his chair and loosened the belt over his paunch. 'The fact is that Avarr is a High-adherent too. Ah, I thought he might have neglected to tell you. It's his task to go out and find youngsters with the Wealdan in their blood. He then brings them here if they and their parents are willing. He can be very persuasive, but in a good way you understand?'

Coryn nodded.

'They're very willing, most of them, as it's an honour to come to Storr for learning of any kind, that it is. We teach many subjects here as well as training the lads in the use of the Wealdan. We even teach those that have no Wealdan at all. Avarr's speciality is to sense the Wealdan and its strength, or potency, in a person. He sent me a message from the port this morning describing you and your lad.'

Coryn stayed quiet, waiting.

'The lad's potency is greater than any I've seen in a child for many years. But it's unusual. Very unusual. He'll be doing well when he joins us here in the Haven, that he will.'

'I'm still thinking on that, on whether this is the right place for Wetham.'

'He's young for entering the Haven,' Daven said, 'this is true. And I know he's been through much in his few years. It'll be hard for him to settle. But the young are nothing if not adaptable.'

'You noted his scars.' Daven nodded but said nothing. Coryn continued. 'But there's other reasons I'm here.' Coryn paused, glancing through the windows. Streamers of white cloud striped the blue dome of the sky. 'I was already on my way to Storr when I met up with the boy.'

Daven nodded. 'Before you say more, I'll tell you this. Three days ago I received a pigeon with a message from Roesette sent by Dame Mureen aef Callan.' Coryn looked up sharp and Daven smiled spreading his hands wide. 'She writes in little detail.' He raised a finger. 'But she tells me you are trustworthy. That you saved her life and the lives of many others including the lad, Wetham.'

'Ah. I had help. It wasn't all my own doing.'

'A man of bravery and honour, yet modest. It is good to know they still exist. But why don't you tell me why else you've come to Storr Haven, Sire Coryn.' Daven steepled his fingers, leaning his elbows on the table. He stared at Coryn with narrowed eyes. 'And why you wish to talk to me in particular.'

Startled, Coryn looked up at Daven again.

'I can see it in your face well enough.'

Coryn rubbed his hand against his neck. He knew he'd got the right man. Still he hesitated. The fear and the longing so strong in him, made it hard to speak. To ask after Lera, to risk hearing this man hadn't any knowledge of her. Then there was Birog's message. He'd hidden it for so many years, it felt strange knowing the time had come to hand it over. Opening his pouch, he pulled out the small roll of vellum.

'Years ago in Kalebrod a woman saved my life. She'd a focus crystal like the one Dame Mureen wears, but a blue-green one. In return, I promised her I'd pass a message on to you.' Coryn paused. 'It was around nine years ago and I don't know if there's much point in handing it over now. But I gave an oath so...'

'Nine years. Kalebrod. Blue-green focus crystal. What...' Daven cleared his throat. He clenched his fingers and what little could be seen of his face turned red. 'Did she give her name?'

'Birog. Birog Llawgoch.'

An explosion of breath burst from Daven. 'Light of Lehot. Please, give me the message. Do not keep me waiting any longer.' He reached out a meaty hand, his eyes imploring. 'I've been waiting to hear from that woman for more years than nine. It's been more like fifteen since she disappeared from Ostorr Haven. I had given up hope. Give it here, lad, even an old message is better than none.'

Coryn reached out and dropped the roll of vellum into Daven's spread palm.

A breeze ruffled loose leaves of parchment on the desk standing in front of one of the windows and the muted noise of the castle wafted into the room while Daven read the message.

'I don't believe this. That woman, she did it! *Blood of his...* Have you read this?' His eyes glittered dangerous and dark, gone was the genial bear.

Coryn felt he might as well be honest. 'I can't read well. Anyhow, it's all riddles and nonsense.'

'Nonsense? It's code, Coryn aef Arlean.' The genial bear was back in a flash. 'She needn't have worried then or now. It's all safe in that mind of yours. But I think she knew this.'

'What do you mean?'

'You are a Wealdan-bearer yourself.'

'No.' The idea was ridiculous.

'Yes. I tested you in the courtyard,' Daven insisted. 'Your Wealdan is strong but strange. It blocked me from Wealdan-reading you.' He gave Coryn a measuring look. 'Perhaps it blocks the blood-magik too. Have you had such magik used against you?'

Coryn stayed silent, his jaw clenched.

Spirits! The man's speaking madness. I've never used the Wealdan. I don't have it!

'I'm unable to read your thoughts and neither could Dame Mureen.' Daven frowned till his eyes almost disappeared. 'You'd know how strange that was if you knew it was one of her strongest abilities in the Wealdan, that you would.'

'It's this amulet, not me.' Coryn pulled out his pouch. His cracked amulet had helped him overcome the blood-magik holding the ifrit, and blocked the residue lingering on the dead Adherent's body. It'd blocked Dame Mureen's Wealdan-healing, and helped kill the blood-hunter-priest by blocking the blood-magik coming from his red gem.

Coryn had survived because of his cracked amulet.

'Birog gave it to me along with the vellum. She said it'd shield me. That's what it does – blocks anyone trying to use any magik on me, even your mind-reading trick.'

'It's no trick, lad.' Daven's eyebrows lowered over his eyes again but the anger passed in a moment as he pondered. 'An amulet Birog gave you? Perhaps you'll let me look at it?'

Biting the inside of his cheek, Coryn took out his amulet. He'd never let anyone touch it before, not even Dame Mureen. He held it tight in his fist and felt the solid, round smoothness of it, the hole in its centre, the slender crack where the sliver of blue-green crystal hid. But Birog had said he should trust Daven and none other. He passed it over. Daven turned it about in his fingers, stroked its surface then held it up to his ear.

'This is interesting. A typical holed-stone as used for amulets in many lands where the spirits are respected, but with an unusual fissure running out from the hole. And in the fissure, a sliver of focus crystal, a link. I sense the weaving of Wefan within both stone and crystal. But it has nothing to do with protection. It is a beacon, but its signal is weak.' Daven gazed into the middle distance. 'She meant to find you again if she could.'

'A beacon? To find me?' The world shifted under Coryn. He'd believed one thing for so long, to believe another was hard, but if it meant what he thought it meant...Birog hadn't abandoned him. She'd intended to find him again. So what had happened to her? 'The amulet didn't protect me?'

'No, you protected yourself.' Daven smiled and handed the amulet back to Coryn. 'No children born with any Wealdan to speak of for decades and then there are two at once dropping into my lap with more potency then a whole decade's worth combined. And with such strange skills. One who can enhance the strength of the Wealdan in another and one who blocks it altogether. There'll be excitement among all the scholars of the Haven when they hear of this. Maybe even an apoplexy or two. We've been researching into the reasons for the decline for years, but have yet to reach a consensus. Perhaps this is the beginning of a reversal of that trend.'

Coryn thought hard as he dropped the amulet back in its pouch. If he'd known the amulet was useless, he'd never have approached the ifrit, never have saved the women, never have met Katleya...he let that thought lie. He almost laughed. He had possessed some strange type of Wealdan all along and never had a clue. Birog was one clever woman. 'Does the vellum say where Birog and the babe went?'

'She had the babe with her? You saw the babe? What did it look like?' If Daven was eager before, he was more than excited now. Unable to contain it, he stood and paced the room. 'Did you notice anything special about it?'

'It was just a babe. It ate, it slept, it looked normal to me but I was young. I didn't take much notice.' Coryn frowned, trying to remember the details. 'It never cried, that was different I suppose.'

'Just a babe? It is more than *just a babe*. It is a weapon.' Daven sighed. 'And as for it not crying, that would have been Birog's doing. Can't have a babe crying when you're being hunted down by blood-priests.'

'A weapon, how could a little girl be a weapon?'

'A girl? It's a girl? Murak's flaming hells and burning bollocks, I wasn't expecting that! None of us were expecting that.' His eyebrows rose at Coryn's shocked look. 'What, am I not allowed to curse?'

'Spirits! Lehotans...I didn't think they did...'

'Some are more pious than others, it's true. But I'm not one of them, which much annoys my wife on occasion.' He grinned, then frowned, glaring at Coryn for a moment. 'Birog trusted you.'

When Coryn shrugged, unsure if it was a question, Daven nodded. He rose and strode across the room then pulled on a thick cord hanging by the door.

'That babe is the means by which we will overthrow the Priest-king of Murak himself. An end to the Murecken religion in the Ruel Mountains and everywhere else they've been inflicting it. An end to the Murecken invasions too. At least, that is one way of reading their prophecy.'

'Their prophecy? There are different ways to read them?'

'It could be that the babe will enable the Priest-king of Mureck to gain the power of one of his forefathers, Baelur Macule.' Daven crossed the room, turned and marched back again. 'Power enough to cover the world in darkness.'

'Why'd he want to cover the world in darkness? Everything would die. He'd rule over nothing but death.' Coryn shook his head, he remembered hearing the old myths about the Era of Shadows when plagues and famine scoured much of humanity from the world. But they were just old stories, weren't they? 'That's madness. Good thing prophecies are hogwash.'

'Sanity was never a strong point in that blood-line, and their abominable blood-rites exacerbate the problem.' Daven raised one furry eyebrow. 'Prophecies might be hogwash, as you say, but those who believe in them will work to make them come true. That's what concerned Birog and me when we spoke of it years ago. This will all have to go before the Assembly of course, but not yet. I must speak to some of the others first.'

'Birog also said...' Coryn swallowed. 'She said she'd get my sister to safety. That whoever she gave Lera to would contact you. Have you heard anything? Do you know her? Is she well? Happy?' the questions spurted out in a jumble now he'd finally released them. 'Can I see her?'

'Slow down now, lad.' Daven held his hands up, as if trying to stem the flow. 'Lera, you say?'

'My sister. Birog took her through that standing stone. She'd nearly reached her fourth name day.' Coryn felt desperate, all that waiting, all that hoping...

'Birog went *through* a standing stone?'

'She called it a *portal*.' Coryn remembered every moment of that day as it'd been branded on his memory. Birog's last wave, Lera clinging to her back as she disappeared into the stone, then the lacert crashing into and bouncing off its surface. 'But what about my Lera?'

'We have much, much more to speak of Coryn aef Arlean, that we do.' Daven crossed the room to stand close to Coryn, putting a heavy hand on his shoulder. 'Birog's brother, Tyme Llawgoch, brought a child to Ostorr Haven last summer, by the name of Lera aef Coryn. There are so few entering the Havens these days, we can remember the names of each one.' Daven quirked a smile.

Coryn's heart skipped a beat. Could it be her? Was it just a terrible coincidence?

'I shall send a message to Ostorr Haven by bird.' Daven sat at his desk. From a small drawer he took a sliver of paper and began to write. 'Take care with your hope, lad. She might not be your Lera.'

Nothing got past Coryn's throat.

'There.' Daven rolled the slip of paper and pushed it into a small metal tube. 'We'll know soon enough, one way or the other, that we will.'

A knock on the door had Daven up again. 'Enter.' He gave the boy who came in the tube. 'For Ostorr Haven. Fast as you can, lad. Then tell Dame Maechin we've visitors to stay and that I need her here.'

The boy disappeared. Daven closed the door behind him. 'Now, Coryn aef Arlean, you must tell me the entire story this time. From the very moment your life changed its course. No detail left out or glossed over, or I'll have you start again from the beginning, that I will.'

So Coryn began with his eleventh nameday. It took a while, what with Daven's interruptions, especially when he got to the part about the portal above Black Rock.

'What tales you'll have to tell your grandchildren on a winter eve's by the fireside.' Daven broke the stretch of silence that dropped on them after Coryn finished. 'Pirates, slavers, high-seers, portals, ifrits, wyrms, lacerts, writhen, blood-priests and even bloodhunter-priests. You've had adventures enough to fill three, four lifetimes, that you have.'

'I could have done with a few less.'

'No doubt about it, lad. But it looks like you'll get a few more before long. Meanwhile, you'll begin lessons here in the Haven, you and the lad.' Daven's face was almost comic with glee.

'Lessons?' Coryn worried.

'Yes. You've come not a moment too soon and years late. We need everyone with even the barest trace of the Wealdan to fill these halls. You know full well there's an invasion threatening Manom and maybe Faran too. No doubt about it, with Murecken blood-priests so deep into the Amalla Heights.' Daven was pacing again, then he slammed his fist against the desk. 'Tunnels! They're tunnelling through the mountains using mal-wyrms. We've already had reports of ors-wyrms as mounts and your story confirms that. Faran, and the city states and nomadic clans of Manom, those we can reach, will have to be warned.'

'I spoke to the authorities in Rosette, they'll be passing on the information to the other city-states there.' Coryn's head felt stuffed with the information Daven dropped so casually as he thought out loud. Different breeds of wyrm? Prophecies? Would staying here mean he'd have that every day?

'Yes, yes of course. In the meantime, we need to study someone with the ability to stop all types of magik. Can you not imagine how much that will help in our fight against blood-priests?' Daven rubbed his paws together, grinning.

'I – I yes. I see.' Coryn felt uncomfortable, he wasn't ready to worship any gods. But...to stay, to learn. To help stop the blood-priests. That'd be something. He stared down at the carpet. 'I've not. That is...I can't...'

Daven looked at him, his eyes sharp. 'You'll do some learning in private before you're sent into the classrooms with the other students. Because of your age, you'd have to join the classes of the oldest students and they'll be well ahead of you. I'll tutor you till you're at a level with them. Together we'll soon have dealt with any lack in reading or writing skills you have, that we will.'

'I...thank you.' Coryn rubbed at his neck and glanced at the books on the shelves and back down again.

'There's no shame in it.' Devan frowned. 'I'm thinking that slaves aren't taught such things. So, you and the lad shall stay with me until we've sorted out a set of rooms for you both. You'll want to stay together, I'm thinking. My wife will be pleased to have a youngster running about the place again.'

'You've a wife?'

'Of course I have a wife. And I have three sons and a daughter too, all grown and with children of their own.' Daven grinned. 'You'll be meeting them all soon enough. They're not coming for Mabon but they'll be here for Houl. They never miss the Midwinter Festival with their old Ma and Da.'

'Does she live here?' For some reason, it hadn't occurred to Coryn that there'd be families here.

'How else would it be? Maechin will be back from the Healer's Wing in time for supper. You'll meet her then. She's a fine woman but you'll have to watch her. I'm afraid she'll try to mother you to death and there'll be no hope for young Wetham.'

Coryn grinned and Daven grinned right back.

It'd take a while for him and Wetham to fit in, but they would. The place felt right. Coryn looked out of the window. The clouds had thickened on the freshening breeze and he smelled rain. He smiled. He liked feeling the rain on his skin and he'd not felt near enough of it for far too long. 'I'll take a walk and see if I can find Wetham. We should explore those moors. It'll remind us of Kalebrod.'

'You're missing your home?'

'Maybe one day I'll go back. See if there's anything I can do to help fight the blood-priests there.' Getting people with the Wealdan right out from under their noses would be good. 'There might be some sort of resistance I could join.'

'Stay here a while first, learn well how to use that Wealdan of yours, then you'll be of more use to those that need help.' Daven placed a meaty hand on Coryn's shoulder again. 'As I've said, war will be arriving in the lands around Elyat soon enough, sooner than many people would like to accept.'

'I reckon I'm ready to learn what I'll need.'

'That's good.' Daven nodded. 'You have a skill, a talent that we'll need in the battles coming our way. A skill that we'll help you develop. In turn we'll learn from you, that we will.'

'Yes.' He'd do whatever it took to beat the blood-priests. It was time to take charge of his life, do something good with it, as a free man. Make Lera proud he was her brother. Maybe even get Katleya to see him in a better light. After all, he had the Wealdan too. 'I'll stay and learn what I need. So will the boy. Long as we don't get Lehot shoved down our throats.'

'There are many here who worship different gods or none at all.' Daven looked into Coryn's eyes, all trace of a smile gone. He could see the sincerity in the large man's face. 'All are welcome to learn what they can do with their Wealdan no matter their faith or lack of it.'

'That's good to know.'

Chapter 59

Katleya jolted out of her dream. Its tattered streamers of light and dark slipped away, its low thrum sank into her bones, fading to nothing. She sat up, trying to shake the anxiety it left behind. Had shapes formed from the Wefan of her dreams? Shapes like, yet unlike, the spirits that tried to speak to her of danger. For the life of her she couldn't remember their warnings.

Spirits! It's just a stupid dream.

Both the bloodhunter-priest and Leveen had targeted her for her Wealdan-blood and that made her worry that she might be important to the Mureckens in a very bad way. As if she didn't have enough to blasted well worry about.

Diaphos had set and the boat-shape of Liatos floated on the curve of the sea sending a faint silver path shivering across the water. The world lay swathed in greys apart from their little fire. Banked for the night, it glowed dull red at its heart.

Katleya rose from her damp blankets, stretched and walked a few paces away from the campsite. She stared out over the mist wreathed grasslands of Manom northwards to where her new life would begin, safe from anyone who wanted her blood. Rias had left them when they'd reached Roesette, returning to the Temple of Daru in Rialt, but they still had Darus accompany them. They'd made good time along the coast road from Manar, a road busy with travellers, that had fishing villages, towns and farms dotting its length. Nomeck was only two leagues away.

The rolling hills rose in fading swells toward the eastern horizon, where the sky played with the opalescence hinting at dawn. Katleya threw some more wood on the fire and hung a pot of water over it for kaffe. Daras wandered into the camp.

'We should reach the border of Faran by the end of this day.' He squatted near the fire.

'Good.' Katleya put oats in a second pot for porridge. Daras made her skin itch. A hunch told her he was a good man but he just made her uncomfortable. She felt far too aware of when his eyes looked her way, of his body when he stripped to wash. It confused and annoyed

318

her. She turned her thoughts to Coryn. He hadn't done or said anything to make her believe he was interested...

Dame Mureen rose from her blankets. She smiled at them both then turned to face east and knelt to meditate as the sun rose. Maisie joined her. Katleya knew the Lehotan life wouldn't work for her. She'd have to find some other sort of life for herself. One that didn't involve meditating on, or praying to, or bowing down and believing in some god that wasn't there when you needed him. She'd still go to the Haven, learn all she could about the Wealdan, but Lehot needn't come into it, and that suited her fine. She was happy enough with the spirits. You could depend on their undependability.

Katleya checked on the children. They still slept. A happy tangle of arms and legs on the mattresses in the back of the wagon. She realised she'd miss them, she hadn't expected that.

'We worship Daru, the Mother Goddess, at moonrise. That is her time.' Daras prodded the fire. He smelled of horse, sweat and damp soil.

'I know. I've seen and heard you. Back in Rophet, they worship the god Atash at noon. I bet Murak is bowed down to in the dark of night.' Katleya stood. Every god seemed to have demands. 'I've got to go.'

She crossed the sandy road and climbed over a low rise pushing through the tall grasses and herbs. Water gurgled in tiny streams threading between the rolling hills towards the sea. On the crown of one long low rise of a hill, Katleya spotted some familiar rocks. She climbed towards them.

Close to, they all stood almost as high as the stones by the oasis. It seemed an age ago since Katleya had touched them. These were made of the same dark grey-blue stone and were covered with similar carvings. They looked old and brutal, hunched into the grasses against the prevalent sea winds.

She walked round them as the rising sun fingered the stones, picking out the uneven surface with pale pink light. She stopped and studied one. In the brightening light, its surface changed from rough rock to a smooth glossiness, like dark glass. Katleya leaned in close, opening her Wealdan. Little flecks of silver flickered just under the surface. She remembered this. She felt rather than heard the thrumming sound coming up from the earth, right through the soles of her feet. It reminded her of her of half-forgotten dreams.

Taking a deep breath, Katleya pushed her hand in and knife-thin ice sliced through her flesh. She gasped, took in another deep breath, leaned forward and pushed her head through.

Formless grey nothingness swirled around her, swallowing all noise apart from the drumming that sounded like the constant drone of distant thunder. Katleya felt it echo inside her own body, deep down into the marrow of her bones. She touched her face with her fingers. Her fingers could feel her face, her face could feel her fingers, but she couldn't see them. She could only see the burning silver latticing of the Wefan running through her fingers.

Spirits! This is...blasted unnerving.

She began to pull back when something shifted. Her fingers felt – something. A thin silver light streamed past. There and gone again. Katleya stepped forward, straddling the space between the grasslands and the fog. She reached forward as much as she could while keeping her back foot grounded. The grey fog deepened into black, more silver threads flared and streamed, wove themselves together into flows, like the currents of a river, then split apart into fine threads again. The Wefan, but wild and chaotic with no lattices or matrices to control its energy. She felt a visceral fear.

It thrilled her.

This is what she dreamed of so often. The half-remembered, ragged ends of those strange dreams returned to Katleya in a rush, almost as if they were real memories. In the deep silence of the silver and black, she heard the roar of blood in her ears, the beat of her heart and the breath in her lungs. And through it all the deep thrum of the wild Wefan.

Someone grabbed her leg, hauling her back, through the fog and the slicing ice. She lurched, stumbling backwards into Daras' arms.

'What are you? You are no Adherent of Lehot!' He turned her to face him, holding tight onto her upper arms and glared into her eyes. 'They know nothing of these places.'

'Let go, blast it.' Katleya struggled against his hold.

'What are you that you can open a Duru?' His fingers dug deep into her flesh.

'I don't know what you mean.'

He stared into her face, searching for a long while before he let her go.

'I see that you do not.' Daras stepped back. 'That was a very foolish thing to do, Adherent Katleya! You do not understand the danger that lies beyond the Duru Stones.'

'Duru stones? Is that what they're called? What's dangerous about them? What do you know about them?' Katleya demanded, shoving him away. 'And how do they open and where do they go? And how come the Derin know about them and nobody else, not even the Lehotans?'

'Duru is our word for door or portal. Death lies beyond these stones, that is all you need to know.' Daras stared down at her, his eyes narrowed. 'If I had not given an oath I would take you back to High-Seer Yaltos and...'

'Why would you want to take her back to your High-Seer? What is it that she does, Daras?' Dame Mureen marched up. She stood next to Katleya, crossing her arms over her chest.

Daras looked from Katleya to Dame Mureen and back, his gaze suspicious and cold. 'The Duru Stones are ancient and they are dangerous. As are those who are able to open them. That is all I can tell you. If you wish to know more you must ask the Seers of Derin. Only they hold the ancient knowledge you require.' He turned and walked back to the campsite. 'It is time to harness the horses.'

Dame Mureen passed Katleya and stopped in front of the stone. Her hand slapped against the surface. It sounded solid. The old woman then produced a Wealdan-flame and touched it against the rock. It flared and disappeared leaving a sooty mark on the stone.

'He said *duru* means door or portal.' Katleya wondered why it'd gone solid again.

'Whatever it is that you did, child, I cannot repeat it.' Dame Mureen looked disappointed. 'I have read of the Portal Stones. Our last Moder, Birog, asked me to find all I could on them. I believe she went to the Derin in the end. That was fifteen years ago and it was the last we heard of her. Can you tell me how it worked for you?'

'I don't know how, it just does.' Katleya paused. Birog? Where had she heard that name before?

'It has happened before?'

'Once, back in the desert. I'd forgotten about it.' Katleya's racked her brain. Birog...Something told her it was important. 'So much has happened...'

'Kat, Kat?' Neima squeaked in her high thin voice. 'Can I have a piggyback, Pussycat?'

'We must talk of this,' Dame Mureen murmured.

'Yes, we must,' Katleya agreed. Moder, Birog...the names itched at her. Uncle Yadoc! He'd said something about a promise. 'My Uncle Yadoc, he knew a Birog! He said her name when he died...apologised for failing a promise. Did you know a man called Yadoc aef Laeft?'

'No, not Yadoc. But you say he knew Moder Birog?' Dame Mureen searched her face, eager.

'Me, me. My turn!' Sica shouted, laughing.

The two girls came running up, their faces fresh with excitement. The change in them was astonishing. Cheeks rounded and pink, hair clean and glossy. And far too much energy. Katleya grinned.

'Pussycat? How do you know what kind of cat I am?' Katleya lifted her hands making claws of them. 'Maybe I'm a big cat, a desert lion with enormous teeth. One that can eat you all up in three easy mouthfuls! That'll show you.'

She roared and the shrieking girls ducked and dodged behind the stone. She leaped after them and crashed straight into Leveen. The woman had grabbed hold of Neima, but dropped her on top of Sica as she staggered back from Katleya.

'Spirits!' Katleya's heart thumped a staccato beat of fear. Her knives were in her hands as she leaped back. 'I wondered what'd happened to you. How did you find me?'

'I drank your blood, girl.' Leveen grabbed hold of one of Sica's plaits and had her tulwar at the girl's throat in a moment. 'I can find you anywhere.'

'You *are* a bloodhunter-priest then, a filthy, stinking bloodhunter-priest. How do you manage to cover the stink, sniffer?' Katleya shifted her balance, waiting, watching for her chance. 'If it's me you want, let her go.'

'I think not. This one will be my guarantee.' Leveen yanked Sica's plait, making the girl scream. 'As for the stink, I am no full bloodhunt-er-priest. The ritual was not completed, the lacert symbiote failed to take within me. Stay still, girl, or I will cut you.'

'Please, just let the girl go.' Katleya tried to catch Sica's eye. 'Stay still, Sica.'

But Sica struggled and Leveen sliced into her neck with the tulwar. Sica screamed again. Though the cut was shallow and little blood seeped out, the memory of Pella's death seared into Katleya's mind.

'Sica, please, stand still, very still like a statue. You remember the statue game?' Katleya tried to sound calm, hoped the panic didn't bleed into her voice. 'I'll come with you, Leveen, let her go.'

'Drop your knives.'

Katleya dropped them on the grass. Sica was shaking like a leaf but stayed still. Her grey eyes stared at Katleya, wide and terrified. 'Why me, Leveen? What is it about me that's so bloody special?'

'The blades at your ankles too.'

'Can't you tell me that at least? Spirits! You've followed me for thousands of leagues, why so much effort for me?'

'Your knives first.'

She bent down and pulled them from their sheaths. Surging up, Katleya sliced through Sica's plait so the girl stumbled to the ground, then shouldered Leveen, making the woman stagger back two, three steps.

'Run Sica! Dame Mureen! Get the girls!' Katleya screamed, keeping her eyes on Leveen.

Sica scrambled up and fled down the slope, crying the whole way, 'Kat, Kat, Kat...'

'You will not escape me again,' Leveen hissed. She steadied and stepped into a fighter's stance again, her tulwar flashing in the light. 'No matter what.'

'We'll see.' Katleya heard Dame Mureen call for the girls, then shout Daras' name.

Katleya dodged back round the stone, but Leveen did the same. The woman raised her tulwar high. It shone bright in the morning sun. From the corner of her eye, she saw the two girls running to Dame Mureen. She knew she didn't stand much of a chance against Leveen but perhaps she could buy a little time. Daras could take Leveen, he had that little crossbow of his. She had one advantage. She knew Leveen needed her alive. All Katleya needed to do was keep dodging and weaving until Daras arrived.

'You know you cannot hope to win against me.' Leveen's lips twisted into a sneer. 'I might need you alive, but not necessarily whole.'

'Don't be so blasted sure I'll let you cut me, Leveen.' Katleya whipped forward and under the tulwar. She sliced the woman's thigh and rolled away. The tulwar smacked into the soil a hair's breadth from her retreating foot.

'You are fast.' Blood seeped through Leveen's leggings. She stood right in front of the standing stone now, her eyes shaded from the rising sun by that blasted veil.

Katleya didn't answer. She was up and waiting. She needed to see the bloody woman's eyes. You could tell a lot from the eyes. She heard the girls' cries. Why hadn't Dame Mureen taken them away by now? And where was Daras when you blasted well needed him? She flicked a look out of the corner of her eye. Down the hill. Dame Mureen was struggling to hold the girls and drag them back to the campsite while Daras sprinted up the hill.

Reacting to a flash of steel, Katleya raised her knife and caught the tulwar on its blade. Deflected down and to one side, the curved blade sank into the soil. She punched into Leveen's other hand with her second knife as the woman made a grab for her.

'No!' Leveen screamed.

What?

Katleya heard the grunt of a man behind her, then the thud of a quarrel hitting flesh. A man in a black cloak hurtled past her, crumpling to the ground. Daras' distinctive fletching quivered between his ribs just under his arm. His rutted, bald head gleamed in the grey light, as did the flint knife he'd dropped. The blood-priest shuddered and lay still. Another blasted blood-priest? She hoped Daras aimed for Leveen next. She didn't know how much longer she could keep this up.

Long enough, she hoped. Katleya moved. Letting go of the knife still stuck between the bones of Leveen's wrist, she head-butted the woman in the stomach. As they both fell towards the standing stone she reached out past Leveen's shoulder to the stone's surface. If she could just shove the woman through then...

A jagged, flint knife closed on her eye.

Katleya twisted away. Too late. A searing explosion of pain tore into her neck. She saw Daras running, but slow, too slow. A sluggish quarrel drilled into the second blood-priest, his blood-smeared knife spun through the air.

Turning and turning.

She saw Dame Mureen drift to her knees her eyes wide and her mouth a round *o*. She saw the girls pull at the old woman's arms, their mouths wide with silent screams.

She saw her own blood spin out in listless beaded strands. The beads transformed into precious gems as the rising sun caught them.

'No, no, no...' Leveen raged.

So close.

With the last of her strength, Katleya half pushed, half fell against the still screaming Leveen. Together, they plummeted through the Portal, through the ice, through the grey fog.

Her life drained away as her bright red blood spilled out into the silver and black.

Chapter 60

'No.' Coryn stood looking out of the window. The distant moors floated above the dawn mists, the highest tors bathed gold by the rising sun. He'd wanted to take her up there. It would've reminded her of home, as it did him. He couldn't look at Dame Mureen. Didn't want to believe what he'd heard, didn't want to see the truth of it in her eyes. It hurt too much. Like someone had clawed his heart right out of his chest and torn it to pieces.

'She is with Lehot.' Dame Mureen closed her eyes for a moment then looked up at him again. 'You must believe this truth, Sire Coryn.'

'Truth? Katleya believed in the spirits.' Coryn turned on her. She stood firm, her robes stained with salt, her hair still wild from sea winds. 'Not any gods. Gods have to be worshipped to exist for a person.'

'I am sorry, Sire Coryn. I know that, but we believe in the spirits also, those within our beings. I believe her spirit will go to Lehot and He will shelter her in His Halls of Light. Whether we believe in Him or not, He accepts us all.' Dame Mureen's hands gripped her focus crystal. The knuckles of her shaking hands bone white. It sounded almost like she was trying to convince herself. 'We are never alone in His Light.'

'Words,' Coryn whispered. The pain bit into him. Now he realised how much she'd meant to him. Now it was too late. Why hadn't he done more? Why hadn't he stayed with them instead of going ahead? He should have stayed with them. Katleya might still be alive if he had. Guilt hammered into him. 'Your words are dead leaves blowing in the wind.'

'I can look after myself, Coryn aef Arlean,' she'd said. Her head to one side, that funny half smile on her lips.

'Now lad, we each believe in our own way what happens after death.' Daven spoke soft, his voice a rolling rumble. 'Dame Mureen and I believe our spirits go to Lehot, you and Katleya believe the cuinannufen will take your spirits to Annufen. We will all pray for her in our own way. Dame Mureen, thank you for coming to tell us of this. You travelled fast and must have had a hard journey from Nomeck.'

'Please, Coryn.' She stood close to Coryn now. 'There will be a memorial service in her honour. Here in the Temple. Adherent Maisie will bring the children. They cross the sea as we speak, something that you know is a feat for them. They will be here soon and it would make them very happy to see you.' Dame Mureen laid a hand on his arm. 'Scholar Daven is right. We will be together, but we can think of her each in our own way. Thank her for all she did and send her our thoughts.'

He couldn't hear any more. Unable to speak, Coryn pushed past Dame Mureen. He tried not to see the yawning pain in her eyes. It mirrored his own too well and he'd no mind to see that. Daven moved to the door, his bulk a solid barrier.

'No, let him pass, Scholar Daven.' Dame Mureen's voice was soft but firm. 'He needs some time alone.'

The afternoon swelled warm over the moors, filled with insect drone and bird song. Coryn ran through the haze. Despair hunted him like a shadow. How could he believe she'd gone without seeing her d...he didn't want to say it, not even think it.

Soon he was panting in the heat. Drawing in deep breaths of dry, windless air filled with the smells of grass, honeysuckle, and warmed earth. There were moments of oblivion when all he heard were his gasping breaths, his boots thudding on earth and rock, his heart beating in his ears.

Time fled as he ran. In the void of the heavens, stars circled, cold and uncaring. Just another part of the emptiness inside.

His race ended on a steep hill its summit crowned with rock piled on rock. The wind picked up. It moaned through the gorse and the tors as he pressed his head to the cold stone, his mind flashing image after image of Katleya laughing, scowling, exhausted, happy.

The last look she had given him was a look that had held a promise. 'We'll meet again soon enough,' she'd said. 'You and I need to talk.' Well they couldn't, not now.

Then the dog was there. Coryn sniffed and opened an eye. The dog sighed and stared at him hard with those almond eyes. He nodded and draped an arm over the dog's shoulders. The dog bore it as long as it could then stood and looked back toward Storr City, gleaming with a thousand flames from street torches and candle-lit windows.

'Time to go back and get on with it.' Coryn frowned and chewed on the inside of his cheek. 'That's what you're telling me, Dog?'

The dog yawned and raked a hind leg through his neck fur.

'We can't have everything, Dog. Got to get on with the life we've got.' He stood, then leaned down and scratched the dog behind one ear.

Coryn knew then what he wanted more than anything else. Revenge. Revenge against those who'd killed his family, Pella and now Katleya too. And yesterday he'd discovered that he might have a talent that could help destroy the Murecken priesthood. He just had to figure out the way to do it. 'I know, Dog. I've got a lot to learn so I can work out what to do next. If I've got a skill that can actually do some good out there, I'll use it. I'll use it to destroy those blood-priests and their damned Priest-king.'

The dog rose and sniffed at the rocks and bushes. It cocked its leg and watered a low clump of gorse. A tiny tree-spirit sprinted out of the gorse and shook tiny fists at the dog. Coryn tried to smile. It didn't work.

'Looks like our journey isn't over yet, Dog.'

Coryn walked back down from the tor. The dog followed.

Scholar Daven opened the door as Coryn raised his fist to knock.

'Come in, lad, come in.' Daven stepped back.

The room, lit with candles and a good sized fire, felt warm and welcoming after the chill night air. Dame Mureen sat on one of the chairs near the fire. Someone sat next to her on the footstool. The old woman stood, turning toward him.

'Sire Coryn.' She'd tidied her hair and changed her clothes, looking more like the Lehotan High-adherent she was. Her face glowed, a smile broke on her lips. 'We have someone here who would very much like to meet you. She rode hard and fast as soon as she heard of your arrival.'

The second person stood, slipping her hood off as she did. Her golden curls glowed in the candlelight. Her blue eyes shone.

'Coryn?'

She looked so like their Ma, Coryn's heart stopped for a beat.

'Lera?'

Then they were hugging and then he swung her round as he'd done so many times before, not caring about the books knocked to the floor or the scrolls flying across the room.

'I knew you'd find me again.' Lera squealed with delight when he finally put her down. 'I knew it! Birog promised Tyme you would, but I knew it in here.' She pressed her hand against her chest.

'And so did I, and so I did.' Coryn finally, reluctantly, let his little sister go. Not so little any more though. She stood almost to his shoulder. 'You and I have a lot of catching up to do, Lera.'

'Yes we do,' Lera agreed.

Coryn felt the prickle of Wealdan as she lifted her hands to show him glowing motes of green and lavender weaving between her fingers.

About the Author

Follow the adventure. Follow R B Watkinson

https://rbwatkinson.wordpress.com
http://www.claretpress.com/#!r-b-watkinson/c16pm

WEFAN WEAVES TRILOGY BOOKS 2 & 3

THE FRACTURED MONOLITH

Evie, searching for answers, finds a monolith in a derelict area of London. How could she have known it was a Portal? Trying to save her, Alan is dragged into Dumnon by a bloodhunter-priest whose sole aim is to capture Evie for his Master, the Priest-king of Mureck. How will they survive this nightmarish world of war and magik let alone get back home?

The Murecken now invade the western lands, all for the glory of Murak, and the Storratian Empire must fight for its survival. Once more, Coryn must face the blood-priests and thwart their aims.

THE RUPTURED WEAVE

War rages over Dumnon. It cannot be long before it ends, but who will win? The Murecken, their blood-priests gorging on the blood of Wealdan-bearers taken in great numbers from the conquered lands, grow ever stronger. Can the Storratian Empire hold against them, let alone push them back?

Someone has to go into the Murecken stronghold of Elucame. Someone must destroy the fulcrum of their power. The Priest-king himself must die.